KU-034-179

THE
JACKDAW

Also By Luke Delaney

Cold Killing
The Keeper
The Toy Taker

THE JACKDAW

LUKE DELANEY

HarperCollins*Publishers*

HarperCollins*Publishers*
1 London Bridge Street
London SE1 9GF

www.harpercollins.co.uk

Published by HarperCollins*Publishers* 2015

2

Copyright © Luke Delaney 2015

Luke Delaney asserts the moral right to
be identified as the author of this work

A catalogue record for this book
is available from the British Library

ISBN: 978-0-00-758568-7

This novel is entirely a work of fiction.
The names, characters and incidents portrayed in it are
the work of the author's imagination. Any resemblance to
actual persons, living or dead, events or localities is
entirely coincidental.

Set in Meridien by Palimpsest Book Production Limited,
Falkirk, Stirlingshire

Printed and bound in Great Britain by
Clays Ltd, St Ives plc

All rights reserved. No part of this publication may be
reproduced, stored in a retrieval system, or transmitted,
in any form or by any means, electronic, mechanical,
photocopying, recording or otherwise, without the prior
permission of the publishers.

MIX
Paper from
responsible sources

FSC www.fsc.org FSC™ C007454

FSC™ is a non-profit international organisation established to promote
the responsible management of the world's forests. Products carrying the
FSC label are independently certified to assure consumers that they come
from forests that are managed to meet the social, economic and
ecological needs of present and future generations,
and other controlled sources.

Find out more about HarperCollins and the environment at
www.harpercollins.co.uk/green

Dedication

I dedicate this book to my three kids – DJ, JJ and NB.

To DJ, an inspiration to us all, who has already overcome so many obstacles in such a short life and proved to us all what we can achieve when we show some real grit and determination. A personality the size of the Empire State Building – funny, sometimes a handful, great company, a magnet for other children and always in the centre of the action, DJ's a genuinely unstoppable force of nature. If anyone can make all their dreams come true it'll be this kid.

To JJ, a beautiful and gentle child – the polar opposite of their older sibling. Clever and resourceful, but shy and thoughtful. Bright and independent, but never boastful or bragging – JJ continues to develop into a wonderful young person, doing things their own way, blissfully untouched by convention and the need to be like everyone else, seemingly unaware of their Hollywood good looks and million-dollar smile. JJ grows and grows as a person – happier and happier with each passing day. A very special child.

To NB, known to my wife and I as our little gift. Super smart and fiercely independent, but very cuddly and funny too.

Their thirst for knowledge is like something I've never seen and long may it last, although everything has to be done their way and watch out anyone who tries to stop them. There's no point in telling NB 'it's the taking part that matters' – this kid's in it to win it. NB is the definition of steely-eyed determination. We already know NB will be anything they want to be.

In many ways my kids are like a flock of jackdaws – intelligent and chatty, brave and loyal to each other – mischievous and inventive – not to mention sometimes troublesome. But we'd have it no other way. You are our everything. So thank you, guys, for all of your awesomeness.

All our love,
Mum and Dad

1

The thick hood was pulled from his head and Paul Elkins squeezed his eyes closed tightly against the bright, white light that tried to penetrate his pain and fear, but the agony of the duck-tape being ripped off his mouth fired them open as wide as if he was being electrocuted. As the shock of the pain receded, his eyes blinked the room into focus, his chest heaving with panic as the sweat poured down the sides of his face and back. His arms and legs were bound with more duck-tape to a heavy, old wooden chair that creaked as he struggled, but didn't move. He bucked and kicked in the chair until the futility of his efforts overwhelmed him and drained him of his strength and determination, the desperation of his situation becoming increasingly undeniable.

The details of the room that was now his prison seeped into his consciousness. It was painted entirely white, with portable lamps providing too much light. Sheets of black plastic hung from the walls where he assumed there were windows, so no natural light penetrated the room. In front of him the man who'd abducted him from the London street in broad daylight stood straight and strong – confident and in control, his face concealed by his black ski-mask and wrap-around sunglasses, his hands in black leather gloves, the rest of his clothes also all black. Only his mouth was partially visible, slightly obscured by a tiny microphone held in place by a head-strap and connected to two black boxes attached to his chest – one about the size of a hardback book, the other the size of a cigarette packet. The man didn't speak. Behind him a foldable table stretched out – upon it a collection of laptops, cameras, phones and other equipment Elkins didn't recognize, all of which were connected to a portable electricity generator.

Elkins stared at the man through his brown eyes for what seemed an eternity, waiting for him to speak and explain his motivation – to tell him why he'd been brought to this intimidating place. But the man said nothing. In all his fifty-one years Elkins had never been treated with anything other than respect and sometimes fear, but now that counted for nothing. Again his slim, fit body writhed in the chair before once more surrendering to futility. He forced some saliva into his dry mouth, moving it around with his tongue before speaking.

'Do you know who I am?' he demanded, but his voice trembled so much he hardly recognized it himself. The man said nothing. Did nothing. 'I know a lot of powerful people. The people I work for will happily pay you whatever you want, if that's what this is about.' The man slowly turned his back on Elkins and began to switch on the various computers and cameras on the table, all of which Elkins noticed were pointing directly at him. 'What are you doing? What's this about? Are you sending a ransom demand?'

The man turned to him and finally spoke. 'No,' he answered, his voice warped by the voice distorter that hung around his neck, electronic and distant – un-human. 'No ransom demand. I'm summoning your jury.'

'What?'

'Your jury, Mr Elkins.'

Elkins blinked in confusion. 'You know who I am?'

'Of course.'

'Then what do you want?'

'Justice, Mr Elkins. All I want is justice.'

'I don't understand.'

'You will,' the man told him before turning his back to examine a computer screen, speaking without looking. 'It appears we're attracting some attention. Just a few hundred people, but this is only the beginning. You are the first, but you will not be the last. In the future thousands will log in as jurors. Thousands will see justice being done. Justice for the people, where money and power can't corrupt the system. Where your influence means nothing. Are you ready to be judged, Mr Elkins?'

'I haven't committed any crime.'

'Is that what you really believe? Why don't we let the people decide?'

The man spun quickly on his heels and walked to Elkins's side, filling his chest with air before beginning to speak in that unearthly voice. He addressed the hundreds who watched from their homes and offices, bus stops and trains – all of whom had stumbled across the live-stream of Elkins taped to the chair while searching the Internet for cheap holidays, news updates, amusing homemade videos and God knows what else. He spoke directly into the camera connected to the computer.

'All of you should know this man you see here is a criminal,' he accused. Elkins bucked in his chair, a look of disbelief spreading across his face.

'I'm no criminal. I've never even been arrested.'

'No. No you haven't, because your type never do get arrested, do they, Mr Elkins? They never get brought to justice, are never punished for their crimes. They are above the law. Not any more. It's time for the people of this country to judge you.'

'I've never done anything to anyone,' Elkins pleaded, his words stuttering and desperate. 'Why are you recording this?'

3

'I'm not just recording it,' the man explained. 'This is being transmitted live, so people like me can finally see justice being done.'

'I haven't done anything. You're not the police. This isn't a court.'

'Haven't done anything?' the man asked, his electronic voice calm. 'Then let me explain your crimes – your crimes against honest, hard-working people who lost their jobs, had their houses taken away from them, lost their wives, husbands and their families while you grew richer and fatter on their misery. You paid yourselves millions in bonuses despite your incompetence, leaving the people to pay for your mistakes and your greed.'

'What?'

'But as your banks came close to collapsing was it you who financed their survival? No. It was *us. The people*. And when the government was emptying our bank accounts and stealing our jobs, did you or any of the other pigs at the trough stop gorging yourselves? No. The feeding frenzy continued whilst we suffered. Some of us lost everything. Many others took their own lives to escape the pain and misery you caused. You continued to not only protect your wealth, but grow it, while we could barely feed our children.'

'Christ. Is this what this is about – the banking crisis? For God's sake, that was years ago.'

'And still we suffer and still the bankers grow fat refusing even to loan us our own money – investing it in houses across London that most of us could only dream about, stealing our money just as surely as if they'd robbed us in the street – and you dare to ask what your crimes are, dare to say you're no criminal.'

Elkins tried to defend himself, but the man talked over him, resting a gloved hand on his shoulder. 'You are Paul Elkins, correct?'

'Yes.'

'You are the CEO of Fairfield's Bank, correct?'

'So?'

'A bank that lost billions because of its failure to properly supervise its own staff – a staff who were knowingly selling mortgages to people who couldn't afford them?'

'We made mistakes, yes, but . . .'

'Because they'd been promised bonuses of tens of thousands of pounds if they met their greed-driven targets?'

'No one was forced to take out one of our mortgages.'

'Weren't they?' Elkins didn't answer. 'Decent people sold into poverty, homelessness and bankruptcy by you.'

'I didn't sell anyone a mortgage.'

'You were the CEO,' the electronic voice snapped at him. 'You were responsible. You were supposed to prevent it from happening, but you didn't, because the money kept rolling in – right into your pockets. And when it went wrong, when the walls of your bank almost came tumbling down and you had to be saved by the government, by money that rightly belonged to *the people*, did you lose your job like we would have? No. You kept your two-million-pounds-a-year salary and even had so much contempt for the rest of us that you paid yourself a three-million-pound bonus. A three-million-pound bonus for failure.'

The man stepped closer to the camera, his hand pointing back to Elkins as he spoke. 'Members of the jury, this man is not just a criminal and a thief – he's a murderer. Every life taken, every suicide committed because of the crimes of the greedy few – this man and others like him are responsible. But have any of them been punished for their crimes? No. It's time to change all that. It's time for justice. My brothers and sisters – it's time to judge.'

Mark Hudson, seventeen years old, sat in the bedroom of his family's council flat in Birmingham hypnotized by the masked man preaching in his electronic voice on the screen of his laptop. His friends, Danny and Zach, messed around in the background, not nearly as interested.

'Shut the fuck up, you two,' he demanded. 'I can't hear what he's saying.'

'It's all just bullshit,' Danny argued. 'It ain't real. Just a couple of clowns looking for publicity.'

'No,' Hudson snapped. 'Listen to what the man's saying. That bloke in the chair's one of them banker bastards.'

'So?' Zach joined in. 'What the fuck's that got to do with us?'

'Just shut up and listen,' Hudson insisted, silencing his friends who had no intention of crossing him further, well aware of his reputation on the estate that had earned him the nickname 'Psycho Mark'.

'Time to judge this man for his crimes against the people of this country,' the man on the screen told them. *'Your job is merely to pass judgement. Once his guilt has been established I will determine his sentence, which I must warn you now – could be death.'*

'Fucking hell,' Hudson declared, his eyes wide with excitement – a grin appearing on his lips. 'He's gonna kill him.'

Gabriel Westbrook leaned in closer to his computer screen when the masked man mentioned death. He didn't know the victim, but they had plenty in common – high-paid careers in the City, beautiful homes, expensive habits – although he was much younger than Elkins at only thirty-four. He considered summoning his wife to watch with him, but decided that was probably a bad idea.

'Is this for real?' he whispered to himself as he listened to the man's words, rendered all the more disturbing by the warped voice.

'If there was another way I would not be doing what I have now been forced to do. But it is the only way these people will ever listen to us. Only through fear and terror will they take notice. I have no choice but to do what I have to do.'

6

'Christ,' Westbrook told the empty room. 'Is this a hoax? Please let this be a hoax.'

'Come and have a look at this, love,' Phil Taylor called out to his wife Cathy in their small home in Hull. She sensed the excitement in his voice and walked the short distance from the kitchen to the cramped office. Her husband was sitting in front of a computer screen that displayed a masked figure next to a man taped to a chair.

'For God's sake, what are you watching?' she asked, shocked that he'd want to share it with her. 'This isn't pornography, is it?'

'Don't be stupid,' he told her. 'This bloke's kidnapped one of them bankers.'

'Not this again,' she moaned, rolling her eyes in disapproval.

'Hey,' he warned her. 'Those bastards cost me my business and our home. We wouldn't be living in this shit house and I wouldn't be doing my shit job if it wasn't for their bloody greed and incompetence.'

'We overstretched,' she reminded him. 'That's why we lost the business and house.'

'You can believe that if you want,' he told her with a snarl, 'but I know the truth. Now it looks like someone else has finally had enough too.'

It's important I make a statement here and now. It's important we show the rich and the greedy this is their new reality. No more can they steal from us and fear no retribution. From this day on, they will be punished for their crimes.'

'What's he gonna do to him?' Cathy asked.

'I don't know,' he answered. 'Said he might kill him.'

'Jesus Christ, turn it off,' she told him.

'No,' he insisted, never looking away from the screen. 'I want to see what he does to him. I want to see the bastard squirm.'

*   *   *

Father Alex Jones sat in the small office in St Thomas More Catholic Church, Dulwich, watching and listening to the continuing monologue of the masked man. Instinct told him that this was no stunt – the man was deadly serious. His original reason for searching the Internet long forgotten, he pressed his hands tightly together and began to whisper prayers for both the victim and masked man – salvation for both and forgiveness for one.

'Now I need you – my brothers and my sisters – to play your part. It's time to judge. If you believe this man is guilty of crimes against the people then simply click on the like icon. If you believe he is innocent then click on the dislike icon. Once the judgement is made, the sentence will be carried out accordingly. One click, one vote. Don't waste your time trying to make multiple votes. The Your View system only allows one vote per user.'

'God forgive you,' the priest whispered as he clicked on the dislike icon, leaning away to watch how other viewers were voting. The like and dislike numbers were growing rapidly – but one far quicker than the other.

Mark Hudson watched the voting just as closely as the priest, but he was praying for a different outcome.

'What's happening?' Danny asked.

'Shut the fuck up,' was Hudson's only reply.

'The people have voted and they have overwhelmingly found you guilty. Have you anything you want to say?'

'This has gone far enough,' Elkins shouted as the masked man momentarily disappeared from the screen. *'You need to let me go now.'* His face twisted with terror. *'You've made your point.'*

There was the noise of metal on metal before the man reappeared with a length of rope – a noose tied at one end while the other looked to go straight to the ceiling, out of shot. The masked man looped the noose over the struggling Elkins, ignoring his writhing and bucking – ignoring his pleas.

'Please don't do this. Please. I haven't done anything wrong. I can give the money back. You can have it. I just want to see my wife and children again. I'm a family man.' But the man ignored him as he reached for another rope that seemed to hang from the ceiling.

'The people have judged you, Mr Elkins. Now I must pass sentence. Your punishment shall be . . . death.' Before Elkins could speak again, the man pulled the rope he was holding towards the floor, the rope attached to the noose around Elkins's neck instantly growing taut, vibrating with tension as it lifted him, chair and all, from the floor. Terrible sounds came from behind Elkins's gritted teeth as he fought desperately for his life.

'Fucking hell,' Hudson exclaimed, unaware that his two friends were backing away from the screen, their faces serious and pale while his beamed and glowed. 'He's hanging the fucker. He's really doing it. Ha. This is fucking brilliant.'

Westbrook watched on as the older version of himself hung from the rope, still taped to the chair – the man's eyes growing increasingly bulbous and grotesque – his mouth now open with his tongue protruding and writhing around like a dying lizard. He felt sick and scared all in the same moment. Someone wanted revenge – revenge against him and all his type. Which one of them would be next? He felt a shiver run up his spine.

'I can't watch this any more,' Cathy told her husband. 'I think I'm going to be sick. Turn it off.' She reached for the computer's power switch, but her husband pushed her hand away, eyes full of hate – although not for her.

'Leave it,' he ordered.

'Please tell me you don't want to watch this,' she pleaded. 'A man's being killed. Murdered. Why the hell do you want to watch it?'

9

'Maybe he had it coming. Maybe he deserved it. Maybe they all do.'

'Jesus, Phil,' she told him. 'No one deserves that.'

'Don't they?' he asked. 'And what about me? Did I deserve what happened to me? Did I deserve to lose everything?'

'You just lost money, Phil. This is a man's life.' She turned and walked from the room. 'I won't be in the same room as this. I hope they catch the bastard and hang him.' She left him sitting staring at the screen – a thin smile spreading across his face as he watched Elkins's body finally go limp.

The priest closed his eyes and drew an imaginary cross over his heart, summoning the courage to once again look at the scene of barbarity he'd just witnessed on his computer screen. Being a priest in modern London was not what the public imagined it to be. He regularly had to deal with abused youngsters and battered women who for whatever reason were too scared or unwilling to go to the police, although he'd always encourage them to do so. And then there was the missionary work he'd done in Africa – teaching men and women who'd had their arms hacked off with machetes how to somehow survive after yet another civil war in the Congo, as well as many other terrible things he'd seen that he never talked about. But this was as repellent as anything he'd ever witnessed. When he finally opened his eyes the masked man was standing in front of the still swaying body and chair.

'Justice has been done. The first of the guilty has been punished. Rest assured, my friends – my brothers and sisters – there will be more.' The man released the rope and allowed the body and chair to crash to the floor before walking towards the camera. A few seconds later the screen went blank.

Father Alex clasped his hands together and began to pray, but found it difficult to focus – his mind still trapped in more earthly matters. The terrible crime he'd just witnessed would no doubt have to be investigated by the police – by detectives.

The thought brought to mind the troubled policeman who occasionally came to see him – DI Sean Corrigan. Would he be the man who'd have to try to catch this remorseless killer?

'Our Father who art in heaven – protect us from this *new* evil in our lives and forgive him who has done the unforgivable.'

2

Detective Inspector Sean Corrigan sat in his office on the seventh floor of New Scotland Yard reading through the latest batch of CPS memos about the soon-to-begin trial of Douglas Allen – a man the media had aptly named 'The Toy Taker'. Allen had been declared mentally fit to stand trial at a previous Pleas and Directions hearing and now it was full steam ahead for the trial. The investigation had been Sean's first as head of the Special Investigations Team and now he waited for the next, praying it wouldn't come until after Allen's trial and the conviction it was sure to bring. The last thing he wanted was to be dashing backwards and forwards to the Old Bailey whilst trying to run a new investigation. DC Paulo Zukov appeared at his door and tapped more times that was needed on the frame, breaking Sean's concentration and making him look up.

'What is it, Paulo?'

Zukov smiled smugly before answering, sure he was for once one step ahead of Sean. 'Just wondering what you thought about that online murder thing that's all over the news?'

'What are you talking about?' Sean asked, not interested in Zukov's games.

'The online murder, boss. Haven't you seen it yet?'

'No I haven't,' Sean told him. 'I've been a little too busy to be staring at the news all day.'

'This happened last night, boss.'

'Paulo, I haven't read a newspaper or watched TV for days and one day, God forbid, if you're in my position, plus two young kids and a wife who works, you'll know what I mean.'

'Just thought you might have had a call from someone.'

'Like who?'

'Superintendent Featherstone. Mr Addis.'

'Why would I?'

'Well, we are Special Investigations, aren't we?'

'Paulo,' Sean asked, losing his limited patience, 'is there something I should know about?'

'The online murder, boss. Just thought it was the sort of thing we might pick up.'

The look on Zukov's face told Sean he needed to find out more. 'Get in here,' Sean told him. 'Go on then. Tell me about it, but keep it succinct.'

'Some bloke from the City gets grabbed from the street in broad daylight,' Zukov began, 'and the next thing he's on Your View strapped to a chair with some nutter going on about how he and all his banker buddies are criminals and how he's going to teach them all a lesson. Keeps a hood on all the time and uses some sort of electronic device to alter his voice.'

Sean stared at him disbelievingly for a while before speaking. 'And then?'

Zukov shrugged his shoulders. 'And then he killed him.'

'How?'

'Looks like he used some sort of pulley system to hang him. Pulled the chair up and everything.'

'And this is genuine?' Sean asked, still unconvinced.

'Apparently. Bloke's family's already been in touch with the local CID. He went missing some time yesterday and hasn't been seen since.'

'Could he be in on it – some kind of prank or publicity stunt?'

'Doesn't look like it. Not the type, apparently.'

'Where you getting all this from?' Sean asked. 'How come you know so much about it?'

'Like I said – it's all over the news, boss. All over the Internet.'

Sean looked him up and down before pushing his laptop across his desk and indicating for Zukov to take a seat in front of it. 'Show me.'

Zukov sat and quickly logged onto the Internet and began to navigate his way around. He soon had what he was looking for and spun the laptop back towards Sean. 'Here you go, boss – the whole thing available to watch on Your View. It's been the most watched video since word got out.'

'Jesus,' Sean muttered as he concentrated on the screen. 'That says a lot about our society. Who the hell would want to watch a man being killed?'

'Thousands,' Zukov answered. 'Maybe even millions.'

Sean didn't answer, the video of the masked man and his victim taking over his world. He watched the entire 'show', until finally the masked preacher drew a curtain of darkness across the screen.

'What the hell is this?' Sean asked himself.

'Dunno, boss,' Zukov said, mistaking it as a question directed at him. 'But some in the media reckon maybe he thinks he's some sort of avenging angel.'

'What?'

'You know – man of the people sticking up for the little guys, striking back at the rich bankers.'

'You've got to be joking,' Sean told him. 'Avenging angel? More like another bloody psychopath looking to make a name for himself. This is all we need.'

'Maybe,' Zukov added.

Sean leaned back in his chair and fixed him with look Zukov knew all too well. 'You don't sound convinced.'

14

'It's just a lot of people seem to agree with him. Not necessarily the murder, but that it's about time something was done to the bankers.'

'What people?'

'People on Facebook and Twitter. They're all saying it.'

'Facebook? Twitter?' Sean asked. 'It's a wonder anyone gets any work done any more. Get hold of Donnelly and Sally for me. Get them back here for a briefing. They'll need to know what's happening. Shit!'

'You reckon we'll get this one then, boss?'

'Does this look like a run-of-the-mill murder to you? Does this look like someone who intends to stop any time soon? Yeah. This one's coming our way. I can feel it.'

Zukov knew he'd used up his usefulness. 'I'll go track them down for you, boss.'

'You do that,' Sean told him, watching him leave just as Detective Superintendent Featherstone entered the main office and headed his way carrying a pink cardboard folder – the colour indicating the contents were confidential. Featherstone appeared to be his jovial self, despite the bad news Sean knew he carried tucked under his armpit. He knocked once on Sean's doorframe before entering and taking a seat without being asked.

'Morning,' he began. 'How's it going?'

'Fine so far, but I'm guessing it's about to change.'

'How's the prep for the Allen case going?'

'Pretty much done,' Sean told him, his eyes never leaving the pink folder. 'Down to the jury as to whether they believe he intended to kill the boy or whether they think it was an accident. Nothing more we can do now. The abductions and false imprisonments are beyond doubt.'

'Good,' Featherstone answered, although he hadn't really been listening.

Sean nodded at the folder. 'Let me guess – the banker who was murdered live on the Internet yesterday?'

15

'You heard then?'

'Only recently.'

Featherstone tossed the folder across the desk. 'Courtesy of Mr Addis. Felt this was right up your street.'

'Thanks,' Sean said without meaning it, pulling the file towards him and flipping it open to be greeted by a professional-looking photograph of the smiling victim. 'Not the usual holiday snap-shot. Someone important?'

'Paul Elkins,' Featherstone explained. 'CEO of Fairfield's Bank based in the City, so yes, he's both important and wealthy, or at least he was. If it hadn't been for the video on Your View and the rantings of the suspect I would have assumed it was a professional hit – some Colombians or Russians making an example of him.'

'You have reason to believe he was laundering money for somebody he shouldn't have been messing with?'

'No, not yet, but it'll need to be eliminated as a possible motive.'

'Of course, but . . .'

'But what?'

'You've seen the video – looks more personal than professional.'

'There you go,' Featherstone told him. 'I knew you were the right man for the job – you're making inroads already.' Featherstone's smile was not returned. 'Anyway, he finishes work late yesterday afternoon and takes the tube home, shunning the use of a company chauffeur, as usual. He's walking along the street where he lives in Chelsea when he's attacked from behind, apparently hit over the head several times and then dragged into a white van that's parked up next to the abduction site. The van takes off and not long after that he's live on Your View. As they say, the rest is history.'

'How do we know all this?'

'We have two witnesses who saw pretty much the whole

16

thing – a housekeeper on her way home and a neighbour who happened to be looking out of her window.'

Sean scanned through the file, noting the details of the witnesses and the fact the victim had been hit over the head several times with something the neighbour described as a small, black bat. 'Looks like he used a cosh.'

'I reckon,' Featherstone agreed.

'Then he's definitely no professional.'

'How so?'

'Because a professional would have taken him out with one hit. This guy's not done this before. He's learning as he goes.'

'Which all fits with him being a disgruntled citizen with an axe to grind with bankers.'

'Well that narrows it down to just a few million suspects.'

'Indeed.' Featherstone shrugged his shoulders and heaved himself out of the uncomfortable chair. 'It's all in the file – what we know so far. I'll leave it with you and good luck. The Assistant Commissioner would of course appreciate a quick result – media's already all over this one.' He headed for the door before turning back. 'One more thing.' Sean looked at him with suspicion. 'Mr Addis has decided he'd like an old friend of yours on this one. Anna Ravenni-Ceron will be joining you shortly. Try to get on with her this time.'

Sean swallowed hard, the excitement in his stomach unwelcome, but it was already too late. As much as he might object to the criminologist and psychiatrist being attached to his investigation, he could never deny his attraction to her – or hers to him. He could almost smell her long dark hair and her soft skin, just as surely as if she was standing in the office next to him.

'I'll try.'

Assistant Commissioner Addis looked over the top of his spectacles at Anna, who sat on the opposite side of his oversized desk in his larger than normal office on the top floor of New Scotland Yard, his stare making her feel uncomfortable and disloyal.

'You understand what I need you to do, yes?' he asked her.

'I understand.'

'Same as before. Watch him, study him, speak to him as much as you can without showing your hand and report directly back to me. In exchange you get unrestricted access to the investigation, including the chance to assist with any interviews with the suspect once he's apprehended, which I'm sure with DI Corrigan in charge won't take too long.'

'I'll get as close as I can,' she told him, 'but it won't be without the risk of DI Corrigan working out what's happening. He's clever and instinctive. It won't be easy.'

'You'll find a way,' Addis leered at her. 'I have every confidence in you.'

She wondered if he knew – somehow knew about that afternoon when Sean had visited her in her office in Swiss Cottage and they'd come so close to giving in to their desires and attraction for one another. But how could he? Then again, how did he know half the things he seemed to know?

'I'll do what I can,' she finally answered.

She felt him studying her for a while, searching for a weakness. 'You think I'm being . . . underhand in wanting him watched by someone from your profession?' She said nothing. 'You see, Anna, Corrigan is an asset. No matter what you may think, I value him as such. But let's be honest with each other, he's not exactly . . . conventional. I've seen his type before – the ones who need to be right on the edge all the time to get the best out of themselves. Trouble with being on the edge is you're more likely to fall. I want to see that coming before it happens with DI Corrigan. I have his best interests at heart here, which is why I value your professional opinion as a psychiatrist.'

18

'Of course. I understand.' Anna didn't believe a word Addis was saying.

'One thing about Corrigan that does concern me,' Addis told her, 'is his compulsion to confront the suspects, once he has them cornered, so to speak. He seems determined to challenge them face-to-face, and *alone*. Any ideas as to why that could be?'

Anna moved uncomfortably in her chair and cleared her throat. Was this Addis gathering evidence against Sean for some reason, or was he concerned Sean would do something to damage the reputation of the Metropolitan Police? The possibility that the Assistant Commissioner could be concerned for his officer's welfare never crossed her mind.

'It's a part of him he can't control. A recklessness that manifests itself in other ways too.' She stopped, realizing she'd probably said too much.

'Other ways?' Addis seized on it. 'Such as?'

'Such as he takes risks that others probably wouldn't, and he can be a little clumsy, socially. Can say things he immediately regrets or sometimes doesn't.' She hoped Addis had bought it.

Addis said nothing for a while before grunting and shrugging his shoulders. 'Indeed. But why does he have this reckless need to be alone with the suspects at all? He was damn lucky Thomas Keller didn't blow his head off.'

'I think he needs it,' Anna told him, trying to tell him the truth while also protecting Sean. 'To have a chance to talk alone with them, before the lawyers and procedure take over – to speak with them in an *undiluted* way. So for a while he can observe and absorb everything about them while they're still their true selves.'

'And why would he want to do that?'

'So next time, if he has to, he can become like them. You have to think like a criminal to catch a criminal. Isn't that what you police say?'

'Maybe twenty years ago,' Addis scoffed.

Anna ignored him. 'Only with DI Corrigan the criminals are murderers. Psychopaths, sociopaths and sometimes just the mentally ill. It can't be easy, having to think like them. It must be a very dark and lonely place to be – don't you think?'

More silence from Addis before he spoke. 'Quite. And this time alone he craves with the suspects is an important part of him being able to think like them?'

'I believe so. He clearly learns from the encounters. I can't see him stopping, unless he's made to.'

'There's no need for that just yet,' Addis jumped in. 'Like I said – he's a valuable asset to me. I wouldn't want to do anything to upset his . . . modus operandi.'

'No,' Anna agreed. 'I don't suppose you would.'

Geoff Jackson sat on his swivel chair with his feet on his desk while he chewed his pen and twizzled an unlit cigarette in the other hand. He'd been staring at his screen all morning watching the footage of Paul Elkins's murder on Your View over and over again, oblivious to the constant clatter of voices and the ringing of phones in the huge office he sat at the centre of. As the crime editor for *The World*, the UK's best-selling newspaper, he could have had a private side office, but he liked to be in the middle of it – it helped him think. He was forty-eight now and had been a journalist all his adult life. The silence of a private office would have driven him mad and he knew it. He also knew that the Your View murder was the biggest story out there and he was determined to make it his. He could smell the paperback already, maybe even a TV documentary. But first he needed to make his name and face synonymous with this murder and the other killings he was sure would follow.

Jackson sensed the editor close by before he saw her, leaping to his feet, his tallish body kept slim by smoking as often and as much as he could in this new non-smoking world, his accent-less voice made increasingly gravelly by the same addiction. 'Sue,' he stopped her. 'Can I have a word?'

Sue Dempsey rolled her blue eyes before speaking. 'What is it, Geoff?' At five foot nine she was almost as tall as Jackson, with the same lithe body, her hair dyed ash blonde to hide the grey. At fifty-one she still turned heads.

'The Your View murder – I need you to hold the front page for me. Tomorrow and the days after that.'

'What?' She almost laughed, walking away with Jackson in pursuit. 'You must be crazy.'

'I need this, Sue,' Jackson all but pleaded, thinking of his above-average flat in Soho and the expensive thirty-two-year-old girlfriend he shared it with.

'You know the score, Geoff. Everything has to be discussed and agreed in the editors' meeting. I can't sanction anything alone, not in this day and age.'

'But you can back me up.'

'And why would I do that?'

'Because this story is the biggest thing out there. It's fucking huge.'

'Bigger than the terrorist attack in LA?'

'If it doesn't happen on our shores the readers soon lose interest – you know that. This Your View thing could run and run. We need to make this story ours. This story needs to belong to *The World*.' Dempsey stopped and turned to him. He felt her resolve weakening. 'The LA story will be dead news in a couple of days. I still have my contacts at the Yard. We could get the inside track. People are already talking about this guy as being some kind of avenging angel. We could even run our own public polls – "Do you agree with what the Your View Killer is doing or not?" It's a winner, Sue. I'm telling you, this is gonna be big. Remember no one believed me when I started digging up the dirt on our celebrity paedophile friends. Look how big that story got. Surely I'm still owed a few favours.'

21

'I have to admit that was good work,' Dempsey agreed.

'It was better than good,' Jackson argued. 'The cops didn't have a clue what was going on – didn't believe what the parents of the children were telling them until I blew the lid off the whole ring.' His expression of self-congratulation suddenly faded to something more serious, as if he was recalling a sad moment from his own life. 'I saved a lot of kids from suffering the same fate as the ones those bastards had already got their hands on.'

'Yes you did,' Dempsey admitted. 'It was good work all around. All right, Geoff. All right, but no funny business. Keep it clean or it might be a journalist this madman comes after next.'

'And exclusivity,' he almost talked over her. 'I get exclusivity. No other journos on the story. Just me.'

'Thinking ahead, Geoff?'

'I just want what's best for the paper.'

'Of course you do,' she answered. 'That's what we all want. OK. You have your exclusivity, but you better bring home the meat.'

'When have I ever not?' he asked with a broadening smile.

'Don't ask,' she told him and began walk away before turning back to him. 'I noticed you still haven't written the paperback about the celebrity paedophile ring. You usually turn the paperback around in a few weeks – strike while the iron is hot and all that bollocks.'

'Not this time,' he answered. 'As much as I'd like to expose those slimy bastard celebs for everything they are, some things are still sacred. I wouldn't write about abused kids for money. Not my style.'

'Not going soft on me, are you, Geoff?' Dempsey smiled and turned on her heels before he could answer.

Jackson made his way back to his desk whistling a happy little tune and wondering whether he should call his publishers now, whet their appetites, or wait until things had really brewed up. Until it was the only thing anyone was talking about.

Sean and Donnelly pulled up on the south side of Barnes Bridge in southwest London. The Marine Policing Unit had found a body floating in the Thames underneath the bridge, trapped by the whirlpool created by the current trying to find a way around. They climbed from their car and made their way to the small gathering of both uniformed and CID officers next to the bridge watching the police launch still trying to recover the forlorn body from behind the sanctuary of a small taped-off area of the pavement. Sean and Donnelly flashed their warrant cards to the uniformed officer guarding the small cordon and headed for the two men in suits.

Sean offered his hand. 'DI Corrigan – Special Investigations Unit.' Donnelly followed suit.

'DS Rob Evans,' the older, shorter, stockier man offered, speaking in a mild Yorkshire accent.

'DC Nathan Mead,' the young, lean, tall one introduced himself in his London accent.

Evans looked back down at the launch struggling in the swell of the river below. The stiff body, arms stretched to the side, face down, swirled in the dark brown water of the Thames by the bridge foundation as another train crashed over above.

'They're still struggling to get the poor bastard out,' he explained. 'Every time they almost have him they nearly get smashed against the side of the bridge, but the current's calming down now. They should be able to get a hook into him soon.' Sean and Donnelly just nodded as they watched the grim spectacle. Bodies fished from the Thames were always tough to deal with – the cold of the water intensifying rigor mortis, while the marine life also took a quick toll.

'Reckon he's your man, do you?' Evans asked.

'Could be,' Sean answered. 'He looks to be suited and

booted. Can't be too many men in suits floating in the Thames today.'

'I bloody hope not,' Evans told him. 'That's the trouble with being posted to Wandsworth – we cover the Thames all the way from bloody Barnes to Battersea. We get more floaters than most. At least this one's still in one piece.' Sean didn't answer, watching the launch inching closer and closer to the body until finally one of the crew managed to hook the dead man's clothing with a grappling pole.

'About time,' Evans moaned. 'We can't get on the boat here. I've told them we'll meet them down by the local rowing club. There's a small pier there, or mooring, or what-ever you want to call it. Anyway, I've said we'll meet them there once they fished him out. You coming?' he asked Sean, who barely heard him, transfixed by the macabre scene of the unyielding body being heaved on board the launch by the crew. The man's head was raised by the rigor mortis in his neck muscles, his eyes and mouth wide open as if staring straight at Sean. 'I said, are you coming?' Evans repeated.

Sean snapped out of his reverie and spun to face him. 'What? Yeah. Sure. We're coming. Where to?'

Evans rolled his eyes. 'Just follow us.'

'Fine,' Sean answered and followed the other detectives back to the waiting cars. Donnelly spoke first as they pulled away from the kerb.

'Think it's our man?'

'Looks like it. Has to be really, doesn't it,' Sean answered.

'Aye. I reckon so. First thoughts?'

'To be honest, I'm trying not to have any.'

'Not like you,' Donnelly pointed out. 'You all right?'

'I'm fine,' Sean lied, the man's staring eyes mixing with images of Anna in his troubled mind – a sense of fear and excitement at the thought of being with her day-to-day distracting him from where he needed to be – preventing him from being able to fully immerse himself in the abduction and

24

murder of the man who now lay dead on the floor of a police launch.

'Well, I don't suppose he dumped him in the river around here,' Donnelly offered. 'Too busy – unless he chucked him off the bridge in the middle of the night.'

'No,' Sean dismissed the possibility. 'Tide brought him here. The Marine Unit might be able to tell us where from.'

'Aye,' was all Donnelly replied and they finished the rest of the short journey in silence, parking up and following the Wandsworth detectives to the small pier of the rowing club where the police launch was already moored.

'We'll wait here for you,' Evans told them, standing at the beginning of the pier. 'Not a lot of room on those things,' he explained, nodding towards the launch. 'If he's not your man you can always kick it back to us, but if it is . . .'

'Fair enough,' Sean agreed and headed off along the short pier.

Donnelly waited until they were out of earshot before speaking quietly. 'I guess he's had his fill of floaters.'

'He could always get a posting to Catford,' Sean told him before pulling his warrant card from his coat pocket and flashing it to the wary launch crew. 'DI Corrigan. Special Investigations Unit. I think this body belongs to us.'

'Come on board,' the sergeant replied. The three white stripes on his lifejacket singled him out as the boat's leader. 'Mind your step though. Deck's a little slippery. Never ceases to amaze me how much water comes out of a dead body – especially when it's fully clothed.' Donnelly rolled his eyes while Sean ignored the comment as they stepped on board.

The river police had already managed to manhandle the body into a black zip-up body-bag, although the victim's arms still protruded somewhat out to his side. They'd left the bag open for the detectives.

'Gonna have a hell of a job getting that zipped up,' the sergeant explained.

'You'll manage,' Sean told him before moving closer to the body and crouching down, the movement of the boat adding to his rising nausea. 'How long d'you reckon he's been in the water for?'

'Hard to say,' the sergeant replied. 'A good few hours at least.'

'Was he dumped close by?' Sean asked.

The sergeant pulled an expression of indifference. 'I shouldn't think so. Tide's been going out for a good while now. Probably somewhere between Teddington and Richmond.'

'Great,' Donnelly complained, aware of the size of area they would now have to consider.

Sean studied the remains of Paul Elkins, the cause of death and exposure to the water making his face appear bloated and grotesque, his eyes bulbous and red – mouth open with a swollen, grey tongue protruding from within. Sean tried not to think of the small marine creatures that would have already found their way into the man's mouth, making his body their temporary home as well as a food supply. The burn marks and bruising left around his neck by the rope used to kill him left no doubt as to the cause of death, although the mandatory post-mortem would still have to officially confirm it.

'When we're done,' Sean told the sergeant, 'I want you to ensure the body is taken to the mortuary at Guy's Hospital. Understand?'

The sergeant drew a sharp intake of breath. 'Tricky. Bodies from this area are supposed to be taken to Charing Cross. Coroner's Courts are very twitchy about jurisdiction.'

'My call,' he snapped at him slightly. 'He goes to Dr Canning at Guy's. No one else.'

'So he is the man you're looking for, then?' the sergeant deduced.

'Yeah,' Sean answered mournfully. 'He's our victim.' He stood and turned to Donnelly.

'Anything catch your eye?' Donnelly asked.

'Nothing particular, although . . .'

'Although what?'

'Although there's only two reasons a killer removes a body from the scene of the murder,' Sean explained. 'One is because the scene links them in some way to the victim, so they have to move it, or . . .'

'Or?' Donnelly pushed, impatient to hear the answer.

'Or because they need to continue using the scene – to live in, to run a business from, although in this case neither of those seem likely.'

'What then?' Donnelly asked.

'He needs it,' Sean explained. 'He needs to use it again for other victims and there will be more. He's as good as told us there will.'

'I was afraid you were gonna say that,' Donnelly told him. 'Why is it with us there's always going to be more?'

'Welcome to Special Investigations,' Sean answered.

'So what we dealing with here? Just another fucking lunatic, or could this one really be some sort of self-proclaimed avenging angel – a normal guy pushed too far?'

'It doesn't really matter right now,' Sean explained. 'What does matter is that he's organized, motivated, clever and dangerous. And we need to find him and stop him, before this whole thing gets completely out of control.'

'Fair enough,' Donnelly agreed. 'D'you want me to sort out a Family Liaison Officer?'

'Yeah, sure.' Sean tried not to think of the pain he was about to put the family through. 'But I need to see them first – let them know what to expect, maybe get some early answers.'

'Want some company?' Donnelly asked.

'Why not,' he answered. 'You can keep me on the right path.'

'Meaning?' Donnelly asked.

'Meaning,' Sean explained, 'this isn't exactly what we've become used to – is it? Not like he's a young woman abducted from her own home or a young child snatched from his bed. They were . . . *vulnerable*. This man had no vulnerabilities – or so he thought. Male, in his fifties, rich, powerful. Can't see the public shedding too many tears over him.'

'Aye, well,' Donnelly reminded him, 'the man's still been killed and anyone who gets murdered in a strange and interesting way on our patch relies on us to find their killer – no matter what their background.'

'I know that,' he agreed, 'but don't expect an avalanche of information if we end up relying on the public to help us solve this one.'

'Sometimes, boss,' Donnelly told him, 'you have a very bleak view of mankind.'

'We'll see,' he warned him more than told him. 'We'll see.'

DS Sally Jones was in her side office ploughing through the huge number of reports the investigation had already generated. She'd spent a good part of the day speaking on the phone with people from Your View, all of whom who were deeply upset and shocked that their 'medium' had been used for such a mindless act of violence, but were powerless to stop it happening again, unless they closed down their entire operation, which of course they were not prepared to do. They were sure the police and public would understand. She sensed a disturbance in the main office and looked up to see Anna standing in the middle of a small group of detectives chatting cheerfully, explaining her sudden, unannounced arrival.

Sally felt the colour drain from her face and an old, familiar sick feeling spreading in her stomach. Her private sessions with Anna had been held in complete secrecy, without the knowledge of anyone connected to the police, but now her psychiatrist was standing in her office talking to her work colleagues.

She practically jumped from her chair and paced into the main office, weaving her way through the small group and seizing Anna by the arm. 'Anna. So nice to see you. What are you doing here?' she faked and began to steer her towards the relative privacy of her own office.

'No one knows, Sally, if that's what you look so worried about,' Anna tried to calm her concerns, 'and no one's going to know. I'm only here to advise on the Your View investigation – that's all.'

'Advise on the investigation?' Sally questioned. 'I seem to remember the last time you did that things didn't work out too well. Not for Sean, anyway.'

'Sally,' Anna explained, looking around to make sure they were out of earshot. 'If me being here is going to cause hostility between us – if it's going to adversely affect our patient-doctor relationship, then I promise you, I'll tell the Assistant Commissioner I can't help with the case.' There was a silent pause. 'You're more important to me than this investigation.'

Sally studied her for a good while, this woman she'd grown to trust with her deepest secrets – secrets she kept even from Sean. 'Jesus, Anna. I'm really sorry. I just didn't expect to see you standing in here, in my office. It threw me a bit.'

'My fault,' Anna admitted. 'I should have spoken to you first. Warned you.'

'You don't have to check with me. Your work is your work. Outside of our relationship you owe me nothing.' There was a silent truce between them for a moment before Sally spoke again. 'So, here we are again. You. Me. *Sean*. A murder investigation.'

'Looks that way. Speaking of which, how is Sean?'

Sally tried to hide her suspicion about the true nature of Sean and Anna's relationship. She barely knew Sean's wife Kate, and didn't particularly like the little she did know, if she was honest, but still she felt strangely compelled to protect

Sean's marriage – some deep instinct in her warning he could be lost into a world of turmoil without her and their two young daughters. In Anna, she sensed a threat.

'Sean's Sean,' she answered. 'He's fine, as usual. Bull in a china shop, all guns blazing, shooting from the hip and God help anyone who gets in the way.'

'Hasn't changed then,' Anna joked.

Sally forced a smile. 'Same old, same old.'

'Well,' Anna told her, getting to her feet. 'I'd better get on with what I'm being paid for. Do you think Sean would mind if I borrowed his office?'

'No,' Sally said and immediately regretted it. 'Or you could share with me.'

Anna looked around. 'Looks like you're already sharing the rent.'

'Ah. Yeah. DS Donnelly,' Sally admitted.

'I think Sean might tolerate me a little better.'

'I take your point. Is there anything you need?'

'No,' Anna told her. 'I already have the file and the video. That's all I need for now. I'll see you later for coffee perhaps?'

'Yeah, sure,' Sally replied, trying to sound a lot friendlier than she felt, watching Anna float from the office and into Sean's. 'This is not good,' she whispered to herself. 'This is not good at all.'

'Are you sure this isn't a professional hit made to look like something else?' Donnelly asked as they approached Elm Park Road in Chelsea – the victim's home street and the place he was abducted from.

'I'm not sure of anything yet,' Sean admitted, 'but if he got caught with his hand in the cookie jar while laundering someone's money, especially if they're Eastern European or South American, they wouldn't want to hide what they'd done. They like to make public statements – keep everyone else in line. And the abduction too doesn't feel right. If it had been organized crime they would have lured him some-where – somewhere quiet and out of sight. But I'm not ruling anything out until we know more.'

Donnelly parked as close as he could to Elkins's home. Sean was out the car before he'd had time to kill the engine, looking up and down the upmarket street – looking for ghosts. Donnelly soon joined him.

'Hell of a place to abduct somebody from,' he offered.

'And in daylight,' Sean added.

'A confident customer.'

'Or insane.'

'Either way the whole thing was seen by a couple of witnesses – both saying the suspect's white van was parked in the street already, waiting for Elkins. So he wasn't followed.'

'Not yesterday anyway,' Sean explained, 'but he was followed at some point, otherwise how could the suspect know where he lived and the fact he regularly walked from the tube station to his home? Unless he already knew him – knew his habits.'

'Someone who worked for him in the past?' Donnelly suggested.

'In the City?'

'No. These people have a lot of hired help. I was thinking more a disgruntled gardener, or maintenance man, or even a husband of a cleaner his missus sacked.'

'Possibly,' Sean agreed. 'It'll all need to be checked out. It'll be nice if it's that easy.'

'Shall we do the witnesses first or the family?'

'The family,' Sean replied. 'Get it over with.'

'If you don't want to see them you don't have to,' Donnelly offered. 'I can always come back later with Sally.'

'No,' he insisted. 'I want to see them, or his wife at least.'

'Fair enough.' Donnelly didn't argue. 'After you.'

Sean walked the short distance along the immaculate street and climbed the short flight of steps to the shining black door of number twelve. He imagined Paul Elkins coming home to this door, day after day, content and confident, untouched by the problems *normal* people had – unable to imagine something like this could ever happen to him. Was that what the killer wanted – to drag the wealthy and privileged into a world where they could feel the pain of everyday life? Had the killer felt too much pain to bear? He took a deep breath and rang the doorbell – avoiding the heavy-looking metal door knocker in the shape of a lion's head that looked like it would wake the dead. The last thing he wanted to do was advertise their presence. It was only a matter of time before the media discovered the victim's home address and came crawling around, but he wanted to keep things quiet for as long as he could.

After a few seconds the door was opened by a short, stocky man in his late twenties wearing spectacles and dressed in an inexpensive-looking dark suit. He eyed them suspiciously. 'Can I help you?' he asked with a slight London accent.

Sean knew immediately he was a fellow detective as he showed him his warrant card. 'DI Sean Corrigan from the Special Investigations Unit.'

'DS Donnelly,' Donnelly told him without producing his identification, 'from the same.'

The other detective seemed to immediately relax. 'Am I glad to see you,' he whispered. 'I was told you'd be taking this one over. Babysitting the family of a murder victim isn't exactly my thing. DC Jonnie Mendham, by the way. You'd better come in.' He stepped aside and allowed them to enter before closing the door and continuing to talk in a whisper. 'They're all gathered in the living room,' Mendham explained. 'Mrs Elkins and her two kids, Jack and Evie. There's also a friend of Mrs Elkins here too, Trudy Bevens – a shoulder to cry on and all that.'

'Fine,' Sean acknowledged as he and Donnelly followed Mendham towards the living room and the desperate sadness he knew he'd find inside.

'Any idea how long it'll be before you send someone to take over from me?' Mendham's voice held a slight pleading note. 'I'm not trained for this family liaison stuff.'

'Soon enough,' Sean answered carelessly. 'Until then just keep a watch out for reporters and make sure they don't speak to anyone they don't know on the phone. Remind them details of the investigations are confidential and not to be shared even with family and close friends until I say it's OK.'

'No problem,' Mendham agreed in a whisper. 'Just get me out of this mausoleum.' He opened the living-room door before Sean could reply and raised his voice to its normal volume. 'Mrs Elkins,' he addressed the attractive woman in her late forties who remained seated as she looked up at them – her appearance still immaculate despite the circumstances, her ash blonde hair framing her tanned face and piercing blue eyes that had reddened somewhat with crying.

'Yes,' she answered as strongly as she could, her voice wavering somewhat.

'This is Detective Inspector Corrigan and Detective Sergeant Donnelly from our Special Investigations Unit,' Mendham explained. 'They'll be taking over the investigation.'

'Why?' she asked in a slightly clipped accent.

'It's the way things work,' Sean spoke to her for the first time as he scanned the other faces in the room – a weeping girl of no more than eleven or twelve who sat close to her mother wrapped in a protective arm, a stoical-looking boy probably about fourteen and Mrs Elkins's tearful friend. 'Most serious and unusual cases get passed on to us. We have a certain amount of experience in dealing with investigations like this.'

'I wasn't aware that anything like this had ever happened before,' she questioned him.

'It hasn't,' he agreed. 'I meant experience in dealing with things that are a little out of the ordinary.'

'*A little out of the ordinary*,' she repeated, looking at him blankly. 'My husband's dead. Murdered by some lunatic.'

'And we're very sorry for your loss,' Donnelly intervened. 'We're here because we're best equipped to find whoever did this and bring them to justice, but we need to ask some questions. Maybe it would be better if the children weren't here for that.'

'No,' she snapped back. 'We stay together. I'm not about to let them out of my sight. Not until you've caught this madman.'

'Fair enough.' Donnelly didn't argue. 'I reckon I'd be the same. Do you mind if we sit down?'

'Sorry,' she apologized. 'Of course not. Please.'

They both sat on the same large sofa opposite Mrs Elkins and her daughter, Sean glad of the large size of the room – just the thought of being trapped in a small room with this many grieving people was enough to make him feel claustrophobic.

'I appreciate this must be very difficult,' Sean tried to say the things she no doubt expected him to say, 'but our questions really can't wait.'

'I understand,' she assured him. 'Ask what you need to. Let's just get it over with.'

'What time did your husband leave for work yesterday?' Sean asked.

'Not long after seven,' she answered. 'His usual time.'

'A hard-working man.' Donnelly tried to ease the tension.

'You don't get to where Paul was working nine to five,' she told them. 'It takes dedication and sacrifice.'

'Yet he was abducted at about five pm – in the street outside,' Sean reminded her. 'So he didn't always work late?'

'No,' she agreed, slightly defensively. 'Not always, but most days. Does it matter?'

Did you know he'd finished work early? Sean asked the killer silent questions. *Did you somehow know?*

34

'Did he call you at all during the day?' he asked, more to try to establish a rhythm of questions and answers than hoping to discover anything useful, 'or contact you somehow?'

'He called me a couple of times,' she answered. 'Once in the morning and again early afternoon – to let me know he was about to leave work.' She suddenly choked up, her tears contagious amongst the other women while the boy looked on blankly. *Was the boy somehow involved?* Sean asked himself, before deciding he was most likely still in shock. The tears would come later. 'It was the last time I ever got to speak to him,' she managed to say.

'Why call twice?' Sean asked, trying to remember the last time he'd called his wife Kate more than once a day just for the sake of it. 'Was something troubling him?'

'No,' she answered tearfully. 'He usually called me twice or more a day just to say hello. No particular reason. I think he worried I'd get bored if he didn't.'

'But he didn't seem worried about anything?' Sean persisted.

'No,' she insisted.

'Didn't mention anything at all?'

'No,' she repeated. 'What could he be worried about?'

'He was the CEO of Fairfield's Bank, yes?' Sean asked.

'So?'

'Not exactly the most popular people in the world right now – bankers,' he reminded her.

'I understand that,' she assured him, 'and I know this madman used that as some type of twisted justification to commit murder, but Paul was a good man. He believed in responsible banking. He was as interested in making extra pounds and pennies for ordinary people as he was millions for multinationals.'

Sean couldn't help but roll his eyes around his salubrious surroundings. 'I'm sure that's true,' he said as tactfully as he knew how, 'but from the outside he would have looked like just another wealthy banker.'

'From the outside,' she pointed out. 'This monster knew nothing about Paul. He gave away thousands to charity. I used to joke that he'd give away everything we had if I'd allow him – make us homeless.'

'Why?' Sean asked, not sure where his questions would take him, but asking anyway. 'Did he feel guilty about his wealth for some reason?'

'No,' she bit. 'Why should he? Why should we? We've worked hard for everything we have. We both have. But there'll always be jealous people who would rather just take what we have than earn it for themselves.'

Sean imagined her and her dead husband's backgrounds – wealthy families sending them to the best schools and the best universities, feeding them in to the network of the privileged to ensure they'd be groomed for the top jobs. He swallowed his resentment.

'So you think your husband was killed by someone who is jealous of him?' he asked.

'Of course he was,' Mrs Elkins insisted. 'What else could it be?'

'Do you have someone in mind?' he encouraged her. 'Someone you know was jealous of your husband?'

'No.' She shook her head and pulled her daughter closer. 'We don't know anyone who could possibly do anything like this. Paul was killed by a stranger – a bitter, jealous stranger.'

'And work?' Sean persisted. 'Was there anyone he'd been having trouble with at work?'

'Look.' She closed her eyes and tried to compose herself. 'Paul was a very senior executive. It would be unrealistic to think there wasn't a degree of professional jealousy, but nothing that would lead to this.'

'You'd be surprised,' Sean told her. 'Jealously can make people do terrible things.'

'And it has,' she agreed, 'but not by someone we know. Paul was liked. He was a good man. He cared about other people – including the people he worked with. No one would have hurt him. My God,' Mrs Elkins suddenly said as she began to sob heavily. Her friend quickly took some tissues from a box on the table in front of her and handed them to her. 'I'm already talking about him in the past tense.' Her daughter's sobbing also intensified as Sean looked on; the need to escape to the sanctuary of the street was beginning to overwhelm him. He breathed in deeply and steadied himself.

'What about someone else?' he asked. 'Someone who worked at the house maybe?'

'No,' she insisted, shaking her head again. 'We only have the cleaners, and Rosemary who helps out with the children, and Simon the gardener, but no one else and they all loved Paul. He looked after them well.'

'Was he having any trouble at work,' he pressed, 'from an unhappy customer – any threatening phone calls or letters – emails?'

'Not that he told me of,' she assured him. 'I mean, when things were at their worst, when the banking crisis thing first started, there were threats to the bank, but nothing Paul seemed worried about. He didn't mention anything specific. But he never talked about work at home. Maybe the bank can tell you more – I'm not sure, but this all seems a bit pointless. He was taken by an insane murdering animal, not a jealous colleague or bitter employee, and if you don't catch him he'll do it again,' she warned them. 'He's as good as said he will.'

Sean and Donnelly looked at each other for a long few seconds before looking back at Mrs Elkins.

'I think we have everything we need for now,' Donnelly intervened. 'A Family Liaison Officer from Special Investigations will come to see you later, and rest assured we'll be in touch as soon as we find out anything. In the meantime, if you think of anything, anything at all, just tell the Family Liaison Officer.'

'And that's it?' she asked. 'Paul is murdered – a brief visit from the police and we're supposed to just get on with our lives?'

'No,' Sean warned her. 'I'm sorry, but this is just the beginning. It won't be over until we find the man who did this.'

Mrs Elkins looked to the ceiling before taking a more conciliatory tone. 'I'm sorry. I've been unreasonable. It's just I can't believe this has actually happened. It all seems so impossible.'

'No need to apologize,' Sean assured her, getting to his feet. 'You've suffered a terrible shock. Best thing I can do for you now is find the man who did this.' He pulled a business card out and placed it on the table in front of her. 'Call me if you need anything – any time. Don't get up. We'll see ourselves out.'

Donnelly pushed himself off the sofa and followed Sean out of the room towards the front door, with Mendham following close behind. 'Any idea when you'll get your Family Liaison Officer here? I don't fancy being stuck here long,' he asked.

'They'll be here when they're here,' Sean reprimanded him.

'Cheer up, son,' Donnelly told him. 'It's not all car chases and kicking down doors. Sometimes we have to *earn* our meagre wages.'

'You won't be here too long,' Sean assured him as he opened the front door and walked into the street without turning to see Mendham's frustrated gestures at being abandoned.

'What now?' Donnelly asked.

'You said there were witnesses,' Sean reminded him. 'We might as well speak to them seeing as how we're already here.'

'Aye,' Donnelly agreed. 'So which one do you want to see – the housekeeper or the yummy mummy?'

'I'll take the mum.'

'That figures. Name's Angela Haitink. Number eighteen.'

'Thanks,' Sean told him and headed off without saying more. A few seconds later he was standing on the steps of a five-storey white Georgian house with a black door so shiny it made his reflection vibrate when he used the ornate chrome knocker.

Interviewing witnesses was never something he'd enjoyed. He always milked them for everything and anything they were worth, but he found their inaccuracies and hesitancy frustrating and annoying. He reminded himself not to treat Angela Haitink as a suspect. After almost a minute the door was answered by a tall, slim woman in her mid-thirties, with short blonde hair in a ponytail, wearing a designer tracksuit and trainers that he guessed would cost him a week's wages. Her similarity to the mothers of the children taken by Douglas Allen reminded him of the impending trial he'd almost forgotten about in the fury of a new case.

'Yes,' she asked, her accent exactly what he expected. 'Can I help you with something?' She looked him up and down as if he was an unwanted salesman.

He opened his warrant card and waited for a change in her expression that never came. 'Angela Haitink?' he asked. She nodded yes. 'Detective Inspector Corrigan. I'm investigating the murder of Paul Elkins. I understand you witnessed his abduction?'

She glanced at her sports watch, her expression finally changing to one of concern. 'Do we have to do this right now? I'm afraid I'm running a little late.'

He swallowed his resentment. 'It is rather important,' he told her. 'A man has been killed. One of your neighbours.'

She looked up and down the street before speaking again. 'Of course. I'm sorry. Please come in.' She stepped aside and allowed him to enter, heading for the kitchen after closing the door – Sean following, taking in the opulent surroundings. 'It was a terrible thing,' she told him without sounding

39

genuinely concerned. 'We're all in a state of shock. I even knew the poor man, for God's sake.'

'You knew him?'

'Well, I mean I said hello to him occasionally and I think my husband knew him a little better, but really – in a street like this. I just assumed he was being robbed, but then he bundled him into the back of a white van and drove away with him . . . I mean – my God.'

'So you called 999?'

'I had to – I mean, I had to do something.'

'You did the right thing,' he encouraged her, reminding himself to go softly.

'I couldn't believe what I was seeing. That's when I phoned the police, but by the time they got here he was long gone and then I saw the news and found out that he'd been murdered – live on the Internet. Terrible. Just terrible.'

'Which is why I need you to remember everything you saw,' he told her as warmly as he could, 'to help us catch the man who did this as quickly as possible.'

'Of course. But I wouldn't want anyone to find out I've spoken to the police. I mean, what if the killer found out? He could come after me.'

'He won't,' Sean tried to reassure her, resisting the temptation to roll his eyes. 'We don't think organized crime's involved here. This one's not the type to go after witnesses.'

'You don't *think*?'

'No. I don't. But we can keep your identity secret, even if you end up giving evidence in court.' He could have kicked himself as soon as he said it.

'In *court*?' she almost shouted. 'I don't think I could give evidence in court.'

How he missed southeast London. He would have arrested her for obstructing an investigation by now and dragged her back to Peckham nick to be interviewed there. 'It'll probably never come to it,' he lied, 'but you do need to tell me what you saw.' She appeared unconvinced. 'I'm sorry,' he eventually told her. 'You really have no choice, but there's nothing to worry about.' Still she said nothing, as if she was still considering the options she didn't have. 'Why don't you start by showing me where you were when you saw Mr Elkins being attacked?'

'I was in my bedroom,' she told him, but made no move towards it.

Why were people always so much more bashful about showing their bedrooms than any other room? he wondered – as if it was the one room that betrayed our personal life more than any other.

'Don't worry,' he tried to joke. 'If it's in a mess I promise not to tell anyone.'

'No it's not that,' she stumbled a little. 'Please. Follow me. It's on the second floor.'

She led him to the stairs and up to the second-floor master bedroom that looked about the size of Sean's entire ground floor. He followed her to the window that overlooked the street below and they both peered down on the quiet road.

'It's usually like this,' she told him. 'Quiet and private.'

'So did you notice the white van parked up before the attack? It must have stood out a little.'

'I did notice it,' she admitted, 'but it didn't bother me. There's always tradesmen of one type or another in the street.'

'Did you notice how long it was there for?'

'I . . . I really couldn't say.'

'When did you first notice it?'

'Again, I'm . . . I'm not sure.'

'Well, what were you doing?'

'Goodness. So many questions.'

He realized he was moving too quickly and tried to back off a little. 'What I mean is . . . try and think back to what you were doing the first time you saw the van. What drew your attention to it?'

41

'Nothing particularly . . . just, nothing.'

'Were you here – by this window?'

'No. No I don't think I was, actually.'

'Then where? Outside? Inside?'

Her eyes began to flicker with recollection. 'Neither. I was neither.'

'Excuse me?' he asked, his turn to be confused.

'I was at the front door, which was open for some reason.' He let her think for a few seconds. 'I remember. I'd just taken delivery of a parcel, something I'd ordered online, some new sheets for the children's beds, so that would have been almost exactly five. Yeah, definitely, because Marie, our nanny, had already picked the kids up from school and was giving them tea when the parcel arrived.'

'Good,' Sean told her. 'Was there anybody by the van or in it?'

'No,' she told him flatly. 'Definitely no one by it and if there was someone in it, which I'm sure there was now, I couldn't see. It had those darkened, tinted windows.'

'Was the window down maybe?'

'No. I don't think so.'

'Perhaps it was down slightly,' he suggested, 'to let smoke from a cigarette out, or maybe you heard a radio playing inside.'

'No. No. Nothing. It was lifeless.'

'So when was the next time you saw it?'

'When the poor man was being dragged into it.'

'And when was that?'

'Just before I called the police – seconds before.'

Sean recalled the time the case file said the 999 call was made at – just after six pm. 'What did you see? Tell me everything you saw.'

'Well, I was here, close to the window, checking the house-keeper had cleaned properly, she doesn't always, and some movement outside, on the other side of the street, caught my eye.'

'That's where the van was?' Sean interrupted. 'On the other side of the street?'

'Yes,' she told him, 'otherwise I probably wouldn't have noticed anything.'

'Go on.'

'So I looked out of the window and saw one man almost lying on the floor while this other man wearing a ski-mask was leaning over him, beating him about the head with this little black bat thing.'

'How many times?'

'I don't know. Several.' *An amateur*, Sean reminded himself. 'Then he picked him off the ground and literally dragged him to the white van and bundled him in the back. I couldn't believe what I was seeing. Anyway, I grabbed the phone,' she pointed to the one next to her bed, 'and phoned the police. By the time someone answered he, the man with the ski-mask over his face, was still at the back of his van. He was there for quite a while actually, and then while I was talking to the police on the phone he closed the doors, ran around to the driver's side, got in, started the van and drove away as calm as you like.'

'Could you see what he was doing at the back of the van?'

'No. Sorry. I was at the wrong angle to see.'

'But he was there for a while?'

'Yes.'

What the hell were you doing, my friend? You abduct a man from a London street in broad daylight. Then you mess around at the back of your van for several minutes. Why would you do that? Why take the risk?

'Did he restrain him at all?' Sean asked. 'Tie him up or use handcuffs – anything like that?'

'No. He just hit him over the head and dragged him to the van.'

A fully grown man, unrestrained in the back of a van, could make a hell of a noise. Did you really risk driving across London with him thrashing around? I don't think so. So is that what you were doing

43

at the back of the van – restraining him, or drugging him? He had a flash back to the Thomas Keller case – a rapist and murder who used chloroform to overpower his victims. *You must have been. You must have been. This was all so carefully planned – victim selection and research, the room you prepared for his murder – you would have planned how to restrain them too – you must have.*

'You all right, Inspector?' Angela Haitink's voice brought him back.

'What?' He remembered she was there. 'Yeah. Fine. I was just thinking something through.' He quickly re-gathered his thoughts. 'And then he just calmly drove away?'

'Well, yes.'

'At speed, engine revving, tyres squealing?'

'No. Nothing. Just pulled out and drove away. I gave the police the number plate. Can't you find him from that?'

'Maybe. If we get lucky. But he planned everything else, so my guess is it's unlikely he used his own van. Probably used a stolen one or one with false plates. We're looking into it. Thanks for your time, Mrs Haitink.'

'Is that it?' she asked.

'We'll be in touch,' he told her and headed for the bedroom door. 'We'll need a full written statement in due course. I'll send one of my team around at a time that suits you.'

'I'm sorry I couldn't have been more help.'

'You've helped plenty,' he reassured her. 'In fact, more than you probably realize.'

3

Geoff Jackson stood in front of the huge whiteboard and surveyed the collection of seasoned crime correspondents gathered in the conference room laughing and joking with each other, half nursing unlit cigarettes. Unbeknown to them, Jackson was already considering their individual talents and assigning them tasks. He'd virtually grown up in the business, getting a first-class degree in Journalism Studies, then straight to work for a local paper in Swanley, Kent, before rising quickly through the ranks to become the crime editor of the most-read newspaper in Britain.

Jackson was good. Really good. He knew many of his colleagues on the broadsheets looked down on him working for a red-top rag, but he didn't give a damn. He could take their jobs any time he wanted, but they'd never be able to take his. He had an almost predatory instinct for a story and let nothing stand in the way of getting it. How he got it – that was his business. The public just wanted the story, with all the unpleasant details, and he was the man to get it for them.

'All right, you lot,' he bellowed across the room. 'Everyone shut the fuck up and listen.' The room fell almost instantly quiet and serious. 'Do any of you pricks know why we're here?'

'To get the smoking ban lifted,' someone called out, causing calls of approval and much laughter.

'Very fucking funny,' Jackson told the comedian. 'You've just volunteered to be the official tea boy.' More laughter until Jackson killed it, turning and writing on the board in letters almost big enough to fill it:

THE YOUR VIEW KILLER

'Drop your other stories,' he told them. 'From now on this is the only story. I want to look into the victim's background. I want to know everything about him. How rich was he? How did he live? Did he have any secrets, or vices? Was he liked, or disliked? Everything. And let's find out what the public are thinking. Do they agree with what the killer's doing, or do they think he's just another sicko? Let's speak to them and find out and get an online poll going so people can tell us if they're for him or against him. And get hold of your sources and see if any of them know anything. Someone must have heard something on the criminal grapevine, so find out what. I'll email you all your assignments within the next hour, so let's get on with it.'

'You reckon he'll kill again, then?' one of the journos asked.

'I bloody hope so,' Jackson answered deadpan, causing muted laughter amongst his audience. 'Not much of a story if he doesn't, is it?' He looked away from them, checking his iPhone for messages. The journos took their cue and started to file out of the room, leaving Jackson alone to think.

He was happy enough with the meeting, but knew he needed more. The Your View Killer was gold dust, but he still needed to make it different – the public were growing immune to press coverage of protracted cases, preferring to get quick updates from the Internet or the multitude of twenty-four-hour news shows on television. He needed something – something no one else had. He pulled up a chair and sat staring out of the window, waiting for that magical moment when an undeniably brilliant idea popped into his head. He didn't have to wait long. A smile spread across his face at the sheer audacity of the idea and he jumped out of his chair in celebration.

'Yes. Fucking yes.' He pumped his fists in front of him. 'Interview the bastard. Just him and me. Sensational, Geoff my old son – fucking sensational, but how? How am I gonna get one on one with this joker?'

And even if I do, how am I going to keep the police off my back?

Sean and Donnelly arrived back at the Yard and headed towards their offices, but Sean froze in his tracks when he saw Anna sitting in his. Featherstone had warned him she'd be attached to the investigation, but the sight of her so close still made his stomach tighten and his head feel suddenly cloudy, if only for a few seconds.

'You all right?' Donnelly asked. 'Look like you've just been made Addis's new bag carrier.' He followed Sean's eyeline until he saw Anna. 'Oh,' he said. 'Well, you did tell me she was going to be with us again.'

'I know,' Sean answered, still looking decidedly uncomfortable.

'Jesus,' Donnelly told him. 'She's not that bad.'

'No,' Sean agreed. 'No she's not.'

'Aye, aye,' Donnelly teased. 'I'll leave you to it then.'

Sean watched Donnelly head toward his office and Sally, before following suit and walking the short distance to his own. Anna still hadn't seen him when he reached the office door.

'Hello,' was all he could think of to say, but at least it made her look up from her file.

'Sean,' she smiled. 'Not too much of a shock seeing me here I hope?'

'No. Superintendent Featherstone told me you'd be with us. It's good to see you again.'

'Thank you, although I sense a *but* in there somewhere.'

'No. Not really. Just I'm not sure this particular case warrants your input. Your expertise.'

'Meaning?'

'Meaning I don't see a psychiatric angle here – not particularly, anyway.'

'You have an offender who's killed someone live on the Internet. I would have thought a psychiatric evaluation would be just what you needed.'

'This one's no Thomas Keller, Anna – no tortured childhood and history of abuse. He's pissed off and he wants revenge. Nice, straightforward, old-fashioned motivation.'

'That simple?'

'Why not?'

'Because he shares his revenge with the world. How does that fit into his motivation?'

'Because,' Sean tried to explain, 'he sees the majority of the public as fellow victims – victims of the system that he believes protects the rich and powerful – no matter what they do. He wants to be their . . . spiritual leader.'

She looked him up and down before continuing. 'You may well be right, but it's a little soon to be settling on one theory and one theory alone – don't you think?'

'I'm not settling on anything,' he told her, sounding frustrated. 'I'm just leaning towards what the evidence supports.'

'Of course,' she agreed, 'and I hear you found the victim's body in the Thames.'

'Correct.'

'So he took the time and effort to remove the body from the scene – meaning he may well offend again.'

'Really? I hadn't considered that yet,' he lied.

'Yes you have. You know this isn't going to be his only

48

crime, so why don't you just tell me why you don't want me involved in the investigation?'

He studied her for a few seconds, trying to give himself some thinking time so that the next thing out of his mouth wouldn't be harmful and wounding to them both. Finally he held up his hands and allowed himself a slight smile. 'You know what, I'm sorry,' he told her and meant it. 'It is good to see you again. I'm sure we'll catch this one quicker with you than without you.'

'It's good to see you too.' She took the olive branch.

He pushed himself away from her and walked quickly from his office and into Sally and Donnelly's.

'Time to brief the team,' he told them. 'Care to join me?' He turned without waiting for the answer and headed to the whiteboard that had a smiling photograph of Paul Elkins attached to it, with some details and notes scribbled all around it. As soon as Sally and Donnelly entered the main office he began.

'All right everybody, listen up,' he called across the room. Within a few seconds everyone had stopped talking or typing – calls put on hold or phones hung up. 'You've all seen the murder that was shown live on Your View some time yesterday evening and by now you all know it was genuine – not some staged publicity stunt or sick joke. We recovered the victim's body from the Thames earlier today. We haven't had the body officially identified yet, but I've seen it and can tell you it's the body of Paul Elkins.' Nobody argued.

'What we know so far is the victim was wealthy. Very wealthy. He worked for a bank in the City and lived in Chelsea, with his wife and two kids. He was abducted by a solitary male late yesterday afternoon – in broad daylight from his own street as he made his way home. He was bundled into a white panel van and driven away. Two witnesses saw the abduction and one provided a registration number.'

'I've got an update on the vehicle,' Sally interrupted.

49

'Go on,' Sean told her.

'It's been checked out by the local CID who cover the address of the registered keeper. Turns out it belongs to a painter and decorator in Guildford who reported having his number plates nicked a couple of weeks ago. The locals say it checks out. Dead end, I'm afraid.'

'Not quite,' Sean explained. 'Put out a national circulation – anyone reports having their number plates nicked off their van we want to know about it immediately.'

'No problem,' Sally agreed.

'Some time later the victim pops up on Your View, with our masked killer who gives anyone who cares to listen a lecture on the wrongs of being overly wealthy and in particular gives it to the bankers and the banking system. He encourages people to vote online as to whether they think Elkins is guilty of greed, corruption, God knows what. The vote goes against Elkins and he's murdered – we all know how. So . . . ideas.'

'Check with his company and wife to see if he had any death threats or other threats. Emails, letters, phone calls,' Sally suggested.

'Yeah. Good,' Sean agreed. 'Anything else?'

'Check if anyone's been seen acting suspiciously outside his home or work,' DC Alan Jesson offered. 'Maybe there's a record of someone causing trouble or some other incidents.'

'Fine,' Sean told him. 'Check it out.'

'Check the rope around the victim's neck,' DC Maggie O'Neil joined in. 'It might be a rare type.'

'Unfortunately the killer didn't leave us the rope,' Sean told her. 'He removed it from the body before he dumped it, but I'll have Dr Canning check the marks around the victim's neck anyway. He may be able to re-create the rope's pattern and then yes, we might be able to tell if it's exotic. Anything else?' he asked the room.

'Search the area where the body was found for the scene –

this white room he used for the killing,' DC Ashley Goodwin added.

'Could be anywhere,' Sean dismissed it. 'We don't have anything specific enough to target an area, but we can circulate a request Met-wide asking everyone to keep their eyes open. Get that out to surrounding forces too, will you, Ash? I don't think he went outside the southeast.' Goodwin nodded.

'This white room,' DC Fiona Cahill interrupted, 'looks pretty unusual. If he'd prepared it in advance someone else might have seen it – a builder, a caretaker. Maybe it's been seen by someone and the suspect doesn't even know.'

'Worth a chance,' Sean agreed. 'Get that out to the media as an appeal for assistance. Anyone thinks they might have seen anything like it to get in touch. Anyone else got anything?' The room was silent, the detectives looking at one another, but no one spoke. 'All right,' Sean told them. 'Dave, find me someone who's a bit of a whizz with computers and the Internet and all that stuff. We're gonna need a bit of help with this one.'

'Where from?' Donnelly asked.

'I don't care,' Sean told him. 'Anywhere. Try the Cyber Crime Unit. They must have someone they can spare.'

'If we look outside the Met I might be able to find you a real expert,' Donnelly argued.

'And wipe out our unit's budget for the entire year?' Sean complained, 'I don't think so. Let's make do with someone who's homegrown and knows what they're doing and keep a little money for a rainy day.'

'Fair enough,' Donnelly agreed.

'And we're going to need to monitor Your View around the clock,' Sean continued. 'Dave, you sort out a shift pattern so someone's always got it covered.' Donnelly nodded he understood. 'OK, that's it for now,' but the meeting didn't disperse as quickly as he expected, telling him something was wrong. 'Problem?' he asked them as a group.

'This could be a complicated investigation,' Donnelly spoke for them.

'So?' Sean queried.

'So how're we supposed to investigate it properly when Douglas Allen's trial's about to kick off at the Bailey?'

'Don't hang around at court,' Sean told them. 'Keep your mobiles on and the CPS will call you when and if you're needed to give evidence. Go to court – give your evidence and get back here.'

'They'll want us there,' Donnelly reminded him, 'for the exhibits alone.'

'We'll manage,' Sean insisted, holding his hands up, palms out, to let everyone know it wasn't up for further discussion. 'We don't have any other choice but to manage, so let's get on with it.' There were a few moans and groans as the meeting finally broke up, but Sean knew they'd be fine. They just needed to become immersed in the new investigation – move on from the last case. It would do them all good to have Douglas Allen out of their heads. He just wished he could get Anna out of his.

Assistant Commissioner Addis stood looking out of his office window on the top floor of New Scotland Yard, over the vast city he had ambitions to be the next Commissioner of – so long as he could outmanoeuvre his rivals. They had their high-profile marches to police, getting their faces all over the TV news, but he had Special Investigations, ensuring he'd be overseeing every prominent murder, abduction or anything else he deemed fit to assign Corrigan and his team. So long as he kept a tight control over media access to information and press conferences, the TV and paperboys would have to come begging to him or miss out on the story. If they kept him nicely in the eye of the public and politicians, he'd keep them up to speed on the hunt for the Your View Killer.

He just needed Corrigan to do what he seemed able to do

better than anyone else and get a quick result without blowing up and turning his trump card into a liability. That was why he wanted to keep a close watch on things – a tight rein. He was pleased with himself for integrating Anna into the team, but would she remember where her loyalties lay? And would Corrigan's team become suspicious of her and start feeding her misinformation? He knew detectives could be a cunning lot – suspicious and instinctive. Anna would be no match for them if they sensed she was there for any other reason than to observe and advise. Maybe it was time he had someone even closer to Corrigan on the unit – someone who was already in place and trusted. Maybe only another detective could be completely relied on to provide him with what he needed.

The landline phone ringing on his desk broke into his thoughts and he turned and strode across the office, grabbing the phone as he sat in his large leather chair, back straight, head high.

'Assistant Commissioner Addis speaking.'

'Assistant Commissioner,' the voice began. 'My name is Nick Poole – I'm the CEO of Your View.' Addis's eyebrows arched high on his brow.

'And what can I do for you, Mr Poole?'

'Well, as you're no doubt aware, in the light of our site being used by what I can only describe as a sick and evil individual, we gave a lot of consideration to *temporarily* closing it down.'

'And then decided not to,' Addis cut in, fully aware of the situation.

'It's just we felt it improper to be dictated to by this individual and hugely unfair to our other users, the vast majority of whom are responsible, decent people.'

'Quite,' Addis agreed, losing patience. 'So why are we having this conversation?'

'Because,' Poole continued, 'we've met with our technical

people and they tell us it would be possible to close the site practically the second this lunatic appears on Your View – should he try to use it again.'

Addis sank back in his chair to consider the offer for a few seconds before leaning forward again. 'No,' he told Addis. 'We'd rather see what we're dealing with, and tracing the source of the broadcast could be our best chance of finding him quickly. No. Should there be another broadcast – let it run.'

'I'm not sure,' Poole complained. 'People might start accusing us of being complicit. We've already had a lot of complaints about the one he's already broadcast. I'm, shall we say, very uncomfortable with giving this *person* a platform to preach from – let alone to commit more serious crimes on.'

'My call,' Addis told him. 'Tell your complainants you're acting on instructions given to you by the police. Absolve yourself of the responsibility if you like, but if he uses Your View again, we want to be able to monitor it. Understand?'

'OK, but it's your call.'

'Of course it is,' Addis told him and hung up. 'It's always my call.'

Sean and Sally arrived at the offices of Fairfield's Bank in Leadenhall Street in the heart of the City of London. It was getting late, but the Acting CEO had agreed to stay and see them. His boss had been murdered live on the Internet – what else could he do? An elegant woman met them in reception and told them her name, although Sean forgot it immediately, his mind wandering to the meeting ahead. They rose high through the tall building in the elevator until they reached the top floor and were led to a large but simple office where a slim man in his late forties rose from his chair to greet them, pushing back his longish, sandy blond hair with his left hand while holding out his right. He wore a dark blue pinstripe suit, the jacket of which hung over the back of his chair. His bold red tie and braces contrasted sharply with his pale blue and white striped shirt.

'Simon Damant,' he told them, eagerly shaking their hands in turn, as if he'd been desperately awaiting their arrival. 'Acting CEO.'

'DI Sean Corrigan and this is my colleague, DS Sally Jones,' Sean replied. 'We spoke briefly on the phone.'

'Yes, yes. Of course. Please. Take a seat.'

'Thanks for waiting around for us,' Sean continued, pulling up a chair.

'Really, don't mention it. Least I could do, frankly. Christ, poor Paul. He was a good guy. Didn't deserve what happened. God, I hope you catch the bastard.' Damant's accent fitted the rest of him perfectly.

'We will,' Sean assured him.

'Glad to hear it,' Damant told him, spreading his arms wide in an expression of openness. 'Well, what do you want to know?'

'Did Mr Elkins have any, to put it bluntly, obvious enemies?' Sean dived straight in.

'Not really,' Damant explained. 'There are always *rivals* once you reach his level of seniority. You don't get to his position in this business without making a few enemies along the way, but Jesus, somebody who'd do something like this – no chance. Professional rivalry – that's all we're talking about here. The papers and TV stations are saying he was taken and killed by some sort of vengeance-seeking lunatic. Someone who blames the banking sector for all the ills of the world. Is that what you think?'

'We're keeping an open mind,' Sean told him. 'What about anyone else threatening him or the company? Anything like that going on?'

'Well, there's always the anti-capitalist nutters and the anarch-ist groups, of course, and since the banking crisis we get the occasional disgruntled member of the public phoning up to have a go or writing poison pen letters, but nothing particularly personal to Paul. Some of the letters might have been addressed to him, but only because he was the CEO.'

'Have there been any incidents here at your offices?' Sally asked. 'Anyone making trouble, threatening anyone, anything like that?'

'Not inside,' Damant answered, 'but we've had the occasional small group protests outside – you know, marching up and down with daft placards, usually stirred up by left-wing agitators and trouble-makers, but again, nothing you could describe as personal to Paul.'

'What about everyday folk?' Sean asked. 'People who lost their life savings and homes?'

Damant moved uncomfortably in his chair. 'Sometimes,' he admitted. 'Little groups of the disaffected. Paul always felt sorry for them. He took no pleasure in their plight. Like I said, he was a good guy and a bit of a philanthropist too – gave a lot of his wealth away to good causes, but never sought to gain out of it. Just did it because he thought it was the right thing to do. Maybe if he'd made more of a thing about it this nutter wouldn't have targeted him. Christ, the whole thing's just unbelievable.'

'What about within the company?' Sean asked. 'Did Paul have to sack anyone lately – make anyone redundant who took it badly?'

'No. No,' Damant replied. 'Paul was too senior to personally take care of things like that, unless the person being sacked or made redundant were also very senior, and that hasn't happened for a very long time.'

'How long?' Sally asked.

'So long ago I can't remember. Even then I'd imagine they were happy to take redundancy and go. Our redundancy packages are very generous, believe me.'

'I'm sure they are,' Sean agreed, losing interest in what

seemed another dead end. 'Does your company keep records of any threatening or malicious calls or letters you receive?'

'We do. Our internal security people take care of that sort of thing.'

'We'll need copies of everything and any records of calls received too,' Sean told him. 'There may be something in them we can use.'

'Of course. No problem. I'll get security to get those ready for you right away.'

'Thanks,' Sean told him. 'It's appreciated.'

'Don't thank me,' Damant insisted. 'Just catch the bastard – before he grabs another one of us.'

The Your View Killer stalked around the white room making sure everything was ready for his next *trial*. The victim had been selected and his plans for their abduction well prepared and even rehearsed – to a point.

He wore the same black work overalls, black leather gloves and even the ski-mask, even though he was alone and the broadcasting equipment was disconnected. There was no one to recognize him, but he wouldn't make the mistake of becoming lazy and leaving his fingerprints or a strand of hair carrying his DNA in the wrong place for the police to find once they discovered the white room, as surely one day they would – one day long after he, the Your View Killer, had already disappeared forever. A smile spread across his lips at the irony of the situation – one day soon he'd practically have to *give* the police the very things that could damn him. And when that day happened it would be a sign that everything was progressing just as he'd planned.

Sean had arrived home late, but early enough to help his wife Kate prepare supper for both of them. They sat at the kitchen table, Kate doing most of the talking and the eating, while Sean pretended to be listening as he concentrated on his wine and thought about the new case. Kate had a lot to get off her chest and talked away happily about the children and her work as a casualty doctor at Guy's Hospital, but eventually she looked at him long enough to notice he wasn't truly with her.

'You OK?' she asked.

'Sorry?' he replied when he realized he was expected to respond.

'Are you OK?' Kate repeated.

'Yeah. Sorry. New case.'

'A new case?' she inquired. 'What is it?'

Sean rubbed his temples and considered his answer, but Kate had already worked it out. 'Don't tell me – it's the one that's been all over the news – the so-called Your View Killer.' Sean didn't reply. 'It is, isn't it?'

'Same as any other murder investigation,' he lied. 'Just because it's on the telly doesn't make it any more difficult than if no one had heard about it.'

'Well that's not true, is it?' she argued. 'The more high profile the case the more pressure you'll be under to solve it, and the more pressure you're under, the grumpier you'll get.'

'I can handle it,' he tried to reassure her, but he knew he didn't sound convincing.

'I know you can handle it,' she answered, 'but only if you push everything else away so you can think of nothing but the case – including me. Including the kids.'

'That's not true.'

'Isn't it? You sure?'

'I do the best I can. Hopefully we'll get this sorted quickly and then you won't have to worry about it.'

'Until the next high-profile case they dump on you.'

'We're Special Investigations only now – they're all going to be high profile. On the plus side there should be less of them – maybe less than one a year.'

'You hope, or maybe you don't.' He didn't answer. 'Anyway,

what's this one about? The people at work seem convinced he's some latter-day Robin Hood, come to make the rich and corrupt pay for their greed. There's not a lot of sympathy out there for the victim.'

'People are quick to judge, but I guess that's the whole point,' Sean told her.

'What d'you mean?'

'The killer – that's what he does. Tells people to judge, although they only have a fragment of the facts. And they're all too willing to go along with it, even if it means a man ends up losing his life.'

'I don't think people believed it was for real,' Kate argued.

'Did some of the people you work with vote?' he questioned her.

'Why?' she asked, a little suspicious of her husband's reason for asking. 'Are they in trouble if they did?'

'Maybe. Probably not – if they thought it was a hoax. But anyone voting in the future could be guilty of conspiracy to murder.'

'You can't arrest everybody,' Kate said. 'You can't arrest tens of thousands of people, maybe hundreds of thousands.'

'We might have to make a few arrests – scare people away from voting.'

'I'd better not say anything else,' she half joked. 'Wouldn't want to get anyone at work arrested. We're short-staffed as it is.'

'Don't worry,' he told her. 'I promise not to arrest any of your work colleagues, or friends, or whatever you call them.'

Kate rolled her brown eyes, making the golden skin of her forehead wrinkle. 'Gee, thanks,' she replied, getting to her feet and beginning to clear the table. 'Speaking of friends, don't forget we're going out for dinner with ours this week.'

'We are?'

'Yes. We are. It's in the calendar on the computer, if you ever bothered to check it.'

He watched her head to the sink, her long, curly black hair tied back in a ponytail. He tried to remember the last time he'd seen her dressed for a night out, but couldn't. 'Who we going out with?'

'James and Kerry, Chris and Sally and Leon and Sophie.'

'So what you're saying is we're going out with *your* friends?'

Kate looked over her slim shoulder as she paused with a soapy dish in hand. 'Feel free to arrange a night out with your friends any time you like. I'd love to finally meet some of them – *properly.*' She went back to washing the dishes.

'Not a great idea,' Sean told her. 'They'd just get pissed and talk job all night.'

'Sounds great. I'll look forward to it.'

'Ha, ha,' Sean mocked, getting to his feet and heading for the stairs.

'Oi,' Kate called after him. 'A hand with the cleaning up would be nice.'

'I'm knackered,' he complained, 'and I need to get back to the office super early tomorrow before anyone notices I'm not there.'

'Fine,' Kate relented. 'Just remember – dinner – this week.'

'Yeah, yeah,' he answered, but he'd already forgotten about it, too tired to care, his mind blissfully still. The case hadn't got into him yet – hadn't taken him over completely. He wondered whether it was because he too lacked empathy with the victim. If it had been a woman or a child killed in the same way but for different reasons he wouldn't have felt as he did. He would have already been consumed by the overpowering urge to keep going until the killer had been caught – he doubted he would have even come home for the evening. *Early days*, he told himself as he climbed the stairs to bed. *It'll get to you soon enough.*

4

Sean arrived at work the next morning early enough to be the first one in the office and was glad of it. He walked slowly across the main room, casting an eye over the tip that was supposed to be the nerve centre of their investigations. Discarded items of clothing hung on chairs and over computer screens, abandoned polystyrene cups of cold, stale coffee littered almost every work surface, while the wastepaper bins overflowed with crisp packets, chocolate wrappers and plastic sandwich boxes. The large brown paper confidential waste sacks that filled every corner fared no better. He shook his head in displeasure and retreated into the sanctuary of his own reasonably ordered and tidy office.

He slumped in his chair and peeled the lid off the black coffee he'd picked up from a nearby café – the grey filth they sold in the canteen at the Yard was wholly undrinkable. Next he placed his own personal laptop next to the coffee and started it into life. Once it was ready he pulled up the video of Paul Elkins's murder and began to watch and listen: the victim taped to the chair, confused and terrified while the killer periodically stalked in front of the cameras, not even his eyes visible as he spoke in that eerie electronic voice – preaching more than appealing.

Sean pressed pause for a second, giving his mind time to absorb what he had seen so far, to analyse it, to pick up on some small thing they'd all missed. His eyes seemed to flicker as he studied the screen before pressing play again, only to pause it a few seconds later, the image of the killer staring out at him.

'Confident bastard, aren't you?' he whispered. 'Is that why you're doing this, because it makes you feel confident – makes you feel good again? Gives you back the pride that they took away from you?' He clicked on play and watched for a few more minutes, the killer's organized and self-assured demeanour never changing as he explained the rules of the 'trial' to the watching 'jury'.

He paused again and stared at the dark figure standing straight and purposeful. 'What are you like when you're not being this *thing*? What are you like when you're just yourself? Are you meek and mild – a broken man too defeated to even stand up for yourself, your wife, your children? Did they beat the fight out of you – took your business, your house, your job? But when you put the ski-mask on, when you hear yourself speaking in that unrecognizable voice, does it give you your self-esteem back? Does it make you feel powerful? And why kill him the way you did? It was slow and painful. Was it the only way you knew how, or did you want it to be like that? Did you want him to suffer – want to make him pay?'

A knock on his open door shattered his concentration and he looked up to see Donnelly standing there with a small man in his thirties he didn't recognize. Sean looked him up and down, taking note of his skinny arms and legs and little pot belly, spectacles balancing on the end of his nose, receding blond hair uncombed and un-styled.

'Who the hell is this?' he asked Donnelly, never looking away from the man who was now flushed red.

'This,' Donnelly explained, 'is Detective Constable Bob Bishop.'

'Where the hell did you find him? And more to the point, what are you doing with him?' Bishop looked from Donnelly to Sean and back again, following the conversation anxiously.

'I abducted him from the Cyber Crime Unit,' Donnelly continued. 'The DI there's an old friend of mine. He said we could have him.' Still neither of them bothered to address Bishop. Sean shook his head in mock disbelief. 'What?' Donnelly played along. 'You said get an Internet expert.'

'Is that what he is?' Sean continued to stare at the very uncomfortable-looking Bishop. 'Is that what you are – an Internet expert?'

'I know my way around the Web as well as anyone from the Cyber Unit,' Bishop stuttered in his Birmingham accent.

'See,' Donnelly jumped in. 'Like I said – an expert.'

'You know why you're here?' Sean asked.

'Something about the Your View Killer. DS Donnelly told me.'

'It's all about the Your View Killer,' Sean told him. Bishop visibly swallowed hard. 'Can he be traced? Can we trace him to wherever he's broadcasting from?'

'Yes,' Bishop answered, 'but it's not like on the telly – it can take a while. But why d'you need me? Can't you use one of your own team?'

· 'Sure,' Sean teased him, 'because my team's full of Internet and computer experts. The Commissioner lets me keep them locked in a room for whenever I might need them – along with thousands of pounds' worth of tracking equipment for the once in a blue moon when I might need that too. Bishop, this is the Metropolitan Police: you don't get given anything until you absolutely need it and then you beg, steal and borrow it before handing it back to wherever it is you got it from. And right now I need you.'

'Well then, I guess I'm all yours,' Bishop gave in.

'Good. Can we trace it even when it's not on?' Sean pressed ahead with his queries.

'No,' Bishop told him. 'We can only trace him when he's connected to the Internet. Every time he's connected we inch a little closer to his location, but he has to be connected.'

'What if he changes computers or changes the location of his broadcasts? Donnelly asked.

'If we've already got a hook into his computer we can trace him even if he changes location – although we'd have to go back a few steps, which would slow us down. But even without a hard modem we can trace his wireless fingerprint via the—'

'Stop. Stop,' Sean interrupted. 'Save the technical jargon for someone who gives a shit. Now try that again in English.'

'Well, like I said, once we're into his er . . . computer, we've pretty much got him, but it'll take time, depending on how long he stays online each time. If he ditches the computer we're buggered, unless he's using er . . . something that sends the signal on that he also used with the original computer.' Sean and Donnelly looked at each other. 'It's like at home, right,' Bishop explained. 'Most people have more than one device that can access the Internet, but they're all getting that access through one modem, right, so even if they ditch the device, we're still into the source. Get it?'

'I get it enough,' Sean told him. 'Dave, get him a desk in the main office and put him to work.'

'He can share with me and Sally. There's enough room. He wouldn't survive in that shark pool.'

'Fine,' Sean agreed.

Bishop's eyes darted around nervously. 'Excuse me,' he began. 'I know my way around computers and stuff, but I'm not qualified to call myself an expert and you sound like you need an expert.'

Sean looked him in the eyes. 'Do you know anyone better than you who also happens to be employed by the Metropolitan Police?'

'Er . . . well no, but—'

'I didn't think so,' Sean cut him off again. 'Listen, you can speak to whoever you need to speak to for technical advice, go and see whoever you want to see, spend whatever you have to spend – but I need you to trace the location of where this madman's broadcasting from. Do you understand?'

'Yes, but it's just that I was right in the middle—'

'You may be our best chance to catch a killer, and if you do, it won't be forgotten,' Sean encouraged him. 'Are you my man?'

Bishop finally straightened as a sparkle came to his eyes. 'Yeah,' he answered. 'Yeah. I'm your man.'

'Good,' Sean told him as Donnelly led him away to the next-door office. Sean hadn't finished shaking his head when he saw Anna enter the main office and start to approach him. He felt a pleasant vibration in his chest and his head became a little light. He pushed the feelings aside and quickly stood, pulling on his coat and gathering his belongings, stuffing them carelessly into his pockets.

Anna entered without knocking. 'Going somewhere?'

'Yes,' was all he said, aiming for the door where he'd have to pass close to her.

'Mind if I ask where?'

He sighed before answering. 'If you must know, I'm meeting Dr Canning for the post-mortem.'

'Can I tag along?'

'No.'

'Oh.'

Sean realized he was being unnecessarily blunt and reminded himself it wasn't her fault he felt the way he did about her. Being close to her made him feel uncomfortable, vulnerable; but he didn't want to hurt her either.

'I'm sorry,' he explained. 'It's just Dr Canning doesn't like additional people coming to his post-mortems. He likes it to be just him and me. Post-mortem's his call. He's the pathologist.'

'That's OK,' she told him. 'I understand. I'd probably be the same.'

'Look,' Sean continued. 'I'll tell you all about it when I get back. I'd be interested in your opinion.'

'I'd appreciate that,' she told him as he slid past. 'I'll see you later then.'

He walked quickly through the main office without looking back and was gone.

Georgina Vaughan sat on the corner of her desk on the seventh floor of Glenhope Investments in the City of London. She kept a sharp eye out for her boss who often stalked the floor looking for employees who were *engaging in social discourse rather than working.* She shared her limited working space with two colleagues, Nick and Oscar, and when they weren't being spied on there had only been one topic of conversation that morning – the Your View Killer.

She peeked over the top of Nick's screen. 'So who do you think he's going to do next?' she asked in little more than a whisper.

He checked they weren't being watched before answering. 'I don't know. Could be anyone. Could be you.'

She gave a short laugh. 'Me? I don't think so. You heard what he said – he's only after the big fish.'

'You're a senior project manager and a rising star,' Oscar joined in. 'Maybe he'll consider you to be a big fish?'

Again she laughed. 'I doubt it. Not yet anyway. I reckon he'll only go for CEOs. Probably doesn't even know what a project manager is. By the time I'm a CEO he'll probably be dead of old age.'

'You're on the senior management fast-track scheme – what more do you want?' Nick reminded her in his slightly effeminate voice that matched his petite build and whisker-less complexion.

'I'm thirty-fucking-three, Nick. Does that sound like fast-track to you? This whole job's beginning to feel like waiting for dead-man's shoes.'

'Then you'll be happy to see him dispose of a few of them,' Nick suggested.

'Ha, ha,' she mocked him.

'The higher you climb the less positions there are,' Oscar chipped in. 'Besides, with this lunatic running around out there, who'd want to be a CEO of anything?'

'I would,' she almost snapped at him in her clipped accent, her long, wavy brown hair falling forwards. 'I just need him to bump off another couple of hundred and I should be fine.'

'I doubt there'll be any more,' Nick argued. 'I heard he was killed by some Eastern European gang he'd been laundering money for. Apparently his *rates* were beginning to piss them off so . . .' He spread his hands as if an explanation wasn't necessary.

'That's bollocks,' Georgina told him. 'Eastern Europeans would have chopped him to pieces.'

'An expert on these matters, are you?' Oscar asked.

'I've heard things,' she told them, trying to sound mysterious.

'More like seen things,' Nick teased her, 'on the telly.' Both he and Oscar laughed at her.

'Well one thing's for certain,' she silenced them, 'none of us have anything to worry about, sitting here doing these shit jobs. Nothing to worry about at all.'

Sean parked in the ambulance bay at Guy's Hospital, leaving the police vehicle log on the dashboard to prevent his car being towed away. He strode off through a part of the grounds rarely seen by most hospital employees, let alone the public, and made his way to the mortuary where he found Dr Canning already examining the body. Canning looked up to see who had entered his domain.

'Good morning, Inspector.'

'Morning, Doctor,' Sean replied, no feeling in his voice. 'Here we are again then.'

'Quite,' Canning agreed. 'I hope you don't mind, but I've already cleaned the victim up. There's plenty of photographic documentation as to the body's state when it first came out of the river. I've already examined it for anything unpleasant the river left behind.'

'D'you find anything?'

'Not particularly. The usual organic life forms and other debris. I've taken samples and plenty of swabs for you. If there's anything deeper in his throat, stomach or lungs I won't find it until I open the poor fellow up later today.'

Sean moved closer and scanned the body slowly from head to toe, the man's face close to unrecognizable from the image in the photographs Sean had seen – his expression in death a tortured grimace, the vivid rope-burn ring around his neck a stark reminder of how he died. The rest of his body was relatively untouched except for some reddening around both his ankles and wrists – from where he'd been taped to the chair, Sean guessed. Other than that the river had left its mark, but nothing of note, the victim's clothing having protected his dead body from too much exposure to other floating debris.

'These other cuts and marks,' Sean checked, 'they caused by being in the river?'

'Almost certainly,' Canning assured him. 'I had a quick look and found most of them to be post-mortem and none that would have contributed to his death even if he had been alive before being disposed of in the river.'

'He was, wasn't he?' Sean interrupted.

'Was what?' Canning asked.

'Disposed of. Like he was nothing. Something to be rid of. An annoyance.'

'Not like the last unfortunate victim we saw together,' Canning reminded him. 'Quite the ritual of guilt.'

'Best not to think of it too much,' Sean told him, trying not to let the images of the small boy on Canning's autopsy table invade his mind.

'Trial on that one must be coming up soon. Had a letter from the CPS putting me on standby.'

'We're just waiting for our slot at the Bailey to be confirmed and then the trial begins,' Sean informed him. 'I'll try to make sure they don't keep you hanging around too long.'

'Appreciated.'

'Anyway.' Sean pulled them back to the matter in hand. 'Apart from the rather obvious cause of death, can you tell me anything else?'

'Ah,' Canning began. 'The cause of death is not as straight-forward as you may think.'

Sean's eyes narrowed. He didn't like surprises. 'Meaning?'

'Cause of death wasn't hanging, it was strangulation.'

He had Sean's interest. 'I'm listening.'

'Technically hanging is when someone falls from a height with a ligature around their neck, causing both a broken neck and fatal restriction of the blood supply. Death is more often than not instantaneous. Strangulation is the compression of the carotid arteries or jugular veins, causing cerebral ischaemia – which is the brain dying as a result of the lack of oxygen – while at the same time there is a compression of the larynx or trachea, causing asphyxia. Strangulation is a much more unpleasant way to leave this mortal coil than hanging. I'm afraid your victim was hoisted to a slow and painful death as opposed to being dropped to a relatively quick and painless one.'

'Then he wanted him to suffer?' Sean asked himself more than Canning.

69

'I couldn't say, Inspector. We both know that's your domain, not mine. But I saw the Your View footage. The killer looked and sounded pretty angry at the world to me. The sort of person who would want to make others suffer.'

'Maybe,' Sean answered.

'Keeping your options open, Inspector?' Sean just shrugged. 'Well, unfortunately the killer took the rope from around his neck before disposing of the body, so we don't have that to work with, but from the video I could just about tell what sort of knot he used.'

'Go on,' Sean encouraged, glad to be discussing simple, tangible, physical evidence.

'I'm pretty sure it was a poacher's knot – used primarily in sailing.'

'Sailing.' Sean took the bait. 'What type of sailing?'

'All types of sailing,' Canning replied. 'Royal Navy, Merchant Navy, a yacht owner. Maybe he had a small dinghy as a child or a rowboat or . . . the possibilities are endless.'

'I can't see this one on a yacht,' Sean told him, squeezing his eyes shut and rubbing them with a pinched thumb and index finger. 'Not a great look for a man of the people – sailing around on a yacht.'

'No. I don't suppose it would be,' Canning agreed, 'but it's definitely the sort of knot someone would use out of habit – without thinking about it.'

'Or they learnt it specifically so they could use it on the victim,' Sean suggested.

'I suppose so,' Canning agreed, 'but there are easier knots to learn, so why pick this one?'

'God only knows, but you're probably right – he knew this knot, so he used it. He could be ex-navy – merchant or royal, or even an ex-docker. Plenty of them have lost their jobs in recent years.'

'Doesn't really narrow it down for you, does it?'

'No, but it might help me know if I'm heading in the right

direction later on.' Sean thought for a few seconds before speaking again. 'When you watched the video, what did you think?'

'Like I said,' Canning answered, 'the killer struck me as being very angry. Angry at the world.'

'In what way angry? What specifically was angry about him?'

'His words,' Canning told him. 'His words were angry.'

Sean thought silently again. 'You're right, his words were angry, but . . .' He stopped, unsure of his own thoughts.

'But what?' Canning encouraged.

'But the killing seemed cold and impersonal. More like an execution. It was slow and the victim suffered unnecessarily. That could have been because the killer didn't know what he was doing . . . and why would he, unless he's killed before?'

'Do you think he has – killed before?'

'No,' Sean answered quickly. 'No I don't.

'So what's troubling you, Inspector?'

'He preached angry words, even acted aggressively, pointing into the camera, accusing the victim, yet the killing was cold. Emotionless.'

'How would you expect an angry man to kill his victim?' Canning asked.

'A knife, a club or bat – something more frenzied and personal – something that let the anger out – true revenge. Not to just stand back and watch the man hang. If he's as angry as he seems to be that couldn't have satisfied him, couldn't have given him the release he needed.'

'Maybe he's more sadistic than you considered?' Canning offered. 'Wanted to sit back and watch his victim suffer rather than being embroiled in an act of frenzied violence.'

'Could be,' Sean agreed, 'but when I watch that video I can't help but feel like I'm watching two different people – the preacher and the killer.'

'Entirely possible,' Canning told him. 'The killer comes in and out of shot – appears and disappears from the screen – so you'd have to consider it.'

'I am,' Sean admitted. 'But he could be two people in one man.'

'Also possible,' Canning agreed enthusiastically. 'Another schizophrenic for you to decipher.'

'Let's hope not.'

'Have you shared your thoughts with anyone else yet?'

'No,' Sean told him, Anna's face suddenly burning in his mind as he wondered how long it would be before she saw in the video what he had seen. 'Not yet. Best to keep it simple. Won't change how we investigate it anyway. The killer's told us he's someone with an axe to grind against the rich and so far he hasn't given me any reason to disbelieve him. I'll play his game for now – let him think he's in control.'

'Why would you do that?'

'Because the more confident he is, the sloppier he'll get and that increases his chances of making mistakes, and that increases my chance of catching him quickly.'

'I hope you're right,' Canning told him as he began to examine his surgical tools before selecting a scalpel, 'because I should think a man capable of killing another human being in this way is probably capable of anything.'

DC Bob Bishop sat at the desk that they'd squeezed into the corner of Donnelly and Sally's office. Sally hadn't bothered to protest as she watched the two of them manoeuvre the desk into the already cramped room, shaking her head and tutting as they crashed around. He was deep in concentration as his fingers typed away on the relatively state-of-art laptop he'd commandeered from his regular unit. A heavy hand falling on his shoulder and a gruff Scottish voice made him jump with fright.

'All right there, Bobby Boy?' Donnelly asked before

72

slumping down in his own chair, which creaked a little under his weight. 'Cracked the case yet?'

'Not exactly,' Bishop replied in his Birmingham tones.

'Why not?' Donnelly asked, half teasing. 'All you got to do is trace this psycho's signal, right?'

'It's not that simple.'

'Thought you were an expert, Bobby Boy.'

'I told you before, I'm no expert and your killer knows what he's doing too. He's using a wireless mobile device and staying off any broadband connections. Looks like he's put in a few levels of encryption as well.' He turned away from Donnelly and resumed his frantic typing, but kept talking, to himself more than Donnelly. 'Yeah, he's a clever bastard, all right, but not as clever as he thinks he is. He may have slammed the front door shut, but he's left the back door slightly ajar.'

'So you can trace him?' Donnelly reminded him he was there.

'What? Oh, yeah. I can trace him. You see, I reckon he thinks that every time he turns his computer off he's breaking the line, so to speak, destroying any connections that had existed and with it our chance to trace him. But he's wrong,' Bishop grinned.

'Really,' Donnelly half-heartedly asked, not remotely convinced.

'Yeah. Very wrong. You see, all those little satellites floating round the world have already been working away to pinpoint his transmission location. Sure, when he stops they stop, but they don't ever go back to square one. So the next time he transmits they're already that much closer to finding him and therefore so are we. It's only a matter of time.'

'Unless he changes location,' Donnelly reminded him.

'Even if he changes location,' Bishop explained, 'although that would slow us down a bit, but DI Corrigan doesn't seem to think that's going to happen.'

'No,' Donnelly agreed. 'No he doesn't, and with good reason.

Our man's invested a lot of time in setting all this up, including the location he uses. I can't see him having multiple sites. He may have Joe Public fooled he's some sort of protector and avenger of the people, but to me he's just another killer. Nothing more. Nothing less. You see, I don't let them get in my head like DI Corrigan does. To me they're all just losers waiting to be taken down and this one's no different. Once he feels safe somewhere he'll stick with it – mark my words.'

'But DI Corrigan does?' Bishop seized on something Donnelly had said.

'Does what?'

'Does allow them to get inside his head?'

'Oh aye. Heard something, have you – the old detectives' grapevine been at work?'

'Just picking up on something you said,' Bishop answered.

'Bullshit,' Donnelly challenged him. 'Come on – what have you heard?'

'Like, that he can predict them – tell what they're going to do next.'

Donnelly laughed short and hard. 'That's fucking Mystic Meg you're thinking of, Bobby Boy.'

'Just saying what I heard.'

'Well you heard wrong. I've seen him do some stuff I've never seen anyone else do, granted, but I've never seen him do that. Be nice if he could, mind – save us all a lot of grief. But just for the record, it's more a case of him getting into the killers' minds than them getting into his.'

'What d'you mean?' Bishop asked, confused.

Donnelly smiled a mischievous smile and leaned further back into his chair, hands behind his head. 'You'll see, Bobby Boy. You'll see.'

Geoff Jackson spotted the woman he'd come to meet as soon as he entered one of the few surviving independent coffee shops in Soho. Joan Varady was, as usual, furiously typing

74

on her iPhone and never once looked up as he approached her, or even when he sat down. Her small build and the simple haircut that framed her pretty but ageing face belied the powerful position she held in one of the world's biggest publishing houses.

'Late as usual,' she accused him, still without looking up.

'Sorry,' Jackson apologized. 'Busy, busy, busy. You know how it is.'

'I do indeed,' she told him in her educated, but not clipped, accent. 'Which is why I don't like hanging around waiting for journalists in coffee shops.'

'Fair enough,' Jackson agreed, 'but you'll realize it was time well spent, once you've heard what I have to say.'

Finally she looked up from her phone. 'Well. I'm listening.'

'I'll assume you've heard all about this new killer – the one they're calling the Your View Killer.'

'Ah,' Varady almost sighed. 'I might have guessed it would be about him. I've seen some of your coverage in that rag of a paper you insist on working for.'

'I didn't know *The World* was your kind of a paper,' he teased her.

'Believe me,' she assured him, 'it isn't.'

'Whatever,' he told her, bored with the jousting. 'Fact is I've got exclusivity on the story – the inside track.'

'Still got a couple of cops in your pocket – feeding you the low-down?'

'Maybe. Or maybe I've got even more this time.' Varady didn't look impressed. 'I can have the book written and ready to go within a week of the killer being caught, clean and no need for major editing. You could have it on the shelves within a couple of months while the story's still hot. Feed the public while they're still hungry for the grisly details.'

'If you really want to feed the public grisly details you need to write the book about the celebrity paedophiles you broke,' Varady told him.

75

'No,' he snapped at her a little. 'That'll never happen.'

'Someone's going to write it. Might as well be you.'

'Forget it,' he insisted. 'Besides, this is the better and bigger story, and I've got exclusivity.'

'That's fine, but just because you have exclusivity with your paper doesn't mean other journos at other papers, not to mention the television boys and girls, won't be covering it. What can you offer that they can't?'

Jackson spread his arms, inviting her to look at him with admiration. 'What can I offer? The best, that's what I can offer, and you know it.'

Varady looked him up and down before speaking. 'OK, Geoff, you're good – we all know it – but the last book got as much stick as it did praise. I had to work my arse off to keep it on the shelves. Did you really have to call that psycho "The Toy Taker"?'

'Public need a handle, Joan – something not too difficult to remember. Something that identifies the story at a glance. Remember "The Crossbow Cannibal"? That was a beauty. Wish I'd thought of it.'

'So what you going to call this one, or are you going to stick with "The Your View Killer"?'

'Don't know,' Jackson mused. 'Might do. Depends what else turns up. Might need something a little catchier. Something that makes him sound more man of the people than crazed killer.'

'Well, whatever you call him, I'm still not sure,' Varady told him. 'I've no great desire to piss off the Met – again. They know some of their own are speaking to you and they were none too happy when you started sniffing around trying to find out personal details of that SIO, whatever his name was.'

'Ahh,' Jackson smiled. 'Detective Inspector Sean Corrigan. He's a slippery bastard, but I have to admit he's more interesting than the usual plastic detective on accelerated promotion.'

'Yeah, well just stay away from him would be my advice.'
Jackson grinned. 'Oh no,' Varady leaned back, 'you're not
telling me he's in charge of the Your View Killer investigation
as well, are you?'

'Don't worry about it,' Jackson reassured her, but she was
already packing her handbag and shaking her head. 'Listen,
Corrigan is gold dust. He's the lead detective on the Special
Investigations Unit. He's gonna get all the juiciest cases across
London – he's like the bear that leads you to the honey every
time. You want the hot crime story, follow Corrigan.'

'I'm your fucking publisher,' Varady reminded him, standing
and stretching to her full five foot two inches, 'not your
bloody editor.'

'You still need stories though, right? You can't always rely
on celebrity autobiographies.'

'Not interested,' she insisted and moved to leave, taking
his publishing deal with her.

'All right,' he told her in a desperate last effort to get her
to listen. 'What if I told you I'm going to *interview* the killer?'

She looked him up and down for a second or two. 'So
what? Interviews with banged-up killers are nothing new.
Still not interested.'

'No,' he told her, smiling again. 'Not when he's banged up
– now, while he's still on the loose. While he's still commit-
ting his crimes.'

Varady sat down again. 'Jesus. You're joking, right?'

'Would I joke about a thing like that?'

'Think you can pull it off?' she asked, her eyes narrowing.

'Of course I can. Do I have your interest again? Ready to
talk about a deal yet?'

'You get the interviews and we'll talk.'

Sean arrived back at the Yard and stuck his head into Sally
and Donnelly's office to ask them to join him and Anna next
door for a catch up of the day's progress – if there was any.

'How did the PM go?' Donnelly asked while he was still emptying his pockets and hanging up his raincoat.

'No surprises yet,' Sean told him. 'Death seems to be by hanging, or strangulation to be precise.'

'The difference being?' Donnelly asked.

'No broken neck to accompany the asphyxiation,' Sean explained. 'He hung until his brain died through lack of oxygen.'

'Nice,' Sally added.

'Dr Canning reckons the killer used a knot used in boating or yachting. He recognized it from the video, so it would seem our man has some knowledge of boating or sailing.'

'And he dumped the body in the river,' Sally reminded them, 'so possibly he has a boat or access to one. Something for us to work with.'

Sean frowned, concerned he'd failed to think of what Sally had suggested. The connection between the knot, the river and possible use of a boat should have obvious to him, but for some reason he'd missed it, as if his mind wasn't fully focused on the investigation. He involuntarily glanced at Anna.

'A good point well made,' Donnelly told Sally. 'He's probably got some knackered little rowboat tied up under a tree somewhere.'

'Well, if he has we need to find it,' Sean told them. 'How's your man DC Bishop getting on with the Internet inquiries?'

'Seems to be getting on all right, although if you want an explanation of what he's doing you're better off asking him yourself – all sounds like technical gobbledegook to me.'

'I'll spare myself the experience,' Sean answered. 'What about forensics?'

'Nothing of note so far,' Sally explained. 'In fact, nothing at all from the abduction site and obviously we don't know where the murder scene is so all we're left with is the body and his clothing, which are currently in the hands of Dr Canning.'

'All right,' Sean told them, pushing his fingers through his short hair, 'Dave, organize the door-to-door in the street he was abducted from and the surrounding ones too. Maybe we're missing a witness or two. Sally, get a Met-wide request out asking for all derelict buildings to be checked – in fact, see if you can get that out to our surrounding forces as well. If the body washed up in Barnes then this kill room could easily be outside the Met area.'

'Anything else?' Sally asked.

'No,' Sean told them, looking and sounding disappointed. 'Right now that's all I've got . . . except for the electronic device he uses to change his voice,' he suddenly remembered. 'Get Paulo on the case,' he told Donnelly. 'He bought it somewhere or made it himself, but we might get lucky.'

'OK,' Donnelly agreed as he and Sally made their way from his office, leaving Sean alone with Anna. She motioned as if to speak, before the phone ringing on Sean's desk stopped her.

Sean wearily answered it. 'Hello.'

'Sean. It's Superintendent Featherstone.'

'Guv'nor.'

'Any progress?' Featherstone asked. 'Everyone would like to put this one to bed early.'

'Me too.'

'I bet – especially with that trial coming up. When's that kick off, by the way?'

'This week,' Sean told him. 'Probably.'

'Fuck me,' Featherstone cursed. 'All the more reason to get this wrapped up sharpish.'

'I'm trying,' Sean answered, hiding his frustration, 'but it's a little early to expect a breakthrough with what's essentially a stranger killing. I have no obvious suspect.'

'I understand,' Featherstone said, 'but as you know, not everyone's as patient as I am.'

'Meaning Assistant Commissioner Addis?'

'No need to mention names. Just make it look like we're making progress. Understand?'

'I understand,' Sean assured him.

'Good,' Featherstone said, sounding like he was about to hang up before Sean stopped him.

'One thing you can do for me.'

'Go on.'

'Get the enhanced images of the room he used out to the media with an appeal to the public. Someone might recognize it.'

'No problem,' Featherstone agreed and hung up.

'Everything all right?' Anna asked.

'Yeah, fine. Why wouldn't it be?'

'You seem a little distant.'

Sean leaned back into his chair, puffed out his cheeks and decided just to come straight out with it. 'I'm sorry. It's having you around,' he tried to explain. 'It's . . . distracting. I'm beginning to miss things. I can't afford to miss things.'

'Such as?'

'The sailing knot and the river – I shouldn't . . . wouldn't have missed that.'

'And you're blaming me?' Anna asked, though she didn't sound accusing.

'Not blaming you . . . it's not your fault. It's down to me, I know, but having you here all the time, seeing you all the time, is distracting. I try to not let it be, but I can't.'

'I thought we'd dealt with this,' she told him.

'Had we?' he asked. 'Really? We agreed it would have been the wrong thing to do, for both of us, but we didn't . . . solve anything.'

'I'm not a mystery to be solved, Sean, like one of your cases. Is that what's distracting you – that I'm an *unsolved case*?'

He looked at her unsmilingly for a long while. 'Yes,' he answered honestly. 'Yes it is. Perhaps it would have been

80

better for both of us if we had, you know . . . got it out the way. We're both grown-ups – we could have dealt with it.'

She moved closer so he could still hear her now quiet words. 'No it wouldn't. We both know it. We all need some things to anchor us in this life, otherwise we can begin to drift. Some of us would simply drift along until we hit land again, where we can rebuild, start over. But some of us would drift to dark places – places we might never find our way back from. You're a danger junkie, Sean. You need it to stay alive, to be who you are. For you, living on the edge is a necessity, not a rarity. But you can't live your private life like you live your professional one – it has to be stable or you might just fall off that edge you like to be on so much.'

His startling blue eyes sparkled and danced as he deciphered the meaning of her words and their implications, knowing that if she knew how deep into his past the darkness ran she might have even worked out that perhaps, secretly, for reasons even he didn't understand, he wanted to destroy the only truly stable thing in his life. He carried the guilt that all the abused carried, making him doubt whether he even deserved to have a loving family. Maybe he did want to cast himself adrift, free from the responsibility of giving and receiving love – free to stop trying to control the darkness inside of him – to finally allow himself to spiral downwards until he crashed and burnt. If Anna truly knew his past, his childhood, then she might understand that for him every day he managed to appear *normal* was like another day for an alcoholic of not taking a drink. But the temptation, the thought of slipping into the warmth of who he perhaps really was, would never leave him.

'You all right?' Anna asked.

'Yeah. Fine,' he lied. 'So what do we do now?'

'We forget it ever happened and get on with our jobs.'

'As simple as that?'

'We have no other choice.'

81

'No,' he agreed, still troubled by his own thoughts. 'I don't suppose we do.'

'Good,' she told him. 'Perhaps we can start with you telling me if you've had any new ideas, any insights as to what the killer may do next.'

'Insights?'

'Yes, Sean. Insights. It's no secret between us that you have them. Remember?'

'If you think I can tell you where and when he's going to hit next then you'd be wrong.'

'I know I would be. I don't believe in psychics. Maybe you remember that too?'

'Not really.'

'But you must have some ideas. An imagination like yours doesn't just stop working. It can't.'

'I know he'll attack again,' Sean admitted, 'but so do you.'

'In all probability, yes he will, for reasons we've already discussed, but perhaps there's something else – something you haven't told anybody else?'

'Nothing solid,' he told her. 'Just loose ideas rattling around inside my head, nothing I can grasp hold of. Nothing that makes much sense.'

'Try me.'

'Look, I don't want to overcomplicate something that's already complicated enough. Last case we had I made my mind up too early and I was wrong. Evidence here says it's a disgruntled member of the public getting some payback on the banks and that's probably going to be exactly what he is, but . . .'

'But what?'

'But I want to keep an open mind. Just in case. I don't want to get fooled again.'

'You sure you don't know something?' Anna persisted. 'I might be able to help. It is what I'm here for.'

'Is it?' Sean found himself asking, unsure of where his own suspicions had suddenly sprung from.

'Of course,' Anna told him. 'Why else would I be here?'

He studied her hard before speaking, looking for the tiny telltale signs of a lie he'd seen thousands of times before. 'Forget it,' he finally answered. 'I'm being an idiot. Forget everything. I'm glad you're here. We'll make it work.'

'Good,' she replied, 'and thank you.'

'Don't thank me yet,' he warned her, his friendly tone and slight smile hiding what his eyes had seen in her face. 'Remember we're only at the beginning. There's plenty more to come from our boy yet. Of that, I'm certain.'

Georgina Vaughan pulled on her expensive training shoes, checked her iPhone was strapped to her bicep properly, selected the music she wanted to listen to, took a couple of deep breaths and then opened the door leading to the communal area of her flat in one of Parsons Green's Victorian redbrick mansion blocks. She skipped down the three flights of wide stairs and exited the building into Favart Road. She enjoyed the spring sunshine on her face as she ran, turning into the King's Road, dodging past the late afternoon commuters and shoppers until she was able to turn into Peterborough Road and jog towards a small park known as South Park. She never noticed the white panel van that pulled away from the kerb as she left her building, nor the same van overtaking her in the King's Road as she headed towards the park where she always went running.

She was enjoying the relatively fresh air of the park, the steady pace of her feet moving to the rhythm of the music that deadened all other sounds, but she was aware the evening was growing late and the sun was moving quickly from the sky. She didn't want to be in the park when darkness descended, so she picked up her pace, the solid tarmac of the park's path turning to the loose gravel of the parking area as she approached the exit.

As she drew closer to the gates she began to feel strangely unnerved, eager to rejoin the streets outside where she'd be back amongst other people. She increased her speed, but the entrance seemed to grow further and further away.

She would have screamed if he'd given her a chance, but his hand hit her hard in the throat as he stepped out from behind the tree and grabbed her, pulling her behind it and slamming her against the rough trunk, her head banging hard and dislodging her headphones. For a second he released her throat and ripped her iPhone from her bicep. He threw it on the ground, smashing it with the heel of his black boot before he again gripped her around the throat hard enough to stop almost any sound escaping. For the first time he showed her the knife, no more than six inches in length including the handle, but lethal looking, bladed on one side, with teeth on the other. Her eyes grew wide with terror, her mind already assuming rape was the least she was about to suffer, until she heard the strange electronic voice that came from the box attached to his chest, his mouth moving only slightly behind the ski-mask, the mirrored sunglasses showing nothing but the reflection of her own fear.

'I'm not here to hurt you. I'm not going to rape you,' the mechanical voice explained as he moved the knife closer to her face, 'but if you try to escape, struggle or make a sound I will kill you, here and now. Do you understand?'

She tried to speak, but he squeezed her throat tight and held the knife to his own hidden lips and shushed her, the voice distorter making it sound like the ocean.

'No sound. Remember?'

She managed to nod as the tears began to roll down her face. Her brain scrambled to remember why this creature with the monstrous voice seemed so familiar, her mind rewinding back through conversations she'd had with colleagues and friends, back through news items she'd seen, until it reached the memory of watching the man being hanged live on the Internet – the Your View Killer.

Panic threatened to overwhelm her and make her pass out and she welcomed the promise of oblivion, but suddenly she was moving, being pushed and dragged across the loose gravel, her legs intermittently giving way, his strength obvious as he held her weight without breaking pace or breathing hard. And all the time the knife was held against her throat, its sharpness causing stinging cuts every time she slipped, until they reached a white panel van waiting in the car park. He slid the side door open and pushed her inside then took hold of her right arm and twisted it painfully behind her, making her call out in pain as he strapped her at the wrist into a leather buckled restraint. Within seconds he'd strapped her other wrist into an identical restraint. She twisted to look into the face she couldn't see and spoke despite his demands.

'Please,' was all she could say. He just placed his finger to his lips and again made the sound of the ocean, grabbing her by the feet and pulling her legs straight before attaching further straps to her ankles. She was about to try one last time to plead with him to let her go, but the thick, sticky tape plastered across her mouth took the chance away. Daylight turned to blackness as a thick hood was pulled over her head.

'Time to go,' he told her and slid the panel door closed, leaving her strapped in the darkness of the back of the van with nothing but terror and the smell of her own urine seeping between her legs.

Sean sat quietly in his office trying to concentrate on the latest influx of information reports. Anna was only a few feet away, studying her own files when suddenly the calm was shattered as Bishop burst into the room, his eyes wild with excitement. He waited a second until both were looking at him before speaking in an almost frantic tone.

'He's back on. He's back on Your View,' he managed to tell them. 'I've got it up on the laptop next door.'

Sean was already up and moving. 'How long?' he asked.

'Seconds,' Bishop answered. 'My alert went off and there he was.'

Sean pushed past him, calling out to Donnelly and Sally who were in the main office checking on the other detectives. 'Our man's online,' he told them. 'Get in here now. Everyone else,' he shouted across the office, 'get Your View online any way you can.' He turned back to Bishop as he entered Sally and Donnelly's office. 'What's he doing?'

'Nothing,' Bishop answered, resuming his seat in front of the laptop with Sean now looking over his shoulder. 'All we're getting so far is this.' He pointed to the screen where a woman dressed in exercise gear was tied to a heavy wooden chair with a hood over her head. Sean watched her wriggling and mumbling under the hood. By now Sally, Donnelly and Anna were also crammed into the room peering at the small screen. 'The suspect hasn't shown himself yet.'

'Why?' Sally asked.

'Because he's waiting,' Sean told her.

'For what?' Donnelly asked.

'For his audience to gather,' Sean explained. 'So the trial can begin.' They all inadvertently cast their eyes to the on-screen view counter that showed the number of viewers growing rapidly as news of the Your View Killer's latest appearance spread across the Internet and the digital world – live texts, emails, Twitter, Facebook all spreading the word like an electronic wildfire that played directly into the puppet-master's hands.

'Bastard took a woman,' Donnelly said. 'I never expected him to take a woman.'

'Neither did I,' Sean admitted.

'Says more about you two than it does him,' Sally told them. 'Plenty of rich women out there too, you know.'

'No,' Sean explained. 'It's just this was as much about his wounded male pride as anything. That doesn't tally with killing a woman.'

'He hasn't killed her yet,' Anna pointed out. Before Sean could answer a dark figure appeared on the screen standing next to the hooded woman before the shot focused in solely on his hidden face.

'That's clever,' Bishop told them. 'He must have rigged something up so he can control the camera's lens remotely.'

'Or someone else is operating the camera,' Sally pointed out.

'Either way it's different,' Sean explained. 'Why change the way he films it?'

'Practising?' Anna suggested. 'Honing his art?'

The disturbing electronic voice began to speak.

'I see you've gathered in greater numbers now, my brothers and sisters. Good. Only together can we defeat the greedy vultures who rule over us. Only together can we change our unfair and unjust society where hard-working people can be cast out of their jobs and homes to save the riches of the rich – the power of the powerful. Only together will we ever be listened to. Only through strength in numbers will we succeed where governments and unions have failed us – us, the common people.'

'The speeches sound prepared,' Sally observed. 'Like he's reading off an autocue.'

'Maybe he is.' Sean considered it was possible.

'Oh he's definitely a pissed-off lefty,' Donnelly insisted.

'Appears so,' Sean agreed. 'The second that hood comes off I want people trying to identify her.'

'Will do,' Donnelly told him and headed into the main office to assign the task.

'And now the wealthy and powerful who own the British media have unwittingly brought us together in our tens of thousands with their coverage of these events. What do the fools call me – "The Your View Killer". What could be a more ridiculous name? Naming me

87

at all undermines the seriousness of what I'm trying to achieve, but if they help to bring us together, then so be it.'

'He's no idiot,' Sally stated. 'Sounds . . . educated.'

'Doesn't mean he's not insane,' Sean pointed out.

'Not long ago I saw a jackdaw flying low in the sky, carrying something in its beak – its next meal, I assumed. Suddenly a huge crow appeared from nowhere and began to attack the jackdaw, stabbing at it with its sharp beak, grabbing at it with its talons, trying to take the very food from its mouth. But just when I was sure the jackdaw would lose its hard-fought prize, a hundred jackdaws rose from the trees and swept into the sky, communicating with each other in a thousand different sounds, mobbing the fat crow, barely letting its wings beat until they'd driven it from the sky. The fat crow was defeated by the might of the many and the determined. That is what we must be if we are to defeat the fat crows that infest our skies. We must become as the jackdaws are – then nothing can stop us.'

'He's completely mad,' Sally offered as they watched the film return to a wider shot, the killer's arm stretching out and ripping the hood his new victim's head, making her turn away and squeeze her eyes tightly shut. 'Christ,' Sally spoke again. 'She's so young.'

'What is she?' Donnelly asked. 'One of those young website millionaires you hear about?'

The man tore the tape from the woman's mouth, making her scream out in pain.

'You bastard. Please. Why are you doing this to me?'

'I'm doing it for the people,' he told her in the cold electronic voice. *'This is for the people.'*

Mark Hudson was happy to be alone in the bedroom of his council flat in Birmingham, glad his moronic mates weren't around to spoil his enjoyment. This one was even better than the last – he'd taken a woman this time and a young, attractive one too. Hudson licked his lips at the thought of what the man might do to her. He wanted to see her humiliated before he killed her and he was sure his new hero would kill her – after he'd had a bit of fun. He and the Your View Killer were cut from the same stone, he was sure of it. He knew the man on his screen wouldn't disappoint him.

'Come on,' he urged the man. 'Fucking do her, man. Do her.'

'Open your eyes.'

'I don't want to.'

'Open your eyes or I'll cut your eyelids off.'

'Please, I haven't done anything to you.'

'Open your eyes.'

Hudson watched as the woman slowly opened her eyes and then tried to lean as far away as she could from the hooded man.

'Yeah. Do as you're told, bitch.'

'You are Georgina Vaughan, yes?'

'How . . . how d'you know my name?'

'That's not important. What are important are your crimes against the people.'

'I haven't committed any crimes against anyone.'

'Wrong. You work for Glenhope Investments, correct?'

'I'm just a project manager.'

'The same Glenhope Investments that needed a government bailout to stop it from going out of business, while at the same time continued to pay its employees grotesque bonuses.'

'I don't know anything about that.'

'Liar. You're a liar and a whore to money and wealth, and soon you will be judged for your crimes.'

'You're so dead,' Hudson said out loud, an ugly smile on his face, eyes frenzied with excitement. 'You're dead, bitch.'

Gabriel Westbrook stood leaning over his desk as he watched the hooded man preaching to his audience on the screen – an audience the live viewer count put at over one hundred thousand and growing. He sensed little sympathy from the watching public for the plight of his fellow financial sector worker, imagining them as a mob, stalking through the City looking for more victims to lynch. Already he sensed an uneasiness spreading across the City. Nothing too serious yet, but people were beginning to talk and the talk wasn't positive. Now, with a second victim taken, fears would increase and spread. Not a wholesale panic, but it didn't take mass hysteria to cause serious financial problems – just a sustained shift in momentum. With the threat of more victims to come, some people would start to choose to take their holidays early, in the hope that by the time they returned the madman would have been caught. Others would take time off sick and many would no longer be comfortable working late – keen to hurry home in the hours of daylight. The streets of the City would hardly be deserted, but the country's financial heart was like a giant old tanker relentlessly carving its way across oceans, driven by perpetual forward momentum. Were the balance to be tipped, no matter how slightly, momentum would be lost and it would be a long hard process before the huge financial institutions once again reached full speed ahead, by which time billions would have been lost. In a time when the sector was still recovering from its first self-made crisis, the effects would cause significant damage – maybe even more.

He wanted to turn off his computer, but somehow couldn't.

'I didn't do anything.'

'You are part of the organization that made our government steal the people's money so you could survive – money that you were supposed to give back to the people, but didn't. Instead you invested it in property, African gold mines, Australian mineral mines, the vast profits of which you shared amongst yourselves like pigs at the trough while decent, hard-working people lost their jobs, their houses and their life savings. And yet you say you've done nothing wrong.'

'Jesus Christ,' Westbrook shouted at his screen. 'Someone

needs to stop you – someone needs to shut you up, before you start a bloody civil war.'

'You should watch this,' Phil Taylor called out to his wife Cathy. 'This man's talking a lot of sense.'

'I don't want to listen to that lunatic,' she called back to her husband who sat in the small office-cum-storage room.

'Don't you want to know what those bastards did with the money they stole from us?'

'Stole from us?' she questioned, continuing their inter-room conversation from the kitchen. 'I was under the impression bad debtors put the business under. That and you overstretching.'

'Yeah, well, if the banks had just lent me a bit more we would have been all right.'

'Sure about that, are you?' she doubted him.

'Whatever,' he mumbled quietly to himself, eager to get back to the hooded man on the screen.

'Nothing wrong indeed.'

'I swear. I haven't.'

Taylor watched as the man walked behind the woman and rested his hands on her shoulders, making her squirm and twist as she tried to see what he was going to do.

'I'm going to ask you a question now and I want you to answer it honestly. If you lie I will know and your punishment will be severe. Do you understand?'

'No. No I don't understand. I just want to go home.'

'Answer the question honestly and perhaps you will.'

'OK. OK, I'll answer the question as honestly as I can.'

The man took a deep breath, the voice distorter making it sound like a rush of wind.

'Have you received any bonuses since the banking crisis? A simple question.'

'OK – yes, yes I have, but it's not what you think.'

The man straightened and took another deep breath, as if he'd unearthed a great truth.

'How much? How much each year?'

'I can't remember, exactly.'

'Try. How much?'

'About . . . about forty thousand pounds.'

'Forty thousand pounds.'

'But it was in shares. I couldn't even spend them. They were just . . . just paper.'

'And your salary, how much do you get paid each year?'

'I told you – I'm not rich. I'm just a project manager.'

'How much and don't lie to me.'

She slumped in the chair.

'About ninety thousand pounds.'

'Ninety thousand pounds and forty thousand bonus, while others can barely feed their families. Shame on you. Shame on you.'

'D'you hear that?' Taylor called out. 'Hundred and thirty grand a year for being a bloody project manager.' His wife didn't answer. 'Greedy bitch,' he whispered. 'Bet you weren't thinking about people like me when you were celebrating your fat City bonus. No – of course you weren't. None of you were.'

Father Alex Jones had received the text message he'd been dreading informing him that the Your View Killer was back live on the Internet. He sat at the altar of his empty church in Dulwich and logged onto Your View on his old iPad and soon found the images he feared, but looked for anyway – the hooded man with the deeply unsettling distorted voice standing next to a terrified-looking young woman. He'd prayed as the man had preached, pleading with God to touch the man's heart with mercy while begging for the woman's safety, but so far neither prayer seemed to have been answered.

'The people have heard enough. It's time for them to judge. Time

for them to decide whether they find you guilty or not guilty.' The man's face grew larger on the screen. *'I know what they're thinking – that they can stop me talking to the people. Think they can stop the people having their justice by shutting down this website. But if they do her fate will be more terrible than they can possibly imagine. The people will not be silenced. I will not be silenced.'*

Father Jones dropped to his knees in front of the altar, pressed his hands together, closed his eyes and began to pray. 'Our Father who art in heaven, hallowed be thy name. Thy Kingdom come . . .'

'Get me someone from Your View on the line,' Sean told anyone who was listening. 'The more senior the better.'

'D'you think they might be trying to pull the plug?' Donnelly asked.

'We can't take the chance they are,' Sean warned him.

'I'm on it,' Donnelly told him and grabbed the nearest phone as the others continued to watch the pictures coming from the small screen.

'The people are beginning to vote. Soon we'll know if this whore of wealth has been found guilty by you, the people. I have nothing else to say while we wait for the judgement.'

'Jesus Christ,' Sally exclaimed. 'What must she be thinking – tied to that chair by this psychopath, waiting for a bunch of voyeurs to pass judgement?'

'She'll be thinking a lot of things,' Sean told her. 'None of them good. But wasting time worrying about that's not going to bring us any closer to finding him, and stopping him. How you doing, Bob?'

'Getting closer and closer. The longer he stays online the closer I'll get.'

'How close are you now?' Sean asked impatiently.

'He's definitely transmitting from the southeast,' Bishop told him. 'If he keeps this up it's only a matter of time before we have him.'

'The southeast?' Sean didn't hide his disappointment. 'Can't you do better than that?'

'Yes, but it'll take time,' Bishop explained. 'We're not just trying to track a mobile phone signal. This is far more complicated. But we're linked into the Internet Crime Unit's tracking software. We'll get him soon enough.'

'So long as he doesn't ditch the computer he's using, or move to another location,' Sean reminded him. Bishop just shrugged, concentrating on the computer in front of him. Donnelly grabbed Sean's attention, holding the corded phone out as far as he could for Sean to take.

'Nick Poole on the phone, boss. CEO of Your View.'

Sean stepped towards him and took the phone. 'DI Corrigan speaking. I assume you're watching this.'

'I am,' Poole answered.

'I'm just calling to make sure you have no intention of pulling the plug.'

'Listen,' Poole told him nervously, 'I know I gave Assistant Commissioner Addis assurances that we wouldn't take this whole terrible business offline, but this is getting too much. We can't be dictated to by this lunatic. I don't want to be a part of this any more.'

'You heard what he said,' Sean snapped down the phone. 'You pull the plug – you seal her fate. Let it play out.'

'And I can tell people you made us keep the site live?' Poole asked. 'We can tell the media it was the police's idea?'

'If you want to use my name to cover your arse then use it. Just don't shut this down.'

There was a slight pause before Poole spoke again. 'OK, but it's your call. Your responsibility,' Poole insisted.

'Fine,' Sean told him with barely disguised contempt and hung up.

'Problem?' Donnelly asked.

'Not now,' Sean answered and moved to better see the

screen, the hooded man still standing silently next to his victim. 'You any closer?' he asked Bishop.

'A little, but not much,' he answered.

'Quiet a second,' Sally interrupted. 'I think he's about to say something.' The group watched as the man moved out of camera shot.

'Look at the voting count,' Sally told them. 'People are voting not guilty.'

'Looks fifty–fifty to me,' Donnelly disagreed.

'Yeah, but with the first victim it was an overwhelming majority finding him guilty,' Sally explained. 'This is a split jury – so what does he do now?'

'I think we're about to find out,' Sean silenced them as the hooded man came back into view.

'*The people have voted. It appears you cannot decide whether her guilt is clear. I am disappointed. Too many of you have allowed yourselves to be seduced by her femininity and false tears. But it's not your fault. The rich and powerful have used their media empires and influence to brainwash many of you over decades and decades – pumping you full of the news they want you to hear as well as mind-destroying soap operas and reality shows to ensure your misplaced sentimentality.*

'*However, your decision is your decision . . .*'

'He's gonna let her go,' Sally said, sounding desperate for it to be true.

'*but I cannot ignore the thousands who have seen through her disguise and recognized her guilt.*'

'*No. No. I haven't done anything. They see that.*'

'*Brothers and sisters – this is no time for mercy. This is a war: a war we must win or forever be trodden under the foot of oppression, growing weaker and weaker as they grow ever more powerful and wealthy. We must be strong, must be prepared to act against our gentle nature and strike back when we are wronged.*'

They watched as he again disappeared from camera shot

before quickly returning and moving behind his victim, holding a set of hair clippers up for the cameras to see.

'My God,' Sally said through clenched teeth, 'what's he going to do to her?' No one answered as they held their collective breath.

'She has humiliated us – the people. Laughing at us as she climbs the corporate ladder to unimaginable riches – fucking us at every turn, her vanity her shield. Now let her feel the bitter sting of humiliation.'

The clippers buzzed as he grabbed her by her long ponytail and scythed it off in one motion, allowing her head to fall forward as it came away. Sean closed his eyes for a second at the sound of her sobbing, saddened by her humiliation but relieved she was suffering no worse. His relief turned rapidly to extreme anxiety as the hooded man grabbed what remained of her hair and yanked her head backwards, exposing her throat.

'Shit,' he muttered involuntarily, imagining the clippers being replaced with a razor-sharp knife sliding across her taut skin. Instead the man gripped her in a headlock and began to saw great chunks of hair from her scalp, leaving multiple cuts and grazes. Finally he stood aside, leaving the victim bowed in her chair, looking down at her own hair gathered at her feet.

'Bastard,' Sally said loudly, her eyes glassy and reddening. No one disagreed.

'Humiliation enough? Perhaps. But hair will grow and her vanity will return.'

Once again he stepped out of view. 'Christ, not more,' Sally pleaded as the man returned holding a relatively small knife. He stood facing the victim, the knife disappearing from view, shielded by his own body as her pleas screamed from the computer's tinny speakers.

'Please, no. Please don't kill me. Please.'

The screaming seemed to last for an age as his elbows and shoulders jerked side to side and up and down, until at last he stepped aside so the world could see Georgina Vaughan slumped in the chair, dead or unconscious, her running top and sports bra split up the middle revealing her small breasts. In the centre of her chest blood seeped from the eight-inch-tall dollar sign he'd carved into her skin. The camera focused in on the wound before pulling back to show a wider shot. The man faced the camera, breathing hard after his exertions, struggling to regain his breath.

'Is she dead?' Sally asked, her voice still shaking.

'No,' Sean answered without conviction. 'I think she's just passed out.'

'Best thing for her,' Donnelly added. 'Fuck. That was hard to watch.'

'We'll be watching more if we don't find him,' Sean soberly reminded them.

Her pain and suffering were necessary. She will live, but this is war. If the rich and powerful fail to heed this warning, next time I will not be so merciful.'

Sean and the others were in a state of shock at what they'd witnessed as the man put a hood back over the victim's head and walked from sight. A second later the link went dead.

'He's gone,' Bishop broke their silence. 'The link's been cut.'

'D'you get any closer?' Sean asked.

'A bit. He's in the Metropolitan area or very close to it,' Bishop explained. 'Which means we have to find his signal in amongst millions of others. Best bet is he's broadcasting from a rural area somewhere just outside London.'

'Could he know we're trying to trace him?' Sean asked.

'I would assume he'd assume we would be.'

'That's not what I meant,' Sean explained. 'I mean, could he somehow see how close we're getting to him? Could he measure that somehow?'

Bishop sucked air in through his teeth like a mechanic presenting a large quote. 'Well, he'd have to have some state-of-the-art software – very difficult-to-get-hold-of stuff – and then he'd have to know how to use it. It's possible, but unlikely. We mainly use this stuff to track paedophiles grooming kids online. Those bastards know their business, but they still never seem to see us coming.'

'I hope you're right,' Sean told him before turning to the others. 'All right. We're all feeling pretty shit right now and so will the rest of the team. I need you to get them out there doing whatever they can to find this fucker. Keep them busy. I want them to remember what they've seen, but not dwell on it. They've all got jobs to do. There'll be witnesses we haven't found yet and we need to intensify our efforts to find this van. Let's have every white Renault Trafic van in London stopped and checked if we have to. If the driver seems even a little strange then have them arrested and held until we can take a look at them. And check on number plate thefts too. Anyone who's reported having their number plate stolen within the last few months we need to know about it – all vehicles, not just vans. And this damn *white room.* Somebody somewhere might have recognized it. Let's pump the public for information – let them know just because they might know where it isn't doesn't mean we do. Some people assume we know everything while others just don't want to get involved. We need people to start coming forward with information. Maybe someone out there even knows who he is. Maybe they're covering for him. Make sure we're pricking their conscience. An anonymous phone call with a name could break this whole thing open.'

'What about the equipment he uses to disguise his voice?' Sally asked.

'Looks homemade,' Sean reminded her, 'but he may have had to buy some of the component parts. If we're lucky he's not competent with electronics and paid someone to put it together for him, although I doubt it. Get Summers or Jesson to check it out from all angles anyway. Find out what shops sell this kind of stuff and start phoning around – see if someone remembers dealing with anyone they thought were a little off and check for CCTV. You never know your luck. As soon as I think of anything else I'll let you know.'

Sally and Donnelly nodded and headed off into the main office to rally the team. Sean tapped Bishop on the shoulder. 'And you just keep doing whatever it is you do.' He felt a presence at the door and turned to see an ashen-faced Addis standing, staring at him.

'A word, Inspector,' Addis insisted. 'Your office will do.' Addis spun on his heels and led the way, Sean following without enthusiasm. 'Take a seat if you like,' Addis told him calmly, but menacingly. Sean took him up on his offer and slumped in his own chair behind his desk. Addis remained standing, looking at the door Sean had left open behind him. 'You may want to close that,' he told Sean, 'unless you want your entire team to hear what I have to say.'

'I have no secrets from them,' Sean lied, hoping the open door might curb Addis's words.

'Really? Perhaps you should,' Addis told him, moving on before Sean could ask what he meant. 'I assume you've just watched the same footage on Your View as I had to watch. For God's sake, Inspector – a young bloody woman this time – one even the public voted to spare. The media will crucify us over this and frankly I don't blame them. Why don't we have anyone in custody yet? Why is this madman still running around out there wreaking havoc across London?'

'With all due respect,' Sean cut in, 'it's only been a matter of days and this is only the second victim he's taken. But we're making progress. We're getting closer and closer to tracing wherever it is he's broadcasting from.'

'Is that all we've got?' Addis snapped. 'Hope that we can trace his signal?'

'No, sir,' Sean explained. 'We're chasing down dozens of lines of inquiry and now we'll have dozens more.'

'Good, because it would be most unsatisfactory to think

99

that all you are doing is sitting around waiting for this lunatic to snatch someone else so you can trace the signal.'

'Well we're not,' Sean assured him.

'And this latest victim – has it been confirmed she is who he said she is yet?'

'Not yet, but it'll only be a matter of time now the broadcast's been out there.'

'Well, let's just pray she doesn't turn up dead somewhere,' Addis added.

'She won't,' Sean told him.

'Really? How can you be so sure?'

'Because if he was going to kill her he would have done it on Your View. He would have wanted everyone to see. That's the point of doing what he does – so everyone can see. So everyone can hear what he has to say.'

'All the more reason to close him down fast.'

Sean looked away from Addis as Anna entered the office. 'Sorry,' she began. 'It's just I overheard you discussing whether he would kill this victim.'

'And?' Addis asked.

'I agree with Inspector Corrigan. He won't kill her. Not now. If he does, the charade that he's doing this out of justice and that the people are the jury will be shattered, making him nothing more than another one-dimensional murderer. That's not what he wants – not what he believes he is.'

'Then we should be thankful for small mercies,' Addis told them and walked from the office, fleetingly halting at the door. 'Let's just get this one solved and put to bed,' he added. 'Before it drags us all down.'

Sean waited until Addis was clear of the main office before speaking again. 'Thanks,' he told Anna.

'What for?'

'For backing me up and getting that clown off my back.'

'I told him the truth – you're right, he won't kill her. Not now.'

'I hope you're right,' Sean told her, 'or Addis is going to use my bollocks to decorate his oversized desk.'

'I doubt that,' she argued. 'Addis needs you more than you think.'

'Maybe,' Sean said doubtfully. 'I'm still surprised he took a woman though.'

'Why?' Anna asked. 'Because you thought this was about male pride?'

'An element of it, yes – if what we're seeing, if what he's telling us is true. You'd have to think he's someone who's lost his job, or maybe a business and then his wife and family as a consequence. As a man, that would hurt your pride.'

'As a woman too,' Anna reminded him.

'Touché,' Sean accepted her point, 'but it was still a mistake.'

'Why?' Anna still didn't follow.

'Public sympathy,' he explained. 'People weren't exactly falling over themselves to help us find Paul Elkins's killer. There wasn't a lot of empathy with him out there. But now he's made a young woman his victim that'll change – even if she was well heeled and well paid. We might get a little more cooperation now.'

'That's a cold way of looking at it,' Anna observed.

'It's a fact,' he told her. 'Cold or otherwise.'

'And you?' she surprised him. 'Did you feel empathy for him?'

He leaned back as far as he could into his rickety chair. 'No,' he answered honestly. 'No I didn't. Does that make me a bad person – a monster?'

'Hardly,' she replied. 'People have empathy for people they perceive to be vulnerable victims – young women, the poor, the elderly . . .'

'Children?' Sean cut in.

'Especially children,' she agreed. 'I guess this case couldn't be more different from your last.'

'No,' Sean sighed. 'Maybe that's why the team's had difficulty getting up and running for this one.'

'You think they are?' she asked.

'Maybe, until now. The mood seems to have changed with this new victim. They seem back to themselves.'

'Their last few cases have been exceptionally trying, physically and emotionally. My professional opinion would be to rotate your personnel more frequently.'

'I can't,' he told her flatly. 'I need their experience. Health and safety. Employee welfare. Just leave all that at the front door on your way in. This is the Metropolitan Police, not Tesco's.'

'And you?' Anna continued. 'You don't think any of this affects you?'

'Think?' he almost mocked her. 'I don't have time to think. Well, not about how things are *affecting* me.'

'You're not immune to it, Sean.'

'Is this a friendly conversation or are you psychoanalysing me?' He was joking, but Anna seemed to tense up a little, and he noticed it.

'I wouldn't try and examine you without your permission and knowledge,' she snapped her answer.

'Fair enough.' Sean didn't push it. 'Besides, right now I've got better things to think about than whether you are or not. I've got to work out what this bastard's going to do next and stop him.'

5

Geoff Jackson sat in the Three Greyhounds pub in Greek Strect, at the heart of Soho in London's West End. A colleague had tipped him off the killer was back on Your View, and he'd immediately ducked into the pub, grabbed a table close to the bar and logged onto the Internet on his laptop. The broadcast had been everything he could have hoped for and the killer had even had the good sense to apparently spare the woman. Her humiliation and torture had been unfortunate, but he was now convinced this was a man he could do business with.

He sipped his pint, oblivious to the crowd building inside the upmarket pub. He could almost smell the cash and celebrity coming his way. But how to make contact with the killer and still keep the police at bay long enough to get what he wanted out of him? He watched the Your View footage over again and drummed his fingers while he whispered to himself. 'Contact. Contact. How the hell do I contact you and keep us both safe?'

He let the ideas swirl around inside his head, confident that eventually the answer would materialize – after all, it always did. Suddenly, almost without warning, he found himself mouthing the answer almost silently. 'Twitter. I'll get you to contact me on Twitter.' He smiled and had to suppress his laughter. 'I'll get you to tweet me, you beautiful bastard.' He kept talking, developing the idea, afraid that silence could chase it away. 'I'll get you to send me a private message, then I'll give you the number of a pay-as-you-go mobile and get you to get one too and call me and fucking bingo – we'll have our own untraceable, private means of communicating, all protected by journalistic material immunity.' He allowed himself a smile of satisfaction as he thought of the police tapping into his usual mobile phone, reading his texts and maybe even eavesdropping on his calls, all of which would be a waste of time. That reminded him – he needed to call an old private detective friend of his. If the police were going to tap his phone it was only fair he did the same, and there was only one phone he was interested in – DI Corrigan's. If his friend could pull it off, he could be tapping into a gold mine.

A waiter standing next to him disturbed his daydreaming. 'Can I get you anything else, sir?'

'What?' Jackson asked, momentarily confused. 'No. No thanks.' The waiter turned to leave. 'Actually,' Jackson stopped him. 'There is something. Do you know where the nearest phone shop is?'

'I need everyone to quiet down and listen for a few minutes,' Sean shouted across the main office. 'I know you're all busy and about to get busier, so I'll be quick.' The room soon fell silent. 'As you all know by now there's been a second victim taken, although it appears she's still alive, meaning our man's gonna have to drop her off somewhere without compromising himself. We need to start checking police stations and hospitals in case she's been picked up in a confused state, which is entirely possible after what she's been through. Hopefully they'll recognize her, but they may not – they may just think she's another victim of care in the community – so we need to check it before we end up with egg on our face.

'As expected, it didn't take long for the phones to light up and we've had confirmation of who she is. Her name is Georgina Vaughan, thirty-three years old, works in the City. Her parents, work colleagues and boyfriend, Freddie Griffith, all saw the Your View broadcast and all phoned it in. Obviously they're all feeling pretty sick right now, so we need to find her and at least let them know she's safe. The rest we'll deal with later. One thing she mentioned in the video was that she was a project manager and this we now know is true, so we're not dealing with a financial big-hitter like the last victim, which means our man's changed his MO slightly. He could be thinking about what we're thinking a lot more than perhaps we first thought – making it as difficult as possible for us to predict his next move. His next victim. Something to bear in mind.

'As of yet no one can tell us about her movements since she left work. We'll be able to track her on any CCTV on her route home, but that'll take time and we need to know sooner rather than later, which again means we need to find her. She has the answers. Boyfriend says her running shoes are missing, so she could well have gone for a run when she was snatched. He told us she usually ran from their flat to a nearby small park called South Park. My money's on the park being the snatch point so we'll treat it as such until she or something else tells us different. Remember – when she's found she's a crime scene. If he releases her without further harm she may have the best evidence we're gonna get already on her. We don't want some kind-hearted hospital employee putting her clothes through the wash. All right, that's it. Dave and Sally will make sure you have your assignments on the hurry up, so don't disappear till you have them.

'And listen,' he told them, the urgency and importance clear in his voice. 'This is our chance to secure a live witness who's seen him up close and personal – who's probably been inside his van and has definitely been inside the white room.

Who knows what she's going to be able to tell us? Certainly more than the first victim – that's for sure. It's imperative we find her and find her as quickly as possible. Dave, make sure every cop in London and the southeast is on the lookout for her. Finding her and securing whatever evidence she may be carrying is now officially our number one priority.' Donnelly simply nodded that he understood. The rest of the team murmured with excitement and Sean knew they understood the importance of finding the living victim and witness as quickly as they could.

'You all know what you have to do so let's get on and do it,' he ordered before turning away and heading to his own office, letting the team know the impromptu meeting was over. He grabbed Sally as he walked.

'I'm meeting the boyfriend at their flat, see what he can tell us,' he told her. 'Want to come?'

Sally looked around the chaotic office, detectives frantically trying to clear their last inquiries before she and Donnelly gave them more. 'I'd better stay here,' she explained. 'Help Dave get the new actions dished out, like you said.'

'Fine,' Sean nodded in agreement. 'I'll go alone. Anything comes up, let me know.'

'Will do,' she answered just as Anna came up on Sean's shoulder.

'I could come,' she told Sean. 'I'd like to.'

'It's fine,' Sean argued. 'I'll do it alone.'

'I want to,' Anna insisted. 'Really. I'd like to come.'

He could feel both Sally and Anna staring at him, daring him to say no.

'Fine,' he relented. 'Grab your things.'

Sean and Anna approached the mansion block that housed the flat Georgina Vaughan shared with her boyfriend of the last two years, Freddie Griffith. Sean was growing frustrated at the lack of parking spaces. Early evening had turned to night-time and most of the affluent, up-and-coming City types had long since returned home and swallowed up the residents-only parking spaces.

'This close to the King's Road we'll be lucky to find anywhere,' Anna commented unhelpfully. 'We should have taken the tube.'

'I hate the damn tube,' Sean snapped back. 'Especially in the evening, when everyone's on their way home stinking of the day. Not so bad in the morning when all you can smell is deodorant and perfume.'

'What a pleasant thought,' Anna said.

'Which one?' Sean asked, looking for a reaction.

'Neither really appeal,' she answered.

'So,' Sean changed the subject, 'what's your guess so far? Do you think she's still alive?'

'I'm not sure,' she explained. 'Probably, but this one's an angry one. He said he'd spare her, but it doesn't mean he's not going to have a fit of temper and change his mind. And he's clearly clever and organized – perhaps he'll decide the risk of letting her go, of leaving a living witness, is too great.'

'Perhaps,' Sean limply agreed.

'You don't sound convinced.'

'I agree he's clever and organized, even articulate, and yes, I can feel the anger in him,' Sean explained, 'but he's a risk-taker too, and this persona he's created is totally dependent on his own belief – the belief that people see him as some kind of dispenser of justice and not just someone who's abducting and killing people. Remember he plays the part of the judge deciding the sentence. As to whether his victims are guilty or not, he leaves that to the people watching – the jury. With this victim the jury was split. If he kills her now he's made himself judge, jury and executioner. That doesn't fit with his plan.'

'What plan?' Anna asked. 'I don't see any particular plan in his actions.'

'There will be,' Sean told her. 'Trust me. They all have a plan.' He spotted a parking space and pulled over, climbing from the car quickly and waiting for Anna on the pavement. They walked along the road until they found number thirty-two.

Sean pressed the intercom button labelled 'C'. After only a few seconds a desperate-sounding voice reverberated from the metal box. Sean could see there was a small camera in the system and knew they were being watched.

'Hello. Who is it?'

'Police,' he said into the intercom, knowing there was little need for further personal details yet, stepping back and holding his warrant card close to the camera.

'OK. Please come up. We're on the third floor.'

Sean waited for the telltale buzz of the door being unlocked before pushing it open and stepping aside to allow Anna to enter first. Once inside he looked around at the opulent surroundings – a wide, sweeping oak bannister, parquet wood flooring, large antique-looking mirrors and everything clean and cared for.

'Very nice,' he said as they climbed the stairs, 'and this is just the communal area. I've lived in a few flats in my time. None of them had communal areas that looked like this.'

'I suppose so,' Anna replied, looking around without much interest. 'Is that relevant – the communal area?'

'No,' Sean answered. 'I was just saying.'

They climbed the rest of the way in silence until they reached the third floor and flat C, where a white man in his mid-thirties was already waiting for them, tall and athletic with short blond hair, but looking agitated, tired and pensive.

'Freddie Griffith?' Sean asked.

'Yeah, sure,' he answered. 'Please come in.' He didn't ask their names or for identification as he led them into the large, spacious flat, decorated simply, but with stylish and expensive furniture and electrical equipment. He showed them to the open-plan living area and clicked off the huge flat-screen TV hanging on the wall. 'Please. Take a seat.'

Sean did as he was told, introducing himself as he sat. 'Mr Griffith, I'm Detective Inspector Corrigan from the Special Investigations Unit and this is my . . .' he looked at Anna, 'my colleague, Anna Ravenni-Ceron.' He hoped Griffith wouldn't pick up on her lack of a rank and start asking awkward questions he didn't have time for. 'We'll be investigating the abduction and assault of, I believe your girlfriend, Georgina Vaughan.'

'Yes. Georgina's my partner. Have you found her yet? Is she all right?'

'Not yet,' Sean admitted, 'but I'm very confident we will soon. I've got the entire Met looking for her.'

'That bastard,' Griffith told them as he finally sat down, intertwining his fingers and rocking slightly in his chair. 'Did you see what he did to her? If only I could find him before you lot do. I'd make the bastard pay. Jesus Christ – he cut off her hair, and then . . . with that knife. How could he do that to her? She's never hurt anyone. You deal with these type of people – why did he do this to her?'

'I understand your anger,' Sean told him truthfully, 'but right now I need to ask you some questions – questions that could help us find the man who took Georgina and find out why he did this to her.'

'I can't think clearly,' Griffith admitted. 'This is like a living nightmare. I mean, I'm working in my office when Lisa comes in . . . Lisa's one of my colleagues, and right away I know something's seriously wrong – she's all pale and upset and she tells me Georgie's on the bloody Internet – on Your View – that the lunatic who killed that other poor bastard's got Georgie. I turn it on and there she is, taped to that bloody chair. Fucking hell, I watched the whole thing. Do you understand? I watched the whole thing and there wasn't a damn thing I could do to stop it.'

Sean saw the colour drain from Griffith's face. He was sure Griffith was about to throw up. 'That must have been very difficult,' was all Sean could think of to say, wishing Sally was there to take care of the compassionate element of the witness interview, 'but I really do need to ask you some questions.'

'If it helps find her,' Griffith answered, 'if it helps find him, then of course, anything. Please. Anything. Christ, Georgie. Why did it have to be her?'

'When you first called the police,' Sean moved him on, 'you told them you'd noticed Georgina's running shoes were missing?'

'Yeah,' Griffith agreed. 'I figured she'd come home, then gone for a run. The sick bastard must have grabbed her when she was out running. I thought it could be important the police knew that as soon as possible.'

'It was the right thing to do,' Sean cajoled him. 'So the first time you called the police was when you arrived home, not when you saw your girlfriend on Your View?' He felt Anna's eyes fall on him, as if she was trying to warn him it was too early to treat Griffith as a suspect.

'That's right,' Griffith agreed again, his eyes still darting around the room, his voice never changing from simple anxiety, his body still restless, his complete lack of reaction to the inference in Sean's question that he'd possibly acted strangely in coming home before calling the police instantly satisfying Sean that he was in no way involved in Georgina's disappearance. 'A lot of people in my office know Georgina. She used to work there. It's how we met, so I immediately asked them to call the police while I came straight home. I had to be sure, you see . . . be sure she wasn't here. I know – stupid isn't it – but for some reason I just had to know for sure it was Georgie on Your View and not somehow, someone else. I suppose that makes me a bad person, doesn't it – wishing this on someone else?'

'It's not unusual,' Anna spoke for the first time. 'In a

situation as rare and traumatic as this it's perfectly normal to want to be absolutely sure what you think is true, is true. It helps us to accept and deal with the reality of the situation.'

'You sound like you know a lot about it,' Griffith told her, almost managing a slight smile. 'Amazing what they teach you cops these days.'

'It is indeed,' Anna told him, drawing a look of quiet disapproval from Sean.

'So you noticed her running shoes were missing.' He tried to get Griffith back on track. 'Then what did you do?'

'Like I said – I called the police.'

'Without checking to see if any of her other running gear was missing?'

'That would've been pointless,' Griffith told him. 'Georgina buys so much running gear it'd be impossible to tell what if anything was missing. Besides, the coat she left for work in, her handbag, her laptop, was all here, on the kitchen table, where she always dumps it, but not her phone. She takes it with her, to listen to music when she runs and for calls and timing herself. So she had to have gone for a run.'

'Yes,' Sean agreed. 'And you said she usually runs in a park not far from here called South Park?'

'Yeah,' Griffith answered. 'It's just the other side of the King's Road, at the end of Peterborough Road.'

'Does she ever run anywhere else?'

'Sure, maybe, but not very often. The park's her favourite.'

You snatched her from the park, didn't you? Sean spoke silently inside his mind. *It had to be the park because that's where you knew she'd go and you knew she ran there because you'd watched her – learnt her routines. But did you follow her from her work or did you wait outside her house and then follow her? Or maybe you took the chance you'd just get lucky and waited for her in the park. No, you didn't follow her from her work – there was no need once you knew where she lived. And you wouldn't wait for her in the park unless you knew she was coming, because you plan too tight for that. No, you waited for her outside her flat and then when you were sure she was going running you drove ahead of her and waited for her in the park. I know you better and better, my friend.*

'Sean,' Anna broke through to him. 'You all right?'

'Yeah. I'm fine.' He quickly turned back to Griffith. 'Have you noticed anyone hanging around your flat? Has Georgina mentioned noticing anything like that?'

'No,' Griffith told him with certainty. 'Nothing.'

'What about a vehicle, specifically a white panel van, but he could have been using any vehicle.'

Griffith's eyes widened. 'Wait a minute. You think he's been watching her . . . planning this. Oh my God. You do, don't you?'

'I have to consider it,' Sean told him flatly. 'Today may have been the first time he'd ever seen Georgina, but I have to consider the possibility he watched her.'

'How long for?' Griffith asked. 'How long has he been watching her . . . us for?'

Sean sighed, realizing Griffith was too smart to string along. 'I don't know for sure – days at least.'

'Jesus Christ,' Griffith exclaimed. 'We're going to have to sell the flat – move out of London, even if she's still . . .' he choked up.

'She's still alive,' Sean promised. 'I know she is. We have every police officer in London and the southeast looking for her.'

'It fits his profile,' Anna explained. 'We really are as sure as we can be she's still alive.'

'Please, God, I hope you're right.'

'We'll find her,' Anna tried to reassure him, 'and she'll heal. With support she'll get past this.'

'So you haven't noticed any vehicles hanging around?' Sean got back to the questioning.

'No,' Griffith answered. 'Not that I've been looking, but I will be in the future, every damn day of my life.'

112

'Was anything happening at her work,' Sean continued, 'or in her social life or family life – anything at all?'

'Like what?'

'An ex-boyfriend, family feud, a problem with someone at work?'

'No. No,' Griffith insisted. 'Georgina's from a normal family, gets on well with everyone at work. No, nothing.'

'And ex-boyfriend?'

'Well, if she was having trouble with an ex she didn't mention it to me, but look . . . I mean, what's the point? We know who's taken her – that lunatic the papers are calling the Your View Killer. Ex-boyfriends, trouble at work – I don't see how any of that could be relevant.'

'Just want to check everything,' Sean told him.

'I understand, but shouldn't you just concentrate on this psychopath?'

'Sometimes,' Sean explained, 'not everything is as it appears.'

Griffith threw his arms open, a little exasperated. 'You'd know more about that than me.'

'Well,' Sean said as he stretched out of his chair and stood, Anna copying his movement, 'if you think of anything, let me know.' He slipped a business card from his wallet and dropped it on the glass coffee table. 'I need to go and check out the park she may have been taken from.' He felt his phone vibrating in his pocket and pulled it free. It was Donnelly. 'Dave.'

'Guv'nor,' Donnelly told him. 'We've found the victim.'

Sean turned away from Anna and Griffith, as if that would somehow stop them hearing his conversation. 'Where?'

'Wandering around Putney Heath. Someone out jogging stumbled across her and called the police.'

'Where is she now?' he asked as his heart rate continued to increase. *What answers would Georgina Vaughan have – knowingly or otherwise? What had she seen? What forensic evidence clung to her body and clothes?*

'You've found her?' Griffith interrupted. 'Is she alive? Is she all right?'

Sean held his hand up to silence him. 'Queen Mary's Hospital in Roehampton,' Donnelly told him. 'I've asked Maggie and Al to go and see her.'

'No,' Sean told him. 'I'll go myself.'

'You sure?' Donnelly asked.

'Yeah. I'll take Anna with me. What about where she was found?'

'Locals have got the area taped off and forensics are on the way.'

'OK, good. Keep me informed,' he told him and went to hang up before Donnelly stopped him.

'Guv'nor – there's something else you should know. When she was found her hands were tied behind her back, her mouth was taped shut and her naked chest was still exposed.'

Sean said nothing for a few seconds, his mind whirling with the facts he was being told. 'Was she blindfolded?' he eventually asked.

'No,' Donnelly answered. 'Why d'you ask?'

You didn't blindfold her because you wanted her to see her humiliation – wanted her suffering to last. 'No reason,' he lied, not yet ready to share his gathering storm of thoughts with anyone else, as if sharing them might somehow weaken his growing connection to the Your View Killer. 'Try and get the local CID and uniforms to canvass the area around the heath, see if anyone saw the drop-off and check for CCTV – we might get lucky.'

'OK,' Donnelly agreed. Sean hung up and turned back to Anna and Griffith.

'Please,' Griffith pleaded, his voice shaking and his eyes increasingly reddening. 'No matter what, I need to know.'

'She's alive,' Sean told him, 'and doesn't appear to have suffered any additional injuries. She's been taken to hospital in Roehampton. As soon as I leave here I'm going to see her.'

'Then I'm coming too,' Griffith told him. 'I need to see her.'

'Of course,' Sean told her. 'I'll get a local CID unit to take you.'

'Can't I just come with you? I mean, wouldn't it be easier?'

Sean cringed inside at the idea of being trapped in a car for God knows how long with a desperate boyfriend of a victim he was yet to see.

'Unfortunately not,' he half lied. 'I need to make a lot of confidential calls en route – things you're not supposed to hear. Sorry, but we'll make sure you get to the hospital as quickly as possible.'

'Should I just get a cab? Would it be quicker?'

'Your choice,' Sean told him, eager to be on his way. 'Just don't try to drive yourself, and you should probably pack a suitcase for yourself and Georgina – stay away from this flat for a while. Go stay with friends or family for a bit, until things settle down. Just let me know where you are.'

'My God. D'you think he could still be watching us?' Griffith asked.

'No,' Sean told him. 'Not him, anyway.'

'Then who?'

'Reporters, Mr Griffith,' Sean told him. 'Reporters.'

Donnelly sat on the side of DC Paulo Zukov's desk and waited for him to finish on the phone. Zukov soon hung up and turned his head towards him.

'Got something that needs my particular skill set, have you?'

'I didn't realize you had a skill, let alone a set of them,' Donnelly cut him down, continuing to talk before Zukov could think of a reply, 'and I hope you weren't wasting the Commissioner's cash using a police phone to call your boyfriend.'

'I'm as heterosexual as the next man,' Zukov told him. 'Not that there's anything wrong with being gay. We are an equal opportunities employer, you know.'

'Save the political correctness for your sergeants' board, son,' Donnelly mocked him. 'Right now I need you to get over to Putney Heath, relieve the local CID and make sure the forensics do what they gotta do. Take someone with you if you need to.'

Zukov sighed dramatically. 'I suppose I'll be stuck there all night,' he complained.

'You're a single man,' Donnelly pointed out, 'no wife, no kids. What do you want to rush home to? Think of the overtime you can waste on wine and women.'

'Normally that's exactly what I do,' Zukov explained, 'but . . .'

'But what?'

'But we've got the Toy Taker trial starting this week,' Zukov continued. 'If I'm called to the Bailey to give evidence I'd rather not be falling asleep in the witness box.'

'You young pups are getting soft,' Donnelly moaned. 'Being knackered comes with the territory, son, and who d'you think you are, referring to it as "the Toy Taker trial" – some kind of tabloid journalist? It's the Douglas Allen trial to you, sunshine.'

'Yeah, well it's not just me that's not happy about it. Half the team's been complaining.'

'Oh aye?'

'Yeah. They should have left us alone until the trial was over. It's pushing it too far running a new investigation and the trial at the same time. Way too far.'

'Aye, well,' Donnelly fixed him with his most intimidating look, 'I'll be sure to share your concerns with Assistant Commissioner Addis when I next run into him. I'm sure you'll enjoy directing traffic in Barnet. Don't forget to shine your boots.'

'Ha, ha,' Zukov answered, 'but it won't be me directing traffic if the trial goes tits-up.'

'Really? Then you must have forgotten that shit rolls downhill,' Donnelly reminded him.

116

'Not this time,' Zukov replied with a grin. 'Addis doesn't care about the likes of me – doesn't even know we exist. It's bigger heads he'll want on his trophy wall.'

'You know what?' Donnelly told him.

'No. What?' Zukov walked into the trap.

'I liked you better when you didn't think too much.' The grin slipped from Zukov's face. 'Now get yourself over to Putney and sort out the locals before I put you on permanent door-to-door inquiries.' Donnelly gave him a victory wink and headed back to his own office. He might have wiped the smile off Zukov's face, but it didn't alter the fact he'd been speaking the truth.

Sean and Anna drove along Roehampton Lane on the fringe of southwest London before it turned into Surrey. The area couldn't have been more different to the other districts that surrounded Richmond Park. Putney, Richmond, Sheen were all wealthy areas, but Roehampton remained an un-gentrified and intimidating place – hideous tower block after hideous tower block infested the skyline as boarded-up shops and cheap, non-franchise takeaway food outlets dominated the local retail businesses. People wandered around like outcasts, the uneducated rejects from a superior society that had exiled them to this strange kind of living hell – hooded gangs of teenagers a plague on the streets as chain-smoking underage girls tried to impress the local gang members by wearing as little as possible.

Sean soaked it all in. 'Jesus,' he muttered. 'What a fucking dump.' Anna didn't answer.

A couple of minutes later he pulled into the huge, virtually empty outside car park that serviced both visitors and staff at the hospital. He had little trouble getting a space relatively close to the entrance, parked and climbed from the car, stretching his stiff muscles. It had already been a very long day. Anna came round to his side.

'Shall we?' she asked, looking over to the large, brightly lit building ahead of them.

'Strange how things turn out.' Sean stopped her.

'What do you mean?' she asked

'The first murder case I was ever involved with was connected to Putney Heath,' he explained.

'Christopher Richards, I remember. Where you developed your dislike and distrust of us meddling psychiatrists and criminologists.'

Sean began to walk towards the entrance, Anna struggling to keep up.

'It's an interesting coincidence that Georgina Vaughan was dropped off there.'

'Go on,' he answered without slowing or looking at her.

'It was just maybe he knows. I mean, the man we're looking for – maybe he knows.'

'Knows what? That my first case was connected to another murder that happened off Putney Heath. I don't see how. I was just a PC at the time, on attachment.'

'You were more involved than that,' she argued.

'Maybe, but the only people who'd know about it are other police. You trying to make me paranoid?'

'Just seemed a little strange, that's all.'

They walked through the main entrance of the modern glass building and headed straight for the reception where an elderly woman in civilian clothes was manning the desk, smiling as they approached, no doubt glad for something to do.

'Hello. How can I help you?' she asked in her strong London accent. Sean held out his warrant card.

'DI Corrigan, Metropolitan Police.' The elderly woman's smile fell away quickly. 'You had a woman brought in through casualty earlier this evening, name of Georgina Vaughan. Can you tell us where she is now?'

'Of course,' the woman answered, instantly typing the information into the hospital computer system. 'She was

118

treated for minor wounds and shock and moved to a private room off the Gwynne Holford ward. Take the lift to the second floor and then just follow the green line on the floor.' Sean knew the coloured lines on the floor system well enough, having been in more hospitals than he cared to remember.

'Thanks,' he told her, moving away before the woman stopped him.

'You'll have to get permission from the ward sister to see her first though,' she told him.

'Of course,' Sean answered. 'Not here to step on anyone's toes.' He managed a smile and headed to the lifts. Anna waited until they were inside before speaking.

'Strange. She never asked who I was.'

'No,' Sean said, 'but the ward sister probably will, so what you gonna tell her?'

'I'm going to tell her the truth,' Anna answered. 'That I'm a psychiatrist employed by the police to check on the victim's psychological injuries.'

'Which is not exactly the truth, is it?' Sean pointed out.

'Must be working with you too much,' Anna teased him. 'Beginning to lose my moral compass.'

'I may not always do the *right* thing,' Sean explained, 'but it's always for the *right* reason.'

'To get the bad guy locked up?'

'If you like.' The lift door slid open and Sean instinctively looked down and picked up the green line on the floor, walking without waiting for Anna, who almost broke into a jog to catch up.

'And about what I mentioned before?' she pursued.

'About the man I'm after somehow knowing the first murder I investigated was connected to one in Putney Heath? I don't think so. Just a coincidence.'

'Aren't you even going to consider it?'

'No,' Sean snapped at her. 'That's the plot of a film you're talking about, not reality. Criminals don't go after cops or try

119

to torment them. It's a coincidence, nothing more. If you're going to help me with this investigation best you stay in the real world.' Anna was about to argue, but Sean had already veered away, following the green line seemingly without looking, heading through a set of swing doors before arriving at another set that were locked. He grabbed the handles and rattled the doors to be sure before cursing. 'Shit. Locked. We'll have to rely on someone answering the intercom now.'

'So?'

'So, in my experience of getting anyone in a hospital to answer an intercom we could be here all bloody night.' He shrugged his shoulders in surrender. 'Still . . .' he told her and pressed the intercom button long and hard. After more than a minute there was still no answer so he pressed the button again, this time keeping it pressed until the face of a middle-aged African woman appeared on the other side of the wire mesh window, her eyes asking all the questions as she looked at them suspiciously. Sean pressed his warrant card to the window and spoke loudly enough for her to hear through the door. 'Police.' After a few more seconds of staring at them the woman opened the door and spoke in a heavy West African accent, her nurse's uniform visible now.

'Can I help you with something?' she asked.

'We need to see a patient here,' Sean explained. 'She's in one of your private rooms – a Georgina Vaughan.'

The nurse looked him up and down one more time. 'You'll have to come and see Sister about that,' she told them, indicating for them to enter and follow her with a nod of her head. They were led along the corridor, Sean not able to resist peeking into the sectioned-off rooms to his left, each containing four hospital beds, a toilet and bathroom area and a small nursing station. He was sure he could sense death hovering around the rooms, hiding in the dark shadows, waiting for the occupants of the beds to grow weak before drifting in unseen to take them away forever. The feeling

120

made him shudder, even more so when he decided he was probably the only one who sensed it. The nurse's voice brought him back.

'Sorry, Sister,' she spoke to a serious woman in her forties wearing a dark blue uniform, trousers instead of a skirt, spectacles perched on her hookish nose. She looked up from her pile of charts, barely disguising her displeasure at being disturbed. 'Some people here to see Georgina Vaughan – the patient in private room five.'

'I know where she is, thank you, Rose,' the ward sister chastised her subordinate, before turning her attention to Sean and Anna. 'Your identification?' she asked bluntly, her face stony.

Sean pulled out his warrant card yet again and held it out for the sister to see, but not satisfied with that she took it from him and examined it like a passport control officer, looking from the identification to Sean and back until she finally handed it back and held out her hand as if she expected Anna to produce the same. 'Well?' she asked.

'I'm not a police officer,' Anna told her, trying to hide her discomfort. 'I'm a psychiatrist.'

'Not from this hospital you're not,' the sister cut her down. 'If you were I'd know you and I don't. If you want to see the patient you'll need permission from our psychiatric department.'

'She's not here to treat the patient in any way,' Sean cut in before Anna could make matters worse for herself by getting involved in a medical pissing contest. 'She's here to advise me, on what sort of man we may be looking for. She won't be treating your patient.' The sister never looked away from Anna as Sean spoke. 'I . . . we really need to see her. We'll be as gentle as we can be.' The sister studied them for a long while before getting to her feet.

'Very well,' she told them. 'Follow me.' She swooped from behind the large, fixed desk of the nursing station and headed off along a corridor leading to the private rooms. She stopped outside one marked only as 'Room 5', knocked twice and then entered the dimly lit room without waiting for an answer, Sean and Anna doing likewise before the sister could change her mind.

'Georgina,' she spoke gently to the sleepy-looking young woman with a shaved head half lying and half sitting in the bed, her hospital gown covering the wound Sean knew lay underneath – the raw and raised mark of a dollar sign carved into her skin. 'Some people from the police are here to see you. Are you all right to speak to them?'

Georgina looked directly at Sean with glassy, but alert eyes – suspicious eyes . . . fearful eyes. He wondered if she'd ever be anything other than suspicious and afraid again.

'Just a few questions,' Sean promised her. 'Just a few questions we really need to ask and then we'll leave you to get some rest. We spoke to Freddie not long ago. He'll be here soon.'

'Freddie?' she asked, trying to sit up more.

'He's fine,' Sean assured her. 'Just worried, but he'll be better once he sees you.'

'I'll leave you to it then,' the sister told them, satisfied that Sean wouldn't push too hard. 'She's had some sedatives, but nothing too strong. Just don't be surprised if she tires easily.' She spun on her heels and left the room.

'Freddie's coming here?' Georgina asked, sounding lucid, but a little confused.

'He'll be here soon,' Sean answered, 'but before he gets here I need to ask you some questions, if you think you can manage it.'

'I don't want to talk about him.' She threatened to lock up. 'I don't want to talk about it. Not yet.'

Sean and Anna glanced at each other. 'I understand that,' Sean tried to sympathize. 'Of course you don't, but there are some things I really need to know now. Believe me, I wouldn't ask them now if I thought they could wait, but they can't – not if we want to catch him quickly.'

She looked away from both of them, eyes downcast, silent for a long time, but he daren't push her and cause her to shut down. Better to wait and hope she would open up.

'It feels like a dream. Like a nightmare. Like something I watched happening to someone else. But it wasn't someone else, was it? It was me.' Her hand drifted slowly up to her head, her fingers crawling across her shaven head, over the occasional cut the medical staff had glued shut. Sean thought once more about the dollar sign cut into her chest. Her hair would grow back relatively quickly, but the scar would never disappear. Treatment would fade it, but it would never leave her fully. 'Why did he do this to me?' she asked, almost matter-of-factly.

'That's what we're trying to find out,' Sean answered, 'and it's why I need to ask you some questions.' She didn't respond. 'Can you tell me where you were when he first attacked you?' he pressed ahead. Still she didn't respond. 'Freddie thinks you may have gone for a run. Can you remember going for a run?'

She blinked rapidly before her eyes widened, as if she was seeing her attacker for the first time. 'I was running – in the park,' she answered.

Sean felt the relief inside of him that she was finally recalling her abduction. 'What park?'

'Where I always run. Same place I always run.'

'I need you to tell me specifically. What's the name of the park?'

'South Park,' she confirmed. 'Close to my home.'

'What happened in the park?'

'I don't want to remember,' she pleaded.

'Take your time,' Sean managed to say, but he was beginning to burn inside. 'I need you to try and remember – to tell me what happened.'

'I was running,' she finally began. 'I was running and I suddenly felt afraid, as if I could sense someone was watching me – waiting for me. I started to speed up, running towards the gates in the car park. They seemed so far away.' She was slipping away from them again.

'Go on,' Sean tried to bring her back.

'Then, as I was crossing the car park, he stepped out, from behind a tree. I didn't see him until it was too late. He grabbed me and pulled me against the tree – he was strong, too strong to fight, and then he showed me the knife.'

'He had a knife,' Sean jumped in and immediately regretted it. Better to allow the victim free-flow recall. His eagerness had got the better of him – like an amateur.

'Yes,' she continued to his relief. 'Not very big, with a serrated side, like jagged teeth. I thought he was going to rape me, but he didn't. He told me he wasn't going to hurt me, but that he'd kill me if I tried to escape.' She paused to wipe away the growing tears in her eyes. This time Sean remained silent, giving her time and space. 'He took me to a van – one that had a side door. Then he pushed me inside and put things, restraints, around my wrists and ankles and then tape over my mouth and then the hood. Then we drove for I don't know how long until he stopped and opened the door. He took the restraints away and I remember being pushed and pulled somewhere outside until we went into a building, but I still had the hood on and couldn't see where. We went up some stairs and he made me sit in a chair – the same chair he then taped my wrists and ankles to. I can't remember what happened next, just there was lots of talking, only in that horrible voice he used, and he sounded like he was talking to other people – not me. I'm really tired now,' she appealed to them. 'I don't think I can tell you any more.'

'When he took the hood off,' Sean ignored her, needing more, 'what did you see? What was in the room?'

She blinked and shook the sleepiness from her head. 'Nothing . . . I mean, we were alone. There was no one else there. Everything was white, except some black plastic hanging sheets, or bin liners hanging in places and the table.' She began to fade again as the nightmare and the drugs started to overwhelm her.

'The table,' Sean almost pleaded with her. 'What was on the table?'

'A computer – a laptop,' she managed to answer, her voice beginning to sound slurred, 'other computer hardware and cameras, things I didn't recognize . . . I can't remember.'

'Did you recognize him?' Sean asked out of the blue, making Anna stare at him. 'Was there anything about him you recognized?'

'No,' she managed to say before her eyes fluttered and closed, her head gently rolling to one side as she sighed into sleep.

'Shit,' Sean quietly muttered before looking over at Anna. 'Sorry,' he told her. 'You didn't get to ask any questions.'

'It can wait,' Anna replied. 'Your need was a little more pressing.'

'Maybe,' he half agreed. 'D'you pick up anything useful?'

'Not really,' she admitted, 'other than the obvious. His victim selection is seemingly random, other than they both work in finance and live in roughly the same area of London. I'll study the Your View video when I get a chance, but with him completely concealing his features, even his voice, it's difficult to learn much. You?'

'Same, although she confirmed a couple of things for me.'

'Such as?'

'Like he has restraints built in the back of his van,' Sean explained. 'It struck me with the first victim, who was conscious when he put him in the van, not drugged or anything as far as we can tell, so I reckoned he had to have something fairly elaborate in there, or he'd be driving across London with a grown man banging around in the back. This one plans too carefully for that.'

'Could he have had the van customized for him?' Anna asked.

'Possibly,' Sean answered, 'but I doubt he'd take such a big risk. We'll check it out anyway, but I'm betting it's all his own work.' He looked at Georgina sleeping in the hospital bed, images of her torturer shaving her head flashing in his mind, replaced by her haunting screaming as he carved the dollar sign into her chest. 'Think she'll recover?' he asked Anna. 'Psychologically, I mean.'

'What is recovery?' Anna questioned. 'Returning to exactly the same person she was before? If that's recovery then no, she'll never recover. But if it's moving on with her life and living comparatively normally, albeit in a changed state, then yes, she'll probably recover, with help.'

'Like Sally?' Sean asked without looking away from Georgina.

'I can't discuss Sally with you, Sean, you know that. But you have eyes. You can see for yourself how well she's doing.'

Sean looked at his watch, struggling to see in the dimness of the room – the lights low to encourage sleep and rest. 'It's late. We're not achieving anything here. We should both go home – get some rest before the storm hits.'

'I'll order a cab from reception,' Anna told him. 'I don't live too far from here.'

Sean finally looked away from the sleeping woman. 'Funny,' he told her. 'I don't know where you live. I never asked before.'

'In Chiswick,' she told him, 'I live in Chiswick.'

'Come on,' he said. 'I'll drop you off, so long as I can take you for a drink first. God knows I need one.'

'You sure that's a good idea?' she asked.

'Why the hell not?' he replied. 'Must be somewhere between here and Chiswick where we can get a drink.'

Anna shook her head, but smiled at the same time. 'OK. Why not? But just the one.'

'Let's make it a good one then,' he told her before looking at Georgina, trying to imagine what must have been going through her mind when she was bound and hooded in the

126

back of the killer's van, fearing imminent death and more – trying to reconcile her fate with the fact that only moments before she'd been enjoying an evening run in a picturesque park. 'None of us really know what's around the next corner, do we?' he mused before turning away from the sleeping woman. 'Come on,' he told Anna. 'Let's get out of here.'

Assistant Commissioner Addis took another sip of single malt whisky from a fine crystal tumbler as he waited for the polite laughter of the men around him to fade – his latest amusing comment about the Mayor of London seemingly appreciated. He leaned forward in the oversized antique leather chair and placed his drink on the low wooden table that he and the other four men sat around. His decorated police cap lay next to the drink, his brown leather gloves neatly crossed over it. Normally he'd never take a drink while wearing his full uniform, but in the private members' club tucked away close to St James's Square, he knew he wouldn't be questioned or photographed and, besides, it felt good to be dressed in a symbol of his power. The other drinkers wore suits and watches he could never afford, even on an Assistant Commissioner's wage, but his uniform carried more influence and veiled threat than their money ever could. It was him they tried to impress over a few ludicrously expensive drinks.

'I tell you,' he continued his anecdote, 'the little prick tells me that if any of the protesters get hurt by one of my officers then *he'd hold me personally accountable*. Believe me, if I'd had a truncheon on me I would have shoved it up his arsehole. Trouble is, of course, he'd probably enjoy it.' More approving laughter. 'So I said, of course, Mr Mayor. Not a problem. And when a few thousand crusty bastards waving anarchist flags come marching over Tower Bridge towards City Hall, I'll be sure to make sure the TSG let them pass without a *confrontation*. Little prick almost shit his trousers on the bloody spot.' More laughter and another chance to take a sip of his whisky, but he suddenly felt a shadowy presence at his shoulder and turned his head. A man in a less expensive suit and less well groomed hair stood just behind him, clearly wanting Addis's attention. Addis beamed before looking back to the other men and speaking. 'Minister. I didn't know you were a member here,' he lied.

'Could I have a word please, Robert?' the slim, grey-haired man in his late forties asked, trying not to sound as sheepish as he looked.

'Of course,' Addis replied, still not looking at him. 'I'll have George pull up a chair for you and a drink of course.' Another murmur of amusement from his audience.

The minister cleared his throat. 'Actually, I need to speak to you in private.'

'Oh,' Addis said, smiling condescendingly, as if he was playing along with a child's game. 'I see.' He stood and looked to each of the sitting men. 'Excuse me, gentlemen. This won't take long.' He walked past the minister and headed for two more secluded chairs in a corner of the club. 'Is there a problem, Minister?' he asked. 'You look a little . . . flustered.'

'A problem? Yes, there's a problem, Robert,' he began. 'What you might call a gathering storm. A gathering financial storm.'

'And this has something to do with me, because?'

'Because you haven't bloody well stopped it.'

'Why don't you get to the point?' Addis told him, the strain of remaining civil beginning to tell.

'This bloody Your View Killer,' the minister explained, 'and the police's inability to either catch him or stop him.'

'It's a new and complicated investigation,' Addis told him, regaining his calm demeanour. 'These things can take time, although I don't see why it concerns you or the government. It's getting a lot of media attention, but it's hardly a matter to affect a government's standing in the polls. Not like this is an election year.'

128

'An increase in absenteeism,' the minister began cryptically, 'people leaving work early to get home before dark, people distracted at work even when they are there and, most damningly of all, a drop in confidence in the City per se. Falling confidence kills business, Robert, and a failing economy kills governments.'

'Then I suggest our brave financiers and bankers grow a backbone and get over themselves,' Addis bit, 'and besides, I can't believe this Your View messiah can be having that serious an effect on the workings of the City.'

'Losses are apparently already in the millions,' the minister explained. 'Another abduction or worse, God forbid, murder, and our analysts believe millions could turn into billions. We can't allow that to happen.'

'Very well,' Addis agreed. 'I'll speak with my colleagues in the City of London Police and ask them to beef up security, see if they can't use their vehicle and face-recognition equipment to help out. He's yet to actually snatch anyone from the City itself, but I suppose he could be following them from there.'

'I don't really care what you do and neither does the PM, just so long as it gets sorted,' the minister told him. 'What about this DI Corrigan fellow? You've got him on the case, I assume.'

'Correct. Special Investigations are taking care of this one.'

'Yet without making any progress.'

'DI Corrigan has my full backing,' Addis told him.

'Then I hope your trust in him isn't misplaced.'

'Are you,' Addis asked, 'doubting my judgement?'

'I wouldn't say that,' the minister lied, 'but you've made your ambitions crystal clear, Robert – Commissioner, Mayor of London and beyond. If your *judgement* were, shall we say, called into doubt, it would not help those ambitions. There are plenty of other Assistant Commissioners and Chief

Constables around the country who have their eye on the top spot.'

Addis leaned forward, but didn't lower his voice, speaking loudly enough for anyone who cared to listen to hear what he was saying. 'I'm sure there are,' he agreed with an assassin's smile, 'but none of them have been the head of Specialist Operations in the Met, have they, Minister?'

'Meaning?' the minister asked, his brow wrinkled and his eyes narrowed.

'Let's just say that you can't oversee covert operations for as long as I have without finding out a thing or two about people in positions of power. I'm sure you understand.'

'Is this . . . are you threatening me?' the minister asked, his voice indignant.

'It's the people we have to deal with, Minister,' Addis told him with mock concern. 'Criminals, drug dealers, informants, prostitutes. The sort of people that would sell their soul to the devil for the right price, let alone the occasional piece of unwanted information. But at least I can prevent them from going to the newspapers and embarrassing the innocent parties involved. Although I doubt their wives and children would see them as being quite so innocent.'

The minister cleared his throat and sank deep in his chair. 'I have no idea what you're talking about.'

'Of course you don't.' Addis took deep joy at his condescension. 'Of course you don't.'

'I think our business here is complete,' the minister told him, getting to his feet. 'Until next time,' he told Addis.

'Until next time,' Addis repeated. 'Oh and, Minister – don't ever threaten me again – there's a good fellow.'

6

Sean arrived at work shortly after eight the next morning feeling exhausted before the day had even begun. He pulled the lid off a polystyrene cup of black coffee and logged himself onto the Met's computer system, going straight to his emails, the sight of so many unread messages making him audibly groan and sink into his uncomfortable chair. He noticed a good proportion were last-minute CPS requests for probably unobtainable evidence for the upcoming trial of Douglas Allen.

'Shit,' he whispered to himself before Donnelly burst into his office waving a copy of that morning's edition of *The World* around, making him instantly forget about the CPS memos.

'You're not going to fucking believe this,' Donnelly announced, laying the paper out on Sean's desk and jabbing his finger into the offending article. 'They've only asked the Your View Killer to bloody well contact them.'

'What?' Sean snatched up the paper and started frantically reading. 'Are they fucking crazy? What the hell are they playing at?'

'If that's not bad enough they've also had roaming reporters out and about in every city up and down the country asking people whether they *sympathize* with this psychopath or not.

Canvassing the opinion of brain-dead chavs to ensure they get the result they want.'

Sean was no longer listening as he scanned the article for the name of the editor or journalist responsible until he found what he was looking for. 'I might have known,' he said to himself.

'Known what?' Donnelly asked.

'Geoff Jackson,' he explained. 'Crime editor for this rag.'

'You know him?'

'I know of him. He covered the Allen case and the Keller case – filled in the blanks with his own version of events rather than worrying about the truth. Wrote books too, apparently.'

'He wasn't the only one who wrote books about those two,' Donnelly reminded him.

'No, but his were the only ones that sold,' Sean told him.

'Aye and he gave you the starring role, I seem to remember.'

'I wouldn't know,' Sean replied. 'I didn't read them.' He snatched up the phone on his desk and called the number displayed under the photograph of Jackson.

'He's even given him instructions of how he wants to be contacted,' Donnelly explained. 'On Twitter, if you can believe that.'

'I can believe it,' Sean told him before the phone was answered by a woman's voice.

'You've reached *The World*, Britain's bestselling newspaper – how can I help?'

'This is DI Sean Corrigan from the Metropolitan Police's Special Investigations Unit. I need to speak to Geoff Jackson as a matter of urgency.'

'I'm afraid Geoff's not in the office right now,' the woman's voice told him. 'If you give me your mobile number I'll get him to call you as soon as possible.'

'Tell him to call me on my landline,' Sean told her. 'I'm

guessing he already has the number.' He hung up without waiting for an answer.

'Nobody home?' Donnelly quipped.

'No. Slippery bastards tried to get my mobile number.'

'They've probably already got it.'

'Maybe.' The phone rang on the desk and Sean grabbed it, expecting a confrontation with Jackson. 'DI Corrigan speaking.'

'Inspector,' Dr Canning began, instantly deflating him. 'Everything all right?'

'Yes,' Sean stammered. 'I was expecting someone else, that's all.'

'I have an update for you re our victim from the Thames.'

'Go on.'

'More confirmation, really. Cause of death is, as suspected, strangulation caused by hanging. He was most definitely dead before being disposed of in the river – the absence of river water in his lungs tells us that – and despite the best efforts of the Thames, I've managed to recover some adhesive from his skin where he was taped at the wrists, ankles, et cetera. We should be able to match it if you can find the roll it came from, but it's probably not exotic.'

'Anything that could help us trace the scene?' Sean asked impatiently.

'I'm afraid not,' Canning told him, 'or at least nothing I can see with my equipment. Once we send his clothing to the lab with the samples I've taken you never know your luck, but you know what it's like once a body has been in the river, Inspector – unless something was deposited inside it then you can't expect to find too much, forensically speaking.'

'OK,' Sean conceded. 'Keep me posted.'

'Naturally,' Canning told him before the line went dead.

'Anyone interesting?' Donnelly asked.

'Dr Canning,' Sean answered.

'Anything from the post-mortem?'

'Nothing that helps,' Sean answered. 'Get the team together for an update on the second victim, will you? Give me a few minutes to get all my shit in one bag.'

'Aye, no problem,' Donnelly told him and walked quickly from the office, almost bumping into Assistant Commissioner Addis who'd somehow ghosted in undetected. 'Guv'nor,' Donnelly acknowledged him and slid into the main office. Sean groaned inside. This was all he needed.

'Inspector,' Addis began, his rarely seen, less than convincing half-smile unnerving Sean more than if he'd been blowing thunder.

'Assistant Commissioner,' Sean greeted him.

'Thought I'd pay you all a personal visit and see how things were progressing,' Addis told him. 'A show of support, if you like.'

Addis's words only added to Sean's suspicions. 'I need a show of support?' he asked.

'From time to time,' Addis explained, sounding almost friendly, 'we all need a little support and I just wanted you to know that you have mine, for now.'

'OK,' Sean answered, still feeling more than a little unnerved. 'That's good to know.'

'And the investigation,' Addis continued, 'progressing satisfactorily?'

'It's progressing,' Sean told him, pursing his lips. 'As much as it can.'

'As much as it can?' Addis questioned.

'This isn't a join-the-dots-up investigation,' Sean tried to explain. 'That much I already know. One minute we'll have nothing and the next we'll have everything. It's just the way these ones work. Progress can be difficult to judge. You never know you're at the tipping point until you're actually there.' He shrugged his shoulders for emphasis and waited for Addis's response. The normal Addis would probably blow a fuse, but this new one . . .

'Well . . . I see,' Addis replied, looking like he was struggling a little to maintain his slightest of smiles, 'but don't take too long to get to this *tipping point*. I have it on reliable information that the City's beginning to get a little nervous about the situation. Apparently the markets are already losing millions and if someone else were to be abducted millions could become billions.' His smile broadened slightly. 'If you have any shares, Inspector, now would be a good time to sell them and buy yourself some gold, or silver perhaps.'

Sean realized it was Addis's attempt at a joke. 'Stocks and shares – not really my thing,' he replied.

'No,' Addis agreed, his smile fading somewhat. 'I don't suppose they are.' Neither man spoke for a few seconds, a silence that Sean knew he was enjoying more than Addis. 'Anyway, I won't take up any more of your time, but if there's anything you need don't hesitate to ask. Anything at all.'

'A press appeal could be useful,' Sean told him. 'No need for the victim to appear in it. We can just put out the facts we know, the use of a van, the drop-off areas, that sort of thing.'

'Of course,' Addis replied. 'Leave it with me.'

'I'll prepare you a brief.'

'Good,' Addis told him and headed for the door, still looking at Sean, talking as he walked. 'Remember – anything you need. Anything at all.' For one horrible moment Sean thought Addis might even wink at him.

Once Addis was clear of the main office Sean let out a long breath he felt he'd been holding since Addis had first arrived. He got up from his desk and headed into the neighbouring room where Donnelly was waiting. 'Problem?' he asked.

'No,' Sean replied. 'Our esteemed Assistant Commissioner's acting a little strange, but nothing I can't handle.'

'Strange how?'

'Strange-friendly, that's how.'

'That's not good,' Donnelly offered. 'Assistant Commissioners acting friendly is never good.'

'All right,' Sean shouted across the main office. 'Listen up and I'll give those of you who are here a quick update on the second victim, Georgina Vaughan.' He gave them a few seconds to end their phone calls and typing before speaking again. 'As with the first victim, she works in the City, but, unlike him, not in a particularly senior position. She was abducted early yesterday evening from South Park in Parsons Green and taken to wherever it is our man is using for his broadcasts. You all saw what he did to her.' He looked around at the serious, determined faces. 'After he humiliated and tortured her he released her on Putney Heath, although he left her with her hands tied behind her back, her mouth taped over and her top cut open with her chest exposed. Clearly he wanted her humiliation and suffering to continue even after her release. She was found and taken to hospital. Her injuries are unpleasant, but not serious. I spoke to her last night and she confirmed the suspect is using a white panel van that's been fitted inside with arm and leg restraints to prevent the victim from struggling or escaping. It's safe to assume he used the same restraints on the first victim – all further evidence that he's been planning this for some time. She remembers being driven for a while and then being taken from the van and walked through an outside location to a building – a building in which the suspect made his broadcast from. DC Bishop tells me the signal from the broadcast puts our man somewhere on the outskirts of London. And that, ladies and gentlemen, is about it. Maggie and Fiona are checking the abduction location and so far we've found the victim's mobile phone and headphones and some partial footprints. They're checking the area for CCTV, but haven't found anything yet, although I'm certain they'll find some footage of the van, as will Paulo who's looking after the drop site at Putney Heath. There'll be plenty of enquiries coming everyone's way – get them done quickly and back to Dave or Sally as fast as you can. The more information and leads we have on this bastard the quicker we'll find him. That's all,' he finished and headed back to his own office, reaching it just as his desk phone began to ring. He grabbed it and sat all in the same motion. 'DI Corrigan.'

'Well, well,' the voice on the other end told him. 'Finally we get to talk. How's the shoulder? I heard they didn't manage to get all the shotgun pellets out. Bet that hurts on a cold day.'

'Who is this?' Sean asked impatiently.

'Geoff Jackson,' the voice told him. 'Crime editor for *The World*, Britain's biggest selling . . .'

'Save the advert,' Sean interrupted him. 'I know who you work for and what you do.'

'Of course you do,' Jackson laughed into the phone. 'Tell me, Inspector, did you ever get round to reading my book about the Keller investigation? Or what about my latest one on Douglas Allen? How d'you like the title – *The Toy Taker*. Stroke of genius, don't you think?'

'Jackson,' Sean told him, 'I wouldn't wipe my arse with one of your books.'

'A bit harsh, Inspector.' Jackson laughed again. 'They were nominated for best true-crime works for their respective years.'

'Congratulations,' Sean said sarcastically, 'but listen to me, Jackson, what the fuck d'you think you're playing at trying to get this psychopath to contact your paper? You trying to encourage him to abduct somebody else?'

'Just doing my job, Inspector.'

'Which is?'

'Covering the story, of course. Nothing more, nothing less.'

'Bollocks,' Sean argued. 'You're trying to create the story, not cover it.'

'Cover – create,' Jackson replied, 'what the fuck's the difference?'

'Plenty,' Sean told him. 'Anything you find out about this son of a bitch you tell me, Jackson.'

'No can do,' Jackson answered. 'Journalistic privilege, Inspector. You can't make me hand over shit, although I may chuck you a bone from time to time.'

'We need to talk,' Sean insisted, snarling into the phone.

'Isn't that what we're doing?'

'Face-to-face. Now.'

'Why? So you can beat the crap out of me to scare me off the story?'

The fact Jackson was probably recording their conversation dawned on Sean. 'You're still living in the eighties, Jackson. That doesn't happen any more. Not sure it ever did, but if it makes you feel better you can pick the location.'

'Errm,' Jackson mused. 'How about a nice little café I know in Wapping? Public enough to be safe – private enough so we can talk.'

'Fine,' Sean told him. 'Where?'

'Café Italia in Pennington Street.'

'Be there in an hour,' Sean demanded and hung up before Jackson could argue. Sean knew he'd be there. He grabbed his raincoat and filled his pockets, poking his head around Donnelly's door. 'Grab your coat,' he told him.

'We going somewhere?'

'To see a journalist,' Sean answered.

Donnelly rubbed his hands with enthusiasm. 'Jackson?' Sean just nodded. 'Oh yes,' Donnelly said excitedly. 'This I do not want to miss.'

Sally sat opposite Anna in a large comfortable chair, resting a glass of water on her thigh while Anna read through her patient notes, Sally still feeling uncomfortable despite their familiarity. Finally Anna looked up and smiled.

'Thanks again for seeing me so early,' Sally told her. 'I know you must be pretty busy, especially now you're attached to another case.'

'No need to thank me, Sally,' Anna replied. 'What are friends for?'

'I suppose,' Sally answered unconvincingly, 'but before we start, I was wondering if you think anyone may have put two and two together and come up with four?'

'You mean do I think anyone has worked out that you're seeing me – professionally?'

'Yes. You know, you and I being so close to each other at work – maybe someone's suspected something. Said something?'

'No,' Anna reassured her. 'No one's said anything. Why do you ask? Has someone said something to you?'

'No. No,' Sally told her. 'Nothing. It's nothing. I just get a little paranoid sometimes. Sorry, have we started now, or are we still just talking?'

'Just talking,' Anna smiled. 'Have you confided in anyone that you're seeing me?'

'No,' Sally lied.

'Not even . . . Sean?'

Sally sighed before answering. 'How did you know? Did he tell you?'

'No,' It was Anna's turn to lie. 'I just guessed you'd trust him. We all need someone to confide in, especially after what you went through. Speaking of which, how have you been? It can't have been easy watching that young woman being hurt on Your View.'

'No,' Sally answered. 'No it wasn't, but I did it.'

'And when you got home – when you were alone?'

'Fine. Like any other night lately. I'm off the tramadol and the codeine, not drinking to excess and staying off the hard stuff – a glass of wine to unwind with now and then, but nothing over the top.'

'And the fear?' Anna asked, the question making Sally flinch.

'Better,' she answered. 'Much better. I still get a little nervous if I get home late, when it's dark, but once I'm in my flat I'm fine. Any feelings I have of anxiety quickly fade. No tears. No depression. No dreading waking up the next day.'

'Any dreams?' Anna asked, making Sally shift a little uncomfortably in her chair.

'Dreams?' Sally asked.

'Yes,' Anna clarified. 'Like the ones we've discussed before.' Sally didn't answer. 'Often our fears linger longest in our dreams – in our subconscious. They sneak in when our guard is down.' She smiled at Sally.

'Well,' Sally began before stalling to take a sip of water, 'there is one that doesn't seem to want to let go – one that seems to get me when I'm particularly tired – when I'm in the deepest of sleeps. Funny, I always thought you only dreamt just before you woke up – when your sleep was at its lightest.'

'No one really knows for sure,' Anna explained. 'The subconscious is still a mysterious place. So what happens in this dream?'

'I don't dream it that much,' Sally tried to explain, fearful of mocking her own proclaimed progress. 'Only now and then.'

'I understand,' Anna told her. 'It's best if you tell me about it and then we can discuss it, but only if you feel comfortable with it.'

'I'm happy to talk about it,' Sally answered, aware of her own feelings of defensiveness and eager to banish them.

'Then, whenever you'd like to begin,' Anna encouraged.

Sally filled her lungs and exhaled before beginning. 'It's always the same house, big, with lots of rooms, one leading to another and then another, but there never seem to be any corridors or hallways, just rooms leading to each other. I don't recognize the house. It's not familiar to me. If I do know it then I don't remember it.' Sally suddenly stopped, as if she was trying to work something out, or place the house of her subconscious in the real world.

'Go on,' Anna brought her back.

Sally gave a little shake of her head and continued. 'The ceilings in the rooms are high and the windows are very tall, but they don't have glass in them, just a . . . a blackness . . . an impenetrable blackness, and the doorways are tall as well, but narrow and difficult to fit through.' She paused again as she recalled more of the house. 'And there are no curtains or blinds, in fact there's no furniture at all of any kind, or carpet, just bare floorboards and a single bulb hanging from the ceiling in each room. And the only colour in the house is . . .' Sally stalled again, covering her mouth with one hand as she swallowed hard to stop the tears as a sudden rush of emotions and memories ambushed her.

'It's all right,' Anna comforted her. 'Take your time.'

After a few seconds Sally recovered enough to continue, battling through the dark demons of the past. 'The only colour . . . everything in the house, including the light is . . . is red.'

She closed her eyes for a second, remembering the night she'd been attacked in her own flat more than two years ago, her would-be killer, Sebastian Gibran, turning the room red by draping a silk scarf over a lamp before burying a knife deep into her chest.

'And I'm running,' she eventually continued. 'Running from room to room, my shoulders hitting the frames of the narrow doorways, and I'm scared. I know someone's in the house, and that they're looking for me – searching for me – getting closer and closer as I run aimlessly from room to room, looking for a way out, but there isn't any, just door after door leading nowhere. I feel him in the house. I can't see or hear him, but I know he's there and he wants me. He wants to finish what he began.

'I'm crying and stumbling, falling down and scrambling back to my feet as I feel his presence growing closer and closer, my fear becoming as real and raw and overwhelming as it's ever been, and then suddenly he's there, looming over me, no matter what direction I turn in he's there, and then I feel . . .' She stopped, pretended to sip water from her glass, hiding behind it until she'd composed herself.

'Can you tell me what happens next?' Anna asked. 'If it's too much then . . .'

'No,' Sally interrupted. 'I want to tell you. I need to tell you . . . Christ, I need to tell someone.'

'Tell me what?'

'I feel the knife go in, but not like it's really happening. In the dream I watch the knife point being placed against my chest and then it's slowly pushed into me, sliding into my chest. There's no pain, so I just stand there and watch it slide deep into me, the red blood almost too faint to see in the red of the room, but eventually I do look up from the knife – I look up from my chest and I see the face of the man who's doing this thing to me and . . .' Once more Sally paused as she tried to make sense of what she was about to say.

'And you saw Sebastian Gibran.' Anna thought she'd answered for her. 'You saw the face of Sebastian Gibran.'

'No,' Sally told her, her face pale and serious. 'It was . . . *Sean*. It was Sean holding the knife. It was Sean doing it to me.' Sally watched as Anna's jaw fell open. 'Funny thing is,' she continued, 'once I see it's Sean I'm not afraid any more, or at least I'm not afraid for me any more – I'm afraid for him. What does it all mean?'

Anna cleared her throat before talking. 'Oh . . . nothing. It's just a dream. They're rarely clear and often confusing. We need to be careful not to overestimate their importance. Both you and Sean have suffered violent traumas in the last

142

couple of years. In your subconscious you probably consider him a kindred spirit, hence he appears in your dreams. A friendly face, perhaps?'

'A friendly face with a knife?' Sally questioned, not believing a word of Anna's explanation.

'Like I said,' Anna tried to convince her, 'dreams can be confusing.'

'I see,' Sally lied. 'Like you said – it's just a dream.'

Sean and Donnelly found the café Jackson had described in Wapping easily enough. One side of the street was dominated by a long, low, brown brick building where numerous small businesses had made their homes in the archways it provided. The other side was a mish-mash of old and new buildings, some seemingly made out of nothing more than plastic and corrugated iron. The decidedly un-Italian-looking café was nestled in amongst the other ugly buildings.

'What a fucking dump,' Donnelly complained as they walked from their car to the café. 'Was it asking too much to meet in the West End?'

Sean smiled, knowing Donnelly would rather be in a place like this than the West End any day – it was very similar to their old stomping ground in Peckham. 'He's a crime journalist,' he joined in. 'Hanging round places like this makes him feel the part.'

'Aye,' Donnelly reluctantly agreed. 'Bet you he doesn't live round here though.'

'No,' Sean agreed, opening the door to the café. 'I don't suppose he does.'

Once inside he scanned the clientele and soon spotted Jackson sitting in the far corner, back to the wall like a cop, but concentrating on the food on his plate, never looking up between mouthfuls, unlike a cop. He and Donnelly crossed the café and sat at Jackson's table, Donnelly right next to him and Sean on the other side of the table facing him.

'Not eating, gentlemen?' Jackson asked without looking up, loading his fork with food while the other hand typed constantly on his iPhone.

'I'm particular who I eat with,' Sean told him.

'Whatever,' Jackson replied, finally looking up, 'but remember, before you get too choosy – if it wasn't for me you lot would still be fumbling around in the dark trying to find out which celebrities were really paedophiles and which ones weren't. I handed you that job on a plate. Evil bastards. I hope they get some serious time in some serious prisons.'

'We weren't involved in that investigation,' Donnelly reminded him. 'Not our sphere of influence, but on behalf of the Metropolitan Police I thank you for the information and your cooperation.'

'Can we cut the shit,' Sean impatiently interrupted. 'Before I decide to tell you what I really think of you.'

'Careful, Inspector.' Jackson smiled a warning at him. 'Every other person in here is a journo, so I'd be careful what you say if I was you.'

'I'm not here to threaten you, Jackson,' Sean told him. 'I'm here to warn you – stay away from this man. He's dangerous. He's already killed one person. This isn't a game.'

'And if I don't?'

'If he doesn't kill you, which he probably will, I'll arrest you for interfering in an investigation.'

'If he decides to talk to me, that'll hardly amount to inter-fering in an investigation. And if he does talk then anything he tells me is subject to journalistic privilege and therefore excluded material – material you couldn't take off me even with a search warrant,' Jackson argued.

'Not with a search warrant,' Sean agreed, 'but I could take it with a production order.'

'Only if you can convince a judge it would be of high

value to the investigation, which you couldn't,' Jackson told him. 'I know my business, Corrigan. I'm not interested in *evidence* – entertainment's my field, so good luck with that production order.'

'Trust me,' Sean warned him, 'if I need a production order I'll get a production order.'

'We'll see,' Jackson smiled, 'but anyway, this is all pie-in-the-sky. He hasn't even contacted me yet – he probably never will, but you can't blame a man for trying. Look,' he threw his arms open, 'we seem to have got off on the wrong foot here. I'm not here to work against you guys. I want to work with you. I can help you.'

'I can't let you meet him,' Sean told him. 'It's out of the question.'

'No problem,' Jackson lied. 'So I won't meet him, but I can still talk to him, and I promise, anything he tells me that could help your investigation you'll be the first to know.'

'And you'll set him up for us,' Donnelly told him more than asked. 'Lure him into a trap.'

Jackson shook his head exaggeratedly. 'Oh no. No way. No can do. I didn't catch your name, by the way.'

'That's because I didn't tell you,' Donnelly said. 'If this psychopath contacts you, we need you to set him up. Tell him you'll meet him somewhere and we'll be waiting for him.'

'Can't do it,' Jackson insisted. 'I do that and I lose all my journalistic credibility. My sources have to know I'll protect them – even from the police. Sorry.'

'Fine,' Sean cut in, 'but if he contacts you I want to know everything and I want to know it immediately. You understand, Jackson?'

'No problem,' he lied and smiled. 'You'll be the first to know.'

Sean began to stand. 'You know how to contact me.'

'A mobile number would be good,' Jackson tried.

'My mobile number?' Sean answered. 'To a journalist? I don't think so.'

'Fair enough.' Jackson shrugged before continuing, speaking a little too loud. 'By the way – I hear the Douglas Allen trial starts soon. Any information for me? D'you think he'll plea at the last minute?'

Sean sat back down, his pale blue eyes burning into Jackson's. 'You've had your money's worth out of Douglas Allen. Stay away from the trial.'

'Don't worry,' Jackson laughed. 'You won't see me hanging around the Bailey – trials can drag on for so long, don't you think? Besides, Allen's yesterday's news. He'll plea to or be found guilty of manslaughter, get a few years in open prison and we all move on. The public don't care about him any more, not when they've got the Your View Killer to keep them entertained. I go where the action is, gentlemen, and that isn't at the Bailey.'

'Glad to hear it,' Sean told him.

'No,' Jackson continued. 'The action is wherever *you* are, Inspector Corrigan. Wouldn't you agree?'

'It's time we were on our way,' Sean told him.

'Douglas Allen, Thomas Keller and before that Sebastian Gibran, although I never covered that one – they all fell into your lap. I wonder why? Not long ago Assistant Commissioner Addis forms the Special Investigations Unit, plucks you from obscurity in Peckham and puts you in charge of every high-profile missing persons and murder case in London. Surely you didn't think it would go unnoticed? You're the action, Corrigan. You're like a fucking shitstorm magnet. Oh, I'll be watching you closely from now on, my friend.'

'Goodbye, Jackson,' Sean told him, pushing his chair away as he stood. 'He contacts you, I want to know, immediately.'

'My card,' Jackson suddenly announced, holding a business card that magically appeared pinched between his thumb and index finger. 'In case you need to contact me.' Sean took the card without speaking and without any intention of returning the gesture.

He and Donnelly walked away from the table and out of the café, leaving Jackson alone to consider his next move. *Fucking police,* Jackson thought to himself. If Corrigan thought he could push him around he was sadly mistaken. He knew the law around journalistic privilege better than anyone. They couldn't touch him. All he had to do now was pray the killer contacted him and set up a meet. Once he got the scoop rolling Corrigan and his cronies wouldn't dare interfere and he'd have everyone exactly where he wanted them – right in the palm of his hand.

Sean and Donnelly climbed back into their car without speaking and pulled away from the kerb, Sean doing the driving.

'Do you trust him?' Donnelly asked.

'Do I fuck,' Sean answered.

'Think he'll actually try and meet this psychopath?'

'He will.'

'Then his might be the next body we fish out of the Thames.'

'I don't think so,' Sean explained. 'Jackson doesn't fit his victim type. He won't go off script and do a journalist and risk being seen for what he is.'

'Which is?'

'I don't know,' Sean shook his head, 'but he's no noble avenger of the people, even if that's what he thinks he is. He'll turn out to be some bitter loser, blaming the rest of the world for his own mistakes, using Your View to appeal to all the other bitter losers who haven't got the courage to look at themselves when things go wrong. Easier to blame everyone else.'

'A little harsh, don't you think?' Donnelly asked. 'A lot of people voted to save the last victim. Remember?'

'Whatever,' Sean dismissed it, the thought of the hooded

man on the Internet and the meeting with Jackson making him feel soiled and corrupted.

'Sneaky bastard all the same,' Donnelly changed the subject, 'trying to get your mobile number. A pound to a pinch of shit he'd have your calls and texts intercepted within twenty-four hours.'

'No doubt,' Sean agreed. 'So why don't we return the favour?'

'Listen in to his phone?' Donnelly asked, sounding a little surprised.

'Why not?' Sean argued. 'If he's gonna be talking to our man then we need to know what's being said. Addis said anything I need, so let's listen to his conversations and read his texts and while we're at it we should triangulate his phone's signal so we can track his movements. If it can lead us to the killer then it's justified.'

'Turn the tables on our phone-hacking Fleet Street friends – I like it,' Donnelly told him as he looked out of the window at Wapping, the new home of the national press. 'Not that many of them are in Fleet Street any more.'

Sean felt his phone vibrating in his pocket before the Bluetooth device echoed its ringing tone around the inside of the car. He pressed the answer button on the steering wheel and spoke. 'DI Corrigan speaking.'

'Mr Corrigan,' the officious-sounding voice replied. 'It's DS Roddis.'

'Andy,' Sean acknowledged the sergeant who headed up the forensics team he always preferred to use. 'D'you have something for me?'

'Nothing to get excited about,' Roddis managed his expectations. 'We've looked at the scene victim number two was abducted from and the scene where she was found. There's nothing other than partial tyre tracks and partial footprints at the abduction site – we got nothing off her mobile and headphones. Similar story at the drop site – some partial footprints that may or may not be the suspect's. No tyre tracks, meaning he probably stayed on the road. Better news on the victim's clothes though.'

'Go on,' Sean encouraged.

'We have a couple of fibres – black nylon I'm guessing, which matches what we believe the suspect wears. They could have come from the good Samaritan who found her – we'll need to get hold of them and seize what they were wearing when they found her.'

'We're working on it,' Sean explained.

'But I'm quietly confident they'll be from the suspect. They're nothing unusual, so they won't help us find him, but they could help us convict him.'

'Well,' Sean sighed, 'better than nothing. Anything else?'

'Not yet. As soon as I know, you'll know.'

'Thanks,' Sean told him and hung up.

'At least he's leaving evidence behind him,' Donnelly offered.

'Yeah,' Sean agreed without enthusiasm, 'but it's evidence he doesn't care about. Evidence he knows will take us nowhere.'

'Until we catch him,' Donnelly pointed out.

'Yeah,' Sean agreed. 'Until we catch him.'

He sat in the white room reading the lead stories of the main national newspapers on his laptop. All were following his story, in varying degrees and styles, the red-tops giving him far more prominence than the broadsheets. But all were clearly aware of who he was and what he stood for, and one thing above all others was clear: the police knew nothing and their investigation was going nowhere.

He was glad not to be wearing the stifling ski-mask and awkward voice-distorting equipment, although he still wore his black boiler suit to contain any exchange of forensics from his clothes to the room or vice versa, the rolled-up

149

ski-mask acting as a hat for the same purpose – just in case by some miracle the police stumbled across the room. Thin leather gloves prevented him from leaving his fingerprints. It wouldn't be long now before he wouldn't have to be so careful.

He started to read the coverage of the Your View Killer in *The World*. 'The Your View Killer' – what a ridiculous name, but if it helped focus the public's attention on him then he wouldn't complain. The coverage was far more extensive than even that of the other tabloids. Clearly someone there had taken an exceptionally keen interest in his quest. He scanned the story for the name of the journalist and soon found not just a name, but a small photograph of Geoff Jackson – crime editor no less. There was something else too – an appeal, small and easy to miss, at the bottom of the page in smaller print than the story, the sort of thing only someone paying special interest to the journalist would notice – someone like him. They wanted him to contact them, to contact the journalist. *Do they really dare to contact him? Are they working with the police – trying to trap him?* He read the brief instructions they'd left: he was to set up an anonymous Twitter account, follow Jackson and send a tweet to him so Jackson could follow him back. When that was done, Jackson would send him a private message via Twitter containing a mobile number. Once he had the number he would close the Twitter account and communicate solely via mobile phone. The number would apparently be secure at their end. Seemingly it would be up to him to make any phone he used also secure. He knew enough about the law to know that any communications between himself and Jackson would be protected by journalistic privilege and therefore out of reach of the police.

He leaned back in the chair his victims had been taped to and considered his options. He doubted it was a trap. Too clever for the police, he decided. But could Jackson be somehow trying to catch him himself – make himself some sort of hero? Again, he decided not – the coverage in *The World* had been as positive as it could be, damning his crimes, but subtly implying he might just be giving the rich and greedy exactly what they deserved. *What should he do? What would the people want their vengeful angel to do?* He read the article again and Jackson's instructions to contact him and thought for a while longer before deciding he had little choice. The followers he already had would want – expect – him to do it and the media coverage would allow him to contact hundreds of thousands more, maybe even millions. The Your View Killer could not refuse such an invitation. *Very well Mr Jackson*, he spoke in his mind. *We'll play your little game, but if you cross me – you die.* He shook any further thoughts of meeting Jackson from his head and began to prepare the white room for the next accused, the next trial – the simplest and yet most difficult yet. The one where he'd need all his strength of conviction to achieve what he'd set out to achieve. It would be at times brutal and horrific, but he'd have to push himself further than ever before or face failure, his need for vengeance forever unsatisfied.

Sean and Donnelly arrived back at New Scotland Yard and headed straight to Donnelly's office where Sally and Anna were drinking coffee from cardboard beakers and reading reports.

'Morning, ladies,' Donnelly told them as he threw his coat on the cheap metal hat stand squeezed into the corner of the room. Sean said nothing.

'Is it?' Sally replied without looking up from the papers in her lap.

'Having a bad morning, Sal?' Donnelly asked.

'Endless useless reports of sightings,' she complained. 'Information reports that have no information. I've had better mornings.'

Sean sensed there was more to Sally's mood than thankless police work, but decided now wasn't the time to find out. 'Anything positive?' he asked instead.

'Well,' Sally leaned forward, 'we have CCTV of what we're pretty sure is the van he's using. One of the council's cameras picked it up as it turned left coming out of Peterborough Road and into the King's Road very close to the time of the attack – a white Renault Trafic panel van. Different registration number from last time—'

'No surprise there,' Donnelly interrupted.

'The new plate comes back to an electrician in Bromley,' Sally continued. 'Local CID checked out him and his van, which was apparently stuffed to the rafters with electrician's stuff – certainly no room for an abducted adult. Locals say he's not our man anyway – not the type.'

'Type?' Sean questioned. 'Not the *type*. We have no idea what *type* of person we're looking for.'

No one spoke for a few seconds, unsure whether Sean was genuinely annoyed or just talking out loud.

'D'you want me to get a couple of the team to check him out? Just to be sure,' Sally asked.

'No,' Sean answered with a sigh. 'Our man's using his own van and borrowing the identities of others, which tells us nothing we don't already know. The registration numbers will always lead us away from him – not to him. He's somehow either making false number plates or he's stealing them. We can add that to any press releases we do, but I doubt it'll help. The CCTV shows him turning left and driving along the King's Road, so he's heading west.'

'Doesn't mean he didn't turn north or south at the next major junction,' Donnelly reminded him, 'or even doubled back and headed east.'

'No,' Sean agreed. 'It does not. But the body of the first victim was dumped in the Thames somewhere west of Barnes and the second victim was found wandering around Putney

Heath. And what do we know about serial offenders – what's one of the basic rules we can nearly always apply to them?'

'They like to stick to geographical areas they know well,' Anna answered. 'No matter how confident they appear and how well they seem to plan, working within an area they know well, even best, makes them feel . . . safe.'

'Exactly right,' Sean replied. 'Get the CCTV checked on all routes heading out west,' he told Donnelly and Sally. 'He'll drop off the grid eventually, but we might be able to track him all the way out of London.'

'Even if you're right,' Donnelly pointed out, 'and west London and further out is his preferred territory, that's still a hell of a big area to cover.'

'It's better than the whole of the southeast,' Sean told him. 'Tell DC Bishop to concentrate his efforts on the western outskirts of London.'

'Fair enough,' Donnelly agreed.

'What about this journalist I hear you went to meet,' Sally asked, 'from that rag *The World*? I hear he's trying to get the killer to contact him. Is he planning on actually trying to meet him?'

'He says not,' Sean explained. 'He's promised that if our man does contact him then he'll restrict it to a telephone conversation.'

'D'you believe him?' Sally asked.

'No,' was Sean's blunt answer. 'He wants to meet him – no matter what he says. He'll want a face-to-face, photographs of our man in his Halloween outfit, the whole thing.'

'Then can't we use that?' Sally continued. 'Put the little prick under surveillance and he might just lead us straight to the killer.'

'Wasting our time,' Sean told her. 'He may be a little prick, as you said, but he's a sly little prick. You don't get to be crime editor of *The World* without learning a few tricks. If our man contacts him and they arrange a meet you can bet he'll

153

be looking hard for surveillance and he's probably gonna spot it.'

'What then?' Sally asked. 'How are we going to use this to our advantage?'

'His phone,' Sean answered, producing Jackson's business card from his pocket. 'Prick gave me his mobile number. I'll speak to Addis about getting him listened to – texts too.'

'Assuming he uses his own phone,' Donnelly reminded them.

'Nothing we can do about that,' Sean told him before turning to Anna. 'What d'you think the chances are our man will take the bait? D'you think he'll go for it?'

All eyes fell on Anna. 'Well, he clearly craves attention – otherwise why use Your View? That being the case, the idea of appearing in a mass-market newspaper may well appeal to him.'

'But he's already getting massive coverage in the media,' Donnelly argued, 'so why take a risk and meet a journo?'

'Because so far the only coverage he's had is what's been written about him by other people,' Anna told him. 'What they write is beyond his control, but if he speaks with them directly presumably they'll predominantly be reporting what he says. His *message*. That, I believe, would be a powerful draw for him, so long as he felt in control. He likes to be in control.'

'He gets his message out through Your View,' Sally reminded them. 'Why suddenly turn to the newspapers?'

'Because he can reach more people through them,' Anna explained. 'His audience on Your View will always be limited to certain demographics, but once he hits the papers – his words printed in *The World* – then he can appeal to a much wider audience.'

'Although he'll still be appealing to a particular type of generic group,' Sean added. '*The World* know their target audience well.'

'Which makes it the perfect paper for him,' Anna continued. 'They've been hammering on about greedy bankers ever since the financial crisis began – how the people suffer while they grow richer, despite their obvious failings. They've practically been spreading the same message anyway, so why not use them? He'll undoubtedly know they're sympathetic towards him, or at least as much as they can be.'

'So you think he'll go for it?' Sean asked.

'I think it's a distinct possibility,' Anna told him. 'He's about communication. How could he resist the opportunity to communicate with so many people, many of whom he already knows are of like mind, even if they object to the violence – and not forgetting there are a great many who don't.'

'If that's what he's about,' Sean threatened to drop a fly in the ointment, wishing his doubts had stayed silent.

'If he's about what?' Sally asked.

'Communicating with the general public,' he replied. 'Maybe his message is more . . . more *personal*?'

'I don't understand,' Anna told him. 'Personal to his victims or personal for him?'

'I don't know,' Sean answered honestly, shaking his head. 'I guess we'll find out soon enough: if he goes for *The World*'s offer then everything that Anna says is probably right, but if he turns it down, then perhaps there's more to this one than we're considering.' He turned quickly to Anna before anyone could question him. 'And Jackson – do you think he's in any danger of becoming a victim?'

'No,' she shook her head. 'His victim selection is too specific and, as I've previously stated, *The World*'s something he may see as an ally and therefore Jackson too. To turn on him wouldn't make sense.'

'I agree. But what about his victim selection?' Sean asked. 'He goes for a CEO, which makes sense, but then he drops down to a project manager.'

'A project manager who's clearly on her way up in the world,' Donnelly reminded him.

'All the same,' Sean replied, unconvinced.

'After Paul Elkins was murdered the other CEOs and senior players probably beefed up their security – got the company chauffeur-cum-minder to take them home. Not the sort of luxury they'd afford to a mere project manager,' Sally suggested.

'Makes sense,' Anna agreed. 'He adjusts to easier targets, but still people from the financial sector. The message is the same.'

'But he's a planner,' Sean told them. 'He picked his targets well in advance of abducting them – watched them, learned their lifestyle, habits.'

'Agreed,' Anna said.

'Then we're saying he *predicted* that the most senior people in the City would become more difficult to abduct and deliberately picked Georgina Vaughan because she was less senior and therefore more vulnerable,' Sean argued.

'It appears so,' Anna agreed.

'Then his intelligence and instincts are not to be underestimated,' Sean told them. 'All of which makes him even more dangerous than we first thought. If he can predict what moves people in the City are going to make, then we have to assume he's cunning enough to predict our next move.'

'Meaning?' Donnelly asked.

'Meaning we're going to have to continually think outside the box – try not to do anything predictable.'

'No,' Anna partly disagreed. 'Better to be seen to be doing the predictable. Show him you're doing exactly what he'd expect you to do – a false front while more covertly doing the unusual.'

'Good work, Doctor,' Sean praised her. 'OK. So the first thing we need to do is stop thinking about the victims he's already chosen and try and think about what type of person could be next.'

156

'Well,' Sally suggested, 'he's gone from a CEO to a project manager, so maybe he'll keep sliding down the scale. A barrow boy, maybe – something like that.'

'Jesus,' Donnelly rolled his eyes. 'Where do we start . . . where do we stop? We can't predict who he's going to take next – if anyone at all, for that matter.'

'He'll take someone else,' Sean insisted. 'There's no doubt about that.'

'Why so certain?' Sally asked.

'Because he hasn't finished yet,' he told them. 'Whatever this is about, whyever he's doing this, he's not finished yet. Of that much, I am certain.'

Geoff Jackson fidgeted at his desk in the large open-plan office of *The World*, trying to concentrate on tomorrow's update on the Your View Killer, although he was beginning to tire of that name – not catchy enough and carrying too much implication that the man he hoped to meet was nothing more than another sadistic loser killing for kicks. The anxiety of waiting for his phone to squeal and vibrate with an email alert telling him he'd just received a tweet was driving him to distraction. For the umpteenth time he checked his phone, just in case he'd somehow missed an alert.

He'd already received more than two dozen tweets from people claiming to be the killer. Most had been transparent enough and he'd simply blocked them, but several had been convincing enough to cause him to reply, sending them the number of his newly acquired anonymous pay-as-you-go mobile phone. However, he had quickly satisfied himself none were the real killer and had summarily dismissed them and blocked their numbers. *What was the matter with these people?* he asked himself. *Pretending to be a murderer for kicks. Christ. Was nothing sacred any more?*

His phone suddenly sprang to life and caught him daydreaming, startling him. He checked the screen. It was another tweet. Despite his scepticism his heart still missed a beat as he grabbed the phone and read the message.

It said simply – *You know who I am. What now?*

Something in Jackson's street brawler instinct told him this one was different. He pressed reply to tweet and typed *Call me on . . .* followed by the number of his pay-as-you-go phone, his finger hovering over the send icon as something made him stall, his heart and breath feeling as if they'd both stopped. *What are you doing, Geoff?* he asked himself. *Are you going too far this time, my old China?*

'Fuck it,' he said out loud and touched the send icon with the tip of his finger. A few seconds later the phone told him the message had been sent. He huddled over his computer screen, eager to keep the call as private as he could, and waited for the mobile to ring, his body frozen in anticipation.

A minute passed and still nothing.

'Come on,' he said through gritted teeth. 'Don't bottle out now, my friend.' He tapped his desk with a pencil, losing hope of grabbing the scoop of the decade with each passing second. 'Come on, come on,' he encouraged the phone until once again it suddenly jumped into life and somehow managed to catch him by surprise. He quickly regained his composure and checked the screen – caller ID withheld. 'Clever boy,' he told himself, allowing the phone to ring three more times before answering it. 'Geoff Jackson speaking.'

There was a silence on the other end of the line – nothing but a strange breathing sound.

'Hello,' Jackson encouraged, increasingly sure he was connected with the real killer. 'Is that you?' he whispered. 'You called, so you must want to speak.' Still nothing but the strange breathing sound. 'Hello.'

'What do you want to know?' the voice suddenly asked in the same strange electronic voice Jackson had heard in the Your View broadcast.

'First I need to know it's really you,' Jackson told him, his mouth dry, 'and not just another fake wasting my time.'

'Do you think me a fake?' the voice asked, pushing him onto the back foot.

'No,' Jackson assured him. 'I mean that you're not just another crank call.'

'You know I'm not.'

'All the same,' Jackson stuck to his guns, knowing he needed to maintain some control, 'I need to be sure.' There was a long silence before the unearthly voice returned.

'Very well. Ask your questions.'

'Tell me something about the case that hasn't been in the papers or on the television,' Jackson demanded. 'Something only the police could know.'

'How would that prove anything?' the voice asked. 'As you yourself are not a police officer, unless of course you're working with the police?'

'I'm not,' Jackson assured him, 'but I have contacts in the police – contacts in the investigation team. I know things.'

'Then you'll know there is nothing,' the voice told him, 'because the police have nothing other than what I have allowed them to see, which is no more than what I have allowed you to see.'

It was the final confirmation he needed and now he knew beyond any doubt he was talking with the real Your View Killer. It wasn't just the words he spoke, but the tone of the mechanical voice – its calm self-confidence – things too specific for some lunatic or joker pretending to be him to fake.

'We shouldn't speak too long on the phone,' Jackson warned him. 'Short conversations for instructions only. They're not safe.'

'I agree,' the electronic voice told him, making the hairs on the back of his neck tingle and uncoil.

'We need to meet,' Jackson told him, expecting some objection, but there was none.

'Agreed,' the voice answered. 'I'll call you on this number at exactly nine am tomorrow and give you instructions as to where and when. Goodbye, Mr Jackson.'

'Wait,' Jackson almost pleaded, but it was too late – the line had gone dead. 'Fuck and bollocks,' he cursed, staring at the phone and for the first time noticing his hands were trembling with both fear and excitement. He dropped the phone and clenched his fists to try to stop the shaking. 'This is it, baby. Get your shit together, Geoff my old son. You're about to land the big one.'

7

Sean was huddled around an oversized computer screen with Sally, Donnelly and most of his team, both Featherstone and Addis standing behind them watching their every move as the scene unfolded before them: the Your View broadcast showing a hooded woman taped to the chair in the white room, a few strands of her raven black hair protruding and snaking onto her pristine white blouse as she struggled and mumbled while the man dressed in black, his face hidden by a ski-mask and his voice disguised by whatever it was he wore across his mouth, pointed and preached into the screen, a small, gleaming knife gripped in his gloved hand. He suddenly turned back to his victim, tore her blouse open and carved an X into her exposed skin, her muffled screams filling the room, seeping from the screen and into the office. Sally turned away as if she was going to vomit.

'Turn this vile exhibition off,' Addis demanded, his voice strange and faded, but Sean refused, unable to look away, the man on the screen once again preaching to his disciples before suddenly pulling the hood from the victim's head. Sean's heart missed a beat as the breath was knocked out of him.

'Anna,' he called out, but there was nothing he could do

to save her. The man held up the knife for all to see before spinning and plunging the blade deep into Anna's abdomen, twisting it and pulling it free, blood beginning to flow freely from the wound, Anna's eyes wide in fear and pain, tears mixing with mucus that spat from her nose as she tried to breathe. But he wasn't finished yet, moving behind her, taking hold of her hair and pulling her head back, her slim, beautiful neck exposed and vulnerable, the knife resting across her trachea – a small trickle of blood beginning to run down her throat. He looked directly from the screen and spoke. *'Her crime is treachery. Her sentence is death.'*

Sean wanted to scream at the screen, plead with the man not to hurt her any more, but it was useless: he couldn't move, couldn't even speak, couldn't even force his eyes shut so he didn't have to watch as the killer slowly, deliberately drew the knife across Anna's throat, the skin parting like a grotesque zip, exposing tendons and cartilage as the blood began to flow from the wound. Anna gurgled and gasped as the life seeped from her, her body convulsing then slumping, her head lolled backwards, her hands and legs twitching slightly before finally lying still.

The killer stepped from behind her and walked close to the camera, so close that his hooded face filled the screen, his hands ripping the voice distorter away and pulling the ski-mask free – revealing his face for the world to see. Sean blinked in confusion and disbelief at what he was seeing – at who he was seeing – his own face staring out at him from the screen, his own eyes, wild and bloodshot, looking back at him as he was finally able to open his mouth and scream.

His body jolted and bucked him from his nightmare-plagued sleep, sweat running from his chest down his ribs, his lungs filling with air as he tried to get his bearings in the dimly lit bedroom. Once he realized where he was he searched for Kate in a panic, praying he hadn't woken her – praying his screams could only be heard in the sleep world. He breathed out slowly once he was sure she was still in a deep sleep and slipped from the bed, padding to the bathroom where he took a cold shower to wash away the sweat and the memory of the nightmare. He dressed quickly and headed downstairs to the kitchen, glad of the peace and quiet as he sipped a strong, piping-hot cup of coffee and tried to eat a slice of toast.

The squeak of a stair floorboard warned him Kate was heading towards him, sleepily walking into the kitchen wrapped in an old dressing gown of his he'd never worn, the tight curls of her hair comically tangled. She sat next to him, yawned, took the toast from his hand and took a bite with no intention of returning it.

'You're up early,' she told him, her eyes still barely open.

'Looks like I'm not the only one,' he answered.

'Busy day at work,' she explained, her eyes threatening to flicker shut. 'How's the new case going?'

Sean gazed into his coffee. 'It's another bitch. Another Chinese puzzle – thousands of pieces to somehow try and fit together and not a lot of clues as to how to do it.'

'Just the sort you like then,' she teased.

'Oh yeah,' he said. 'I can't get enough of them.'

'Don't worry,' she reassured him casually. 'You'll get your man, Detective Inspector. You always do.'

'Maybe,' he answered without conviction, 'but this one's clever. Really smart. There's an element of prediction about him that I can't remember seeing before or even hearing of. Most react to their changing situations, even the planners, but this one sees it coming days, maybe even weeks, before it happens and already has his plans in place – keeping himself one step ahead. This one worries me. I can't get a feel for him. His motive's laid bare, his anger, his frustration, his want for some kind of vengeance . . . I should be able to get inside his head, but I can't and I don't know why.'

'It'll come,' she promised him, more awake now – more

concerned. 'Why are you dressed so smart?' she asked him, changing the subject.

Sean looked down at his best tie and suit. 'Douglas Allen trial starts today at the Bailey,' he told her.

'The Toy Taker,' she said with mock horror.

'His name is Douglas Allen,' he reprimanded her for using his tabloid title.

'Trust me,' she told him, 'I remember his name and I hope he gets life.'

'Maybe you'd just rather hand him over to the mob and watch them hang him from the nearest lamppost?'

'He killed a child,' she reminded him unnecessarily.

'Not intentionally,' he told her.

'Then why is he on trial for murder if you think it was manslaughter?'

'He's been charged with both,' Sean explained. 'It's just the way it's done. If the jury find him not guilty of murder they can always drop down to manslaughter.'

'But doesn't there have to be intent to kill to prove murder?' Kate asked, awake now.

'Not necessarily,' he explained. 'If he meant to do the boy serious harm which resulted in his actual death, then it can be deemed to be murder, even without intent to kill.'

'And do you think he meant to do him serious harm?'

'Who knows?' Sean answered. 'Douglas Allen was a schizo-phrenic who wasn't taking his drugs. I doubt he even knows himself what he intended to do.' He looked at this watch. 'I'd better get going. I need to pop into the Yard before court and pick up some case papers.'

'Remember we're going out tonight,' she reminded him. 'Court or no court. It's been in the diary for weeks so don't act like you don't know about it.' His heart sank as some vague memory warned him Kate had told him about it and that he'd agreed to go. His expression betrayed his forgetful-ness to Kate who snatched his phone from the table and entered the screen code, quickly flicking through to the calendar before fixing him with a look of amazement. 'Sean. You didn't put it in your phone. I told you to put it in your phone so you wouldn't forget.'

'I'll be there,' he promised, getting to his feet, easing the phone from her grip and slipping it in his inside jacket pocket.

'You'd better be,' she warned him. 'Il Forno. London Bridge at seven thirty. You know where it is – we've been there before.'

'Yeah, I know it,' he assured her, bending to kiss her softly on the cheek. 'See you later.'

'Seven thirty,' she warned him again. 'Do not be late.'

Anna saw Assistant Commissioner Addis as soon as she entered the restaurant of the Eccleston Square Hotel not far from Victoria Station. He sat with his back to her, sipping orange juice and reading a broadsheet newspaper, his civilian suit perfect camouflage amongst the other breakfast takers. She straightened her suit jacket and picked her way past the other tables until she reached Addis who looked up and smiled his reptilian smile, neatly folding his newspaper as he spoke.

'Anna. So good of you to agree to meet me so early in the morning. Please, have a seat.' He gestured to the seat he wanted her to take with a wave of his hand, allowing her to settle before speaking again. 'Will you take breakfast?' he asked, too formally.

'I'm fine,' she told him. 'Maybe just some coffee.'

'Of course.' He summoned the waiter with a flash of his eyes. 'Coffee for my guest, please.' The waiter gave a little bow and scurried away. 'I thought it would make a change to meet away from Yard,' he explained, still smiling. 'In fact, I think it's best that from now on we always meet away from police premises – away from prying eyes and enquiring minds.'

'Are we expecting to have many more meetings?' she asked, trying to hide her concern at the prospect.

'Well,' Addis told her, pausing as the waiter returned with a fresh pot of coffee that he laid in front of Anna before quickly drifting away. 'That rather depends on the subject of our mutual interest, don't you think?'

'Meaning Sean? DI Corrigan?'

Addis's eyes narrowed and hardened for second before softening. 'Who else?' he answered. 'So long as he's under my supervision, I would appreciate you keeping a watchful eye on him. Think of yourself as his . . . safety net.'

She tried to decide whether this was genuine concern for Sean, or just Addis wanting an early warning system to give himself a chance to jettison Sean before he could be tarnished.

'You sure he needs a safety net?' she asked. 'He seems to be coping fine with this new investigation. In fact, I'd say he seems to be coping better now than I've ever seen him. Less hostile, more open and he seems to be having far fewer episodes of involuntarily placing himself in the mind of the offender, which makes him emotionally more stable.'

'So you're saying he's investigating a little more conventionally?' Addis asked.

'Yes,' she answered directly.

'That's not entirely what I was hoping to hear,' Addis said to himself more than Anna. 'He's not much use in charge of Special Investigations if he's stopped doing what we both know he can do.'

'So you want him to be unstable?' Anna asked. She was increasingly struggling not to be seen to be too obviously protecting Sean; her feelings towards him made just discussing him with Addis feel like a betrayal. But she'd already made her decision: she would tell Addis whatever she needed to tell him to protect Sean – even if it meant lying to him.

'No. No.' Addis was quick to dismiss the suggestion. 'But

the fact remains DI Corrigan works best when he's walking close to the edge. As you know. It's just the way it is for some people.'

'Well,' Anna told him, not entirely sure herself of how much she was telling the truth, 'he certainly seems to have stepped away from the edge somewhat.'

'Really,' Addis mused. 'But his *insights* – would you say they've entirely stopped?'

'Apparently,' she answered, 'although he still remains very instinctive and intelligent. If you want my professional opinion I would say you couldn't have a better qualified person in charge of Special Investigations.' She swallowed drily and tried to keep her poker face while Addis looked at her hard.

'Indeed,' he at last appeared to agree. 'And his tendency towards self-destruction – this desire to rush into potentially dangerous situations on his own. Have you been able to learn any more about that?'

'I hold the same opinion as before: he's not self-destructive, but he can be, at least in the past he could be, overwhelmed by a compulsion to come face-to-face with the offender.'

'So he can learn from them?' Addis asked. 'A little one-on-one time, so to speak, before the lawyers sanitize everything. A final chance to prove to himself that he was right all along.'

Anna felt increasingly uncomfortable – Addis's understanding of Sean meant it would be more and more difficult for her to protect him without Addis smelling a rat. She needed to get out of her arrangement with the Assistant Commissioner as fast as she could, but suspected it would be no easy task. Addis would not take kindly to being snubbed and there was a very real chance he would tell Sean all about the *true* reason why she'd been attached to two of his investigations. Could he – would he – ever forgive her? She wasn't prepared to take the chance, not yet. Better to keep Addis close for now. Keep him where she could see him so she could best protect Sean.

'Yes,' she answered Addis's question. 'I believe it's something like that.'

He watched her for a while once more before speaking. 'Good. I think it's important you remain in your current position, attached to the investigation where you can keep a close eye on DI Corrigan and report back to me any significant changes in his behaviour, specifically if he once again shows an ability to . . . to share the offender's point of view.'

'I understand,' Anna assured him, her head hurting with the desire to be away from Addis.

'Very good,' Addis told her with his unpleasant smile. 'I'm sure you'll agree that our relationship has been mutually beneficial? You have after all been given unprecedented access to high-profile murder investigations and of course the suspects once arrested.'

'Of course.' Anna forced the words from her constricted throat.

'Excellent,' Addis replied, raising his glass of orange juice to her. 'Then here's to a long and productive relationship.'

She swallowed the bile in her mouth and faked a smile as she raised her cup of coffee to Addis. 'To us.'

Geoff Jackson drove along the quiet rural roads following the Your View Killer's instructions exactly, just as he'd been told to do early the same morning when the killer called him on the pay-as-you-go mobile number at precisely nine am. He'd barely given Jackson time to grab a pen and write down the instructions before he hung up. No matter now as he neared the location.

He'd had a heated debate with his editor over whether he should be allowed to drive off into the middle of nowhere to meet a killer at all. Once Jackson had won that battle he then had to try to persuade her to let him go alone. Apparently she knew a couple of guys – ex-SAS or something. They could shadow him all the way and be his security. Her security, more like, but there was no way he was going to let a couple of goons blow this for him. He went alone or nothing. In the end she agreed – how could she not? This was potentially far too big to risk missing out on.

Jackson followed the satnav directions all the way to a small car park on Ruislip Common in Hertfordshire, a few miles west of London, scanning his surroundings before allowing his car to roll to a halt, his eyes searching the trees and thick bushes for any signs of life, the doors still locked as a precaution until he decided it was no longer needed. If the Your View Killer was watching from the treeline he'd never spot him. Better to bite the bullet and get out the car – show himself to the killer he hoped to meet – relying on his instincts and animal cunning to keep himself alive.

As he opened the door the sounds and smells of the common washed over him for the first time – crisp air that tasted so much sweeter than London air, the sounds of the trees gently swaying in the light breeze audible instead of being drowned out by traffic. He breathed in deeply, the clean air making him feel a little dizzy and lightheaded. He decided he didn't like the sensation and lit a cigarette before hauling himself out of the car, closing the door quietly and taking another good look around. This was the sort of place where the bodies of murder victims were found. Was that why the killer had brought him here? He shivered and pulled hard on his cigarette as he watched the dog walkers off in the distance, too far away to hear their whistles and calls. For a second he imagined his naked body lying in a shallow grave as a dog sniffed and scratched around him. Again he shivered and sucked on his cigarette. 'Fuck,' he spoke out loud to be heard; if only there'd been someone around to hear him.

The distant sound of a vehicle's engine coming along the country road towards the car park made him turn from the dog walkers and concentrate on the lane. In the distance he could just about see the occasional white flash as the vehicle passed gaps in the trees. He took one last drag and crushed the cigarette underfoot as the white flashes grew ever closer, moving fast along the road, the engine screeching under the strain. Classic counter-surveillance driving, he thought to himself – drive hard and fast. If anyone's following you they're going to show out pretty quickly moving at that kind of speed. This had to be his man. He'd expected him to be on the plot way before he arrived, watching him from the trees, but clearly he was cleverer than that. He'd probably been parked and hidden further down the road, waiting for him to pass before he approached the car park himself – checking Jackson hadn't been tailed before moving in, just in case he'd brought his own security or cooperated with the police. He'd probably already walked the plot checking for cops, but as an everyday person going for a walk, not as Jackson was certain he would be now – dressed in his full Your View Killer uniform.

'Clever boy,' he said quietly as the white van came fully into view, slowing dramatically, coming to an almost halt at the entrance to the common, like a large herbivore cautiously approaching a watering hole.

Jackson strained to see into the cabin, but the tinted windows made it almost impossible, although he could make out the dark shape of a man . . . or woman, behind the wheel. He swallowed drily as his stomach tightened and his bowels loosened, the van inching into the car park and heading straight towards him, the gravel sounding like crunching snow under the slow-turning wheels.

'Shit,' he whispered through gritted teeth as the van finally stopped only feet in front of him. Jackson watched, almost unable to move with fear as the driver's door opened and what looked to be a man stepped out, not as tall as he'd expected, but stockier than he'd looked on the Your View videos, dressed in the now familiar black overalls and ski-mask, the voice-distorting device across his mouth, connected to a black box on his chest. But what held Jackson's attention most, what made him realize he might have made a grave mistake, was the sawn-off shotgun that the black figure was pointing at his chest.

The man stepped closer and spoke, the voice all the more unreal at such close quarters, and coming from the box on his chest rather than his mouth. 'Well, Mr Jackson, do you still want your interview?'

Say something, Jackson told himself. *For God's sake say something before he blows you away.* He felt his legs would give out from under him at any moment, but somehow managed to speak.

'Yes.' The hardest word he'd ever had to say.

The dark figure fished in a trouser pocket with a gloved hand and pulled a piece of black material from inside, throwing it at Jackson.

'Put that on,' the robotic voice demanded as Jackson allowed the cloth to open into its natural shape.

'Jesus,' he said quietly, his hands beginning to shake even more as he looked up at the figure. 'You don't need to do this,' he pleaded. 'You can trust me.'

'Don't worry, Mr Jackson,' the voice answered, his amusement and confidence detectable even through the voice distorter. 'If I was here to kill you you'd be dead already.' Jackson looked pleadingly at the hood in his hands and back at the figure. 'Just a precaution,' he explained. 'So you can't tell anyone where you've been.'

'I won't,' Jackson begged. 'I promise.'

'The police have their ways, Mr Jackson, so if you please – time is against us.'

Jackson raised the mask in front of his face and closed his eyes. If he told the killer he wasn't prepared to go with him he could kill him there and then. If he agreed to go with him then anything could happen to him . . . But if he could survive, if he could survive and get the story, get the interview – an interview with a killer who was still on the loose, not one who was already banged up for life and willing to talk to anyone to alleviate the boredom of prison – then he'd be a legend. He would have done what no other journalist had done before. This could win him News Reporter of the Year and guarantee him a bestseller.

'Fuck it,' he swore and pulled the hood over his head. The sudden darkness almost made him panic enough to pull it straight off, but he managed to resist as the man took hold of his arms and pulled them around his back. He felt something tightening around his wrists before a surprisingly gentle hand took hold of his upper arm and began to lead him away.

'Don't be alarmed, Mr Jackson,' the terrible voice told him. 'I've always been a big fan of your work.'

Oh my dear God, Jackson screamed in his own head. *What have I done? What have I done?*

Sean arrived at the Old Bailey shortly after nine am, battling his way through the crowded front entrance, holding up his warrant card, but still being forced to queue with the mixture of defendants, witnesses, lawyers and God knows who else, as they were all funnelled through the metal detectors and scanners. Once he was past the bottleneck he hurried up the stairs and went through a door marked 'CPS and Police Personnel Only'. He soon reached the CPS office and searched around for the barrister who thus far had been representing the case for the prosecution – Jonathon Richman, QC. He'd met him several times before and it wasn't long before he spotted the tall and handsome Richman sitting at a cluttered desk already wearing his black gown, although his wig was yet to be perched on top of his longish grey-black hair. Richman took a slurp from his takeaway cup before denouncing the contents to the room in his public schoolboy accent.

'God, this coffee's bloody awful,' he declared loudly. 'Sandra. Sandra darling,' he summoned one of the young CPS clerks. 'Be a love and pop out to Starbucks for me, will you. Large soya milk latte, please.' He held out the offending cup. 'I can't drink this poison.' The clerk took the cup away with a grin. Sean worked his way across the crowded office and sat down opposite Richman.

'Coffee no good?' he asked to get Richman's attention.

Richman barely looked up from his files. 'Bloody awful,' he replied, 'just like this case.'

Sean felt his frustration and anger already beginning to rise. 'The case is solid enough,' he reminded Richman.

'Well,' Richman argued, 'as I *tried* to point out at the case conference there are always difficulties where there are doubts over the defendant's mental state.'

'The case is strong.' Sean refused to yield. 'His mental state's not in doubt.'

Richman sighed. 'Listen. I spoke to his barrister this morning. They'll plead to all four abductions, three counts of false imprisonment, four counts of common assault and . . .'

'And what?' Sean pressed him.

'And to the manslaughter of Samuel Hargrave.'

'Manslaughter?' Sean asked, his anger and frustrating growing, swelling up from the dark place of his blackest secrets. 'He was a five-year-old boy.'

'I'm well aware of that, Inspector, but . . .'

'Taken from his bed in the middle of the night,' Sean talked over him, 'and killed by Douglas Allen's hand.'

'But we can't prove Allen's intent,' Richman argued, the truth of his words calming Sean's rising temper. 'You know that.'

'He deserves a trial.' Sean refused to relent. 'The boy. His parents. They deserve a trial. If the jury finds him not guilty of murder, but guilty of manslaughter then so be it. I can live with that. But they deserve a trial.'

'He's a diagnosed schizophrenic.' Richman tried another approach. 'The jury could easily find him not guilty on the grounds of diminished responsibility. They may even decide he's not even guilty of manslaughter or the abductions – God knows with juries. Do you really want to take the risk of going to trial?'

'R v Chambers,' Sean began. 'The psychiatric report stated, yes he's schizophrenic, but not so much that he didn't understand what he was doing – not so he didn't feel guilt and remorse. Where a hospital order is not recommended, and it wasn't, but the defendant constitutes a real danger to the public for an unpredictable period of time, then the right sentence will in all probability be one of life imprisonment. Correct?'

'You don't have to lecture me on the law, Inspector,' Richman complained.

'Nor you I,' Sean bit back. 'No deal. If he wants to plead guilty to everything, that's his business, but no deal.'

'Fine,' Richman relented. 'Have it your own way. I'll inform the defence there'll be no deal.'

'Good,' Sean told him, getting to his feet and handing Richman his business card. 'If you need me, call me on this mobile number.'

'Need you?' Richman said incredulously. 'I do need you – here – for the duration of the trial.'

'Sorry,' Sean told him. 'I can't hang around here for the next three weeks. I'm in the middle of a murder investigation. I leave you with DC McGowan. He's more than capable of looking after things here. I just popped in this morning to assure you that everything's good to go. To make sure you have everything you need and that we're all singing from the same song sheet. When you need me to give my evidence I'll be here. If I'm needed before then I'll come if I can.'

174

'Oh,' Richman faked a laugh, 'you'll be needed, Inspector. I can assure you of that.'

Sean looked him up and down expressionlessly. 'Goodbye, sir.'

'Just one thing,' Richman stopped him. 'Your new case – anything interesting?'

Sean remembered Richman knew he was running the Special Investigations Unit and that meant high-profile cases – just what every barrister wanted. 'The Your View Killer,' he told him.

'Ooh, now there's a case I'd really like to get my hands on,' Richman admitted.

'Really?' Sean asked. 'Defence or prosecution?'

Richman smiled broadly and held his arms wide apart. 'Like I'd bloody well care.'

Sean looked him up and down one more time. 'Call me if you need me.'

Jackson blinked against the brightness of the light that reflected and magnified off the white walls, its harshness conflicting with the darkness of the hood that his captor had just pulled off his head. He gave his eyes a few seconds to adjust, opening them a millimetre wider every two or three seconds until they were all but wide open, the mistiness clearing as he focused on the dark figure sitting casually on what looked like a fold-out table – the type decorators used for pasting wallpaper. This one was covered with electrical equipment: at least two laptops, several webcams and other items he didn't recognize, most of which were plugged into a small electricity generator. At the man's side was the object that attracted most of his attention – the sawn-off shotgun. The dark figure seemed to notice him looking at the gun, gently resting his hand on it as if to make the point, but the gun remained on the table.

Jackson looked down at his wrists and ankles. He was

sitting in a heavy wooden chair that he immediately recognized from the Your View videos. Memories of the man's violent death and the young woman's torture made him want to leap from it immediately, but the shotgun kept him firmly seated, despite there being no bindings to hold him.

'You haven't . . . you haven't tied me to the chair?' he asked.

The electronic laughter filled the white room. 'Why would I do that? You're my guest, Mr Jackson.'

'Were the others guests?' Jackson nervously asked, still afraid the same fate awaited him.

'No,' the man answered, his distorted voice sounding calm, but serious. 'They were necessary hostages. Necessary sacrifices.'

'Are you going to kill me?' Jackson couldn't stop himself from asking. He'd rather know straight away than try to avoid the subject until it was too late. He'd rather know it was coming and prepare himself than be ambushed and suddenly slaughtered like a free-range pig.

'Why would I do that?' the man asked. 'Do you think I'm insane, that I'm doing what I do for some kind of perverted satisfaction?'

'No,' Jackson spluttered. 'No. Of course not.'

'It's important you understand I have nothing *personal* against the people you call victims,' the dark figure explained. 'I hate what they are, not necessarily who they are. They've never insulted me or spat in my face, but they are more than complicit with the institutions they work for in piling misery and suffering on the normal, hard-working people of this country, many of whom who have lost everything. They screw up, but it's we who pay the penalty. Why should that be, Mr Jackson?'

'It shouldn't,' Jackson stuttered. 'You're right. I agree with you. They should pay for what they've done. But aren't there others more deserving of your justice?'

'Such as?'

'What about paedophiles? People who hurt children?'

'Ahh, yes. Of course,' the masked man nodded. 'It was you who uncovered the vile scum who were using their celebrity to abuse the young and innocent, was it not?'

'It was,' Jackson proudly admitted.

'But that would make me a vigilante, Mr Jackson,' he explained. 'Do you think all I am is another misguided vigilante?'

'No,' Jackson quickly answered.

'They will be adequately punished by the justice system. Who will make the bankers pay – the government, the unions, the police? None of them can touch these people.'

'I understand now,' Jackson told him, sounding a little more confident. 'So you punish them because no one else will?'

'It is necessary,' he explained, 'to address the imbalance of power and wealth. To punish the guilty who are yet to be punished. It is right that they should live in fear – that they should feel the fear working people live with all their lives, never knowing when they will be left jobless or homeless, cut adrift from society, trying to survive day to day, hand to mouth. That's living in fear – a fear the rich will never know. So I bring to them a different type of fear.'

'So you're avenging the working people of Britain?' Jackson asked, warming to his task.

'Why just Britain?' the man replied. 'The whole world has suffered at their hands.'

'Isn't there some other way of punishing them,' Jackson asked, 'other than violence and murder?'

'I only wish there were, but these people only respond to such extreme acts. If you threaten them with taking away their wealth they'll only hide it where it can't be found: property, overseas investments, blood diamonds, gold mined by people who are little more than slaves. They've been

177

protecting their wealth for almost two hundred years now. This is the only way to strike back.'

'You seem to know a lot about it,' Jackson couldn't help but comment. 'Wealth, commodities, investment.'

'I have spent years researching these institutions,' he answered, 'and the more I learnt the angrier I became and the angrier I became the more convinced I was that this is the only way to make them truly notice us – we *the people*.'

'So why come to me?' Jackson asked. 'Why accept my offer of a face-to-face interview? Why not stick to Your View?'

'Because my message isn't just for those with access to a computer or device. My message is for everyone, young or old, able to use a computer or not. Many of the people I speak for can't even afford such luxuries – but they can, however, afford your newspaper. Through you I can reach millions who would otherwise never hear my words. Do you understand now?'

'I understand,' Jackson nodded.

'Although there is one thing you can do for me,' the man told him, 'in exchange for your exclusive.'

'Of course,' Jackson agreed without even checking.

'The media, *The World* included, have taken to calling me the Your View Killer. I have killed, but that doesn't make me a *killer*. This is a war and in war we are required to kill, even if we find it abhorrent.' Jackson had to suppress a grin: he'd seen this one coming. *We all have our vanities,* he spoke to himself. *Even the Your View Killer.* 'This ridiculous name belittles everything I'm trying to achieve.'

'I agree,' Jackson jumped in, 'and I have an idea. I was going back over your previous broadcasts on Your View.'

'And?'

'You mentioned that working people should be like jack-daws, flocking together to defeat the bigger, stronger crow. It's perfect. It's perfect. We'll call you . . . The Jackdaw. Trust me, once people see this interview they'll all follow our lead.

178

Soon everyone will be calling you The Jackdaw. Maybe even you will?'

The man watched him in silence for a while before lifting the shotgun from the table. *Oh, Jesus*, Jackson thought to himself. *Bastard's lied to me. He's lured me out here on the pretence that he wanted to talk, but now he's just going to kill me anyway.*

'Maybe,' the figure finally answered. 'Call me The Jackdaw if you must. But that's enough for today.'

'You mean there'll be other times?' Jackson asked, recovering his composure slightly, both excited and terrified at the thought of having to endure anything like this again.

'We shall see, Mr Jackson,' the figure answered, throwing the hood into his lap. 'In the meantime, just keep watching Your View. Something will happen soon. Very soon.'

8

Sean arrived back in the office at the Yard later that morning. He passed Anna who was chatting with DC Cahill and paused to acknowledge them.

'How's it going?' he asked.

'Getting there,' Cahill answered.

'Anna?' he asked, sensing her unease and wondering what was behind it.

'I'm fine. Thank you,' she replied.

'OK,' Sean told her and made his way over to Sally who was deep in discussion with DC Jesson.

'What's happening, Sally?'

'We're getting a lot of CCTV coming in from council and TFL cameras. He's definitely using a white Renault Trafic panel van. We've managed to track him out as far as junction two on the M4, around Ealing, but we haven't been able to come up with a decent picture of the driver yet. The lab are working on it. Looks like the van windows are tinted or darkened and, as you know, it appears he's switching number plates between abductions.'

'And the victims?'

'They don't appear to be connected in any way,' Sally explained. 'They don't work for the same firms, don't seem to know each other, don't have any mutual friends or family. They appear random.'

'Anything else?' Sean asked, a little forlornly.

'No witnesses have been found to the second victim's abduction, or her drop-off. We've received umpteen calls from members of the public giving names of possible suspects based largely on the fact they own white vans and not much else. We've got local cops checking them out. There's a list on your desk.'

'Thanks,' Sean answered sarcastically before turning to Anna. 'Can I see you in my office a second?' Sally's look of suspicion wasn't wasted on him.

'Of course,' Anna answered and followed him to his office where he took the unusual precaution of closing his flimsy door. 'Everything all right?' she asked.

'You tell me,' Sean replied. 'You seem a little . . . *uncomfortable*. Anything I should know about?' He circled his desk and sat down, looking up at Anna, waiting for an answer.

'No. Why? Should there be?'

'Is it a problem for you – working so closely with me? I don't want you to feel awkward.'

'No,' she insisted. 'It's not an issue. I've just had a bit of a strange morning.'

'OK.' He let it slide. 'Then if you're going to be working with me I might as well get some use out of you.'

'Please do,' she told him, smiling slightly.

'This man we're looking for,' he began, 'what d'you think he is, mad, bad or just misguided? D'you think he'll stop?'

'I don't see mental health problems here,' she told him. 'And for what it's worth I don't see him *behaving* like a criminal, meaning I don't believe he's ever committed any serious crimes before.'

'What makes you think that?'

'Just the way he conducts himself. The way he speaks. The way he moves. It doesn't scream at me *criminal*.'

181

Sean studied her for a while, but knew exactly what she meant. 'Misguided it is then,' he deduced.

'Maybe,' she answered unconvincingly, 'but he's made several references to being in a war.'

'So?' Sean asked.

'It's possible he believes that, I mean really believes it.'

'And if he does?'

'Then he probably considers his actions, the killing of the first victim and the torture and humiliation of the second, to be necessary and therefore justified, in order to win the war.'

'Then we're back to mad or bad,' Sean argued.

'Are we?' Anna said. 'You know, during the Vietnam War the Americans used to go into villages and vaccinate the children against various diseases, as part of their hearts and minds campaign. When the North Vietnamese arrived in the same village the first thing they'd do would be to cut off the vaccinated arms of the children, not because they wanted to harm them, but to send a message to the Americans that they would stop at nothing to win the war. The men who did this were normal men who'd become soldiers – men with families and children of their own. Were they all mad or bad, or were they just determined, with so much belief that their cause was right that they were prepared to do anything to win?'

'That was different,' Sean answered weakly.

'Not to our man. To him it's exactly the same thing.'

'Maybe, but will he stop?'

'Like the Vietnamese, maybe he'll stop when the war is over.'

'Great,' Sean told her. 'And this invitation from *The World* – will he do it?'

'If he's as much about communication as I think he is then I'd expect him to do it.'

'But not hurt Jackson?'

'No. I'd be surprised if Jackson became a victim. He's too valuable an asset.'

'Uhmm,' Sean grunted, leaning back in his chair as he considered Anna's observations. 'Could his need to communicate with as many people as possible be about ego?' he asked.

'Ego?' Anna asked, a little confused. 'In what way?'

'In any way.'

'Well, I suppose possibly, if he's lost his job, maybe his business or home, it would be a blow to his ego, particularly if he's a male and we're fairly certain he is. So yes, feeling he has a huge audience hanging on his every word may very well be his subconscious effort to repair his damaged ego.'

'Wasn't exactly what I was thinking,' Sean told her without sharing his own stirring thoughts further.

'Then what were you thinking?'

'I'm thinking there has to be a connection between the victims.'

'Sally said there isn't,' Anna reminded him. 'She looked into it and, other than they both work in the City, there's nothing there.'

'Then we're missing something. Not going deep enough into their backgrounds.'

'If he's a disgruntled member of the public who's suffered because of the banking crisis then the fact they both worked in the City could be enough.'

'I'm not so sure,' Sean admitted. 'I think there could be something else. I just don't know what.'

'And this is related to you asking about his *ego*?' Anna asked. 'What's going through that complicated mind of yours?'

He rubbed his face with both hands trying to make sense of his own questions, but the pieces of the puzzle were still too random, floating in his mind like snow – snow that melts as soon as it falls to the ground.

'I don't know,' he confessed. 'Not yet.' His mobile phone buzzed on his desk, distracting them both. Sean read the text message and raised his eyebrows.

183

'Problem?' Anna asked

'No,' he answered a little sheepishly. 'Just Kate reminding me we're supposed to be meeting some friends for dinner tonight.'

'You have friends?' Anna asked only half jokingly.

'Kate's, not mine,' he answered a little too quickly, causing a moment of awkward silence between them. Sean shuffled the reports on his desk, names of white van owners who various members of the public had decided were the Your View Killer.

'Want to help me pick a winner?' he asked.

She pulled up a chair and sat opposite him, pulling a pile of the reports towards herself. 'Why not?'

After he'd dropped Jackson back at the car park, he returned to the white room. He'd been careful enough to check his mirrors from time to time, but he was already sure he wasn't being followed. Jackson had come alone – greedy for the story – greedy for the exclusivity. He continued to think of Jackson while he prepared his technical equipment for the next broadcast, ensuring the cameras could be operated remotely, checking the newly installed motion sensors were working correctly.

Despite Jackson keeping his word and coming alone, he still didn't trust him. How could he? He was a journalist, making his living reporting on the suffering of others. But he had no choice but to deal with him. It was one more thing he simply had to do to keep the public on his side and the police off balance.

The police, he thought to himself. *What did he know about the police who were hunting him? Not enough*, he decided and immediately logged on to his personal laptop – not the one he used for his broadcasts. He looked up his own case, reading through various online newspaper articles, quickly discovering that his crimes were being investigated by the Special

184

Investigations Unit. He continued to search through the stories, many mentioning an Assistant Commissioner Addis and a Detective Superintendent Featherstone, but they held little interest for him: he knew enough about the police to know they would just be the front men, the bureaucrats. What he needed to find out was who was actually *investigating* him. *Hunting* him.

Inevitably he turned to the article written by Jackson. If anyone had cut to the core of the Special Investigations Unit then he had to admit it would probably have been Jackson. Within a few minutes of reading through his coverage of the Your View Killer case he had the name he was looking for. Detective Inspector Corrigan. But why no pictures? Did he have a past to hide, or wasn't he interested in nurturing a high profile to use as a tool to climb the ranks? Maybe a bit of both, he decided. But in that case, if he'd been entrusted to head up the Special Investigations Unit, it meant Detective Inspector Corrigan was interested in only one thing – hunting down his man.

Jackson had thoughtfully mentioned other recent cases DI Corrigan had been involved in: Sebastian Gibran, Thomas Keller, Douglas Allen, all names vaguely familiar to him from things he'd heard or seen on the news, but nothing more. The exploits of madmen held no interest for him, but Corrigan . . .

He entered the names of the previous cases into the laptop and commanded the Internet to search for them, the hundreds of thousands of hits immediately coming back to him as he selected the most informative-looking site and read about the men DI Corrigan had already hunted down and locked away: a motiveless sociopathic killer, a psychopathic rapist and murderer from a predictably abused childhood and, last but not least, a schizophrenic who apparently heard the voice of his dead wife telling him to abduct children from their beds. They were nothing, he decided. Easy prey for a man like

185

DI Corrigan. Whereas he, he was the voice of the people – little less than an avenging angel come to punish the rich and greedy. The public had wanted these other men found and punished, but not him. If they wanted him, first they would have to fight their way past his growing army. He smiled to himself. He'd never given any consideration to what type of man would be sent to hunt him. The realization it was an obsessive made him feel suddenly a little uncomfortable. But he wasn't afraid of DI Corrigan. He leaned back and stared at the ceiling for a while, a slight smile spreading across his lips as he considered his preconceived plan – his idea to keep the police where he could see them. When the time was right he'd lead them directly to where he needed them to be. And now the police had a face, the face of Detective Inspector Corrigan – a hunter of men.

Sean was still in his office with Anna reading through the seemingly endless files of potential Your View Killers. They'd long since dismissed suspects suggested by members of public because they didn't like the look of the man down the street who owned a white van, or the builder they'd used who owned a white van, who did a terrible job of their extension. Hours wasted on other people's petty vendettas. Now they were focusing on real suspects – people with cautions and convictions for threatening banks and bankers. Some had threatened arson, physical violence or even death, others simply revenge and retribution. All were potentially dangerous in their own right, but none leapt from the pages and shot Sean between the eyes with a crystal-clear bullet of purpose. None made his heart race as soon as he began to read their background, although some were so clearly disturbed, so full of hate and loathing, that they couldn't be completely discounted. A number of them clearly saw themselves as avenging angels. But Sean was becoming increasingly convinced the man he hunted had never come to police

186

notice before, at least not for attacking or threatening bankers or banks. The man he hunted had been keeping his powder dry, playing the long game – the patient game – and, as he knew all too well, patient killers were the ones who didn't want to be caught . . . ever.

He looked up from the files and tried to rub the stiffness out of his neck. 'Found anything interesting?' he asked Anna.

'There's some real hatred here,' she answered, glad of the chance to take a break from reading, 'and hatred is a powerful motivator. But there's not enough in these reports for me to properly profile them. Without seeing their psychiatric reports, those that have them, or transcripts of interviews, I can't narrow much down.'

'I'll get them for you,' Sean promised before being distracted by DC Bishop walking past his office. 'DC Bishop,' he called out, stopping him mid-stride.

'Yes, guv'nor?'

'Any luck on tracing where this joker's broadcasting from?'

'No,' Bishop replied. 'Nothing more since last time he went online.'

'Can't you speed things up?' Sean asked impatiently. 'You're still our best hope of finding him.'

'I'm trying, guv'nor, but we just don't have the equipment to do it any faster. We're not the CIA.'

'Then get hold of the CIA,' Sean told him. 'Call the American Embassy and see if they can help, or anybody else for that matter.'

'Really?' Bishop asked, unsure if Sean was being entirely serious.

'Yes,' Sean answered. 'Really.'

'OK,' Bishop agreed and moved to walk away before Sean stopped him again.

'Wait a minute,' Sean demanded. 'Why aren't you monitoring Your View?'

'I don't have to,' Bishop explained. 'I've flagged the website. If our man comes on it'll automatically send a text to my iPhone and I'll log on and watch it.'

Technology, Sean thought to himself, shaking his head. 'Fine,' he dismissed Bishop. 'Anything happens, let me know immediately.'

'No problem,' Bishop assured him in his Birmingham accent and wandered off just as Sally appeared at Sean's door.

'Boss,' she told him. 'I've got our first victim's work on the phone, wanting an update on the investigation.'

'Paul Elkins's work?' Sean asked with surprise. 'Jesus. They'll get an update when it's safe and proper to give them one. What's the matter with these people? They think they have the right to know everything.'

'Georgina Vaughan's family and work have been on the phone too,' Sally informed him. 'All wanting to know what's happening – what we're doing – how close we are to catching the Your View Killer.'

'Christ,' Sean said, shaking his head. 'Palm them off for me, will you, Sally. Tell them we're making good progress, but it's all confidential – we'll update them when we can.'

'No problem,' she told him and spun away from the door, immediately being replaced by DC Jesson.

'What now?' Sean snapped, impatient to get back to his own thoughts, to clear his mind of the detritus of the investigation and interference of outsiders – to give himself the clarity of thought that could lead him all the way to the suspect's front door.

'Geoff Jackson from *The World* newspaper on the blower for you, guv'nor,' Jesson answered.

Sean felt a little surge of excitement, sensing Jackson was about to tell him something important. 'OK,' he told Jesson. 'Put him through.' Jesson hurried back to his desk to transfer the call.

'Your journalist friend?' Anna asked.

'Not a friend,' Sean had time to tell her before the phone on his desk started chirping. He snatched it up. 'DI Corrigan.'

'Detective Inspector Corrigan,' Jackson began. 'Just a courtesy call really – to let you know I met with the Your View Killer, or as he now wants to be known, The Jackdaw.'

Sean was pretty sure he knew whose idea the change of name had been. 'Damn it, Jackson,' he exploded. 'If he contacted you, you were supposed to inform us immediately. You don't know anything about this man. He's dangerous. I've got enough to do without having to investigate the murder of a bloody journalist.'

'Relax,' Jackson told him. 'Clearly I know more about him than you give me credit for.'

'How so?'

'I'm still alive, aren't I?' Jackson almost bragged.

'More by luck than judgement,' Sean answered.

'Whatever.'

'We could have used this,' Sean explained. 'If you'd arranged to meet him we could have tailed you and taken him out.'

'It's not my job to catch him,' Jackson laughed, 'or to help you catch him. My job's to report and that's what I'm doing.'

'Any notes you made, any recordings, anything and everything you remember, I want it all, Jackson,' Sean insisted.

'No can do,' Jackson mocked him. 'Journalistic privilege, remember? You want it, you need a production order and good luck with that.'

'Don't play around with me,' Sean warned him, his voice serious enough to momentarily silence Jackson. 'We need to meet. I need to know everything you learnt – off the record if you want, but I need to know.'

'Fine,' Jackson relented, 'but not yet, although there is something you need to hear right now.'

'I'm listening.'

'He told me . . . he told me to keep watching Your View. Said something was going to happen real soon.'

'Like what?' Sean asked.

'I don't know, although I'm sure we can both guess what he meant. I've done for you, Inspector, now you need to do for me.' Jackson hung up.

'Shit,' Sean swore, forgetting Anna was there.

'Problem?' she asked.

'When is there ever not?' he replied before his mobile started vibrating, distracting him. He read the message and swore again. It was another reminder from Kate about dinner that evening. 'Shit.'

'And yet another problem?' Anna enquired.

Sean pushed deeper into his uncomfortable chair. 'No,' he told her. 'Nothing I can't handle.'

Detective Superintendent Featherstone sat in one of the front rows of the lecture theatre at Scotland Yard, his hands tired from applauding the parade of lower ranking officers marching to the slightly raised stage where Assistant Commissioner Addis was presenting them with commendations for everything ranging from bravery to detective ability. Featherstone couldn't wait to get the whole ceremony over, grab a pint at a little pub he knew close to the Yard and then escape back to Shooter's Hill police station, away from prying eyes. He watched Addis hand out the last of the awards, smiling his crocodile smile and reminding Featherstone of just how much he wished he'd never met him in the first place.

The ceremony over, everybody slipped out of the theatre and into the large function area just outside, past the portraits painted in oil of previous commissioners. Featherstone was in no doubt that one day Addis's picture would be amongst them. He tried to avoid catching Addis's eye as he hurriedly congratulated his own detectives who'd been awarded commendations and began to look for an exit strategy, but

190

somehow, like a panther in the night, Addis was suddenly on top of him.

'Alan,' Addis ambushed him, almost making him drop his cup of unwanted tea. 'Here to show solidarity with your hard-working officers?'

Featherstone looked around at the detectives he'd been congratulating, all of whose eyes were firmly fixed on him, all of whom he knew would be thinking the same thing: *Rather you than me, sir.*

'Something like that, Assistant Commissioner,' Featherstone replied, the frustration at being captured before he could escape gnawing at him.

'Good. Good,' Addis told him, having not listened to his answer. 'And are any of these officers part of DI Corrigan's team?' he asked, making Featherstone even more concerned. 'Anyone part of the Special Investigations Unit?'

'No, sir,' Featherstone answered. 'They're all attached to other southeast London murder teams I look after.'

'I see,' Addis told them. 'Well never mind. A quick word, if you don't mind, Alan.' Featherstone's blood ran cold as he followed him to a quieter corner of the function room where Addis wasted no time in getting to the point. 'So, tell me, how's the Your View investigation coming along? Has Corrigan come up with any useful *insights* as to how we're going to catch this lunatic?'

'Nothing particular that I know of,' Featherstone confessed. 'I'm sure you know as much about the investigation as I do.'

'Come, come,' Addis disagreed. 'I know what you detectives are like – never too keen to share everything with us wooden-tops, eh? Is there anything going on that I don't know about, that I should know about?'

Featherstone could almost feel Addis's eyes cutting into his soul, reading his innermost thoughts, secrets and fears.

'Not that I'm aware of,' he answered truthfully, glad that if Sean was up to something he hadn't shared it with him.

191

What he didn't know he couldn't betray. 'But it's early days and not much to go on yet,' he said, trying to throw Addis off whatever scent he was following.

'I'm not sure I entirely agree with your assessment,' Addis told him, making him swallow hard. 'Two victims. Two broadcasts. CCTV footage of the suspect's van and, unless I misunderstand, at least two eyewitnesses. Seems to me there's quite a lot to be getting on with.'

'And we are, sir,' Featherstone tried, 'but you have to understand this is a very difficult investigation and—'

'I don't have to understand anything,' Addis hissed across him, 'but what *you* need to understand is that this case has the highest of profiles. People in the City are growing increasingly alarmed at our failure to bring this matter to a close, and that's beginning to cost the economy money, Alan – lots of money. And that makes the politicians worried and that's when they beat a path to my door, with their unrealistic demands and petty threats, but still . . . they have a point.'

'I understand,' Featherstone told him, desperate to conclude their business and be on his way.

'I hope you do,' Addis added quickly, 'because I've already protected DI Corrigan more than you could imagine – given him every support, but . . .' He left his unfinished statement hanging in the air.

'I'll speak with him,' Featherstone assured him. 'Make sure he understands the urgency of the situation.'

'You do that,' Addis added threateningly, 'and make sure he knows I created the Special Investigations Unit for my purposes, not for his.'

Sean paced around the perimeter of the small car park in South Park from where Georgina Vaughan had been abducted. Despite being a stone's throw from the King's Road it was remarkably peaceful, just far enough off the beaten track to be forgotten. As he walked he tried to imagine what it would be like at dusk, the time when she was taken – the time when a small green oasis could quickly turn into an intimidating forest, the sound of the leaves in the breeze drowning out any warning sounds of approaching danger, the shadows hiding lurking violence – just as it had for Georgina.

He reached the tree the killer had stepped out from behind and paused, staring at the trunk as if for invisible clues, trying to place the man he hunted there, trying to see him for himself, but nothing came – nothing anyone else wouldn't have been able to see.

'Come on,' he whispered to himself. 'Get it together. Think. Think.' He scanned the park: a large central area of grass surrounded by mature trees and a path Georgina Vaughan would have jogged around – just the sort of location he'd expect a madman or rapist to stalk. But an avenging man of the people?

Is that all you really are? he asked himself. *A madman? A murdering madman who can't accept what you really are, so you give yourself a cause to justify your need to kill?*

He wasn't so sure, but the park reminded him of so many scenes of rape and murder he'd been called to, going right the way back to his first ever murder investigation in Putney Heath – the one Anna had been so interested in. It had become his life: violence, murder, victims with their lives torn away by people who were more often than not tragic figures themselves. Was he becoming the final victim in the desperate triangle, consumed by his job as his wife drifted away from him and his children grew up without him? He thought of Kate and his two girls and then he thought of Anna and was left feeling mournful and displaced. He pulled the sides of his thin raincoat together against the early spring chill and walked to the edge of the grass area, allowing the fresh breeze to clear his mind.

He considered the evidence from the scene, such as it was – some indistinct footprints, some drag marks where the

193

victim had resisted and *possible* tyre marks, although even if they did come from the abductor's van, they were nothing unusual. If he was going to find The Jackdaw he would have to rely on evidence of another kind. Evidence of the mind.

No matter what this killer thought of himself, he was a serial offender and therefore he'd have a pattern, following predetermined psychological rules that he probably didn't even know existed. But Sean did. He knew them all too well. *You're nothing special*, he tried to convince himself. *You'll make the same mistakes they all do – your kind.* He took another sweeping look around the park. *And your kind like to stick to areas they know well, so they can feel safe.* He could just about make out some of the houses that ringed the park, tall terraced houses, well maintained, some undergoing loft extensions – all the homes of the wealthy. *This is the King's Road*, he continued the conversation with himself, *where the rich and privileged live and play, so how come you're so comfortable here? Why did you choose this place? Not the sort of place the avenger of working people would know to the point of being comfortable here, not even the sort of place they'd know about, unless they'd worked here, or spent weeks watching their victim here or, or, or . . .*

'Fuck it,' he cursed loudly enough to be heard by a passing cyclist who gave him a wide berth.

There was nothing here for him. He'd have park employees checked over once more, but his instinct already told him it was a dead lead. He slid his hands in his pockets and headed back to his car feeling like he was on a different planet to everyone else. Despite the lack of any new evidence, he felt that the dam had begun to show its first cracks – invisible to the naked eye, but there nonetheless. *Patience*, he told himself. He knew not to even try to work out what his mind had discovered, not yet. It was too early to make sense of what was little more than a feeling. Just keep punching at the dam, over and over, until suddenly the invisible cracks turned to seeping wounds as more and more water gushed through, the bricks tumbling away faster and faster, until the puzzle that seemed so difficult became so blindingly obvious he would chastise himself for having not seen it earlier. If he could just get into this one's mind, start to think like him then soon the dam would collapse.

Donnelly and Featherstone sat tucked away in the corner of the Prince of Wales pub in Wilton Street, Victoria – far enough from the Yard to prevent it becoming a police pub, but close enough to the train station for it to be a convenient place for a drink before heading home or, in Featherstone's case, back to southeast London. They lifted their full pint glasses and chinked them together with a subdued 'Cheers.'

'Thanks for meeting me,' Featherstone told Donnelly. 'Thought it would do us both good to catch up over a pint.'

'No problem.' Donnelly assured him, before sipping his drink. 'Any reason to get out of the Yard for a bit is a good reason.'

'Life at the Yard not suiting you, then?' Featherstone grinned.

'Feel like I'm living under a microscope.'

'I know what you mean,' Featherstone agreed. 'Uniform top-brass can make you feel that way.' He shook the image of Addis away before it ruined the taste of his beer.

'Aye. You're not wrong. How did I ever end up there?' Donnelly asked, shaking his head with bewilderment at his situation.

'I could get you out, if you want?' Featherstone offered. 'But it'll mean leaving the Special Investigations Unit. I could get you on one of the MITs closer to home.'

'Nah,' Donnelly dismissed it and took a mouthful of drink. 'The travelling and the Yard's a pain in the arse, but the work and the team suit me fine. I'm not sure I could go back to investigating domestic murders and gang bangers now. It'd bore me to tears.'

'Very well,' Featherstone told him, 'but if you change your mind . . .' He let the offer hang.

'Aye. Thanks anyway.'

'Speaking of your team,' Featherstone shifted gears, 'how's Sally doing?'

'Sally?' Donnelly asked, sounding surprised Featherstone would even ask. 'She's fine. No problems. Back to her old self. She's a tough one, that hen.'

'Good,' Featherstone told him, sounding pleased. 'And DI Corrigan?'

'Corrigan? He's fine. Still one of the best I've worked with and I've worked with a few. It's the investigation that's a bitch, but we'll get there – eventually.'

'But you're making progress?' Featherstone asked.

'As much as we can,' Donnelly assured him. 'Although we've got the Douglas Allen trial started today, so we'll no doubt be up and down to the Bailey while we're trying to sort this new one out. Could slow things down a little.'

'I hope not,' Featherstone told him, deliberately not hiding the concern in his voice.

'Oh.' Donnelly picked up on it. 'Problem?'

'Just the aforementioned uniform top-brass – Addis in particular. They're getting twitchy for a result.'

'We all want a result,' Donnelly reminded him.

'Yeah, but for different reasons,' Featherstone pointed out.

'Go on,' Donnelly encouraged him.

'Apparently your boy's costing the City millions in absenteeism and that's got the politicians worried and they in turn have got the brass worried. They won't let this investigation turn into an open-ended book,' he warned Donnelly. 'If Corrigan can't get it done they'll find someone who can.'

'If Corrigan can't get it done quickly then no one can.'

'That's as may be,' Featherstone told him, 'but these aren't detectives we're dealing with – they're politicians in police uniforms. Don't expect them to be fair and understanding.

They play a short game of media-friendly results. They're not interested in long drawn-out investigations. Know what I'm saying?'

Donnelly nodded his head slowly. 'Aye. I know what you're saying.'

'Then you'll also know that I have Corrigan and your team's best interests at heart. But if I'm to protect him from the likes of Addis, I need to know what's going on before he does.'

'And you're telling me this why?'

'Because I need someone I can trust keeping an eye on things for me,' Featherstone explained. 'Someone who'll let me know if Sean's struggling with the investigation, or anything else for that matter.'

'Meaning?'

'Come on, Dave. You know as well as I do that Corrigan sails bloody close to the wind sometimes. Maybe a little too close.'

'So,' Donnelly cut to it, 'you want me to keep an eye on him. Let you know if anything's going pear-shaped.'

'Exactly,' Featherstone told him. 'So I can protect him. Protect the whole team. We're detectives, Dave. We need to stick together.'

'I understand,' Donnelly answered, nodding sagely.

'Good,' Featherstone said with a smile. 'Now finish your pint and let me get you another.'

Quickly and quietly he moved about the white room preparing everything for his next defendant. He wore his usual black overalls, with the ski-mask rolled up so it looked like a small woollen hat. His voice-altering device was lying on the table next to the various laptops and hardware. He felt safe and relaxed, until he thought he detected the sound of an approaching car engine coming towards the derelict building along the dirt road – the sound making him freeze on the spot, his head cocked slightly to one side as he strained to tell if it was getting closer or fading away. After a couple of seconds he knew beyond doubt – it was getting closer.

It had only ever happened once before, weeks ago when he was still preparing the room inside the building he'd found that seemed so perfect for his needs. On that occasion he'd watched from a window, peeking through a small circular gap in the dirt he'd hurriedly made as the car parked no more than thirty feet from the building, but for the entire time it was there no one got out. Instead he heard a man's voice and a woman giggling. Young lovers with nowhere to go, or an unfaithful couple with the same problem. No threat to him. After an hour it had left. Was this the same couple returning after all these weeks, driven back to his domain by illicit lust?

As the sound of the car drew ever closer he turned off the generator, sending the room into darkness, before hurrying to the same window, peeling back the covering bin liner and staring out through the same hole in the greased smeared glass. His eyes zeroed in on the vehicle as it came into view, expecting the same car as before to roll to a stop and the giggling to begin, but his already pounding heart froze as the blue and yellow markings of a police car became clear. He instantly ducked away from the window and rolled his ski-mask down to better hide amongst the shadows, before slowly returning to the spyhole, the sight of the police car parking only feet from the entrance making him want to recoil, to run and hide. But he needed to see them. Needed to watch them.

He struggled to control his rapid breathing, glancing over his shoulder at the table laden with the most damning of evidence, before the sound of car doors slamming made him look back. There were two of them, both men, of about the same size and age, young and strong looking, acting casually and confident, looking all around and talking to each other, although he couldn't make out what they were saying. Occasionally their radios would crackle into life, but again he couldn't hear what was being said. Did they already know he was there? Had they been sent to take him down? No. There weren't enough of them and they were both in uniform and acting too casually – not on edge enough. Maybe they were just searching for vandals or local drug users looking for some privacy. No, he decided. They might not know he was there, but they were looking for him, of that he was sure – checking possible buildings where he could be broadcasting from. He'd accepted that this particular white room could be discovered by the police before he'd completed his quest, but it hadn't concerned him – he could simply move to another location and begin again. But he'd never expected to be unlucky enough to be present when the room was found. The spy camera he'd concealed in the old air vent would have alerted him to their presence, saving him from walking into a trap, but now he was cornered anyway – like a rat surrounded by feral cats which circled ever closer.

At least they hadn't spotted the van. It was close by, but well hidden, even from helicopters searching from above. They were still heading towards him, making him once more look over his shoulder at the equipment laid out on the table, as damning as any dead body. A dozen unbelievable and irrational excuses he could give them flashed through his mind but he realized there was no way he could talk his way past them. He looked from the window again and saw they'd reached the building and were already peering through the ground-floor windows, working their way towards the main entrance he'd left unsecured. He cursed himself for having not brought a padlock to lock it from the inside with. Perhaps that would have been enough to deter police who came half-heartedly snooping around, but without it surely they would come inside.

He felt like a hunted animal, trapped in a rat-hole, a fox

cornered in a riverbed, surrounded by a pack of dogs, and he hated it. Hated the feeling of fear – the feeling of not being in control – the feeling of weakness – all the things he'd felt on the day when his life changed forever. The day he'd sworn to make those who had made him suffer pay for what they'd done. Pay for his humiliation.

He looked down from the steep angle as one of the policemen tried the front door before speaking to the other one. 'It's open,' he heard him say.

'Probably being used by some homeless crack-head,' his partner replied.

'Still,' the one by the door called back. 'We'd better take a look around.'

'Why not?' the less enthusiastic one agreed.

He ducked under the window and moved deeper into the white room, carefully and quietly lifting the sawn-off shotgun from the table as he listened to the sounds coming from below – footsteps and voices echoing around the empty building that had long ago been used by the electricity board as a training centre before cut-backs caused its abandonment.

He looked at the shotgun in his hands as the footsteps moved to the staircase and climbed towards him. What choice did he have? He'd ambush them as they entered the room – a shot for each of them. If he cleaned out the room and torched the building no one would ever know the murders were committed by The Jackdaw. But if it was even suggested they could have been, he would lose all public sympathy. People had to believe in The Jackdaw, or it would all be for nothing.

No. He would wait in the darkest corner of the room. If they entered he'd take them by surprise, strip them of their radios and other equipment before marching them into the woods where he'd secure them to a tree with their own handcuffs before clearing out the white room and setting it on fire. He'd contact the journalist and let him know where

200

the police could be found. The Jackdaw's battle was not with hard-working police officers who'd suffered as much as anyone during the banking crisis. His battle was with the rich and greedy. Within a few days he'd find a new building and The Jackdaw would return. He walked to the far corner of the room as if through a minefield, crouching down, back against the wall, gun pointing towards the door and then he waited. Waited for the unlocked door to open.

The footsteps on the stairs grew louder and louder, getting closer and closer – the occasional exchange of words becoming clearer and clearer until he could understand everything they were saying as they moved along the corridor kicking and pushing doors open, confirming to each other they were empty. Surely it would be the door he was pointing the shotgun at that was next to fly and bang open. He tightened his grip and braced himself, but the next sound he heard wasn't the sound of the door smashing open, it was the sound of splintering wood, cursing and laughter coming from the corridor. His eyes were wide and wild, staring from the holes in the black ski-mask, trying to make sense of what he was listening to – more cursing, more laughter and then the footsteps again, only this time they were moving away from his door, heading back down the stairs and towards the exit until the voices were once more coming from outside.

He quickly scrambled to his feet and rushed to the same window, staring down in disbelief as the policemen walked back towards their car – one laughing and one limping – the mystery of what could have happened making his head hurt with bizarre possibilities as he watched them climb into their car and slowly drive away until they were eventually out of sight and the engine noise nothing but a memory.

He breathed for what seemed like the first time since he'd heard the car approaching, his lips curling into a smile under the ski-mask that he promptly ripped off his head, the cool air exhilarating against his hot, sweating skin, his smile turning to a quiet laugh of relief. *Why had they left before checking the entire building?* He gave himself a few minutes for his ragged nerves to settle and to be sure the police wouldn't return before he dared to venture from the white room, collecting his torch from the table and pulling the door slowly open. He paused in the doorway, shining the beam from the torch along the corridor, searching for any unseen foe hiding in the shadows until he was sure there were none.

He ventured into the corridor, the cone of light sweeping one way and then the other until it fell upon the cause of their retreat: a broken, rotting floorboard the one who'd cursed had seemingly put his foot through. He examined it more closely with the torch and found a few small shreds of dark material. Pieces of the unfortunate policeman's trousers? His broad smile returned, all fear swept away. It appeared luck was with The Jackdaw. Near disaster had quickly turned to his advantage. To save face and avoid a return visit to the treacherous floorboards, the two policemen would no doubt report that they'd searched the building and that it was empty. It would be crossed off the list of buildings to be searched – eliminated from their inquiries. The building was now a complete safe haven. He didn't have to worry about the police finding the white room again – until he wanted them to. He walked back to the room and sat in the chair he kept for the defendants and began to gather his thoughts. He had much to do. Much to prepare.

9

Sean arrived at the expensive-looking Italian restaurant close to London Bridge and stood on the opposite side of the street, watching people coming and going. He was already late, but needed a few minutes alone before entering, trying to become a *normal* person before crossing the road, even if it was just for one night.

'Shit,' he whispered to himself. He knew he didn't have time for this – for dinner with Kate and her *normal* friends. The killer was moving fast and with it the investigation was growing bigger all the time and he was already struggling to keep up. Scenes, witnesses, CCTV, forensic submissions, the endless chasing down of existing leads that only led to more leads was already beginning to swamp them. He needed the Your View Killer to slow down and he needed to be at his desk or stalking one of the crime scenes trying to become the man he needed to find and stop – anything but dinner with a bunch of civilians. But he couldn't let Kate down again and hope to get away with it. Over the last couple of years he'd done little other than disappoint her – the job threatening to finally overtake and drown him. He'd seen enough detectives drift into divorces to know he had to give her something – even if it was just dinner with her friends.

Just walk in, he told himself. *Just walk in, kiss Kate, smile, shake hands and if absolutely necessary double-kiss the other women on their cheeks. Don't look them up and down like they're suspects. Get it over with and get back to work.* He looked at the name of the restaurant: Il Forno. *What the fuck did that mean?* No doubt Kate's friends would all know. He decided his metamorphosis into a normal person was never going to happen, so swallowed a sick feeling and dodged the traffic as he crossed the road, taking one last deep breath before pushing the door open and walking inside where he was immediately met by an Italian-looking man in his thirties wearing a suit that looked like it cost a month of Sean's wages. He got the distinct impression the man's eyes were telling him he didn't look like he belonged in Il Forno.

'Can I help you, sir?' he asked in what sounded like a genuine Italian accent.

'I'm here to meet my wife and some other people,' Sean explained. 'Kate Corrigan.'

'Ah, yes,' the man acknowledged with a smile. 'May I take your coat?'

Sean thought for a second, trying to remember if he had anything in his coat pockets that he could neither leave there nor empty out in the entrance to a crowded restaurant. He was pretty sure most of his everyday cop things, his warrant card, his phone, his telescopic truncheon, had already been transferred to his jacket or clipped to his waistband.

'Yeah, sure,' he told the man, slipping his coat off and handing it over.

'This way, please,' the man told him and headed off across the restaurant, leading him to a table he heard before he saw. 'This is your table, I think,' the man told him, pulling out a chair for Sean to sit.

'Yes. Thank you,' Sean answered, looking at the slightly uncomfortable half-smiles on the faces of the people who

204

stared up at him: James and Kerry, old university friends of Kate's, now married with one child. Chris and Sally, Chris being a fellow doctor from Guy's Hospital, Sally his long-term partner. No kids. Leon, the Polish doctor and his doctor wife, Sophie. Married with two children. And then there was Kate who was barely smiling at all.

'You're a bit late,' she pointed out, trying to sound casual.

'Sorry,' he told her, sitting in the seat the man offered, feeling it being pushed into the backs of his legs, making him forget all about the handshakes and kisses he'd rehearsed in his mind. 'Got stuck at work.'

'Just for a change,' Kate added loud enough for everyone to hear. Sean tried to let it go.

'Can't expect London's finest to drop everything just for dinner,' James, Sean's least favourite of the people gathered, joined in. 'Isn't that right, Sean?'

'I guess,' he answered without looking at him.

'So what important case are you working on at the moment?' Chris asked.

'Sorry,' Sean tried to finish the conversation, hoping for once they'd all get back to talking about things he neither knew nor cared about – just so long as he wasn't at the centre of it. 'It's confidential.' He turned to Kate before anyone else could speak to him. 'How long you been here for?'

'About forty-five minutes,' she answered. 'Which is how long you should have been here for too.' He looked down at his clamped hands and said nothing, hoping she'd move on. 'D'you want a drink?' she finally asked.

'Yeah, sure,' he answered. Maybe alcohol would make everything a little more bearable.

'Red wine?' she offered, reaching for a bottle.

'That'll be fine,' he agreed, watching Kate pour the blood-coloured drink into an oversized glass. As soon as she'd finished he took a large swig, but the lack of an alcohol kick was immediately disappointing.

'Nice to see you anyway, Sean.' Leon appeared to be trying to help him.

'You too,' he answered without feeling.

'Well it's certainly been a long time,' Kerry joined in.

'Too long,' James added with a sarcastic smile.

Sean smiled unconvincingly for about a second before grabbing a passing waiter. 'Can you get me a Jack Daniel's?' Sean asked him before he could speak. The waiter nodded once and disappeared.

Kate leaned closer to him as the others began to talk amongst themselves again. 'It's a little early for that, isn't it?'

'Just catching up with you guys,' he explained.

'This is the first drink we've had,' Kate told him. 'We were waiting for you to get here.'

'Then you shouldn't have,' Sean snapped back in little more than a whisper before James piped up again.

'What do you think of this Your View Killer, Sean? He seems to be the talk of the town.'

'I think he's a loser and a coward,' Sean answered, looking hard into James's eyes. 'Just like they all are, at the end of the day.'

'But he has popular support, right?' Chris joined in, the attention now squarely back on Sean.

'Media crap,' he told them, thinking of Jackson. Wait until they saw the newspapers tomorrow, with Jackson's one-on-one interview splashed all over the front cover. 'Don't believe what the papers tell you.'

'So you're involved in the investigation?' James accused him with a satisfied smile.

'I didn't say that,' he replied. 'Just telling you what I think.'

'But you know details of the investigation?' James insisted.

'No,' Sean lied, 'but if I did I wouldn't be able to tell anyone.'

'What's the point of having a policeman as a friend if he

won't spill a few juicy details now and then,' James told the group.

'I'm not your . . .' Sean managed to stop himself before he said 'friend'. 'I don't know anything more than you do.'

'No great loss to the world, a few bankers,' Sophie added.

'They have families,' Sean reminded her. 'The first victim had a wife and children.' The table fell quiet for a while until he was rescued by the waiter bringing him his bourbon. He drank half of it immediately, enjoying the sensation until he felt Kate's gaze. 'What?' he asked her. She just handed him a menu and he pretended to be reading while the others inevitably began to chat about medical matters and Guy's Hospital. But other voices were now invading his mental space, loud and obnoxious – yet he seemed to be the only one to notice. He took another mouthful of bourbon and tried to ignore the noise coming from behind him, but it was no good – unless the voices stopped he'd be distracted all night, even more than he already was.

'Anything grab your fancy?' Kate asked, but he barely heard her.

'Sorry?' he asked.

'On the menu,' she told him. 'The menu you've been staring at for the last few minutes.'

'Yeah, sure,' he lied as the voices kept boring into him. 'It all looks good.'

'Then cheer up and relax,' she encouraged him. 'Who knows, you might even have a nice time.' Her words only added to his increasing irritation – reminded him all the more of how different he was to everyone else sitting around the table, probably everyone else in the restaurant. And still the voices pounded in his head, making him look over his shoulder to find the source of his annoyance: four well-dressed men in their forties, although they were beginning to look a little dishevelled, with their jackets slung over the backs of their chairs and their ties loosened – all wearing belts and brightly coloured braces. Several bottles of wine adorned their table and each had a glass just like Sean's in front of him containing a golden-coloured liquid. Their lascivious laughter grew louder as one of them accosted a passing young waitress, holding her by the forearm and inviting her to sit on his lap. Her smile was full of fear and embarrassment as she tried to pull away, but was held firm. One of the male waiters quickly came to her aid, bowing and smiling, trying to cajole the man into releasing her, but his appeals were only met with a torrent of abuse, much to the amusement of the other men. Sean could tolerate it no more. One thing he could never stomach was a bully.

'We went to a restaurant in Venice last year called Il Forno, didn't we, Kerry?' James seemed to address him. 'The owner told me what Il Forno means. Obvious really. Do you know what it "Il Forno" means, Sean?'

'No,' Sean told him, pushing his chair away from the table and standing. 'No I don't.' He drained his glass and placed it on the table in front of the bewildered-looking faces. 'If you'll excuse me,' he added before heading off towards the four drunks. When he arrived at their table he just stood in front of them and said nothing – waiting for them to notice him and one by one fall silent.

'Can I help you with something?' the ringleader asked in a fake cockney accent, smiling and looking to his friends for reassurance.

'Let her go,' Sean told him, his pale blue eyes burning with intensity. 'Right now.'

'Or?' the ringleader asked, something about Sean's eyes making his smile fade.

'Let her go,' Sean warned him. 'Before you find out.'

'Listen, mate,' the ringleader told him, 'why don't you fuck off back to your table with your wife and her girlfriends and leave us alone.'

'Why don't you make me?' Sean challenged him. The man

released the waitress but as he tried to get to his feet Sean moved too quickly for him, one hand grabbing him around the throat, twisting and pushing his head forward until it slammed onto the table while his other hand whipped his warrant card from his jacket pocket. Sean flashed it around at the stricken man's friends before holding it close to the face that was still pinned to the table. He released his grip on the man's throat and grabbed him by the hair, lifting his head from the table slightly before banging it back down. 'Police, arsehole.' He turned to the waitress, still keeping the guy pinned to the table. 'Do you want to press assault charges?'

'No,' she shook her head, rubbing her arm. 'Thank you. Maybe they should just leave.'

'You heard her,' he told the silent gang of four. 'Now pay your bill and disappear, and don't forget to leave a tip.' He released the ringleader with one last shove on his head and casually headed back to his table, while the four drunks re-gathered their senses and quickly began to pull on their jackets and ask for the bill.

When Sean returned to his table he sat down as if nothing had happened, turning to Kate who was staring at him open-mouthed. 'What?' he asked with a shrug of his shoulders, but before she could answer he was distracted by his phone vibrating in his chest pocket. He checked the caller ID. It was Sally. He immediately knew something had happened. 'Sally.'

'Guv'nor,' she answered. 'He's on Your View now and it's live. Boss, he's taken another one.'

'Shit,' he cursed, oblivious to the attention he was receiving from the other diners and staff. 'How long?'

'Less than a minute.'

'Who's he got now?'

'A white male in his fifties,' Sally told him. 'We don't know anything else yet.'

'OK. Stay on the phone,' he ordered. 'Have you got your laptop with you?' he asked Kate.

'Yeah,' she answered, shaking her head. 'Why?'

'I need it,' he demanded.

'But—' she tried to argue.

'Now. Please,' he insisted. She shook her head more vigorously, but leaned down by the side of her chair and pulled her laptop from its bag and slid it across the table to Sean. He flipped it open, entered the same password they used for everything and waited less than a second before the screen sprang to life. A few seconds later he was looking at the images on Your View, a man taped to the same chair in the same white room as before. 'Shit,' he swore again and turned the volume to maximum, drawing more looks of despair from Kate and the others. The killer stood next to his victim, his terrible metallic voice preaching as before while the terrified-looking man squirmed and struggled in the chair, a hood still over his head and the tape that Sean assumed was across his mouth turning his pleas to little more than incoherent mumblings.

'What's going on, Sean?' Kate asked, but he just held up a hand to silence her.

'Is Bishop tracing this?' he asked Sally.

'He's on it now,' she assured him. 'The signal seems to be coming from the same general area as before – on the outskirts of southwest London – possibly Surrey.'

'Good,' he told her, turning his full concentration back to the screen as the man in his black ski-mask pointed from the victim to the screen and back again. What wouldn't Sean have given just to see the torturer's eyes – just his eyes . . .

This man no doubt felt he was safe,' the mechanical voice preached, '*retired and living his life of privilege, surrounded by the wealth he'd accumulated after years of stealing and lying to the people – one of the ones who thought they were so smart, getting out of the business before they could ever be held accountable for their crimes. But now you, the people, have a chance to make this thief pay for this injustice – pay for his greed and incompetence.*

While he fled to live in luxury, in his mansion in one of London's most exclusive areas, we struggled to feed our children and keep a roof over their heads. He may look like any other man,' he told his audience, pointing to the victim who was still taped to the chair, *'but don't be fooled. These people are as expert at hiding their guilt as they are the money they stole from us.*

'You may wonder why I have left his face covered and his mouth taped shut. Let me explain: for years his mouth has been used for nothing but telling lies and his eyes for nothing other than deceit. I will not allow him the chance to once again lie to the people through greedy lips or to falsely appeal to you for mercy through deceitful eyes. That is why he will remained hooded and helpless, so he too can feel what it's like to be unable to control what is about to happen to him, just as we were unable to prevent being swept into poverty by his greed and that of others like him. He deserves nothing more than humiliation. But you, the people, deserve to know this criminal's name before you make your judgement. Under this mask hides Jeremy Goldsboro – one-time vice president of King and Melbourn Capital Associates, who now lives off the grotesque amount of money our so-called government gave to his company – money that should have been ours, to educate our children and treat our sick.'

'At least we know the name of the victim now,' Sally told him.

'Find out everything you can about Jeremy Goldsboro,' Sean instructed. 'The phones will probably start ringing off the hooks any minute now anyway.'

'Will do,' Sally assured him.

'How's Bishop doing?' Sean changed tack, just as the restaurant manager appeared at the table.

'Closer and closer,' Sally answered, 'but he's still looking at a hell of a big area.'

'Excuse me, sir,' the manager tried to get his attention, 'but I'm afraid I'm going to have to ask you to turn down or turn off your computer.'

Sean glanced up before looking back at the screen. 'What?'

'Your computer, sir. I'm afraid it's disturbing the other customers.'

Sean slid his warrant card from his pocket and showed it to the manager without looking from the screen. 'This is important police business,' he told him. 'Now go away.'

'You all right?' Sally asked.

'Just civilians,' he dismissed everyone around him, making them look even more uncomfortable, especially Kate, who the manager had turned to out of desperation, not that Sean noticed. 'Wait,' Sean told her. 'What's he saying now?'

It's time for you the people, the jury, to vote. Remember, the balance of your vote dictates the harshness of the criminal's punishment. Be strong, brothers and sisters, for if we're not willing to get blood on our hands then we will never change this corrupt system and we will always be under the heel of our oppressors. And let me warn the police – especially you, Detective Inspector Corrigan – if you try to tamper with the online vote I will know and the thief's punishment will be the most severe. The most severe. Time to vote.'

Sean could hear the victim's awful mumblings as the preacher's words struck new terror into him – terror that would have been even greater if he'd been able to see the garden pruners that the masked man pulled from his trouser pocket and held up for the watching audience to see.

'Jesus, Sean,' Sally told him. 'He's talking to you.'

'I heard,' Sean replied.

'Did he just say your name?' Kate asked, moving closer to better see the screen.

'Don't worry about it,' he tried to reassure her.

'But he said your name,' Kate repeated. 'That means he knows who you are. What else does he know about you, Sean? Where we live? Where I work? Where the kids go to school?'

'He would have seen my name in a paper or something,' he said, Jackson's face flashing in his mind. 'He's just trying to mess with me – playing mind games.'

'Mind games?' Kate asked, increasingly upset. 'He could have followed you, Sean. He could have followed you home.'

'They don't do that,' he promised.

'Maybe this one did?'

He stopped for a second, thinking about the research this one did on each of his victims – *watching them. Following them.*

'You should go home,' he told her. 'Make sure everything's all right. Phone the babysitter and let her know I'm sending someone over to check the house.'

Kate grabbed his face and made him look her in the eyes. 'Tell me, Sean,' she demanded. 'Do I need to be scared here? Should I be afraid?'

'No,' he tried to convince her. 'It's only a precaution because he's mentioned my name. I just want you to know you're safe.'

She let go of him, tears leaking from the sides of her eyes. 'Damn you, Sean,' she said, 'and damn your bloody job.' She grabbed her bag and stormed out of the restaurant without speaking to anyone else.

Sean blew out his cheeks then returned to the screen. 'Sally,' he spoke into the phone.

'Yes, boss?'

'Get someone round to my house as fast as, can you?'

'Already done,' she assured him. 'You seen the votes?'

He looked down at the thumbs up and down icons. Almost two hundred thousand people had voted, with the jury seemingly split down the middle. 'He's not interested in the votes,' he told Sally. 'He's going to kill or maim him no matter what the votes say.'

'The people have voted,' the electronic voice spoke from inside the screen, *'and it is clear a great many of you understand this man's crimes and that he must be punished.'* The man tied to the chair kicked and bucked – his mumblings all the more disturbing for their lack of comprehensibility. The man in the ski-mask was now holding the pruners closer to the

213

camera so that everyone other than the victim could see them. *'His life will be spared, but every time he looks down at his hands as they count the money he stole from us he will be reminded of his crimes.'*

Mark Hudson licked his lips involuntarily when he saw the man in the ski-mask on Your View show the camera the pruners. He imagined the horrendous injuries the instrument could cause – even death.

He heard his mum calling up the stairs. 'Mark. Come and have your tea before it gets cold.'

'Not now, Mum. I'm busy,' he screamed back from his bedroom before muttering, 'Stupid bitch', his full attention immediately back with the image of the dark figure holding the pruners. 'Yeah. Cut his fucking fingers off. Cut his fucking fingers off and make the fucker eat them,' he encouraged with a thin smile, his face now as close to the screen as it could be without losing focus, the sound of the victim's anguished mumblings making the hairs on his skin stand up with excited anticipation. This was even better than throwing cats off the tower block's balconies or stabbing stray dogs. The only thing better than watching it would be doing it himself.

The dark figure turned to his victim and grabbed one of his hands, demanding he unclench his fist, beating on the back of his hand when he did not, threatening him with death unless he did as he was told. When the victim finally relented and uncurled his fingers his torturer grabbed his hand and folded all his fingers away – all except for the little one. Hudson's eyes widened as the masked man placed the finger between the blades of the pruners and began to slowly squeeze them together, the victim's skin and flesh surrendering too easily as the blood flowed over the metal shears, the screams of agony through the tape across the victim's mouth drowning out the sound of the bone being cracked and split. It was everything Hudson had been dreaming about seeing ever since the humiliation and torture of the previous victim had filled his empty life.

'Yes,' he hissed to himself as the severed finger dropped into the masked man's waiting palm.

The muffled screaming gradually subsided, dying into sobs of pain, the man's ordeal apparently over . . . for now. The torturer approached the camera until his head and shoulders alone appeared on the screen, holding up a severed finger for the world to see.

'A small price to pay for the crimes he has committed against the people of this country and beyond. I do this to show that I too can be merciful – can show restraint. I do this to prove to you all that I, we, are better than they can ever be. I also understand the people's need to call me something – to have a name they can rally around. From this moment forward you should call me . . . The Jackdaw.'

Hudson stared wide-eyed, silently mouthing the same words over and over without realizing: *The Jackdaw. The Jackdaw. The Jackdaw.*

Phil Taylor watched as the dark figure held up the severed figure and spoke to the watching thousands about mercy and restraint, but for the first time he was beginning to feel very uncomfortable even just watching the man who now called himself The Jackdaw. There was something about the victim's muffled screams that cut through to him and made him feel sick. If someone tied him down and cut his finger off with pruners, he knew he'd scream just like the man in the chair.

His wife suddenly popped her head around the door of his small, crowded office. 'You all right, love?'

'Yeah,' he told her too quickly. 'I'm fine.'

Gabriel Westbrook watched the man in the chair, slumped and quiet now, seemingly close to unconsciousness – the missing finger clearly visible as a small amount of blood dripped to the floor. Although the injury seemed relatively minor in comparison to the previous broadcasts, the coldness of the act, the brutal determination of the masked man to cut through the bone and sinew of another person's finger while they writhed and struggled, left him feeling chilled and displaced, nauseous and a little dizzy as he imagined himself taped to the chair while the dark figure cut through his finger with nothing more than a set of garden pruners.

'You bloody animal,' he accused the figure. 'You're just a bloody animal.'

Father Alex Jones sat in the dark of his office inside St Thomas More Church, a small circle of light from his desk lamp and the hue of his computer screen the only illumination. He prayed thanks to God that the latest victim's life had been spared and for his safe return to his family and loved ones and he prayed for the soul of the man who'd coldly mutilated another man in the name of some misguided cause. And finally he prayed that the police would find the man whose hate had turned him to evil, before he could take another soul.

Sean watched till the very last second when the Your View footage went dead, leaving a frozen picture of the victim slumped in his chair.

'Did you see everything?' Sally's voice snapped him back.

'Yeah,' he answered. 'I saw it.' There was a slight pause before she spoke again, both taking a moment to think about what they'd just witnessed. 'At least he's still alive,' Sean finally spoke.

'For now,' Sally warned him, 'but we have a probable confirmation on the victim. Apparently his wife's called and told us Jeremy Goldsboro went for a walk in Holland Park earlier this evening and hasn't been seen since – until he appeared on Your View.'

216

'Anything else?'

'Dribs and drabs,' she told him. 'He used to work in the City, but retired a few years ago. It's pretty confusing here at the moment.'

'OK.' Sean understood. 'I'll get back to the office as fast as I can.' He hung up and began to gather his things, his mind whirling with the events of the last few minutes, oblivious to everyone else in the hushed restaurant until he looked up and saw the faces of Kate's friends staring at him. He looked at them one by one, their eyes slipping to the side as his own seemed to challenge them, until he returned to gathering his belongings, more urgently now, eager to be away from people who would never be like him, and back amongst his own kind. He pushed his chair back and stood, tucking the laptop under his armpit and taking one last look at the faces around the table.

'Enjoy your dinner,' he told them and headed for the exit where the same man who'd greeted him now handed his coat back. Sean grabbed it while already heading out the door.

At his desk in the offices of *The World* newspaper, Jackson worked frantically, while other members of his team did the same – relentlessly ringing phones mixing with the sounds of their urgent voices and rapid typing as they tried to change the entire first six pages of tomorrow's newspaper to cover the story that had just broken – The Jackdaw had taken another victim.

Jackson had watched the whole broadcast – the white room and the chair the victim had been taped to all too familiar to him now, but the excitement at having his interview with The Jackdaw running right alongside the story of the new victim's ordeal chased away any feelings of fear he might have had. As far as he was concerned this was journalism at its best – something that could compete even with

217

the twenty-four-hour news channels. He had the interview and would be sure the readers fully understood the risk he had taken in meeting such an obviously dangerous man. Although he had to be careful not to go over the top and alienate the killer – after all, he still hoped for further exclusive interviews.

He checked the pay-as-you-go mobile that lay next to his keyboard, almost willing it to ring or even receive a text message, but it remained dormant. 'Come on,' he ordered it. 'Ring, God damn you.' After a few seconds he gave up on it and returned to watching another re-run of the latest torture and mutilation, making a note of every detail for tomorrow's story.

He'd almost forgotten about the phone until suddenly its ringing and vibrating made him visibly jump on his desk stool. 'Fuck,' he swore involuntarily and loudly before recovering and snatching the phone up. 'Hello.' There was a pause before anyone answered, the only sound that of breathing, magnified and distorted. Jackson held his nerve and waited.

'I assume you saw my latest . . . *offering*?' the voice asked.

'I did,' Jackson answered, keeping his voice low so as not to attract attention. The Jackdaw was for him and him alone.

'There's a lot of noise where you are. You are not alone?'

'No,' Jackson admitted. 'I'm at work. But no one knows I'm speaking with you.' There was another few seconds of silence.

'Tell me – what did you think of what you saw?'

'In what way?' Jackson asked, stalling, unsure of what the Jackdaw wanted him to say. More silence.

'Do you understand why I spared his life?'

'Because,' Jackson struggled, 'you're merciful?'

'Merciful,' the voice laughed mechanically. 'You make me sound like a god. No, Mr Jackson. I spared him because I could see it's what the people wanted. I act only on behalf of the people.'

'I understand,' Jackson lied.

'You understand, but you don't believe,' the voice told him. 'Do you think that my act of *mercy* was simply to hide some murderous insanity? Do you think I do this solely to satisfy a need to kill and torture my fellow men?'

'No,' Jackson tried to convince him. 'I just need . . . want to understand more. If we met again you could help me understand. Phones aren't safe for long conversations.' He waited, unable to breathe, until the answer finally came.

'Very well,' the voice conceded. 'I'll call you in a day or so. Goodbye, Mr Jackson.' He hung up before Jackson could say any more. Jackson sat with the phone still pressed against his ear until a colleague slapped him on the back and made him drop it in fright.

'Bit jumpy tonight, Geoff?' his colleague asked. Jackson turned to face him, the colour drained from his face. 'Christ. You look like you've seen a ghost.'

'Yeah,' he replied. 'Something like that.'

'Wait a minute,' the other journalist caught on. 'That was him, wasn't it – on the phone, just now. It was the bloody Jackdaw, wasn't it?'

'Maybe,' Jackson answered.

'You meeting him again?'

'Maybe,' Jackson said again.

'You are, aren't you? Jesus, Geoff. That's bloody risky.'

'Yeah, well,' Jackson shrugged, 'I've already rolled the dice on that one.'

'Why not just interview him on the phone?' his colleague asked. 'Who cares if the police are eavesdropping? Might even be a good idea to have them close by.'

'You joking?' Jackson asked, a look of disbelief on his face. 'On the bloody phone? Make sure the Old Bill are close by? The public want to know I sat opposite a stone-cold killer

– they want to know I could have been taped to that chair any second and had my throat cut. They need to be able to taste the fear – feel the danger. They want a show, not a fucking telephone conversation. And that's exactly what I'm going to give them. The Jackdaw and The Showman. What could possibly go wrong?'

'He could kill you,' the journalist reminded him coldly.

'He could, but I don't think he will.'

'Don't *think* he will! Bloody hell, Geoff, it's one hell of a risk to take just for a story – no matter how big it is. I know you'll make a nice few quid out of the book and TV stuff, but is it really worth it?'

Jackson leaned back in his reclining office chair, flipped his feet up onto his desk and wrapped his hands around the back of his head. 'It's not about the money,' he explained. 'It's about the story and the *prestige*, my old friend. Always about the *prestige*.'

Sean's arrival back in the office went barely noticed, such was the buzz of detectives collating information and getting on with their assigned tasks. The entire team seemed to be there. Clearly everyone had seen the latest Your View video and were desperate to move the investigation forward as fast as possible. He moved quietly across the room gathering Donnelly, Sally and Anna with taps on shoulders and nods of his head as he went, leading them to his office where he threw his coat over a hook on the back of the door, slumped in his chair and rubbed his face with the palms of his hands before looking up at the others.

'All right,' he asked them. 'What do we know for sure?'

'First things first,' Sally told him. 'Are Kate and the kids safe?'

'Yeah,' he assured her. 'Local CID are round there now checking it out. They phoned me when I was on my way here to let me know. Thanks for arranging it, by the way.'

'No problem,' Sally replied.

'Wouldn't you rather be at home?' Anna asked. 'Just to be sure?'

'He's not coming after my family,' he told her, 'or me. That's fantasy. That's films and TV shows. Kate knows that.'

'He mentioned your name in the video,' Anna reminded him unnecessarily.

'So he read my name in a newspaper and spouted it out during one of his rants,' Sean suggested. 'Big deal. He's not coming after me or my family and the best way I can stop Kate from worrying is to catch him sooner rather than later. And to do that I need to be here, not sitting at home. So, like I said, what do we know for sure?'

'Victim's definitely this guy Jeremy Goldsboro,' Sally told him. 'We've had literally dozens of calls from people saying they know him or knew him, so we have no reason to think otherwise, and we know he's a retired banker – left his job as one of the vice presidents of . . .' she checked her notebook, 'King and Melbourn Capital Associates, one of the City's big boys, apparently. He went for his evening walk in Holland Park, close to where he lives, and wasn't seen again until he was seen on Your View.'

'Wasn't his wife worried,' Sean jumped in, 'when he didn't return home?'

'Apparently it's not uncommon for him to go for very long walks,' Sally explained, 'so she wasn't unduly worried.'

'Poor bastard,' Donnelly added. 'He must have heard about the other victims and been thinking, thank Christ I got out of the City before this lunatic hit the scene. Next thing he knows he *is* the next victim.'

'Has he been found yet?' Sean asked.

'No,' Sally told him.

'Well, if our killer sticks to his usual method it won't be long before he turns up wandering around some park or common somewhere. Has the park Goldsboro was taken from been secured?'

'It's closed and locked after dark,' Sally explained, 'but the locals are babysitting it for us until we can get to it.'

'Good,' Sean answered just as he spotted DC Bishop wandering past his open door. 'Bishop,' he called out, making him take a couple of steps backwards before he popped his head around the corner of Sean's office.

'Yes, guv'nor?'

'You got a trace on this joker's location yet?' Sean asked.

'Not yet, guv, but I'm working on it – getting closer and closer,' Bishop answered. 'I'm as sure as I can be the signal's coming from somewhere in east Surrey or thereabouts. He's trying plenty of tricks to cover himself, but I'll get him eventually – it's only a matter of time.'

'Did you try to borrow some gear off the CIA like I told you to?'

'I phoned the embassy,' Bishop explained.

'And?'

'They told me to go fuck myself,' Bishop told them.

'So much for the special relationship,' Donnelly added.

'OK,' Sean told Bishop. 'Just keep on it.'

'Will do,' Bishop assured him and headed off. Sean turned back to the others.

'In the absence of a positive trace what else have we got?' he asked them.

'The new video,' Sally reminded them.

'The new video,' Sean repeated, leaning forward to turn on the laptop and calling up the latest Your View footage, the picture frozen where he'd left it after folding it shut in the restaurant, showing the victim slumped in his chair with blood dripping from the wound where his little finger had been severed. He clicked on the replay icon and watched with the volume turned down from the beginning. 'Christ. What's going through his mind?' he questioned. 'Why change his . . . his reaction again?'

'His reaction?' Sally asked. 'In what way?'

'The relatively minor injury caused to the victim,' Sean suggested, 'despite the fact about fifty per cent of viewers voted guilty.'

'I don't know,' Donnelly reminded him. 'That was a nasty wee video. It was pretty brutal. Maybe he decided it was enough to get people's attention?'

'But he already has people's attention,' Sean argued, 'and what's this about – it's about crime and punishment, isn't it? And this victim's "crimes" seem much more significant than Georgina Vaughan's. He's an ex-vice president, whereas she was just a project manager, yet her "punishment" was argu-ably more severe than his. So why is he easing off?'

'It could be a sign he's becoming increasingly media savvy,' Anna suggested. 'He would have seen that people are voting to spare the victims in as many numbers as they are to punish them. He would see this as a direct vote against him and what he believes he's trying to do. It's possible he's trying to appease his audience.'

'So he's moving away from more gratuitous acts,' Sean recapped. 'Relatively small, but nasty acts of violence.'

'That would be my guess,' Anna answered.

'Wait a minute,' Donnelly suddenly told them. 'He met with that slippery bastard Jackson, right?'

'So?' Sean asked.

'I bet he bloody well briefed him,' Donnelly explained. 'Told him to ease off on the gratuitous stuff if he wanted to keep the public, or at least a significant section of it, on side. This was all bloody Jackson's idea.'

'Well, if it saves lives . . .' Sally spread her arms.

'If it is Jackson's idea, he's not doing it to save lives,' Sean told them. 'What d'you think, Anna? Think Jackson could persuade our man to tone things down for the sake of positive press?'

'He's always been publicity minded, otherwise why use Your View, why publicize yourself at all?' Anna explained.

'Just quietly go about your business of revenge, or retribution, or whatever it is he's motivated by.'

'But his first victim was murdered,' Sean reminded her. 'A serial offender whose crimes get less and less serious or brutal? I've never come across that before. They always escalate.'

'Then you'd be assuming he's just another serial offender driven by his desire and need to kill for killing's sake,' Anna pointed out.

'Is that what you think?' Sally asked Sean. 'That this is all an act, a camouflage for something a hell of a lot more basic – that underneath all this he's just another serial killer?'

'I don't know anything for sure right now,' Sean admitted. 'I'm neither buying into the whole avenging hero persona, nor am I discounting it. I'm just trying to keep an open mind until we know more. What I do know for sure is the shit'll hit the fan once the top-brass get wind of what's happened, assuming they don't already know.'

'So what now?' Sally asked.

'No need for an office meeting,' Sean told her. 'Everyone's seen the latest video and they all look up to speed. Bishop seems sure the location of the broadcasts is somewhere in east Surrey, so let's get the area swamped with whatever the Met and Surrey Old Bill can spare. He has to be using a derelict building or something similar and it must be rural or someone would have seen or heard something by now. There can't be that many places left to check. Get on to it, will you, Dave?'

'No problem, boss,' Donnelly assured him.

'Anna,' he told her. 'Keep working on the suspect's profile. I'll take anything you can give me that'll help me get in his mind.'

'OK,' she agreed, but quickly looked away. Sean knew what it meant: did he really want to be in the mind of another killer? DC Jesson suddenly appeared at the door and distracted him before he could challenge Anna.

'Guv'nor,' Jesson said urgently.

'What is it?'

'They've found the victim,' Jesson announced, 'walking around the back streets of Acton – hands tied behind his back, mouth still taped over. A good Samaritan found him and called us. Local uniforms took him straight to Charing Cross A&E. No life-threatening injuries.'

'He let him go then,' Donnelly said what they were all thinking.

'A man of his word,' Sally added. Sean was already standing, once more pulling on his raincoat and loading his pockets. 'Charing Cross, I presume.'

'Yeah,' Sean told her, 'and you're coming with me.'

Sean and Sally entered the A&E department at Charing Cross Hospital through the entrance used by the ambulance crews wheeling patients on stretchers. They had their warrant cards already in hand on the off chance someone challenged them, although they knew the staff would know exactly what they were, even without their IDs.

'You all right?' Sean asked Sally. 'You were a little quiet in the car.'

'Yeah, I'm fine,' she lied. 'It's just . . . I haven't been here since my final outpatient visit. I wasn't planning on ever coming back.'

Sean remembered all too well the months Sally had spent in the hospital. Intensive care at first and then a private room on a ward – recovering from the wounds Sebastian Gibran had inflicted on her.

'Unfortunately,' he told her, 'given your line of work, that was never going to be likely.'

'No,' she answered. 'I don't suppose it was.'

'You'll be fine,' he encouraged her as they approached the main nursing station where three female nurses wearing a variety of uniforms sat behind the large desk. After being ignored for what seemed a long time the youngest nurse eventually looked up.

'Can I help you?' she asked.

Sean and Sally both let her have a long look at their warrant cards. 'We're here to see Jeremy Goldsboro,' Sean told her without saying who they were or where they were from. He knew she wouldn't be interested in the details. The nurse looked at her colleagues without answering him.

'Do you know where Dr Mantel is?' she asked the other nurses, one of whom leant forward and picked up a phone and spoke into it after a few seconds.

'Can you page Dr Mantel for me?' she asked whoever she was speaking to. 'Let her know the police are here and want to see one of her patients. OK. Thanks.' She hung up and nodded to the only nurse who would speak to them.

'She should be here in a few minutes,' the talkative one told them. 'You can take a seat in the waiting area outside.'

'It's OK,' Sean told her. 'We'll just wait here.' The nurse looked at her colleague who'd made the phone call; she shrugged.

'Fine,' she replied and sat down without saying anything further.

Sean and Sally moved far enough away that their whispers couldn't be heard. 'Looks like somebody's been briefed not to speak to the Old Bill,' Sally suggested.

'It's not their fault,' Sean excused them. 'If they accidentally say too much they'll be in the shit with the hospital board. Better to say nothing.'

'I remember there was a time a visit to an A&E department was a guarantee of a cup of something warm,' Sally reminisced.

'A long time ago, maybe,' Sean reminded her. A very slim woman in her thirties, brown hair tied in a ponytail, wearing glasses, grey trousers and a white blouse with a stethoscope draped around her neck, drew his attention.

He watched her pause at the desk and talk briefly with the nurses before turning her head in their direction. 'This is our doctor,' he told Sally and walked towards her, warrant card once more in hand. As they came near the woman seemed to stiffen.

'Can I help you?' she asked.

They both showed their IDs. 'I'm Detective Inspector Sean Corrigan and this is Detective Sergeant Jones from the Special Investigations Unit, Metropolitan Police. Are you the doctor who's treating Jeremy Goldsboro?'

'I am,' she answered curtly.

'Can you tell me anything about his condition?' Sean asked, before quickly adding, 'Sorry. I didn't catch your name.'

'Dr Sara Mantel,' she told him, 'and Mr Goldsboro appears to be fine, more or less. His left little finger has been amputated . . .'

'Amputated,' Sean interrupted. 'You mean cut off?'

She looked him up and down. 'Whatever word you prefer,' she told him, 'but it wasn't hacked off, if that's what you mean. The wound is relatively clean. It's a shame we don't have the finger – we could probably have sewn it back on. Other than that he's suffering from a degree of shock – nothing life-threatening – and mild blood loss, although he won't need a transfusion. Must have been a terrifying experience though. He may need some psychiatric assistance at some point in the near future.'

'Can we see him?' Sean quickly moved on.

'Very well,' she agreed, 'but usual rules – not too long and not too much.'

'Fair enough,' Sean conceded.

'Cubicle ten,' she told them and started to move away before Sean stopped her.

'One more thing.' Mantel turned towards him without speaking. 'Does anyone know he's here – friends, family?'

'His wife's been informed.'

'How?' Sean asked, confusing her further. 'Did he call her – on his mobile perhaps?'

'No,' she answered. 'We called her. He said he'd had his mobile taken from him.'

'By his abductor?'

'I really don't know,' Mantel told him with growing frustration. 'Such things aren't my concern. Now if you'll excuse me.' She turned on her heels and headed off along the sterile corridor.

'Not exactly a bundle of information, was she?' Sally complained.

'Once Goldsboro's signed his medical release form she'll be more forthcoming,' Sean reminded her. 'Whether she likes it or not.'

He gestured that she should go first and they both walked the short distance along the corridor to the cubicle marked with a '10', the thick, light blue curtain pulled across the entrance. Sally pulled it open only slightly and half stepped inside.

'Mr Goldsboro? Jeremy Goldsboro?' The well-built man in his early fifties lying on top of the bed, still wearing his own blood-spattered clothes, looked up at her with sharp grey eyes, although they were slightly bloodshot and tired.

'Yes,' he told her in a stronger voice than she'd expected, his well-spoken accent matching his square jaw and straight nose. 'I'm Jeremy Goldsboro.' Despite his pallor and dishevelled appearance, Sally could imagine that on any other day he would be handsome and healthy looking.

'We're from the police,' she told him, moving deeper into the cubicle with Sean following her in. She pointed at herself. 'Detective Sergeant Sally Jones and this is Detective Inspector Corrigan from the Special Investigations Unit. Do you mind if we ask you a few questions?'

Goldsboro looked at Sean. 'DI Corrigan. That name rings a bell.'

'Coincidence,' Sean suggested.

'I don't think so,' Goldsboro replied, before wincing with pain and holding his heavily bandaged hand across his chest. 'Ah yes. I remember now. You're in charge of catching the man who did this to me, aren't you?' It almost sounded like an accusation.

'I am,' Sean admitted.

'Pity for me you didn't catch him sooner,' Goldsboro added.

'I'm sorry,' was all Sean could say.

'Don't be,' Goldsboro told him and sounded like he meant it. 'If you could have, I'm sure you would have.' He winced again. 'Please – ask your questions – anything you like if it'll help catch the bastard. Damn animal cut my bloody finger off, for Christ's sake.'

'I know,' Sean answered. 'I'm sorry for what you've been through.'

'What's happened, happened. It's over now and I'm still alive where others are not. I won't let this ruin my life.'

'I'm glad to hear it,' Sally told him, 'but sometimes the worst effects of what we've been through don't manifest themselves until days, even weeks later. If you begin to feel a little . . . down, don't wait. Get help straight away.'

'I'll be fine,' he assured her. 'Once I get home and things settle down, I'll be fine.'

'We need to know where you were abducted from,' Sean changed the subject, keen to press on, 'and how it happened.'

Goldsboro took a breath and tried to sit more upright until the pain seemed to stop him. 'I was just coming to the end of my evening stroll in Holland Park – it's right next to where I live – and was crossing the small car park there when he stepped out from behind a tree and pointed a shotgun at me. He was already wearing the ski-mask pulled over his face and spoke through the voice-altering thing he had across his mouth.'

'What happened next?' Sean asked.

'I'm trying to remember,' Goldsboro told him, looking more confused now. 'It's more difficult than you'd think.'

'Take your time,' Sally encouraged him. 'It'll come.'

'He threw me a hood,' Goldsboro continued, 'and told me to put it over my head and face. I tried to talk to him, but he wouldn't listen – just kept pointing that damn shotgun at my head and telling me he'd blow my head off if I didn't hurry. Needless to say, I put the hood on. Next thing I'm being pushed across the car park – can't see a bloody thing. I hear a car or more likely a van door slide open, definitely a sliding sound, and he pushes me inside. He strapped my ankles and wrists to some sort of leather-bound restraints and pulled the hood off. My first thought was that he wanted me to see that he was going to kill me, but instead he slapped a piece of sticky tape over my mouth and pulled the hood back on. Then we drove for what seemed like hours before we stopped. He took me out of the van and frogmarched me into some kind of building. It was cold inside and smelt of damp, like it had been long since abandoned. We went up some stairs and he pushed me into a chair and taped me to it. I didn't hear the tape being ripped, so I guessed he'd already prepared it. He left the hood on me and the tape across my mouth. I guess he didn't want me to see or say anything, but I could hear sounds like he was turning on electrical equipment that made the sort of whirring sound computers and digital cameras make when they're warming up. A few seconds later he started going on about greedy, criminal bankers and how we've been stealing from "the people" and all that nonsense. Then the bastard grabbed me by the arm and demanded I hold my fingers out. I thought maybe he was going to start breaking them or pull my finger-nails out, but then I felt the cold metal closing around my finger and . . . well, you know what happened next.' He looked down at his bandaged hand. 'At least he strapped a basic bandage around it before taking me back to the van.'

'He strapped it?' Sean asked.

'Yeah,' Goldsboro confirmed. 'Not properly, but enough to stem the bleeding.'

'Then what?'

'Back on with the hood and back out to the van. Again we drove for what seemed like forever, a motorway or dual carriageway at first, and then the traffic got slower and heavier, so I guessed we were somewhere in town. Eventually I heard him get out and slide the door open. He undid my wrists, but then taped them behind my back before releasing my ankles and removing the hood. Christ, I thought I was going to suffocate in that damn hood. Once my eyes adjusted to the streetlights I saw I was in some residential street. He gave me a shove and I kept walking in that direction while he got back in his van and drove off in the other. I was confused and disorientated. I guess I wandered about until somebody found me and called the police. It was only later I realized I should have just called at the nearest house.'

'That's understandable,' Sean reassured him before quickly following it with another question. 'When you were in the van, could you tell if he was separated from you?'

'He definitely was,' Goldsboro answered without hesitation. 'The driver's cabin was cut off from the rest of the van by what looked like wooden boarding and the section I was in looked and felt like it had been padded.'

'Soundproofed,' Sean spoke to himself.

'Could have been,' Goldsboro agreed.

'Was there anything about him that looked . . . familiar?' Sean asked.

'In what way?'

'In any way,' Sean told him. 'Anything at all.'

'You're asking me if I think I *know* him?'

'I have to consider it,' Sean explained.

Goldsboro shook his head slightly as he considered the question, his eyes squinting with concentration, taking his time before answering. 'No. Nothing. If there had been I would have noticed. My powers of observation are well known. I don't know this man.'

'Then what about his other victims?' Sean asked. 'Paul Elkins and Georgina Vaughan. Do you know them?'

'No,' he told him a little unsurely. 'Paul Elkins sounds vaguely familiar. I may have crossed his path when I worked in the City, but it's been years since I was there. Georgina Vaughan means nothing to me.'

'What about someone who may have had a personal grudge against you?'

'Not that I know of,' Goldsboro answered. 'I had my fair share of threatening emails and letters when the banking system had its little wobble, some more personal than others, but nothing too close to home – all just sniping from a safe distance, although . . . there was one who was a little more *troubling* than perhaps the others were.'

'In what way?' Sean asked.

'I had plenty of threats to do this and do that, even threats against my family, but they were all so over the top you knew they weren't serious – not really.'

'But?' Sean encouraged.

'Well, there was one who was always a lot more specific, and calm . . . cold. There was structure to his threats – I don't know, an intelligence about him, I suppose, and he seemed to know personal details. Nothing too specific, but enough to cause concern.'

Sean and Sally glanced at each other. 'Can you remember his name?' Sean asked.

'No,' Goldsboro told him. 'It was a long time ago now. I gave the City of London Police a statement, just like we all did and let them get on with it. I heard later he was arrested and charged or cautioned – I don't remember which. I'm sure they'll still have a record of it somewhere.'

'*Like we all did*?' Sean repeated Goldsboro's words.

'Yes,' Goldsboro confirmed. 'Apparently I wasn't the only one he threatened.'

'OK,' Sean promised. 'We'll look into it, but right now you look like you could do with some rest. They may keep you in for the night, but you should be home by tomorrow. I'll send one of my team round to take a full statement, if you're up to it.'

'I'll be fine,' Goldsboro assured him.

'Sorry,' Sean said, shaking his head. 'Before I forget, did you have a mobile phone with you, when he first approached you?'

'Yes,' Goldsboro told him. 'He took it off me just before he forced me into the van.'

'I see,' Sean replied. 'Oh well – we may yet find it. He may have thrown it close by. You get some rest.'

He headed for the curtained exit before Goldsboro stopped him. 'You will keep me informed, won't you, Inspector? My wife, you see. She won't sleep now until he's caught. Anything I can tell her to ease her fears.'

'Of course,' Sean agreed and once more made for the exit before pausing and turning back to Goldsboro. 'One last thing, Mr Goldsboro – are you right-handed or left?'

Goldsboro frowned slightly at the question. 'Right-handed. Why? Is it important?'

'Probably not,' Sean answered, not knowing whether he was telling the truth or not yet. 'Goodnight, Mr Goldsboro.' He escaped back into the corridor with Sally in pursuit.

'What's with the right-handed, left-handed question?' she asked, struggling to keep up with Sean.

'What?'

'The right hand, left hand question,' Sally repeated.

'Goldsboro's right-handed,' he told her, as if that alone would answer her question.

'And?'

'But our boy cut his left little finger off.'

233

'Which matters why?'

Sean stopped and looked at her. 'Doesn't that strike you as being a little odd?'

'Odd how?'

'Our boy tells the world he wants Goldsboro to be reminded of his greed every time he looks down at his hands as he's counting his cash – so why take his left finger and not his right?'

'I doubt he was even thinking about it,' Sally argued. 'When you're about to hack someone's finger off I don't suppose you'd be worrying about whether they're right- or left-handed.'

'I suppose not,' Sean agreed and started walking again. 'But perhaps he did consider it and decided to take the left finger as a sign of . . . mercy. Perhaps he's losing the stomach for what he's started, or . . .'

'Or what?'

'I'm not sure,' he told her. 'Not yet. Best thing I can think of is he's trying to send us a message. By de-escalating the level of violence in his crimes he's trying to tell us something.'

'Like what?'

'That he's not insane or that he's had enough. That he's trying to stop.'

'Or maybe he's just messing with us,' Sally suggested. 'Breaking a few rules to keep us off balance.'

'Maybe,' Sean replied without conviction, swooping through the ambulance bay exit and unlocking their car.

'What now?' Sally asked, opening her door.

'Where else?' Sean answered with a question. 'Holland Park.'

Sean parked in Abbotsbury Road, Holland Park, he and Sally walking the short distance to the small car park inside the park itself where they showed their warrant cards to the uniformed constable guarding the taped-off entrance and ducked under and inside. They could see someone moving around inside the car park, shining a torch at the ground as they did so, as if searching for something. Sean already knew who it was.

'Paulo,' he called out, pulling his own mini-Maglite torch from his belt pouch as Sally did the same. 'Over here.' The beam of light froze in the darkness, then bounced its way towards them, the shadowy figure becoming clearer until it was close enough to be recognized.

'Guv'nor,' Zukov greeted him before quickly turning to Sally, 'Sal.'

'Been here long?' Sean asked.

'Long enough,' Zukov moaned.

'Forensics?' Sean questioned.

'Be here in a couple of hours,' Zukov answered. 'DS Roddis is sending a couple of his team over and technical support are sending over some lighting, but they won't get down to the nitty-gritty of it until morning.'

'And have you found anything?' Sally asked.

'Nah,' Zukov told her. 'Nothing to find if you ask me. Geezer grabs him in the car park and forces him into his van, probably threatening him with a knife or something and they're away. What's to find?'

'It was a shotgun,' Sean filled him in on the details.

'See,' Zukov triumphantly declared. 'Clean and fast. Nothing for forensics.'

'Except his mobile phone,' Sean told him. 'Suspect took it off him and probably tossed it somewhere in this car park.'

'Best we give it a ring then,' Sally suggested, pulling out her phone, talking as she dialled. 'His eighteen-year-old son gave us the number when he called in saying the victim was his dad. I thought it might come in useful.' She held the phone to her ear to make sure she was getting a dialling tone and waited, all three of them standing absolutely still and silent, aware that even the slightest sound carried a long way in the quiet of night.

'Over there,' Sean told them and turned in the direction of the chirping, ringing sound coming from some bushes on the edge of the car park. After seven rings the noise stopped as the answer phone clicked in – Jeremy Goldsboro's well-spoken voice, asking Sally to leave a message. 'Ring it again,' Sean ordered. She pressed redial and followed Sean who cocked his head to better track the ringing that had started again. He reached a thick bush just in time to see the illuminated screen before it disappeared. 'In here,' he told them. He pulled a single latex glove from his inside jacket pocket and stretched it over his fingers. 'Now ring it again,' he told Sally. This time he could both see and hear the mobile as he reached into the bush and pulled the phone free. It was locked, but the display screen showed it had received dozens of missed calls. 'That's a lot of missed calls,' he told the others. 'We're lucky the battery wasn't dead.'

'Concerned family and friends,' Sally suggested.

'No doubt,' Sean agreed. 'You got an evidence bag?' he asked Zukov.

'Just a couple,' Zukov answered, pulling a small plastic bag from his trouser pocket and opening it for Sean to drop the mobile inside. 'Waste of time though. This one always wears gloves. We'll get nothing from it but the victim's prints.'

'You never know your luck,' Sean reminded him. 'He may have got sloppy.'

'Not this one,' Zukov disagreed, folding the phone in the bag and slipping it into his pocket. 'I'll make sure Roddis gets it anyway.'

'You do that,' Sean told him, no longer really listening, looking up at the black trees that barely moved in the deadly still night – trees that ringed the entire car park. *Did you sit in your van the whole time*, Sean asked. Or *did you hide in these trees, watching him as he strolled in the park, waiting for him to get close enough to strike? And the shotgun, where did that come from? Only three types of people have shotguns: farmers, rich people and criminals. Which are you, my friend? Which are you?* For a second he could see the dark figure striding across the car park, shotgun down by his side, quickly stepping behind the nearby tree out of sight until Goldsboro was almost on top of him. But the figure had no face, no feeling, no anything. *Who the hell are you? What's this really about?*

'Sean. Sean.' Sally's voice brought him back to the present.

'Sorry. What?'

'What now?' she asked.

'Well,' he answered, 'Goldsboro said he had his phone taken off him just before he got into the van, so we can be fairly sure this is where it was parked.' He looked at Zukov. 'Make sure forensics pay special attention to this area. I want everything seized and taken to the lab: food wrappers, cigarette butts, apple cores, everything. He could have been waiting here a while before Goldsboro got close enough to snatch.'

'Or he could have followed him from his home,' Sally argued. 'In which case he would have only been waiting here a short time.'

'Maybe,' Sean agreed, 'but we're not in a position to assume anything, so let's give every scene the full works. Hoping he makes a mistake, or DC Bishop getting a trace, are our best chances to find him fast.' He turned to Zukov. 'Stay here and look after the scene, Paulo, and while you're hanging around you can get on your phone and check something out for me.'

'Why not?' Zukov answered. 'Give me something to do while I'm stuck here on my jack.'

'Goldsboro said a man who threatened him a few years ago was arrested and charged or cautioned by the City Police,' Sean explained, 'but he can't remember the suspect's name. Get hold of them and see if you can get a name and current address.'

'A few years ago?' Zukov questioned.

'It's the City Police,' Sean reminded him, 'not the Met. If there's one thing they're good at, it's keeping records.'

Zukov nodded as Sean looked at his watch. It was almost one in the morning. 'You should go home and get some rest,' he told Sally. 'I'll drop you off before I go back to the Yard.'

'You're not going home?' she asked.

'Not yet,' he answered. 'I've still got a few things to take care of.'

'After everything that's happened tonight, Kate would probably appreciate you getting yourself home, even at this hour,' Sally advised him.

'I'm not exactly her favourite person right now,' Sean explained, 'and to be honest I'm not in the mood to go home and walk straight into a domestic. Better to give her a little time and space.'

Sally rolled her eyes. 'Men,' she told him. 'You just don't understand women, do you?'

'What's that supposed to mean?' Sean asked, feeling affronted.

'You'll see,' she warned him.

10

Early morning and Sean had used the showers in the gym at the Yard to clean up, dressing in the clean shirt and underwear he, like all experienced detectives, kept in his office for the times when getting home proved impossible or simply not worthwhile. Better to grab a few hours' sleep on the office floor than waste valuable time travelling between work and home. After several cups of strong coffee he felt functional, if not great, although he knew the tiredness would come earlier each day the investigation dragged on. He should eat, but his stomach wasn't yet ready to deal with solids. He looked around his desk and office at the various piles of files. He decided he couldn't bear to plough through more potential suspect reports and opted for a file containing buildings that had been checked in the ever decreasing target area. Some included printouts of photographs conscientious officers had taken on their own phones, but most were just a description of the property and the fact it had been searched with no trace of the man he sought. He was just reaching for a new file when he sensed a presence at his door and looked up to see an ashen-faced Assistant Commissioner Addis glaring at him. Despite Addis's polished appearance, Sean suspected he hadn't been the only one to spend the night in his office.

'I've tried to help you.' Addis got straight into it, his lips thin with anger. 'Tried to protect you from powers you couldn't even understand – gave you one of the best and highest-profile jobs in the police service – but let me tell you, DI Corrigan, I'm beginning to have serious doubts about your ability to run a major investigation such as this.'

'I didn't ask you,' Sean reminded him, too tired and frustrated not to defend himself and just take it. 'You came to me, remember? I never said I wanted this.'

'Don't give me that old bollocks,' Addis told him, baring his teeth. 'If I hadn't stepped in when I did you'd still be rotting in Peckham, investigating dead drug dealers and teenage gang murders. If that's what you want to go back to, just say the word.' Neither spoke for a while. 'I didn't think so,' Addis eventually said. 'There's DIs and DCIs out there would bloody well kill for your job and don't you forget it.'

Addis's words hit Sean far harder than he could have imagined. For the first time since the Special Investigations Unit began he realized how much he needed it, how much he now lived and breathed it, how much he *loved* it – almost more than anything else in his life. Addis was right: he couldn't go back to investigating join-the-dot murders any more than Addis could go back to walking the beat – if he ever had done. He lived for the chase now more than ever.

'So what's your point?' he asked.

'Your failure to catch this bastard is costing the country tens of millions, maybe even hundreds of millions of pounds,' Addis explained. 'Absenteeism in the City is now at an all-time high, with those who are still turning up for work all scurrying home before dark for fear of becoming the next victim. I tried to warn you about this before. When the City starts losing millions that creates pressure – pressure that heads down the line, all the way to my fucking office door. There's only one way to stop the rot, and that's to find this arsehole. And that, Inspector, is your job.'

'I'm doing my job,' Sean tried to assure him, 'but the man we're looking for is clever and careful. As of yet I don't have a single decent suspect, and I can't just pull one out of a hat because the City's losing money. I have to follow where the evidence, the leads, take me.'

'What about the van?' Addis asked.

'He false plates it every time,' Sean explained. 'Impossible to trace.'

'And that . . . *thing* he uses to disguise his voice,' Addis continued, 'we must be able to find where it came from?'

'We're on it,' Sean told him, 'but right now it looks to be homemade – from a mixture of phone and toy parts and God knows what else. We're checking all the electrical stores across London and Surrey – the major ones and the small independents, just in case someone remembers someone or something. Maybe our man stood out for some reason. If we're really lucky we might get some CCTV, but I'm not holding my breath. With a little help from the Internet and a basic grasp of electronics he could have put it together from almost anything.'

'You have photographs of him driving from the scenes and witnesses,' Addis argued. 'Can't you get them enhanced?'

'Stills of him wearing a black boiler suit and balaclava, and when he's not wearing the balaclava the windows are so heavily tinted we can't get a decent shot of him. I have people going through footage from hundreds of CCTV cameras, so we may yet get lucky, but don't hold your breath. Even his driving position is designed to minimize his chances of getting caught on camera: he stays pressed back against the headrest, in the shadows. He's planned this meticulously – d'you really think he's just going to let us have a nice clear photograph of him?'

'What about the victims' backgrounds?' Addis persisted. 'Have you checked to see if any of them are linked?'

'Of course we have,' Sean answered, unable to hide the

growing irritation in his voice, 'but there's nothing. Different companies, different positions, different everything.'

'Perhaps you haven't been back far enough?' Addis accused him. 'Perhaps you need to go back years into their pasts?'

'And how am I supposed to do that?' Sean bit. 'The investigation's moving forward so fast we're struggling just to cover the basics. Every abduction site is another crime scene we have to cover, as is every drop-off point, every body or survivor we find – more and more witnesses and potential witnesses to find and speak to – more and more door-to-door inquiries to complete – more and more CCTV to seize and examine – more and more Your View footage for the lab to plough through. We're stretched to breaking point and with every new abduction we get even thinner on the ground – so why don't you tell me where I'm supposed to find the people who can spend days, maybe even weeks, going years back into the victims' backgrounds? Right now I've got enough people to cover the urgent inquiries and no more.'

'Then use borough CID officers,' Addis naively told him. 'You have my authority to use whoever you need.'

'Christ.' Sean massaged his temples. 'Boroughs don't have anyone to spare. They can just about keep themselves going. They can't give me what they haven't got.'

'So what in the hell do you need?' Addis barked.

'I need him to slow down,' Sean answered honestly. 'Stop the abductions – ideally for two weeks, but I'd take one. Give us time to catch up with ourselves, maybe even get ahead.'

Addis shook his head. 'Sean,' he told him, the anger gone from his voice. 'These are the sort of excuses I'd expect from *any* DI, but you're not any DI, are you?'

'I don't understand.' It was partly a lie; Sean was uncomfortable with Addis's sudden calmness.

'We both know I didn't bring you here to follow the leads and wait for the evidence to present itself. I brought you here because of what you are. You're different and we both know it.'

'Different how?' Sean asked, curious to find out how much Addis understood.

'You have a . . . *gift*. You see things that others do not – you don't need as much evidence to progress an investigation as others do.'

'I can't get anyone convicted solely because of what I might think,' Sean pointed out. 'I need evidence.'

'Of course you do,' Addis agreed, 'but once you know what to look for, the evidence is so much easier to find – agreed?'

'I'm no magician,' Sean told him. 'I'm no psychic. I can't just shut my eyes and wait for the suspect's name and address to pop into my head.'

'Of course not,' Addis replied. 'Do I strike you as being a man who believes in mumbo-jumbo?'

'No,' Sean answered. 'No, you do not.'

'Quite,' Addis agreed, 'but you do have something I've rarely seen and that's why you're here. But if that something is no longer part of you – if you can't do what you used to be able to do – then you're no use to me, Sean. Now, can you still do what I need you to do?'

Sean took a breath and sighed, taking his time to answer the question he'd never been so honestly and directly asked before. 'Yeah, I can still do it,' he finally answered. 'I just need more time to get inside this one's head.'

Addis leaned forward and rested his hands on Sean's desk. 'Time,' he told him, 'is the one thing you don't have.'

Geoff Jackson was still in the throes of a disturbed and fitful sleep when the sound of the pay-as-you-go mobile phone ringing began to stir him from his tortured slumber.

He'd worked late and then headed for a quick drink at a pub close to his office where he knew the landlord was good for a few after-hours drinks – so long as you worked for the right paper. He'd bumped into some journalist friends and a quick drink had turned into a heavy session before he finally took a cab home to his flat and girlfriend who was sixteen years his junior and very much planning on becoming the next Mrs Jackson. His first wife still lived somewhere in north London with their two kids, while he was unsure where his second wife was right now. Somewhere in America, he thought.

Finally, the realization that the ringing phone was *the phone* cut through the remaining effects of the alcohol and shocked him awake. As he grabbed the phone from the bedside table he realized that Denise was no longer in the bed next to him. *Thank fuck for that*, he thought. Now he could talk freely.

'Hello.'

'Good morning, Mr Jackson,' the awful electronic voice greeted him. 'Are you alone?'

'Yes,' Jackson scrambled, trying to clear his head enough to think, regretting switching from beer to vodka the night before. 'I'm alone.' There was a pause, as if the man at the other end of the phone didn't entirely believe him.

'You sound,' the voice told him, 'troubled.'

'No,' Jackson assured him. 'Just a little tired, that's all . . . I was working late . . . on your story. I wanted to get it in today's issue.' He rubbed his face, trying to wake himself up and think.

'I see,' the voice answered.

'I wanted to do your story justice,' Jackson told him. More silence while The Jackdaw considered his words.

'That's very considerate of you,' he eventually answered.

'Just doing my job,' Jackson lied, thinking faster now. 'I'm glad you called, but I thought the last time we spoke you said it would be a few days before you would contact me again.'

'I did,' the voice admitted, 'but things have changed, Mr Jackson. I need to see you now. This morning.'

'Changed?' Jackson asked, his mind awash with possibilities

and none of them good. 'What's changed?' He endured yet more silence before the voice answered.

'Corrigan,' he told him. 'He concerns me.'

Jackson jumped out of bed and started pacing around the room, the floor still littered with his clothes from the night before, as well as the underwear he'd *relieved* Denise of on his arrival home.

'Corrigan?' he asked. 'Corrigan concerns you how?'

'I looked up some of his recent cases,' the voice explained. 'Difficult investigations it appears, yet seemingly Corrigan solved them quickly enough. He strikes me as being a very determined man.'

Shit, Jackson silently mouthed to himself, afraid The Jackdaw was about to abandon his cause for fear of Corrigan and along with it the story. *Think*, he told himself, *think*. He needed to get what he could while he could from The Jackdaw – even if it was just the lead into the next story he had in mind. 'Do you see Corrigan as your *adversary*?'

Yet more painful silence.

'No,' he answered. 'I'm not at war with the police. I'm not a criminal. But Corrigan is a threat – an unwitting tool of my would-be oppressors and tormentors. If I am to complete what I must complete before being brought to my knees by the attack dogs of the greedy and powerful, then I must accelerate my plans.'

'Plans?'

'We've spoken long enough on the telephone, Mr Jackson,' the voice told him. 'To speak any longer could be dangerous for us both. There's a cemetery near Fulwell train station, in Strathmore Road. Meet me there at ten.'

'Where?' Jackson tried to catch him, but it was too late. The Jackdaw had gone. 'Shit,' he swore to himself before tossing the mobile onto the bed and scampering to the bathroom to empty his bladder and the contents of his stomach.

*　　*　　*

245

Sean looked up from the latest report of buildings that the searching officers had deemed as being possible locations for the white room, but nothing had leapt out at him as particularly likely. He looked out into the main office and decided enough of the team were gathered to make an office meeting worthwhile. He pushed his chair back and, standing up on tired, aching legs, walked from his own office into the communal area which, owing to the earliness of the hour, hadn't yet been turned into a tip.

He stood by the large whiteboard, more from habit than a need to use it, and called across the office. 'All right, everybody – I need your attention please.' He waited for the conversations, discussions and phone calls to be put on hold before beginning. 'OK, people. Let's go over what we've got so far, which isn't exactly a lot. What we do know is he's abducting people who do or have worked for financial institutions and so far all the victims' workplaces have been based in the City. He likes to snatch them from open spaces and appears to have a preference for park car parks, although remember he snatched the first victim straight from the pavement. He doesn't appear to be put off by the presence of other people, although clearly it's not going to be his preference. Once he has them he uses the same white van, fitted with different stolen number plates to move them to this white room.'

'Guv'nor?' DC Maggie O'Neil asked. 'How do we actually know it's the same white van?'

'We've had CCTV of the van fleeing all three abduction sites enhanced and compared,' he explained. 'Small imperfections in the paintwork, marks on the wheel covers, even the resting position of the windscreen wipers are identical. It's the same van.' O'Neil nodded she understood. 'Once he has them in the white room, they're taped to a chair while he, for want of a better word, *preaches* online before getting the viewers to vote. Depending on how the vote goes they're supposedly freed unharmed or punished, only our boy doesn't seem to be taking too much notice of the votes any more. This room he uses, it's the same over and over, and we know this for the same reasons we know it's the same van – imperfections on the walls, the exact same positioning of the black bin liners in the background, even the light quality – the lab rats have looked at it all and are telling me it's the same room, no question. So whoever it is we're looking for has found himself a place where he feels safe enough to keep returning.' He looked around the room until he found who he was looking for. 'Paulo. Any luck tracing the name of the man who threatened Goldsboro?'

'He was threatened?' Jesson asked, reminding Sean that only he, Sally and Zukov knew about it.

'Sorry,' he apologized. 'Goldsboro told us he was threatened several years ago – threats that led to someone being arrested.'

'I imagine he was threatened by more than one person,' Jesson argued.

'He was, but apparently this one stood out,' Sean explained. 'Paulo.'

'The man the City Police arrested is a guy called Jason Howard – male, white, in his late forties. Apparently he lost his business shortly after the banking crisis and then his house and then his wife and kids. The City Police told me he blamed the banks.'

'Sounds like we have someone with a clear motive,' Jesson told the gathering.

'What happened to him?' Sean asked.

'They cautioned him and released him,' Zukov answered. 'Apparently no one was too keen to go to court over it so . . . He's not been in trouble since, according to the PNC, but by all accounts the threats were pretty heavy – appeared to have some substance to them instead of just ranting. I took the chance to give them the names of our victims too and, surprise, surprise, Goldsboro wasn't the only one he threatened. He also threatened our first victim – Paul Elkins.'

''Allo, 'allo,' Jesson chipped in.

'But not Georgina Vaughan?' Sean asked.

'Apparently not,' Zukov confirmed.

The image of a man sitting alone in a small room spending years plotting his revenge began to form in Sean's mind, his heart rate jumping as he saw the possibility of a tangible connection between at least two of the victims.

'Where was Elkins working at the time the threats were made?' He held his breath and prayed it would be the same company that Goldsboro had been working for – King and Melbourn.

Zukov took a second to check his notebook. 'Not his present company,' Zukov explained, further exciting Sean's sense of anticipation. 'He was with the Bank of Shoreditch at the time of the threats.'

Sean's heart sank at another dead end. He only hoped his despondency didn't show too obviously on his face. 'And since then this Jason Howard's not come to anyone's attention?' he managed to ask.

'Seems so,' Zukov told him. 'Dropped off the face of the planet. The City emailed me over his photo and details. D'you want me to circulate them?'

'Just within the team. Then find him, if he's still alive, and arrest him. I want him brought in for interview,' Sean demanded. 'And search wherever he's been living.'

'You think he's our man?' Cahill asked.

'I think he needs to be found,' was all Sean would tell her. He searched the room for his next target. 'DC Bishop – any update on where the suspect's broadcasting from?'

Bishop cleared his throat before replying. 'Nothing more since last time. I'm pretty sure he's based in east or southeast Surrey somewhere, but can't get any closer than that until he goes back online.'

Sean looked around all the faces gathered in the room. 'East or southeast Surrey,' he told them. 'It's big, but it's not exactly the Amazon, so can somebody please tell me how come we haven't found this building yet? I've got a pile of reports giving me the details of properties searched, but still we have nothing. How so?' For a few seconds no one answered. 'Does this not strike you as a little strange?'

'Maybe we're looking in the wrong place,' DC Jesson offered in his Liverpudlian accent. 'Maybe he's using something that messes up our tracking equipment – making us look in the wrong place.'

Sean looked back to Bishop. 'Is it possible?'

'Highly unlikely,' Bishop answered, looking and sounding somewhat affronted. 'I mean, don't get me wrong, such equipment does exist and he is using it, but we've already broken through his encryption and re-direction. The signal's source is solid. I know it is.'

'And we have CCTV footage from traffic-monitoring cameras that show the van travelling west out of London,' the tall, well-spoken DC Fiona Cahill reminded them.

'And a limited time span,' DC O'Neil added. 'Between the time he snatches the victims, drives west, shows them on Your View, then kills them or releases them, he has to be somewhere west of London.'

'So southeast or east Surrey looks good.' Sean took over. 'So why the hell haven't we found this damn white room?' No one answered. 'We need to increase the scope of our search – consider the possibility he doesn't have the luxury of an isolated, derelict building. Maybe he's doing all this from his garage or even his house or flat.'

'He'd need a house with a decent-sized garage at least,' Sally joined in, 'and a house with a garage usually means a family. Hell of a job to keep something like that from your family. As for a flat – I can't see how it could be possible.'

'A house with a garage then,' Sean agreed.

'His family?' Cahill asked. 'I thought Howard's family had left him?'

'Don't assume Howard's definitely our man,' Sean warned her, 'or that he doesn't have a new family.'

'OK,' Sally argued, 'so say it's a house with a garage – what are we supposed to do? Call on every house with a garage in Surrey? It's not even inside the Met. They don't have the manpower and nor do we. They're already helping us out with roadblocks on as many main roads in and out of London as they can. I don't see how this is helping us move things forward. We should stick with the derelict buildings until we've exhausted it,' she continued. 'At least it's something we can manage – on a scale we can manage.'

'But it's not getting results,' Sean snapped back at her. 'We have to be prepared to look further afield. Assume nothing, bring some fresh thinking to this investigation. This bastard's running rings around us. We need to put the pressure on him for a change.' For a second he was tempted to share Addis's not so veiled threats with them, but thought better of it. Instead he turned to DC Summers. 'How we getting on tracing anything he could have bought to build this damn contraption he uses to change his voice?'

'Sorry, guv'nor,' Summers apologized. 'You're talking hundreds of shops – big and small – too many to cover on foot, so we've spoken to the regional managers of the big chains and they've circulated emails to all their store managers who they've asked to play detective and quiz their staff about any suspicious sales or characters. The independent stores – we've got the local CIDs checking on them for the same, but it'll be a long, slow haul. We haven't had a bite yet.'

'Keep on it,' Sean encouraged before turning back to the rest of the room. 'You all know what to do, so let's get on with it.' He headed back to his office with the beginnings of a migraine growing in the centre of his brain. Sally followed him in without waiting to be invited.

'You all right?' she asked him. 'You seemed a little tense out there.'

'I'm fine,' he lied. 'I just don't like wandering around in the dark – which is exactly what we're doing here.'

'Getting some heat from above?'

'When am I not?'

'Ah, but this is different,' she told him sagely.

'Meaning?' He couldn't resist her intrigue.

'Meaning this time it's money the powers that be are truly worried about,' she explained. 'Bad press, the potential for more victims, we've dealt with that sort of pressure plenty of times before, but when it comes to governments losing money – that brings a whole different kind of pressure.'

'So Addis tells me,' he confided in her, 'although I'm not entirely convinced of the connection.'

'It's real enough,' she warned him. 'I've spoken with plenty of people from the City the last few days and they all tell me the same thing – the City's in a perpetual state of fine balance: when things tip into the positive, no matter how slightly, everybody makes heaps of money and money means taxes for the government, business growth, high employment. But if it tips into the negative, even fractionally, the opposite can happen. It's not a case of the City losing money – more that it's just not making *enough* to sustain itself and all that it brings to the economy.'

'You sound like you're auditioning for the Serious Fraud Squad,' he tried to joke.

'I just found it interesting,' she admitted. 'I never realized just how finely balanced the country's finances are. Think of it as a single business – a factory for making money. Like all businesses it relies on a degree of flexibility from its workforce – people putting in extra hours, not always taking their holidays when they would prefer or coming to work when they could just as easily stay at home when they're not feeling too good.'

251

'I know,' Sean interrupted. 'So some people are taking their holidays early or calling in sick and the others are all scuttling away early to get home before it gets dark. It's hardly going to bring the City crashing to its knees, is it?'

'No,' she agreed, 'but it could hurt it badly – in the short term at least. At the moment it's like an accidental work-to-rule and it's having an effect. It's tipped the balance into the negative which means the money's not there to be taxed and that makes the government nervous.'

'Well, if it brings the government down it'll be their own fault for relying on a bunch of self-serving money grabbers.' The phone on his desk rang before Sally could argue. He snatched it up. 'DI Corrigan.'

'Boss,' Jesson's voice told him. 'I've got Jeremy Goldsboro on the line wanting to speak with you. Shall I put him through?'

'No,' Sean barked. 'I haven't got time for tea and sympathy with victims. Put him in touch with whoever's taking care of family liaison. I'm trying to run an investigation here.'

'There isn't a family liaison officer yet,' Jesson argued.

'Then put him through to Victim Support.' Sean tried not to shout. 'Just don't put them through to me.' He slammed the phone down and sat heavily in his chair. 'What's with these people wanting updates all the time?' he complained.

'Well, we're not in Peckham any more,' Sally reminded him. 'Some of the people we deal with now actually have a fairly high opinion of the police,' she added somewhat sarcastically, 'and they all have high-powered jobs or are employed by powerful corporations. They're not used to not knowing what's going on – not used to not being in control. They're not going to accept being kept in the dark until we deem it necessary to tell them anything. It's just not going to happen.'

'Yeah, well I've got better things to do than chat to victims on the phone all day,' he told her. 'So they're gonna have to get used to it.' DC Cahill appeared at the door before Sally could reply. 'What is it?' Sean asked impatiently.

'Got the boyfriend of Georgina Vaughan on the phone, guv'nor,' Cahill answered. 'Wants an update on the investigation.'

Sean threw his arms up in the air. 'You must be fucking joking,' he called out loud enough for people in the main office to look up.

'I'll take it,' Sally told them. 'I feel a woman's touch may be required.'

'Unbelievable,' Sean continued to complain as he watched Sally follow Cahill out. *Why couldn't these people leave him alone? Just leave him alone to do what he needed to do*. He regretted ever handing them his business card.

Jackson sat in the darkness, more scared than he'd ever been in his life before, the silence and stillness of the room he felt around him even more terrifying than the first time he'd met with The Jackdaw – when he'd ended up looking down both barrels of a shotgun. The hood over his head was beginning to become unbearably stifling. His hands and feet had been left unsecured – he could pull the damn thing off any time he liked – but the man who'd brought him here, the man he'd named The Jackdaw for the good of the story, had told him to leave it on until he returned, that it was a test of whether he could trust him. Jackson had asked him where he was going and why he was leaving, but the man never replied. There was just the sound of soft footsteps and then a door closing. Could he even know for sure that he'd really been left alone? For all he knew the bastard could be standing only feet away, shotgun at the ready to blow his head off the second he betrayed his trust and removed the hood. If he took the hood off and The Jackdaw was in front of him – not wearing his mask – he wouldn't be allowed to live for long. No. He'd keep the hood on until he was told otherwise.

The sound of the door creeping open chased his thoughts away, but not his fears, as the soft footsteps moved towards him. The next thing he knew he was blinking against the light, holding his hands in front of his face to ward off the worst of the brightness, trying to see where the other man was in the room. Through his squinted eyes he could see he was back in the same white room as before – the same table covered in equipment, the same black bin liners over the windows. After a few seconds his sight had recovered enough to see the man who'd brought him here move across the room and sit casually on the table with the equipment, laying the shotgun he'd been carrying down by his side.

'I want to thank you for coming to meet me this morning,' he told Jackson in the dreadful voice he'd made his own. 'I appreciate how busy you must be.'

'Don't mention it,' Jackson managed to reply, his eyes never leaving the shotgun. 'Where did you go, by the way – after you brought me here? Why did you leave me alone?'

'I had something I had to do,' he answered. 'Something that couldn't wait.'

The curiosity and tenacity that made Jackson such a successful journalist began to resurface. 'Like what?' he pushed.

'I'm afraid I can't tell you that,' The Jackdaw replied. 'For your own good.'

'Fair enough,' Jackson played along. 'Then perhaps you can tell me where I am?'

'It would be foolish of me to tell you and dangerous for you to know.'

'Then perhaps you can tell me why I'm here?' Jackson persevered.

'I read your piece in your newspaper today.' The dark figure seemed to ignore him. 'The piece you wrote about *me*.'

Jackson's heart sank. Was that why he'd been lured here instead of just speaking on the phone – because the man he wanted the world to call The Jackdaw didn't like what he'd written about him and now he was going to make him pay? But then he remembered he was neither bound nor gagged.

'You read it?' Jackson asked. 'And . . . what did you think?'

The man in black stood and began to slowly pace around the room, leaving the shotgun behind on the table. 'I thought it was very . . . fair,' he answered after a while. 'Although I thought you dwelled on my unfortunate but necessary acts of violence too much. I suppose it's what the people have been conditioned to demand.'

'It sells papers,' Jackson boldly replied.

'My message will sell papers,' the man contradicted him, his electronic voice a little more urgent and passionate. 'Your interviews with me will sell papers. You do not need to dwell on such *unpleasant* things – things I do not for my pleasure, but because they have to be done to make anyone take notice of us – *the people.*'

'I understand,' Jackson lied. 'I'll do better next time.'

'Ah. Next time. Next time.'

Jackson sensed doubt in the man's distorted voice. 'There will be a next time, won't there?' he asked.

'That, Mr Jackson, depends on the public mood. If I no longer speak for the people, then I can't carry on.'

'The people are still with you,' Jackson encouraged him. 'The public mood is still with you. Trust me.'

'Have I not gone too far though?' he asked. 'Have I not crossed the line of what is acceptable to most people? Tell me, Mr Jackson – what is *the mood of the nation*?'

'I don't understand your doubts,' Jackson told him. 'No one's crying over a few bankers and why should they? You're not doing anything a significant proportion of the population wouldn't like to do. They just don't have the courage that you do.'

'Courage. Is that what it is?'

'Yes,' Jackson urged him. 'You're The Jackdaw. The people admire you.'

'Maybe,' the man behind the balaclava and strange voice answered without conviction.

'Definitely,' Jackson kept going.

The dark figure walked back to the table and sat next to the shotgun before speaking again. 'Are you telling me I should take more people, Mr Jackson? Hold more trials?'

'I can't tell you anything,' Jackson replied. 'That would be . . . unprofessional of me. I'm just saying . . .' He let it hang.

'I see. If you wouldn't mind,' he told him, pushing himself off the table and tossing him the hood. 'Time to get you back, Mr Jackson. I have much to do and less time to do it in than I'd hoped for.'

'Less time?' Jackson picked up on it. 'How so – less time?'

'I've decided to move my schedule forward,' he explained. 'I fear the time available to achieve what I set out to achieve is now more limited than I thought. I must strike these final blows before I . . .'

'Before you what?' Jackson asked, wide-eyed.

'I can't tell you. Not yet.'

'Then can you tell me why you have less time than you thought?'

He breathed in deeply before answering. 'DI Corrigan concerns me.'

'Corrigan?' Jackson almost laughed.

'I researched his background,' The Jackdaw explained. 'His previous cases. Persistent, isn't he? Not a man to give up until he gets what he wants.'

'Don't worry about his previous cases,' Jackson tried to reassure him. 'They were all lunatics and losers just waiting to be caught. You're different. Very different.'

'All the same,' the dark figure insisted, 'he represents a danger to my plans. Things will have to be moved forward.

Now, Mr Jackson, if you would be so good.' He lowered his head, his mirrored sunglasses looking at the hood in Jackson's lap.

Jackson lifted it then hesitated for a second. 'How do you know?' he asked. 'How do you know I didn't take this off – when you left me alone?'

'Because, Mr Jackson, I trust you. If I didn't, you'd already be dead.'

Sean walked quickly through the main entrance of Guy's Hospital and headed towards the food court, the type that had sprung up in every major hospital around the country in the last few years. Early lunchtime and it was already busy enough to make him want to turn around and flee, but he'd promised to meet Kate and discuss the situation his latest investigation had put them in. He passed the more fashionable and therefore more crowded chain outlets and made his way to a far less popular self-service café in the far corner where he knew Kate would already be waiting for him. He found her easily enough, sitting alone away from the crowds, and bent to kiss her on the lips as she looked up to acknowledge him.

'How's it going?' he asked her as he sat. 'You made it to work then.'

'I did,' she answered, but didn't sound happy, 'and the girls made it to school too, with their police escort.'

'Oh,' Sean answered. 'It's just a precaution – to stop you worrying about anything. This man I'm after, he's no threat to any of us. He mentioned my name, that's all. It means nothing.'

'Christ, Sean,' she asked, her voice more worried than hostile. 'Are you sure?'

'Sure I'm sure,' he reassured her. 'They don't come after cops or their families, even the really bad ones. It just doesn't happen. You know that.'

'It happened to Sally,' she reminded him. 'A bad one came after her. She was lucky to survive. Remember?'

'Of course I remember,' he told her, 'but that one was . . . different.'

'Maybe this one is different,' Kate argued.

'No,' Sean dismissed the possibility. 'Sebastian Gibran was the rarest of breeds: the closest thing you could get to pure evil. Perfect childhood, power, wealth, beautiful wife and family, yet he chose to kill – because he thought it was his right to. It made him feel like a god.'

'I don't know, Sean,' she told him, looking down at her pre-packed tuna salad. 'Sometimes I feel like these monsters you hunt are getting ever closer to our front door. Like they're somehow *drawn* to you.'

'They're not,' he promised her. 'Look, this one's not like that. He's just trying to throw me off balance – maybe even get me to hand the investigation to someone else, all of which probably means I've got him worried, which means I'm getting closer. If he was going to come after me or my family do you really think he would have mentioned my name – warned us? He'll know that you and the kids will have a police watch now. He won't be stupid enough to try and get close, and even if he is, we'll have people waiting for him. He's just trying to exert some kind of control. Right now he's probably feeling a bit like a rat in a barrel. Saying this crap about me makes him feel better.'

'You sure?' Kate asked, not letting her eyes leave his. 'You absolutely sure he's no threat to us – to you?'

'Completely,' he reassured her and believed it. 'Listen, you just got spooked last night when this joker mentioned my name, and me behaving like an arsehole didn't help.'

'Jesus,' she answered, trying and failing to suppress a smile. 'The look on everyone's faces. Oh my God, I was so embarrassed.'

Sean smiled too. 'Think they'll ever forgive me?'

'No,' Kate laughed, to relieve her tension as much as anything.

'Oh well,' he shrugged. 'Fuck 'em. Won't do them any harm to see a bit of reality up close and personal for once.'

'Your reality isn't necessarily reality,' she warned him.

'What's that supposed to mean?'

'It means the things you deal with, day in, day out, is not most people's idea of the real world.'

'But it is the real world,' he argued. 'It's just not many people get to see it.'

'Sean,' she pointed out, 'half the people there last night are A&E doctors. They've seen their fair share of *reality*.'

'Point taken,' he sighed. 'Anyway, when you see them tell them I apologize, and I apologize to you too. I could have handled it better. I guess I just got carried away when everything started kicking off live.'

'Apology accepted,' she told him. 'Now get yourself something to eat. I don't like it when you get too skinny.' He was about to answer when he felt his phone vibrating in his jacket pocket, making his heart jump and his stomach sink. He tried to ignore it, but just couldn't. The number had been withheld. He answered it cautiously.

'Hello.'

'DI Corrigan,' Jackson's voice came back. 'We need to meet. Have I ever got something for you.'

'How d'you get my mobile number?' Sean asked in a moment of fear.

'Relax,' Jackson told him. 'I called your office number and got diverted to your mobile.' Sean remembered setting the call divert.

'Just tell me what you want, Jackson.'

'The Argyll Arms – Argyll Street in Soho. One hour. Don't be late.' The line went dead.

'Shit,' he cursed.

'Is everything all right?' Kate asked.

'No,' he told her. 'I have to go and see someone.'

'Straight away? You haven't had anything to eat yet.'

'I'll get something on the way,' he promised.

'No you won't,' she argued. 'Sean, this is getting ridiculous. You're going to make yourself ill.'

'I'm sorry,' he told her, 'but I have to meet this guy. He could have important information.'

'About the man you're after?'

'Could be.'

'Sean. I've barely seen you in days and the kids haven't seen you at all. You need to find some time for us in your life.'

'I will,' he assured her, although he wasn't sure how. 'I have to go.' He stood and thought about kissing her again, but the look on her face told him it wasn't a good idea. 'I'll try to get home at a sensible time,' he promised. 'Maybe even early enough to see the kids. I'll call you later.' He walked away without looking back.

'No you won't,' Kate told him once he was too far away to hear. 'You never do.'

Sean entered the Argyll Arms, scanned the customers for Jackson and found him sitting alone reading his own newspaper at a corner table in the old pub that had been lovingly restored to its original glory. He weaved and pushed his way past the lunchtime customers and joined Jackson without asking or pleasantries.

'What did you want to see me about, Jackson?' he demanded.

Jackson lowered the paper as if he'd only just noticed him, but Sean knew Jackson had no doubt clocked him as soon as he'd entered. Journalists like Jackson weren't too dissimilar from cops in their habits: they liked to have their backs to the wall, sitting where they could keep an eye on all newcomers, and they liked to be aware of what was going on all around them, at all times. Jackson's stories had seriously pissed off some powerful and dangerous people in their time.

'DI Corrigan. So glad you could make it.'

'Cut the shit, Jackson – I'm not in the mood. I've already had a bad day and it's going to get worse, so what did you want to see me about that couldn't wait? It better be worthwhile me dragging my arse into the West End to hear about.'

'Know what you sound like?' Jackson asked with a grin.

'No,' Sean answered. 'What do I sound like?'

'A cop,' Jackson told him, his grin now a full-blown smile.

'Fuck you, Jackson,' Sean cursed and began to stand to leave.

'I met him again,' Jackson hurriedly explained, his smile vanished. 'The Jackdaw.'

Sean sat slowly back in his seat. 'I told you to stay away from him. He's more dangerous than you think. You're gonna get yourself killed. And what's worse – I'll probably be the one who'll have to investigate it.'

'I don't think so,' Jackson told him smugly. 'I've met him twice now and I'm still here, aren't I? He's not going to harm me – he needs me.'

'Needs you? What for, exactly?'

'Publicity,' Jackson explained. 'Needs me to spread his message to a wider audience.'

Sean studied him for a few seconds, his eyes narrowing as he suspected the worst of Jackson. 'Jesus, Jackson. Have you been encouraging this lunatic to take more people – so you can keep the story going?'

'No,' Jackson answered none too convincingly. 'Of course not. That would be unethical. Maybe even criminal. I know my boundaries better than that.'

'I swear, Jackson,' Sean warned him. 'If I find out you've so much as indirectly suggested he keeps doing what he's been doing I promise I'll have you for conspiracy to murder.'

'Bullshit,' Jackson smiled. 'I know the law too, you know. You can't do me for shit.'

'Just try me,' Sean threatened him. 'Just try me.'

'I take it then you don't want to hear what I have to say.'

Sean felt unclean and compromised. He wanted to get away from Jackson before his dark temper rose and over-took him – before he dragged Jackson across the table and beat him senseless. 'I'm all ears,' he managed to say.

Jackson leaned forward, his eyes fixed on Sean's. 'He said he was going to have to speed things up if he was to achieve what he wanted to achieve. Move his timetable forward.'

Sean felt a little confused. It was the first time he'd consid-ered that the killer could be working to a specific timetable. It meant he'd set himself goals – but what were they? He decided not to share his confusion with Jackson.

'Did he tell you what he wanted to achieve?'

'Not exactly,' Jackson asked, looking a bit puzzled, 'but it's obvious, isn't it? He's said it often enough. He wants to make the greedy bankers pay for their crimes.' Jackson leaned back, smiling, as if The Jackdaw's motive was some sort of sick joke.

'You don't believe him then?' Sean asked. 'Don't believe in all this working-class-hero shit?'

'Do me a favour,' Jackson answered. 'He'll turn out to be just another nutter, although . . .'

'Although what?' Sean encouraged him.

'Well I've met a few, you know, once they're behind bars. Interviews for the paper and research for the books. They're all pretty much the same, wouldn't you say?'

'Keep talking, Jackson.'

'Yeah, this one's definitely got something about him. Something a little different.'

'Different how?'

'Control,' Jackson told him. 'He always seems to be in total control – confident – like he's absolutely sure of what he's doing. I didn't sense any madness in him, just clarity of purpose. Even his voice is controlled – the way he speaks – his sentence construction and intonation – nobody really speaks like that. Probably just one more thing he does to keep you lot off his scent.' For a moment Sean thought Jackson looked genuinely spooked before he re-gathered himself. 'Still – probably just the mask and weird voice making him appear more than he is. He'll turn out to be just another loony. But right now he's the hottest story in town. The readers just can't get enough of him.'

'But he says he needs to speed up his *timetable*? Did he say why?' Sean asked.

'Absolutely,' Jackson grinned.

'And?'

'It's because of you, *DI Corrigan*. He looked up your old cases. He thinks you're very determined. To be honest – I think you've got him worried. Great angle to the story: "The Jackdaw versus London's top detective". I was thinking give the readers a little background about yourself first, you know – how you got your man and all that stuff – how Thomas Keller almost killed you. What do you reckon?'

'Don't even think about it,' Sean warned him, imagining what Kate would say if his name appeared on the front page of *The World*.

'Come on,' Jackson tormented him. 'We haven't had anything this interesting since the Yorkshire Ripper sent tape recordings to the chief investigating officer, and even that turned out to be a hoax.'

'I don't know who's crazier,' Sean told him. 'You or him.'

'Think of the positive publicity,' Jackson tried to persuade him. 'The top-brass would love it: "Hero cop pitted against merciless killer". You'll be famous.'

'You put me all over that arsewipe you call a newspaper and I'll come for you, Jackson,' Sean warned him through thin lips as he got to his feet.

'Just think about it.' Jackson smiled. 'You have my business card. My number's on it. And in case you were thinking of listening in to my conversations, that's not the phone I use to speak to The Jackdaw. You'd be wasting your time.'

'Stay away from me,' Sean insisted, taking the card and slipping it into his jacket pocket, 'and stay away from this joker who's got you convinced he's the real killer. You want to get yourself killed, fine. Just do it on someone else's patch.'

'Oh, he's the real killer,' Jackson told him, his eyes a mixture of excitement and terror. 'Believe me, he's the real deal and when you finally come face to face with him, you'll see it for yourself.'

'We'll see,' Sean snarled and turned to leave before Jackson said something he couldn't ignore.

'You know we're a lot alike, you and me. I see it, even if you don't.'

'We're nothing alike,' Sean protested. 'You're imagining things.'

'Sure we are,' Jackson argued. 'We both love our jobs, even when they're destroying everything around us – our families and friends. We're both determined to get the job done, no matter what it takes – even if we have to bend a few rules. I never quit until I have my story and you never quit until you have your man. We're both prepared to take risks others would never dream of to get what we want. And why do we do this? For money or celebrity? No. We do it for our own satisfaction and peace of mind, because if we didn't, we just wouldn't be able to live with ourselves. Ring any bells?'

'Similar traits don't mean we're alike,' Sean replied.

'Come on, Corrigan. Your colleagues look at you just the same way mine look at me – like you're crazy. Like you're insane for taking the chances you do. But it's what makes you you – just as it's what makes me me. We're lost to our professions, Corrigan, and ultimately it'll probably destroy us both.'

Jackson's words cut deep, but Sean managed to hide how much they had disturbed him. He reminded himself he still had Kate and his girls – clinging to them like a drowning man clinging to a rock.

'Have a nice day,' he told Jackson and headed for the exit.

Sean arrived back in the office at the Yard with Jackson's words still dancing around inside his mind. *Was that what Jackson wanted, was that what The Jackdaw wanted? To bring them face to face – to turn the investigation and its ultimate end into some kind of public entertainment – just so long as they could watch it all from a safe distance?* But maybe, just maybe, he could still use Jackson to lead him straight to The Jackdaw.

He burst into the main office and headed for his own goldfish bowl of a room, palming off the efforts of both Sally and Donnelly to get his attention, for the moment at least. Right now there was only one person he wanted, *needed*, to see. As he entered his office she was already sitting on the opposite side of his desk, once more watching the videos from the Your View broadcasts.

Anna looked up when she heard him enter. 'You've been gone a long time,' she told him. 'Anywhere interesting?'

'You could say that,' he replied. 'I met with Geoff Jackson.'

'The journalist from *The World*?' she asked. 'The one covering our investigation?'

'Yeah,' he answered. 'He met with the killer again.'

'How d'you know?' Anna argued. 'How d'you know he's meeting with the real murderer? How does Jackson know?'

'He seems convinced,' Sean told her. 'I may not like the little prick, but he's smart enough and experienced enough to make sure he's speaking to the real deal.'

'So what now?'

'Said the killer's working to some kind of timetable,

implying he intends to achieve certain targets he's set himself. D'you think that's possible – that he could reach a point that satisfies him and then stop?'

'Interesting,' Anna answered, pursing her red lips as she considered the question. 'I suppose I'd have to say it's possible, based on the fact he killed his first victim, but not the next two, which tells us he's not in a state of rage or frenzy. He's in control – he has discipline and restraint. But it means he's even more organized than we thought he was. He may be trying to balance the number of victims he can claim with the chances of eventually being caught. Not something your typical serial killer can do. Most will offend until they're caught or killed.'

'But he's not a serial killer,' Sean reminded her. 'He's only killed one of his victims. If anything he's becoming less violent, not more.' He slipped off his raincoat and slumped into his chair. 'I don't know,' he admitted. 'D'you buy all this vengeful voice of the oppressed crap?'

'Why not?' she asked. 'If this is a man who's potentially lost everything because of the banking collapse, then yes, it could psychologically destabilize him enough to make him act out his fantasies of revenge in a violent way. Even commit murder.'

'And want to broadcast it to the world?'

'For some people revenge is an intensely personal thing. For others, they want the world to know it was them.'

'But he hides behind a mask.'

'When he sees the masked man on the videos, he sees himself.'

'But he would have to have had some underlying psychological issues already, right? He hasn't gone from nought to a hundred in one go. The screws were already loose. Whatever effect the banking crisis had on him it just finished the job. If it hadn't been that it would have been something else – his wife leaving him, losing his job, someone looking at him the wrong way while he's queuing with his kids at Legoland – something would have set him off. If he is in fact just another psychopath, albeit a particularly patient and clever one.'

'Having doubts?' Anna asked.

'Let's just say I like my psychopaths nice and straightforward. You know, start with pulling legs off spiders then a slow and steady descent into complete violent madness – each crime worse than the last, sort of thing.'

Anna smiled. 'Not all people with psychopathic tendencies end up as violent criminals,' she explained. 'A significant number of company CEOs have psychopathic personalities, only they *kill* people in the boardroom and in business deals, but they still do so without feeling the same sort of compassion a normal person would for their victims. They enjoy the power. They enjoy being able to control what happens to the life of another person.'

'Well, this one's certainly turned the tables on your boardroom psychos. I bet they're not feeling quite so in control right now,' he told her, before being distracted by DC Bishop wandering past his door. 'Bishop,' Sean called out, stopping him in his tracks and making him look up from the latest technical data sheets he was studying while walking. He retraced his steps backwards and poked his head into Sean's office.

'Something I can do for you, guv'nor?' he asked.

'Yeah,' Sean told him. 'How you getting on tracing the source of the signal?'

Bishop looked puzzled for a second. 'I've already traced the source, guv'nor,' he answered. 'It's the *location* of the source that's the tricky bit.'

Sean's eyes narrowed. 'Don't play with me,' he warned him.

Bishop nervously cleared his throat. 'No change since the last broadcast,' he explained. 'I can't get any closer until he's—'

'Online,' Sean interrupted. 'Yeah, yeah. I get the picture,' but as Bishop was about to walk away an idea came from

267

nowhere and jumped into the front of Sean's mind. 'Hold on a second,' he stopped him, fishing in his jacket pocket for the card Jackson had given him. 'Can you track a mobile phone signal, even if it's on the move?'

'You should go through technical support for that,' Bishop reminded him.

'I know technical support can,' Sean answered. 'What I asked is can *you* track a mobile?'

'So long as it's turned on and I have the number. All I have to do is triangulate the signal and bingo.'

'Number's on there,' Sean told him, handing him the card.

'Geoff Jackson?' Bishop queried. 'The journalist? I doubt he's using his own mobile to communicate with the suspect.'

'He's not,' Sean agreed, 'but he's a journalist. He's no more likely to be without his own mobile than we would.'

'So,' Bishop surmised, 'when he goes to meet with the suspect he'll still have his mobile with him.'

'Of course he will,' Sean told him.

'*If* he goes to meet him again,' Anna argued.

'He will,' Sean assured her.

'The suspect took the phones from the other victims prior to abducting them,' Anna reminded him. 'At the very least I'd expect him to be cautious enough to make Jackson turn his phone off and with it your chance of tracking it.'

'He probably will,' Sean agreed, 'but if the surveillance can stay close enough to the signal before that, it could be too late. Jackson might just lead us straight to him, even if he doesn't know it himself.'

'But why not technical support?' Bishop asked. 'They've got better equipment for this than I can cobble together.'

'Because I need it now,' Sean insisted. 'Jackson isn't gonna hang around. Technical support will take too long to get themselves sorted. Don't worry about the authority – I'll get Addis to sort it ASAP. He won't argue if he thinks it'll bring a result.'

'And the surveillance?' Bishop asked.

'Let me worry about the surveillance,' Sean told him. 'You just get a fix on Jackson's phone.' Bishop shrugged his shoulders and headed off to find people who had access to the equipment he would need and who owed him a favour or two. Sean stood and walked to his door, summoning Sally and Donnelly from the main office. A few seconds later they were all gathered in his office waiting for the news. 'We're going to triangulate the signal on Geoff Jackson's mobile phone and put a surveillance team up his arse. Next time he goes to meet our boy we'll be there with a welcoming committee.'

'Sneaky,' Donnelly observed. 'Very sneaky.'

'Dave,' Sean ordered, 'get hold of Addis and get me a surveillance team on the hurry up. With Addis ordering it – it'll happen fast. He has that effect on people.'

'I'm on it,' Donnelly told him and immediately headed off to hunt down Addis.

'What d'you want me to do?' Sally asked.

'Stay close,' Sean told her. 'If Jackson looks like he's heading to a meet I want you with me, and Bishop too. If he leads us to our man I want someone with me I can trust – someone to handle Jackson while I handle the suspect.'

'What if he's armed?' Sally questioned. 'Goldsboro said he was armed with a shotgun.'

'Then I'll be careful,' he answered flippantly.

'Like you were with Thomas Keller?' she asked.

'That was different.' Sean tried to dodge the subject.

'Promise me you won't try and take him on your own,' Sally insisted. He looked from Sally to Anna and back, unable to decide who looked the most concerned.

'OK,' he assured them. 'If this works and it looks like there's even a chance he might be armed, then I promise we'll just box him in and wait for an ARV to take him down.'

'You'd bloody better,' Sally warned him. 'You'd better.'

*   *   *

269

Zukov and DC Tessa Carlisle turned into Cecil Road – an unattractive dead-end street in Colindale, north London, full of ugly grey houses thrown up after the Second World War.

'I hate it around here,' Zukov complained. 'Gives me the creeps. Reminds me of being at training school.' He was referring to the nearby Metropolitan Police Training College – a place that held little other than bad memories for him.

'It wasn't that bad,' Carlisle disagreed. 'I had a pretty good time there.'

Zukov eyed the pretty young detective from behind his sunglasses. He had his own ideas why Carlisle, with her sparkling blue eyes, heavy chest and long blonde hair, had enjoyed her time at training school more than he had, but he kept his thoughts to himself. He found the house he was looking for and parked up.

'This is it,' he told her, 'number fourteen – flat number five.'

'Can't be much of a flat in a house that size,' Carlisle deduced.

'More like a bedsit, I reckon,' Zukov agreed. 'Probably going to be a right shithole too. Don't know why they make us wear suits all the time when we spend half our lives crawling around dumps like this. Some immigrant carved up his council house with plaster board and now charges other immigrants a fortune to live like pigs.'

'Let's not make any judgements just yet,' Carlisle warned him and climbed out the car before he could reply, waiting for him to join her on the pavement. 'Shall we?' She smiled at the grumpy-looking Zukov before heading towards the front door of number fourteen. She pressed the cheap white doorbell that electronically chimed a classical tune she vaguely recognized and waited for sounds of life to come from beyond the frosted double-glazed glass that dominated the white PVC door. A few seconds later she heard footsteps and saw the distorted silhouette of someone approaching. She heard a lock turn and the door was opened by a slim man who looked to be in his mid-sixties, although she guessed he was probably a lot younger – a hard unprivileged life having taken its toll. He wore a grey shirt under a burgundy cardigan, with matching grey trousers and comfortable grey shoes. The smell from inside the house was immediately unpleasant – too many people trying to co-exist in too small a domicile, the cooking smells from at least three continents mixing in the overly warm central heating. Carlisle almost gagged, but recovered quickly enough.

'Can I help you with something?' the man asked, friendly enough.

'Police,' Zukov told him, holding out his warrant card to prove it. 'DC Zukov and DC Carlisle from the Special Investigations Unit – New Scotland Yard,' he added for extra credence. 'Do you live here?'

'Yes,' the man nodded.

'Is it your house?' Zukov continued.

'I own the house, yes,' he answered, looking increasingly confused.

'Does anyone else live here?' Zukov laboured.

'Yes,' he admitted without concern. 'My tenants.'

'Your tenants?' Zukov asked as if he'd made a significant discovery.

'Does a Jason Howard live here, Mr . . . sorry I didn't catch your name?' Carlisle took over.

'My name is Peter O'Meagher and yes, Jason lives here – has done for a few years now. He's not in trouble, is he?'

'Is he in now?' Carlisle asked as quietly as she could – the thought of calling for back-up going through her head before O'Meagher dispelled it.

'No,' he told her. 'In fact, I haven't seen him in a good few days. I don't think any of us have – although he left me an envelope with enough cash in it to pay for several weeks' rent before he left.'

'So you're not expecting him back?' Zukov asked.

'Until I hear otherwise I expect him to return. All of his things are still here.'

'You checked his room?' Carlisle probed.

'Just once,' O'Meagher explained. 'A couple of days after he first left – just in case.'

'Just in case what?' Zukov pushed.

'Not everybody who stays is happy, Detective,' O'Meagher pointed out. 'It's happened before – sadly. I started thinking maybe the cash in the envelope was more his way of paying for the *inconvenience* rather than rent up-front.'

'But it wasn't?' Carlisle checked.

'Thankfully not,' he half smiled.

'Glad to hear it,' Carlisle agreed and meant it. 'Can we come in – can you show us his room?'

O'Meagher looked uncomfortable. 'Do you have a search warrant?'

'No, but we could get one,' Zukov warned him.

Carlisle tried to a softer approach. 'If we find something important I promise we'll get a warrant before we seize anything. We don't want to put you in a compromising position.'

O'Meagher stood aside to let them in. 'Fair enough,' he agreed, closing the door behind him, 'but I doubt you'll find anything useful. Jason didn't have much of a life, from what I could see. He had some sort of a job at a local warehouse and didn't earn very much from what I could tell. Kept himself very much to himself.'

'Did you ever talk to him at all?' Carlisle asked.

'A little – not that he said much,' O'Meagher explained. 'I believe he owned a small business before he lost it during the banking crisis – along with his wife and children. She's left him and now he's reduced to this.' Zukov and Carlisle glanced at each other knowingly.

'Did he ever say anything about getting his own back on

the banks?' Zukov asked as they climbed the threadbare carpet on the narrow staircase.

'Not to me,' O'Meagher answered, 'but, like I said, we really didn't speak at any length.'

'I understand,' Carlisle said as they reached a plain wooden door on the first-floor landing. 'But about this money in the envelope – Jason handed that to you himself?'

'No,' O'Meagher told her. 'It was just left for me. I found it in amongst the other post.'

'So although he lives here, he posted it to you?' Carlisle continued.

'It hadn't been through the post,' O'Meagher explained. 'It was just an envelope with my name on it – on the floor, in amongst the other mail.'

'So it came through the letter box?' Zukov joined in.

'Possibly,' O'Meagher considered it, 'or it could have just got knocked off the sideboard and fell there. I'm afraid not all my tenants are as careful as they should be.'

'I guess not.' Carlisle ended the discussion, aware O'Meagher couldn't pour any more light on how the letter came to be amongst the other mail. 'Shall we?' she encouraged him, nodding at the single key he was holding.

'Sorry. Of course.' He slid the key into the lock and turned it, pushing the door and allowing it to swing open, revealing the stillness inside. Carlisle could immediately sense no one had been inside the room for some days at least – it felt cold and abandoned. She stepped past O'Meagher and entered the room closely followed by Zukov, who let out a long whistle as he scanned the interior.

'This was not what I was expecting,' he admitted, shaking his head.

Carlisle too was surprised, the squalor she was so used to finding replaced by an immaculate space. Even the window had been left slightly open to allow fresh air to circulate. The bed had been made with fresh sheets and blankets, books were

273

stacked neatly on the limited shelving, personal possessions arranged tidily on the sideboards and the mantelpiece over the ancient electric fire. She walked to the cheap wardrobe and pulled the doors open. The few clothes that he had were clean, pressed and either hung or folded neatly.

'Did you do this?' she asked O'Meagher.

'No,' he insisted. 'This is how Jason lived.'

'Did he have a military background?' Zukov asked.

'I don't think so, but I can't be sure. Like I said – he never talked much.'

Carlisle walked to the alcove that served as the kitchen and examined the small two-hob cooker where she found more of the same cleanliness and order. It was the same in cupboards – everything clean and neatly stacked – as if it had never been touched. Finally she opened the fridge, almost afraid what she might find – a severed hand or head perfectly pickled and left in a spotless but empty space, like a piece of modern art in an exhibit. But there was nothing – nothing but shining cleanliness.

'Were you ever aware of him cooking in here?' Carlisle asked.

'Not really,' O'Meagher answered. 'He mainly chose to eat out at the local cafés. I guess cooking wasn't his thing.'

'No,' Carlisle agreed. 'I guess not. Did he ever have any visitors?'

'No.' O'Meagher sounded sure. 'Never. He was a loner – a quiet loner.'

'Ever come home the worse for wear and moan about the hand life had dealt him?' Zukov pried.

'No,' O'Meagher shook his head, smiling. 'I never ever smelt drink on him – morning or night. I have no idea how he spent his private time.'

'Looks like a social life isn't the only thing he was missing,' Zukov added as he pulled open the last drawer to reveal nothing but neatly folded clothes.

'Meaning?' Carlisle enquired.

'Meaning there's no correspondence in the whole place,' he told her. 'Not a letter, not a bill, not a bank statement – nothing.'

'There must be something,' Carlisle argued. 'Everybody has something.'

'You won't find any banking documents,' O'Meagher explained. 'After what happened Jason didn't trust banks. As far as I know he dealt in cash only. He was paid in cash and that's how he paid me.'

'But he must have had a bank account to pay his bills,' Carlisle pointed out.

'He didn't have any bills, as such,' O'Meagher continued. 'I pay for all the heating and water and so on and my tenants give me cash to cover what they use.'

'What about a car?' Carlisle probed. 'Cars create paperwork.'

'He didn't have a car.' O'Meagher dashed their hopes again. 'I think most of the time he walked to work.'

Carlisle and Zukov looked at each other before scanning the disturbingly ordered room. 'A difficult man to find,' Zukov declared. 'Almost like he was *planning* to disappear.'

'He's made himself a ghost,' Carlisle agreed. 'How d'you find a ghost?'

'I don't know,' Zukov answered, 'but I know we need to tell the guv'nor – see what he makes of all this. Not sure if he's going to love it or hate it.'

'Only one way to find out,' Carlisle encouraged him.

'Fair enough,' Zukov agreed and slipped his mobile from his jacket pocket, 'but no matter what he thinks – I reckon we've just found our prime suspect.'

Jackson sat in a small café in Berwick Street, Soho, drinking his way through another espresso while he typed the next day's headline story into his laptop and wondered how much of the piece should be about The Jackdaw and how much DI Corrigan. *Corrigan*, he thought to himself. *The killers came and went, but Corrigan – well, he was just the gift that just kept on giving.* His fingers hesitated over the keyboard. *Go all out on Corrigan now – make him an unwitting celebrity detective, or give him a little more time and wait for him to come of his own accord. Fuck – Corrigan was the story.* He could just feel it.

The pay-as-you-go mobile vibrated in his trouser pocket and made him jump and forget what he was about to write. He fumbled to free the phone, hurrying to answer it before the caller gave up. 'Hello.'

'Ah, Mr Jackson,' the unmistakeable electronic voice replied. 'Are you alone?'

'No,' Jackson answered, half hoping to hear the line go dead as the familiar fear quickly crept over him. 'I'm in a café, but I can speak.'

'I need to see you,' the voice told him. 'I have something I need you to see. Something I want you to witness.'

Jackson's mind spun with possibilities. *Did The Jackdaw want him to witness the torture or even murder of another victim? Had his luck finally run out and it was his turn to be the victim? Should he tell the police – lead them to the sick bastard? What the fuck*, he decided. *He'd come this far.* 'When?'

'Two hours from now,' the voice instructed him. 'Drive to the Queen Mary Reservoir, Ashford Road, Walton-on-Thames, and wait for my call. Goodbye, Mr Jackson.' The line went dead before he could argue.

'Bollocks,' Jackson muttered to himself as he flipped the phone closed and slipped it back into his trouser pocket. 'What now, you bastard? What the hell have you got in mind now?'

11

David Barrowgate paid the black cab driver in cash and then watched it drive off along Brunswick Gardens, Notting Hill Gate, as he began the short walk to the old mansion block that housed his state-of-the-art, all-mod-cons flat. The walk would have been even shorter if cars hadn't been parked along both sides of the street and he hadn't ended up with the only black cab driver in London who cared about blocking the road while his punter paid the fee. The suitably small tip reflected his displeasure. Still, the brief exposure to some fresh air would do him no harm after an afternoon spent wining and dining some of his firm's most important clients – the sort that never touched a drop when back in their own countries, but never held back when in London. He couldn't stand half the people he had to do business with – ignorant peasants from Eastern Europe and North Africa, who just happened to have stumbled across black gold or some other valuable commodity and now wanted to invest their excess cash in the London markets. But it was all worth it: he was only thirty-two, but he already had a flat to die for with no mortgage and a couple of million stashed in the BVIs, not to mention a position as a senior trader for the Chaucer and Vale Bank. Life was good.

All good things came to those who waited for them or, as he liked to believe, *all good things came to those who worked their arses off for them*. Somehow he'd worked hard enough to overcome the oversized classes and poor teaching standards at his inner-city primary school and win himself a place at the nearest grammar school where he'd excelled at maths and even become the captain of the rugby side – his courage overcoming his physical slightness. After achieving straight As at A-level he'd waltzed into Cambridge University where he continued to star in mathematics. Before he'd even obtained his degree he'd been recruited by Antrobus Bank on a starting salary of a hundred grand . . . plus bonus of course. Now he was earning ten times that and why not – he was one of the best at what he did. With his mathematical skills he could predict the markets quicker than almost anyone and that meant he could make money – lots of money – and that made him a valuable commodity. Sure, he'd deliberately changed the way he spoke – dropping his slight Yorkshire accent for something that sounded as if he was a product of Harrow or Eton – and, sure, he never talked much about his upbringing, school or the fact his parents still lived in a small council house in Leeds, but it was all just part of the game. He was sure he wasn't the only one whose life seemingly only began once he reached university – everything in the past neatly packed away in a large suitcase and pushed under the bed of history. Only thing was, he increasingly wanted to unpack the old case and become something of what he used to think he was, or at least could be.

He was growing tired of the game the City played – sucking in the brightest and the best from the top universities and putting them to work for the world's biggest banks with the sole purpose of making money. He was becoming increasingly confused the more he looked around at the larger world: carpenters made things from wood, for which they were rewarded with money. Doctors cured the sick, for which they were rewarded with money. Everybody did something for which they were rewarded with money and the satisfaction of what they produced or changed. But he made money, for which he was rewarded with money. He had no *product* – nothing to stand back and admire before it went to market. His product was also his reward and it was leaving him feeling increasingly unsatisfied. *A few more years*, he told himself, *a few more years and he'd be out – free to do something more rewarding*. First he'd travel the world, staying in backpacker hostels, hiding his wealth and past, with perhaps the occasional overnight stay at a five-star hotel. And then he'd decide what he was going to do with the rest of his life. The thought of returning to academia interested him most – becoming a professor of mathematics and dedicating the rest of his life to solving at least one of the world's great unsolved mathematical problems. Time would tell, but for now he'd stay on the treadmill. No matter what the future held, he had no desire to be anything less than extremely comfortable.

Even if he hadn't been a little drunk and even if he hadn't been daydreaming about what the latest deal would net for him personally, he probably wouldn't have noticed the white Renault Trafic van parked in the residents-only bay outside the entrance to his building, bold blue letters on its side proclaiming the name of a plumbing company that didn't in fact exist. He also probably wouldn't have noticed the door of the van opening as he began to climb the short flight of steps to the front door or the man in black clothes and a black balaclava who moved quickly and silently across the pavement, closing the distance between them until there was no distance, until too late he sensed his presence and tried to turn. But a hard, dull blow to the back of his head made him crumple to his knees, dizziness and nausea sweeping over him as he felt hands slide under his armpits and begin to pull him away from the building. At only five foot eight and of slim build he was easily dragged down the steps and across the pavement. His head began to clear as he realized he was being bundled into a van or large car, but another blow, this time across his temple, all but knocked him unconscious as his ankles and wrists were strapped into restraints, his mouth taped over and a hood pulled over his head. He thought he heard a door sliding shut and an engine starting, but mainly there was just darkness and the sound of his own blood rushing around inside his head. Mainly there was just confusion and terror.

Sean sat in his office trying to concentrate on the reports of yet more white vans being driven in a suspicious manner or having been parked in a suspicious area or way, but he was paying them little attention. He kept glancing at his mobile phone, waiting and praying it would deliver the message that Jackson was on the move and heading west – towards The Jackdaw. It rang while he was looking at it, making his heart miss a beat before he grabbed it up. The caller ID told him it was Zukov.

'What's happening?' he asked without niceties.

'I found Jason Howard's last known address,' Zukov told him. 'A bedsit in Colindale. Very salubrious.'

'Get on with it, Paulo,' Sean hurried him.

'Landlord let me in, but there's no trace of Howard. Landlord and the neighbours say no one's seen him for a week or so, not that anyone was looking.'

'Have you searched it?'

'Yeah,' Zukov answered. 'It's as clean as the Pope's knob. Neat, ordered, bed made, washing-up done, clothes folded in the wardrobe, dry food in the cupboard, but the fridge is empty and cleaned. Looks like he's gone on a little trip.'

Sean chewed the loose skin around his thumbnail. *Organized. Deliberate. Forward thinking. Just like The Jackdaw.* 'Any idea where he's gone?'

'No,' Zukov admitted. 'He left without telling anyone. Stuffed an envelope full of cash, left it for the landlord and took off, apparently leaving his worldly possessions behind – such as they are.'

Sean's eyes narrowed as he imagined Jason Howard making his final arrangements before slipping from the house and into the dark night – the birth of The Jackdaw?

'We'd better find him, and quickly,' Sean insisted.

'Easier said than done,' Zukov explained. 'He has no bank accounts, credit cards, no utilities he has to pay for – not even a car. He's completely off the grid. I can check his workplace, but I reckon I know what we'll find. I'll get the locals to check with his ex-wife too, but again, I won't be holding my breath. Think he's our man?'

'Maybe,' Sean answered without the enthusiasm Zukov expected.

'Only maybe?' Zukov checked. 'He's got to be perfect – hasn't he? Why go to such lengths to make himself untraceable if he's not up to something serious? We've checked out dozens of suspects with form for threatening bankers, but no one's shaped up this well.'

'Maybe he just doesn't like the modern way of life,' Sean found himself answering as he wondered why his heart wasn't jumping into his mouth at the further damning evidence pointing towards Howard. Was it fatigue? Was it because it seemed too easy? Or was it because The Jackdaw always seemed to predict their next move – so how come he hadn't predicted they'd find his bedsit? *Or had he?* Excitement always came to Sean when he sensed he was beginning to run down his quarry, but he didn't feel it now. At best he sensed a trap.

'Circulate him as wanted anyway,' Sean told him. 'Right now he's the best we've got.'

'Already done,' Zukov informed him.

'Good. Do whatever you have to do to find him.'

'Will do,' Zukov replied and the line went dead, but the

phone started chirping and vibrating again before Sean had even put it down.

'Yes,' he barked.

'Jackson's on the move,' Bishop answered. 'Heading west.'

Now Sean did feel his stomach tighten with excitement. 'You with the surveillance team?'

'Yeah. DS Donnelly hooked us up.'

'Stay with them and the target,' Sean told him. 'Jackson will be looking for you, so hang back out of sight and use the signal to track him. Understand?'

'No problem,' Bishop assured him, 'but what if he's not going to meet our man? What if he's up to something else?'

'Where is he now?'

'On the A4, approaching Earls Court.'

Sean felt his heart rate suddenly accelerate, some primeval alarm telling him something was about to happen.

'No,' he told Bishop. 'He's on his way to meet him. I can feel it. Keep close, but out of sight. I'm coming to meet you.'

Mark Hudson lay fully clothed on top of his bed in his room in the council flat he shared with his mother. A cigarette burnt in the ashtray next to him while he played the most violent video game he had been able to find in the shop to steal. The room was beginning to smell rancid from the pile of unwashed clothes on the floor, leftover takeaway food and stale smoke. The windows hadn't been opened since the previous summer, more than six months ago. The stench was even beginning to keep his friends away, that and his increasingly violent and unpredictable mood swings. Not that he cared. He had his games and now he had a role model too.

His mobile phone vibrated next to the ashtray and played a short burst of an underground rap song exalting the act of rape. He idly checked the message from one of his friends, the contents of which made him jump up, knocking the ashtray and cigarette flying as he scrambled to his desk and

282

computer. His filthy fingers typed quickly and smoothly until he found what the text had told him to check out. He breathed a sigh of relief as he realized he hadn't missed any of the action – the man on the screen sitting taped to the same chair as before, the hood still over his head as he fidgeted and tried to free himself from his bindings.

Hudson barely dared breathe as he waited for his idol to appear on screen, but he didn't have to wait long until the dark figure he'd come to admire so much came into view standing proud and confident. How Hudson would have loved to be alone with the man they called The Jackdaw for a while. He'd already fantasised about what he'd do to his idol, all shown live on Your View – the pupil taking his master's place as he became the worshipped one – the most feared shark in the ocean. He licked his cold-sore-infected lips and settled down for the show. The dark figure walked to his victim and pulled the hood from his head, making him squint and squirm away from the light of his own future. He grabbed him by his short light brown hair and ripped the tape from his mouth. There was a silence for a few seconds while Barrowgate caught his breath and realized the full extent of his predicament.

'*Please,*' Barrowgate managed to beg. '*Don't kill me. I can pay you. Just tell me what you want.*'

'*Justice,*' the dark figure spat the word at Barrowgate before turning to the camera to speak to his audience. '*I want justice, Mr Barrowgate. But even here, even now you think you can buy whatever you like – think that if you pay me enough I'll forget about the injustices I and people like me have had to endure at the hands of the greedy few. The greedy few like you, David Barrowgate.*'

'*I've done nothing to you,*' Barrowgate pleaded. '*I haven't done anything to anybody.*'

'*Wrong,*' the dark figure told him. '*You and your kind have hurt a great many people and now you will be judged and punished for your crimes. But not in a courtroom, where your money would buy you the best barrister to get you off on some technicality. No, Mr Barrowgate. You will be judged in this room and by the people.'*

Hudson's eyes grew wide with excitement and anticipation. The last two victims had been a bit of a disappointment, but somehow he sensed this was going to be different.

Sean and Sally finally caught up with the surveillance team not far from Walton-on-Thames, just to the southwest of London. Jackson had come to a stop and therefore so had they, parking up far enough away that they couldn't possibly be seen by Jackson or the suspect if this was where they were to meet. Sean spotted Bishop sitting in one of the lead cars and headed for him, tapping on the side window before he and Sally climbed into the back seats.

Bishop turned to the thirty-something woman next to him dressed in smart-casual clothing and spoke. 'DS Howland, this is DI Corrigan and DS Jones, from the Special Investigations Unit. They're the ones who arranged this little jaunt in the country.'

Howland offered her hand to the new passengers. 'Lara. Good to meet you.'

Sean shook her hand first. 'Sean. Likewise.'

Sally did the same. 'Sally.'

'Any movement?' Sean asked.

'Not for a few minutes,' Howland answered. 'He drove all the way out here then took a side road and parked up down by the reservoir. I've got a couple of foot units out and about hiding in the grass who've got an eyeball on your boy, but he seems to be on his own.'

'Then he's waiting for further instructions or the suspect's watching him – checking he hasn't been followed,' Sean explained.

'Looking for us,' Sally added, silencing everyone for a few seconds.

'What's the terrain like where the target's stopped?' Sean asked.

'My people tell me it's open ground – flat with a few ditches and a lot of knee-high grass. But if you're worried about them showing out, don't be. It's getting dark out there and they're keeping a safe distance, carrying out their obs from a water ditch. No one's going to spot them,' Howland assured them.

'That's not what I'm worried about,' Sean explained. 'This one likes the woods and trees. He won't come here. Not to meet Jackson anyway.'

Bishop's laptop suddenly began to emit a shrill, piercing sound. 'Uh oh,' was all he said as he moved the tracking equipment from his lap and replaced it with the computer, flipping it open, the Your View broadcast playing on the screen without him having to do anything more.

'Problem?' Sean asked, leaning forward to look over Bishop's shoulder.

'See for yourself,' Bishop answered, passing the computer to Sean.

'Shit,' Sean swore as he looked at the images of Barrowgate squirming in the same wooden chair, the man in the ski-mask with voice-altering equipment across his mouth preaching into the camera. 'He's already taken another one.'

'Then he's not coming here,' Sally surmised.

'No,' Sean agreed, 'but Jackson could still be going to him.'

'Why?' Sally asked.

'To witness it for himself. See it up close and personal,' Sean answered.

'*You can't buy me with your money, Mr Barrowgate,*' the masked figure told him. '*I am above and beyond your lust for wealth and material goods. I am a soldier – a general leading his army of the people towards a better, fairer system where the wealth is shared and used to benefit all, not just the greedy few.*'

'Is it just me,' Sally asked, 'or does he sound like he's beginning to lose it?'

'He's beginning to believe his own press,' Sean explained. 'Jackson's been pumping him up to be some sort of people's champion and now he's beginning to believe it.' They watched as the man disappeared from view, leaving the terrified Barrowgate to face the camera alone. 'Now what's he doing?'

'Hold on a second,' Howland interrupted, pressing the covert earpiece deeper into her ear. 'I'm getting an update from one of my units with an eyeball on your target.' Everyone in the car held their breath. 'Looks like he's reading a text.' Sally and Sean looked at each other. 'Now he's back to the vehicle and it's an off, off, off.' Howland pressed the transmit switch on her radio and spoke to her team. 'Target's moving off in his vehicle. We'll close on him when he's back amongst traffic on the main road and pick up a visual for a follow. Everyone else follow us, but don't bunch up.' Howland started the car and headed along the road on course to inter-cept Jackson as he re-joined the main road.

'D'you really think it could have been the suspect texting Jackson?' Sally asked, reading Sean's thoughts.

'You don't see him on screen, do you?' Sean replied, but before Sally could answer the dark figure returned and stood next to a pale and sick-looking Barrowgate.

'*Please,*' Barrowgate appealed to him. '*I don't feel well. My head hurts. I think you might have fractured my skull. You hit me so hard.*'

'*What I have done to you is nothing compared to what you have done to the people of this country,*' his captor replied. '*While the banking sector collapsed and we suffered, you were paid a million pounds as a bonus, weren't you?*' Barrowgate said nothing, his eyes blinking at what he was being told. '*Weren't you?*' his tormentor shouted, making him jump.

'*Yes,*' Barrowgate admitted under the pressure, before rallying and trying to explain. '*But my bank was never in diffi-culties. We didn't sell mortgages.*'

'*I know,*' the warped voice told him. '*I know, but the crisis caused property prices to collapse and you then encouraged wealthy foreign investors to buy up property at knockdown prices, selling it a few years later for vast profits, taking affordable housing away from those who really needed it. You're a profiteer and a thief, Mr Barrowgate, and now you must pay for your crimes.'*

Barrowgate looked stunned for a few seconds before he could speak. *'How did you know?'* he asked. *'How did you know?'*

'Good question,' Sean told Sally. 'How does he know?'

'Are these things a matter of public record?' Sally suggested. 'Could he be hacking banks' computers – raiding their bins for confidential waste? I don't know.'

'No,' Sean agreed. 'I don't know either.'

Mark Hudson watched transfixed by the writhing victim and the words of his idol, although he was slightly disappointed the victim wasn't a woman. He preferred it when they were women.

'How did I know, Mr Barrowgate?' his idol repeated Barrowgate's own question. *'Because I know everything. I know everything about you people – about your self-serving greed and arrogant, shameless, fraudulent taking of what belongs to us, not you.'*

'Yes,' Hudson encouraged. 'Dirty, thieving bastard,' he almost shouted, forgetting about the countless vulnerable victims he robbed and assaulted in the dark streets around the fringes of Birmingham city centre, lying in wait for out-of-towners who took a wrong turn looking for their car park. 'Now do him,' he demanded. 'Make the bastard pay. Fucking do him.' But instead The Jackdaw walked from the screen, the camera tracking his movements for a few steps before switching back to the victim. Moments later The Jackdaw returned with a sawn-off shotgun that he levelled at Barrowgate's head, making him flinch and lean away as if that could somehow save him from the gun's blast. Hudson felt his testicles coil and tighten with excitement. He'd never

287

seen anyone's head blown off with a sawn-off before. But suddenly the dark figure pulled the gun away from his victim and tucked it up under his own chin, his thumb resting across the triggers.

'No,' Hudson screamed. 'No. Don't do yourself – do the bastard in the chair. I need you,' he begged. 'I need you.'

'Oh shit,' Sally cursed as she watched the dark figure on the screen push the barrels of the sawn-off shotgun under his chin. 'He's going to shoot himself.'

'I don't think so,' Sean assured her as he bounced around in the back of the surveillance car. 'He needs to finish what he's started.'

'Finish what?' Sally asked.

'I'm not sure,' Sean answered. 'Not yet.' He held up his hand to stop Sally speaking again as the figure lowered the shotgun and let it hang by his side.

'*Relax*,' he told his audience. '*The time for that is not yet here, but it will be soon enough. I know that the police are hunting me down – that they've been ordered to find me and silence me – even if they don't want to. But I have no intention of letting them take me alive so their rich and powerful masters can humiliate and persecute me, building a web of lies to try and belittle me and my work. No. I won't allow that to happen.*' He hung his head, as if behind the mask he needed time to compose himself.

'What's happening?' Sean asked Bishop. 'Is he still on the move?' But Bishop didn't answer. 'Well?' Sean pressed impatiently.

'Give me a second,' Bishop snapped back, deep in concentration, staring at the tracking monitor on his lap. 'Yeah, he's definitely stopped. I thought he might be stuck in traffic, but he's been stationary too long. He's definitely stopped.'

'Where?' Sean demanded.

'About half a mile straight ahead,' Bishop explained. 'Give me a second to cross-reference the signal position with a map grid.' Bishop frantically adjusted the device and input the data. After a few seconds he had what he was looking for.

'Up ahead,' he told them. 'On the edge of Carpenters' Wood.' Sean and Sally looked at each other and both knew they were thinking the same thing: *this one likes his woods and trees.*

Hudson was relieved when The Jackdaw finally looked up again, standing straight and filling his chest before speaking.

'This is a war and as I have said before there are always casualties in war, as there are sacrifices to be made. Sometimes the ultimate sacrifice. And it is the ultimate sacrifice I am prepared to make – when the time is right. When that moment comes I shall not hesitate and they will finally realize my strength. My death at my own hands, not the hands of those who would have me publicly humiliated and destroyed, will give rise to a thousand more just like me: soldiers prepared for war – prepared to follow my example and tear down the walls of this unjust and unequal society and build a new and better world.'

'Yes. Yes,' Hudson agreed, barely able to control his enthusiasm and excitement. 'That's what I am. A soldier. A general. Wait until the world hears about me.'

'But now it is time to judge. To judge this man who arrogantly sits here,' he pointed to Barrowgate who winced as The Jackdaw spoke, *'and tells us he is innocent of any crimes. Well, we shall see. Time for the jury to vote.'*

Before the figure had even finished talking Hudson was eagerly clicking on the like icon, casting his vote of *guilty.*

'The woods are just up ahead,' DS Howland told them. 'What's the signal doing now?'

'On the move again,' Bishop answered, 'but slowly. I think he's out on foot and moving deeper into the wood.'

'Close on where you think his vehicle came to a stop,'

Sean instructed. 'Slow and steady,' he added, 'lights off once we're off the main road.'

'Understood,' Howland replied and soon pulled off onto a dirt road, slowing down and killing the lights. The car was silent as they bounced along the increasingly rough-surfaced road.

'The target's still on the move,' Bishop almost whispered, 'but if I'm not very much mistaken his car should be just a little further along.'

'Slow down,' Sean told Howland, but she already was, rolling along in neutral, keeping the engine noise to a minimum, the road becoming more and more difficult to see as the faint light from the main road behind them faded into blackness.

'I can't see a damn thing,' Howland complained, keeping her voice as low as the engine noise.

'There,' Sean suddenly called out as loudly as he dared, leaning forward and pointing ahead towards a clearing in the trees at the edge of the woodland, what light there was reflecting off something metallic. 'Is that Jackson's car?'

Bishop strained to see in the darkness. 'Yeah. That's it,' he finally confirmed.' Howland let their car roll to a silent stop next to Jackson's.

'What do you want to do?' Howland asked Sean.

'Is he still moving?' Sean whispered to Bishop.

'Yeah. Slowly. Definitely on foot.'

'Then we follow him,' Sean told them. 'We keep our distance and use the signal to track him.' *What are you up to, Jackson?* he asked himself. *Where you taking us?*

'Maybe we should wait for the rest of my team to catch up?' Howland suggested. 'Just in case.'

'We'll be fine,' Sean assured her, sounding more confident than he felt.

'He does this a lot.' Sally tried to ease the tension.

'OK,' Howland agreed and all four detectives silently

climbed from the car into the cold night air, the sound of the trees swaying in the light breeze suddenly amplified and intimidating. Sally pulled her thin raincoat tight against the chill, but Sean didn't even notice it as his surroundings enveloped him – the sounds, the scent of the trees, the feeling of the breeze against his skin. For a second he allowed himself to close his eyes and flare his nostrils. *Do you hear the same leaves I hear? Do you smell the same trees I do? Do you feel the same breeze against your skin? Am I close now? Am I finally close to meeting you?*

'Sean,' Sally hissed a whisper to bring him back to them. 'Sean,' she repeated when he didn't respond.

'What?' he replied, trying to sound as if he'd never been away.

'You need to see this,' she whispered, holding up her phone and drawing Sean towards her. 'I ran Carpenters' Wood through the Internet.'

'And?' Sean hurried her, looking at the screen on her phone.

'The Forestry Commission used to use it as a training site. It's abandoned now,' she explained, 'but the building they used to use is still there.'

'A derelict building in woodland,' Sean spoke their thoughts, his heart rate beginning to build as the chances of coming face to face with The Jackdaw seemed to increase.

'Where's the laptop?' Sally asked.

'I left it in the car,' Sean answered, pulling his own mobile from his pocket and searching for Your View. 'It's too big to carry. We'll monitor it on my phone.' He turned to Bishop who was still holding the tracking device. 'Which way?'

'Down this path,' he answered, pointing to a barely visible dirt path that snaked into the woods and the darkness beyond.

'Can't see a damn thing,' Howland complained. 'We need to use a torch.'

'No torches,' Sean whispered urgently. 'No light.' He covered the screen of his phone to hide its dim glow and focused on the transmission from Your View – the victim sitting taped to the old wooden chair, his eyes wild with fear. 'Damn it,' he cursed, attracting Sally's attention.

'Problem?' she asked.

'He's already started the voting,' Sean told her.

'Then we don't have much time,' Sally answered.

'No,' Sean agreed, moving to the beginning of the path and stepping into the thick ranks of the black trees. 'Stay close and stay together,' he told the others. 'We could be walking into anything.'

Mark Hudson watched the like and dislike icons with increasing trepidation. Hundreds and thousands of people were now voting as jurors in the court of the people, but the majority were voting 'dislike' – *not guilty*.

'Fuck,' Hudson swore at the screen. 'What's the matter with you people? Don't you want justice?' He checked the voting again, but it was no good – the *not guilty* votes were far exceeding the *guilty* votes. 'You weak bastards,' he complained. 'Fuck you all. Fuck all of you.' As the voting continued the dark figure reappeared on the screen holding an old-fashioned-looking glass syringe – not the disposable ones of today.

'*The people have voted,*' the electronic voice boldly announced. '*As the judge I must now interpret the results. My brothers and sisters, you have shown more mercy than was ever shown by those who have ruled over us for too long, but your mercy is your weakness as well as your strength. The time for mercy and understanding will come, but it is not now. Now is the time to put aside your compassion and strike at those who have wronged us. I have decided that you have voted in this way not to show that you believe this leech to be innocent of the crimes I have alleged, but as a sign that you wish for clemency.*' Hudson's idol filled his chest with air, readying himself to deliver his verdict. '*Very well. His life shall be spared,*' he said almost mournfully, before raising his voice in the tone of a preacher, '*but never again will his eyes look*

292

down on us with contempt. Never again will they see the material things he has surrounded himself with – things he has bought with wealth stolen from the people. Blind and disfigured he will be shunned by his own kind and cast aside.'

'*No,'* Barrowgate pleaded. '*Please don't do this. I'll do anything you ask, just please don't do this. I'm begging you not to do this.'*

Hudson watched wide-eyed as The Jackdaw moved quickly behind his victim, gripped him in a headlock and twisted his head violently backwards so his face pointed to the ceiling. Barrowgate continued to try to beg for mercy through clenched teeth. The Jackdaw stared into the camera through blacked-out sunglasses as he held the tip of the oversized syringe over his victim's right eye.

'*An eye for an eye.'*

Barrowgate's pain screamed from Sean's phone as his captor released drops of liquid that burnt through his eyelids and then the thin membrane of the eye – the vitreous gel bubbling from the wound and causing an even more severe chemical reaction as it came into contact with the sulphuric acid from the syringe.

'Jesus Christ,' Sean pleaded. He muted the phone, but he could still hear the screaming. At first he thought he was imagining it, hearing nothing but the residual ghost of Barrowgate's agony, but then he heard it again – faint, but not that far away – as if it was coming from inside a building they couldn't see.

'D'you hear that?' Sally asked.

'Yeah,' Sean whispered and inched further along the path through the woods until without warning he came across a clearing in the trees in which he could make out the shape of a building about sixty feet long and two stories high. All the while the screaming continued, leaking from the building that remained in complete darkness. 'It's the old training centre,' Sean told them.

'Can you see anything moving?' Sally asked.

'No,' he admitted.

'Jackson?' Sally reminded him.

'No. Nothing,' he answered before turning to Bishop who he could only just make out in the darkness. 'What's his signal doing?'

'Stationary,' he confirmed. 'My bet is he's in the building.'

'We should wait for the rest of the surveillance team,' Howland insisted. 'Keep close obs on him until we can get an armed unit out here.'

Sean heard more screaming coming from the low building and glanced at his phone. The killer still had hold of his victim, the syringe hovering over his left eye now. Sean forced himself to look away.

'No,' he told Howland. 'We don't have time to wait for anybody. I'm going in.'

'But he's known to have access to a shotgun,' Howland argued.

'I won't risk letting him slip away,' Sean angrily told her. 'Out here, in this darkness – it would be too easy for him to escape. And the victim – he still has the victim in there.'

'And Jackson,' Sally added. 'He could be walking into a trap.'

'I'm going in,' Sean repeated and moved into the clearing, pulling his telescopic truncheon, known as an ASP, from its belt holster and extending it with a practised flick of his wrist.

'Then I am too,' Sally insisted and followed close behind.

'Me too,' Bishop joined in and stepped into the clearing.

'Shit,' Howland cursed before following the others as they moved quickly towards the building, walking bent over to lessen the chance of detection and improve their chances of not falling prey to a blast from The Jackdaw's shotgun.

Mark Hudson grinned broadly as he stared at the image on his screen of the man kicking and bucking in the chair. The

Jackdaw finally released his grip and allowed the man's head to fall forward – burning, smoking, bloody holes where his eyes used to be – his screams filling Hudson's bedroom – screams like he'd never heard before – real screams, not the screams of an actor in a horror film, but screams that made every hair on his body vibrate with the ecstasy of what he'd been privileged to witness. His future was clear to him now. The path he must take was clear.

Sean and the others moved as quietly as they could around the outside of the building until he finally found an entrance, all the time the victim's screaming coming from somewhere inside. The door was already ajar. *Jackson*, Sean thought. *You're either very brave or very stupid.* He slipped inside knowing the others would follow and tried to make out the layout of the interior in the darkness. The screams led him to a staircase. *You're close now*, he told himself. *I can feel you.* He moved quickly and quietly up the stairs, faint footsteps behind him encouraging him forward, the screaming growing louder, leading him to the top of the stairs and a landing. Then he saw it, a chink of light leaking from one of the rooms off the corridor.

He paused only for a brief second to tell the others. 'Twenty feet along,' he whispered. 'On the left. We go in fast and hard.' He raised his ASP for emphasis. The others raised theirs in unison. He checked his phone one last time and could see the man he longed to face still standing over his victim. Crucially he was not holding the shotgun. He held up three fingers and counted them down. 'Three. Two. One.' As his last finger dropped he launched himself along the corridor and sprinted to the door, the sound of his own loud steps making him shudder inside. Everything now depended on how quickly the killer reacted and how far the shotgun was from his reach.

Without hesitation Sean burst into the room, ready to

scream 'Police' and hit anything that moved with his ASP, but as his mind tried to process the rush of information quickly enough to make a conscious decision the bewildering truth froze him mid-stride. The others behind him almost ran into his back before they too froze as Jackson turned towards them, looking as confused as they did.

'What the hell's going on?' he asked. Sean pulled the phone from his pocket and checked the screen on which the dark figure moved closer to the camera, his image growing larger until only his face and shoulders were visible, his eyes unseen behind the black shields of the sunglasses – yet somehow Sean knew the killer was staring straight at him.

'What the fuck?' Mark Hudson asked no one as the Your View image he was watching started to flicker and distort until it eventually split into two distinct halves – The Jackdaw on one side and on the other a similar-looking room with at least five people milling around inside looking confused.

'The people you see on the other screen are police officers and the Judas traitor who tried to betray me to them. Only they walked head-first into the trap I set for them. And now I know – now we all know – we can trust no one but ourselves.'

The Jackdaw's half of the screen flickered again before turning to darkness, the other half still showing Sean, Jackson and the others as they paced around the room looking for something. Anything.

'Fuck you, pigs,' Hudson snarled before quietly singing to himself. 'The Jackdaw's gonna get you. The Jackdaw's gonna get you,' he repeated over and over, rocking in his chair. 'The Jackdaw's gonna get you.'

'What the hell are you doing here?' Jackson demanded to know. 'How the hell did you find me? How did you find this place?'

Sean and the other detectives ignored him as they

instinctively began to search the room for anything that could help unravel the mystery of why they were there, while The Jackdaw wasn't.

'I have the right to know,' Jackson continued. 'If you've used me then I have the right to know.'

Sean walked to the only furniture in the room – a small decorator's table that held two old-looking speakers wired into a semi-dismantled iPad that was in turn connected by numerous multi-coloured wires to a smallish black box.

'I think I've found where the screaming was coming from,' he told the others. He moved closer and examined the iPad without touching it. Half the screen was blank, but on the other he could see himself staring into its camera and being streamed live on Your View for the whole world to see. Sally and Bishop moved to his side, both staring down at the home-rigged equipment. 'Bastard's set us up,' he explained. 'He worked us out – predicted what we might do. Somehow he knew we'd find a way to track Jackson. He wanted to make us look like fools while he now looks like a genius, and we walked straight into it. Son of a bitch.'

'The iPad. The speakers,' Sally said. 'Maybe we can trace them?'

Sean shrugged his shoulders. *This one didn't make stupid mistakes.* 'We can try,' he told her anyway. 'Bishop. What d'you make of this?'

'We'd have to get it back to the lab,' Bishop explained, 'but at a first glance it looks like he's put together a simple but effective set-up. The speakers have been wired together and probably plugged into the headphone socket and this black box,' he pointed to the device with the numerous wires snaking out of it, 'is probably an adapted modem or router. I'm guessing he rigged it so he could control this iPad remotely using a three or four G signal – probably done with a pay-as-you-go SIM card and therefore virtually untraceable.'

'And the iPad,' Sean asked. 'Can you do anything with it?'

'Only if he's stupid enough to have used his own,' Bishop answered. 'Which I don't suppose he is.'

'Can you at least turn the damn thing off,' Sean checked, 'without compromising it evidentially?'

'I should think so,' Bishop replied.

'Then do it,' Sean insisted. 'I've had enough humiliation for one day.'

'A quote for *The World*, Inspector?' Jackson asked, appearing at Sean's shoulder. 'The people have a right to know what's happening.'

'Fuck you, Jackson,' Sean dismissed him.

'You already have,' Jackson reminded him. 'I had a sweet thing going here, Corrigan, until you trampled all over it. No way will I get another interview with him now. He probably thinks I was actually trying to lead you to him – that I set him up. Your clumsy, fumbling antics have screwed me big time. I would have set him up for you, when the time was right, but not yet. Not yet.'

'I'm not here to give you a story,' Sean snarled. 'I'm trying to save lives.'

'Then you should have worked with me,' Jackson told him, 'because now you've got nothing. Nothing at all.'

12

Sean arrived back in the office late in the evening, but it was as busy as if it was a normal time of day. Earlier events meant the entire team would be working late into the night, including Sally and Bishop who he had left at the abandoned building in Carpenters' Wood to await the arrival of forensics and to see what else they could find that The Jackdaw might have left behind for them; not that Sean was expecting much.

Donnelly intercepted him as he headed towards his side office, keeping his voice low as they walked. 'What the hell happened out there?' he asked. 'Christ, boss – I thought we had him.'

Sean waited until they reached his office before answering. 'He set us up.'

'That much I already know,' Donnelly told him, 'but how?'

'A mixture of luck and cunning,' Sean tried to explain, sitting heavily in his chair. 'He thought Jackson was working for us, so he set a trap to see if he was right.'

'And was he?' Donnelly asked.

'No,' Sean told him. 'If Jackson had been working for us you'd have known about it, but he didn't know that – didn't know we were tracking Jackson's phone. As far as he's concerned Jackson was trying to lead us straight to him.'

'So his trap worked, but for the wrong reason,' Donnelly spelt it out. Sean just shrugged. 'Oh well – look on the bright side – we won't have to worry about Jackson doing any more *interviews with a killer.*'

'No,' Sean agreed, 'but we've lost the only person that could have led us to him and it also means he's even more clever and cautious than we thought. His trap might have worked for the wrong reason, but it was an effective trap all the same. It's another sign he's trying to predict our next move and nullify it before we can use it effectively. Conventional is not going to catch this one. We need to become unpredictable. This one's not just interested in covering his tracks or hiding anything that might give him away – he's playing a forward game, always staying a few steps ahead of us. By the time we think of what to do next he's already predicted it and taken steps to deal with it. You seen Anna around?' he suddenly changed the subject.

'No,' Donnelly told him, 'but I have seen Addis and he didn't look happy.'

'Good news travels fast,' Sean sighed as he leaned forward and flipped his laptop open. Within a few seconds he was watching a recording of Barrowgate's torture and punishment. After watching in silence for a while he paused the clip. 'This is the first time we've had a proper look at his shotgun, right?'

'As far as I can remember,' Donnelly agreed.

'Get Bishop to enhance the shots of the gun, will you, and get them circulated ASAP,' Sean told him.

'No problem,' Donnelly agreed.

Sean stared at the screen, the sawn-off shotgun hanging at The Jackdaw's side. 'You know Aden O'Brien, don't you?'

'DS from the Arts and Antiques Squad,' Donnelly clarified, 'or at least he was, until Addis decided they were surplus to requirements.' Donnelly looked around his surroundings. 'This used to be their office.'

'I know,' Sean told him, 'although O'Brien spent most of his time undercover buying nicked antiques from organized crime. Probably still does. SO10 should be able to tell you where he is. Tell him I need a favour. I need him to look at this shotgun and see if he can't ID it for us.'

'You thinking it's an antique?'

'I'm thinking it's a lead,' Sean answered. 'One we haven't looked into yet.'

'OK,' Donnelly agreed. 'I'll find him.'

DC Jesson appeared at the door looking serious. 'Something I should know?' Sean asked.

'The victim's been found,' he told them in his Scouse accent, 'wandering around Bushy Park in Hampton, gagged and with his wrists bound together. In a bad way from what I'm being told.'

'Life-threatening?' Donnelly asked.

'Local CID are saying no, but the medics reckon his eyes are beyond saving.'

'Where is he now?' Sean wanted to know.

'Queen Mary's in Roehampton. Intensive care. The locals are providing a guard for him, just in case, but apparently the doctors aren't allowing anyone to speak to him.'

'Queen Mary's again,' Donnelly stated, remembering that the second victim, Georgina Vaughan, had also been taken there.

'What shall I tell the local CID?' Jesson asked. 'They're pretty keen to hand the whole thing over to us.'

'Tell them we'll send someone as soon as we can,' Sean instructed, although he had no intention of sending anyone until the morning: no point wasting detective manpower if the medics weren't even allowing anyone to speak with him.

'Will do,' Jesson told him and wandered off.

'What else do we know about the victim?' Sean asked.

Donnelly pulled out his CID report book, referring to the notes he'd been making since he first knew another victim had been taken. 'Name's definitely David Barrowgate, thirty-two years old and a high-flying trader for Chaucer and Vale Bank. Lives alone in a flat in Brunswick Gardens, Notting Hill Gate. Took some clients out earlier today for, and I quote, a *business lunch*, unquote, and wasn't seen again, or at least not by any of his colleagues or friends. They say he took a black cab from the restaurant and told them he was heading home. We're still trying to find the black cab driver. So far, that's about it.'

'Any connection to any of the other victims?'

'Only that he worked in the City, but we haven't done much digging yet.'

'OK,' Sean told him. 'Let's get digging and see if we can't find a connection. Maybe his victim selection won't be as random as we believe.'

'I'll get on it. But doing full profiles for the victims, going back years into their lives, takes forever,' Donnelly warned him. 'We're struggling to keep up with this bastard's rate of offending as it is.'

'I know, I know,' Sean agreed, 'but let's at least go back a few months. We might get lucky profiling them short term. If they are somehow connected to each other then they'll be connected to the suspect too.'

'Leave it with me,' Donnelly assured him.

'Bollocks,' Sean suddenly cursed.

'Problem?' Donnelly asked confused.

'Addis,' Sean told him. 'Just walked in the main office. Do yourself a favour and make yourself scarce.'

'You sure?' Donnelly offered.

'I'm sure.'

Donnelly moved as fast as he could without looking obvious, but Addis was already at Sean's door before he'd escaped. 'Assistant Commissioner,' he nodded to Addis as he slipped past him. Once Donnelly was gone Addis stepped into the office and closed the door. Sean thought he could detect a slight twitching in Addis's right eye.

'Assistant Commissioner,' Sean acknowledged him without standing. 'Please, take a seat.'

'Do I look like I've come here for a sit-down chat?' Addis snarled.

'No,' Sean agreed, knowing there was no point in pulling the tail of an already angry dog. 'No you don't.'

'I told you, Inspector – no more bloody victims.'

'It was a little bit beyond my control,' Sean argued as gently as he could.

'And if that wasn't enough for the public to completely lose confidence in us, you walk straight into a trap and end up looking like a bumbling fool.'

'You're right,' Sean admitted. 'He set me up. He got the better of me – this time.'

'Every time,' Addis told him. 'It seems to me he gets the better of you every time. Have you any idea of how much pressure I'm being put under to resolve this matter? Any idea at all?'

'I can imagine,' Sean answered.

'No, you can't,' Addis insisted. 'How could you possibly *imagine*?' The two men stared at each other in silence for as long as Sean could bear it.

'If I don't have your full confidence to carry on with this investigation, then perhaps you should replace me with someone else,' Sean suggested.

'Don't play double-bluff with me,' Addis warned him. 'You may have got away with it in the Douglas Allen investigation, but lightning rarely strikes the same place twice.'

Sean pursed his lips and considered Addis with more clarity than he'd done since the first time they met. One question burned too brightly in his mind not to be asked.

'One thing I don't understand,' he said. 'You set this unit up, you put me in charge, but then you do nothing but jump all over my back. You've even threatened to replace me. Why give me the unit and then act like I'm the last person in the

303

world you actually want here? I don't understand. It makes no sense.'

'For God's sake,' Addis answered with barely hidden contempt for Sean's naivety. 'What do you think this is? The bloody Boy Scouts? You're here because I want you to be here. Because you're an asset. Because at this time I believe you can get results when I need them quicker than anyone else. But if you think that gives you some sort of immunity from criticism or protection from failure then you're sadly mistaken. You're subject to the same scrutiny as everybody else who works for me and I find people work best when they fully appreciate my *expectations*. But remember, Inspector – if you don't work for me then you're nobody. Just another DI rotting on some murder squad investigating domestic killings or sitting in some outlying borough dreaming of your retirement, only to die within a few months of leaving. We play for high stakes here. Any time you don't believe you can handle it, be sure to let me know.' Addis moved slowly to the door and pulled it open before looking back at Sean. 'We're in a results-orientated business, Inspector. So get me a result.' He walked through the door and strode across the office and was gone. Sean just gazed into the space Addis had occupied until Donnelly popped his head tentatively around the corner.

'You all right?' he asked.

Sean blinked the image of Addis that was seared in his mind away. 'I'm fine,' he answered, standing and pulling his coat on. 'Nothing a little time away from here won't fix.'

'Want some company?' Donnelly offered.

'No,' Sean answered too quickly. 'I need time and space to think. I'm better on my own.'

Jackson sat at the basement bar of a West End strip club, the sort of place that only people who were looking for it would find. For the average customer the drinks were extortionate, but as an old *friend* of the owner, Jackson was rarely asked to settle his tab. He drank with his back to the stage where failed actresses who'd long since given up on fame and fortune danced until they were naked just to survive.

Jackson came here when he didn't want to be seen, nicely hidden away in the dark of the bar amongst other men who didn't want to be seen either. He often ended up here after a bad day at work and this had definitely been that. God damn Corrigan for using him to try to take down The Jackdaw. He'd still give the story full coverage and his follow-up book would still sell, but without the one-on-one interviews it would never stand out – never net him the sort of cash he'd been banking on. Bastard Corrigan had cost him tens of thousands, maybe even hundreds of thousands by the time you'd factored in the TV deal he now wasn't going to get. Son of a bitch. But still, he couldn't help but have a sneaking respect for him. Clever boy tracking his personal mobile and not wasting his time trying to find the pay-as-you-go's signal. Jackson couldn't forgive himself for not seeing it coming, though. If he'd just left his mobile phone behind – for once in his life. He drained his glass of whisky, tapped the empty glass on the bar and jutted his chin at the barman who quickly headed his way with the bottle.

'Just keep 'em coming, Frankie. Just keep 'em coming.' The barman filled his glass and glided away. Jackson raised the glass to his lips just as the pay-as-you-go mobile began to vibrate and flash on the bar, the sound of the club's music all but drowning out its ringing.

Jackson froze for a second before slowly lowering his glass and staring at the phone. What sort of game was this? Had Corrigan somehow managed to get hold of the number? Or could it really be *him*? He quickly raised his glass and drained it in one before answering the phone, his heart racing.

'Hello,' he tentatively answered, but there was nothing but silence. 'Hello,' he repeated. 'Who is this?' More silence. He covered the ear the phone wasn't pressed against to block out the music and waited for an answer. After what seemed the longest time he heard the familiar electronic voice.

'You betrayed me,' the voice accused him, rocking Jackson back.

'No,' he spurted out. 'It was the police. It was Corrigan. He set me up – used my mobile phone to track me.' Jackson listened to the silence. 'Why would I betray you? You *are* the story. Why would I want it to end?'

'Why should I believe you?' the warped voice eventually asked.

'Because it doesn't make any sense,' Jackson tried. 'Just think it through yourself. Why would I help the police?'

'To gain favour with them. In exchange for *insider* information for your book. You are planning on writing a book, aren't you, Mr Jackson?'

'Maybe,' Jackson partially admitted, 'but I don't need to help Corrigan to get information. I have my sources.'

'Just as I no longer need your help to spread my message. My followers now number in the hundreds of thousands.'

'And my readers number in the millions,' Jackson snapped back. 'Come on. We've been through all of this. I can help you and you can help me. We both know it.'

'What's to stop him tracking you again?' the voice asked.

'I've already changed my mobile,' Jackson explained. 'Even had the number changed, which is a real pain in the arse, let me tell you.'

'And this phone? What do the police know of this phone?'

'They know it exists,' Jackson answered, 'but it's journalistic material, which is why I still have it and not Corrigan.'

'And the number?'

'They don't know it. Trust me.' More silence.

'Very well,' the voice finally answered. 'I'll contact you when the time is right. But if you cross me, I won't be as merciful with you as I have been with others.' The phone went dead before Jackson could answer.

'Shit,' he whispered while attracting the barman by waving his empty glass in front of him. Excitement rising in his chest, mixing with the fear of once again facing The Jackdaw. 'Just think of the money, Geoff old boy. Just think of the money.'

Sean stood outside St Thomas More Church in Dulwich. It looked black and forbidding in the darkness, although he was surprised to see some yellow light behind several of the windows. At this late hour he hadn't expected to see any signs of life at the church. So why had he come here? Truth was he didn't really know himself. He'd been heading home when suddenly he found himself taking the longer route past the church. He tried to tell himself he just needed the fresh air to wash away Addis's poison, but deep inside he knew it was more.

After several minutes of looking up at the building he moved forward and tentatively rested his hand on the black iron gate that led into the small courtyard. He gently pushed the gate and almost recoiled with surprise when it swung slightly open. He looked up and down the deserted street, feeling like a criminal, before pushing the gate open wide enough to be able to slip through, holding his warrant card in his pocket as he walked to the arched wooden door of the church itself. He rested the palm of his hand on the door and once again gently pushed, expecting the door to be locked shut and unyielding, but this too opened slightly – just enough for the dim light from inside to leak into the darkness outside. Even if he'd not really wanted to enter the church, finding the door open in the middle of the night ensured the policeman in him took over. Now he *had* to enter, even if it was just to make sure the church wasn't being relieved of its charitable donations box.

He slowly pushed the door open enough to slip inside,

cringing at every creak it made. Once inside he closed it behind him, the sound of the latch lock clunking into place, filling the modest church and echoing off every surface. Sean froze by the door and waited for the ghost sounds to fall silent before daring to step away. His eyes continually searched for any sign of movement as he moved deeper inside the church, his ears pulled slightly backwards by the tension in his face muscles as he listened for the slightest sound. But all he could hear were his footsteps, harsh and brutal on the solid wood floor. Betrayed by the sound of his own shoes he decided to announce himself, even if it was just to the paintings and statues of Christ, the Virgin Mary and God himself.

'Hello,' he called quietly, tentatively into the dimness. 'Hello,' he repeated with more conviction, but nobody suddenly appeared to welcome or challenge him. He kept walking towards the altar and statue of Christ on the cross that dominated the space, pulling him further and further forward, only stopping once he'd reached the few wide steps that led to the bleeding feet of the Messiah.

He looked around nervously before speaking to himself. 'What the hell am I doing here?' The sudden sound of a voice made him spin on his heels and reach for his ASP.

'Perhaps you came to pray,' the man's voice offered. Sean squinted in the poor light as the dark figure came towards him, like a floating aberration, until he was close enough for Sean to see who it was. 'I didn't mean to startle you,' Father Alex Jones apologized. 'I heard someone moving around down here and thought we might be having a visit from one of our not-so Christian flock.'

'The door was open,' Sean explained. 'I was just checking it out.'

'Well, you are a policeman, after all,' Jones teased him.

'I didn't expect the church to be open this late,' Sean told him.

'I like to keep it open as late as I can,' Jones replied. 'You get a better class of sinner this time of night.'

Sean looked the young priest over and allowed himself a wry smile. 'Yes. I suppose you do.'

'I haven't seen you in a while.'

'I've been busy,' Sean explained.

'Of course. So what brings you here now?' Jones asked. 'Forgive me, but I doubt you really came to check on my rather lax security.'

'I'm at work,' Sean tried to explain. 'I guess I just needed to clear my head.'

'What strange work hours we keep, you and I.'

'Comes with the territory, I guess.'

'I suppose,' Jones agreed before allowing a silence to fall between them for a while. 'So what is it you're trying to clear your head of, if you don't mind me asking?'

'People,' Sean answered bluntly.

'I see,' Jones replied, looking at the floor.

'And a case,' Sean continued. 'A case I'm working on.'

'And this case troubles you?' Jones asked.

'No,' Sean told him. 'It's my inability to solve it that troubles me.'

'Nothing worse than an itch you can't scratch,' Jones replied. Sean said nothing as he stared up at the crucifixion scene. *Was that how The Jackdaw saw himself – as a latter-day messiah, prepared to allow himself to be crucified to make his point?*

'So what's the case?' Jones interrupted his thoughts. 'If I'm allowed to ask. One of the benefits of speaking to a priest is they can't tell anyone about it.'

'Like a journalist,' Sean explained, drawing a slightly confused look from Jones.

'Indeed,' he agreed. 'Although you'd need more than a court order to persuade a priest to give up what he's been told.'

'You seem to know more about the law than most,' Sean answered.

'I have a law degree,' Jones told him. 'The Church put me through university before I completed my vows.'

'Any regrets?' Sean found himself asking.

'About joining the priesthood? No,' Jones answered unwaveringly. 'Never. It's what I was meant to do. And you?'

'The police?' Sean asked. 'It's more something I have to do than want to do.'

'I see,' Jones answered, 'but it's not all plain sailing, I suppose. Like your current case.'

Sean looked from Christ to the young priest. 'I'm investigating the man some people are calling the Your View Killer and others The Jackdaw. To me he's just a man I need to find and stop.'

'Ahh,' Jones nodded his head slowly. 'I know the case. I've been following it on the Internet.'

Sean struggled to hide his surprise. 'You've been watching it?'

'I have,' Jones admitted. 'Such terrible videos. Those poor people and their families.'

'You don't seem the type to be watching such . . . *graphic* videos,' Sean told him.

'But I have to,' Jones replied.

'Why?'

'To pray for them,' Jones told him. 'So I can pray they don't come to any harm and to pray for forgiveness for the man you hunt.'

'Prayer doesn't look like it's working,' Sean pointed out.

'Who can say?' Jones argued. 'Perhaps if I and others hadn't been praying for the victims things would have gone even worse for them.'

'Maybe,' Sean said without really believing it, 'but it'll take more than prayer to make him stop. That's my job – not God's.'

'Oh, I'm sure the Lord will guide your hand.'

'I don't think so,' Sean dismissed the possibility and hoped Jones wouldn't pursue it.

'Well,' Jones continued, looking at the ground for a second, 'all the same, the man you're looking for must have been terribly aggrieved to become as angry as he is.'

'Or at least he thinks he has been,' Sean argued, 'and now he wants his revenge.'

'Apparently so,' Jones agreed. 'God loves a sinner and this one's certainly that.'

'Because he hurts people?' Sean asked. 'Because he's killed?'

'Thou shall not kill is one of the ten commandments, not one of the seven deadly sins.'

'Does it matter?' Sean questioned.

'Just a technical point,' Jones told him with a slight smile. 'The Catholic religion is one of the few things that has more technicalities than the law.'

'So what makes him a sinner,' Sean asked, '*technically* speaking?'

'Pride,' Jones answered. 'He can cover his face and disguise his voice, but he can't hide his pride.'

'You mean his damaged pride?' Sean asked.

'No,' Jones told him. 'I mean pride in what he's doing now. He's proud of what he's doing, otherwise why would he seek the assistance of that newspaper – *The World*?'

'To reach more people with his message,' Sean offered.

'Perhaps,' Jones partially agreed, 'but I also see envy and vanity in his actions and words. He's envious of those he hurts while his vanity tells him he deserves to be more than they should ever be.'

'Really?' Sean asked, squinting his eyes. 'I don't see it. He hates the victims as he hates everyone connected to the banking industry. He doesn't envy them. He doesn't want to be like them. He wants to destroy them.'

'Indeed,' Jones replied, 'but some people, if they can't have something they desire, they would rather destroy it.'

'That I have seen,' Sean told him, 'but *envy*?'

'Trust me, Sean,' Jones insisted, 'I've seen plenty of envy in my time and I see it here.'

'I don't disbelieve you,' Sean answered. 'I just haven't considered it before.'

'Sometimes all it takes is a different perspective,' Jones explained.

'But what does it mean – if he's driven by envy and not revenge?'

'Perhaps he's driven by both,' Jones suggested. 'Envy and revenge.'

'Envy and revenge,' Sean shrugged. 'I suppose. I've seen them together before, but in simple cases, easily solved cases: an ex-husband's envy of his ex-wife's new, happy life, while also wanting to avenge the wrong he perceives she's done him. The less successful of two business partners who went their own ways, envious of their more successful rival and quick to blame them for their own failings . . . But here, with this man – I don't think so.'

'An inner turmoil,' Jones suggested. 'A man being ripped apart by his own demons. Hating the thing he most wants to be because he knows he never can be.'

'No.' Sean continued to shake his head slowly.

'Why?' Jones asked.

'Because that sounds like confusion,' Sean argued, 'but with this one I sense no *confusion*, only clarity and an absolute sense of purpose.'

'But envy leaks from his every word,' Jones told him. 'His bitterness pours through the screen every time I listen to him. In this world we live in today, I see envy everywhere and I see it in him.'

Envy, Sean asked himself. *What did it mean and who was the man he hunted envious of? The people he abducted and tortured, or something else?* He waited, but no answers came, only more questions.

'I have to go,' Sean told the priest.

'Of course you do,' Jones assured him, 'but bear in mind what I said. The man you're looking for carries envy around with him on his back like a . . .' He looked at the crucified Christ. 'Like a cross.'

'Then I need to relieve him of his burden,' Sean replied, 'and then nail him to it.'

Addis sat alone in the semi-darkness of his office high in the South Tower of New Scotland Yard, the only light coming from a small, underpowered desk lamp and the glow of his computer screen. Every now and then he took a break from the numerous files all marked 'Confidential' or 'Secret' that were neatly stacked on his desk awaiting his attention and signature. He liked working alone and late, when most offices were dark and deserted, the phones quiet except for the occasional distant ring that went unanswered. It was a chance to catch up on the gargantuan amounts of paperwork that specialist operations created, such as the report he was currently reading – a request by the Anti-Terrorist Unit to try to put an undercover officer into a mosque suspected of trying to convert British-born Muslims to radical Islam. His desk phone suddenly rang shrilly, but Addis's heart never skipped so much as a beat as he casually stretched out an arm and lifted the receiver, his eyes not leaving the report.

'Assistant Commissioner Addis speaking.'

'Robert. It's me.' The familiar voice of the cabinet minister made Addis groan inside and lean back deeply into his privately purchased leather desk chair.

'It's late,' Addis unapologetically replied. 'What do you want?'

'Progress,' the minister answered. 'We all want progress.'

'With regards to what?' Addis stalled.

'Don't play dumb with me,' the minister demanded. 'You know exactly what I'm bloody well talking about. This bastard

313

who now calls himself The Jackdaw, of all bloody things. Listen to what I'm about to say, Assistant Commissioner – his murdering antics are now officially costing the City of London tens of millions of pounds every single damn day. All of which the media are taking great delight in reporting to anyone and everyone who'll listen. Damn, I hate that bloody newspaper.'

'Then why don't you use your influence to silence them?' Addis asked. 'You have more friends inside these organizations than I do,' he continued, although he wasn't entirely sure he was speaking the truth.

'*The World*'s the one that's really blabbing on about it – trying to turn this arsehole into some kind of working-class hero,' the minister complained.

'Then fire a political shot across their bows,' Addis suggested.

'Wouldn't do any good,' the minister explained. 'They're backing bloody Labour right now. Weren't too keen on our last attempt at press regulation. Word has it they've done a deal with the back-stabbing Marxist bastards. Wankers, but the point remains: we need a result and quickly.'

'We're doing everything we can,' Addis tried to assure him.

'That's not good enough any more,' the minister complained. 'Just find this murdering bastard and do it quickly, or I'll find someone who can.'

Addis heard the line go dead before he could answer, his anger rising at even the small defeat of allowing the minister to hang up first. No matter – he had something in mind that would keep the minister off his back and in his pocket forever.

Sean paced around his small office reading through more reports naming possible suspects, all of whom had convictions or cautions for threatening people from the world of banking, from managers of local high street banks to CEOs of major international financial institutions. None were setting his mind on fire with potential, firing electricity through his body in a way that might suggest he had caught the scent of the

314

man he hunted. The reports left him with nothing more than a feeling of emptiness. The sudden sound of a voice startled him.

'Having a bad day?' Anna asked before walking deeper into his office and taking a seat. Sean glanced at his watch. It was gone two in the morning. *Why was she in the office at this ungodly hour? Was it so she could be alone with him?* He quickly looked into the adjoining main office that was almost empty, but not quite. *If not to be alone with him, then why?*

'Have you ever known me have a good day?' he asked somewhat mournfully.

'Oh, some.' She tried to sound positive.

'Maybe some,' he agreed, rubbing the back of his neck to relieve the stiffness. 'Anyway, what are you doing here at this time of day, night, whatever it is? Shouldn't you be at home tucked up with your husband?'

'I had a lot of things to take care of,' she answered.

'Such as?' he asked, unable to suppress his instinctive suspiciousness.

'Files to read,' she replied, 'reports to prepare, you know – stuff. Same as you.'

'Uh,' Sean grunted, deciding not to press the issue, 'and what do your reports say – about the man I'm looking for? That he's just another murdering psychopath or sociopath?'

'Not exactly,' Anna told him, looking a little insulted at his suggestion a report of hers could ever be so blunt, 'and the words "murdering" and "psychopath" don't always have to appear side by side.'

'They do in my world,' Sean insisted, 'or at the very least psychopath and dangerous criminal.'

'I know to you your world feels like the only real world,' she explained, 'but there is a world beyond that, equally real.'

'Are you counselling me, Doctor?'

'No,' Anna reassured him. 'I was just saying.' Neither spoke for a few seconds. 'I think I've mentioned this before,' she

315

eventually continued, 'but quite a high proportion of company CEOs are diagnosable as psychopaths – ruthless, emotionally detached, highly motivated and organized – it's what got them to the top. In a dangerous survival situation, you want a psychopath by your side, not a meek and mild also-ran.'

'The only CEOs I know are the heads of organized criminal gangs,' Sean told her.

'Same qualities as any other CEO,' Anna explained.

'Yeah, only the CEO of Tesco didn't have to cut anyone's fingers off with a set of pruning shears to get to the top,' he reminded her. 'As interesting as this conversation is, it isn't getting us any closer to finding the so-called Jackdaw.' There was another uncomfortable pause between then before Sean broke the silence. 'I spoke to someone earlier this evening,' he told her. 'Someone who's watched the Your View videos of this bastard – someone who's got experience dealing with people at their best and their worst.'

'And?'

'And they told me they saw envy in our man. Envy in his words and his actions.'

'I'm not sure I do,' she dismissed the possibility. 'Everything we've seen indicates he despises what the victims are, so why would he be envious of them?'

'I don't know,' Sean admitted. 'Envious of their wealth perhaps?'

'He abducts, murders or mutilates people because he's envious of their wealth?' she considered. 'I don't think so. Have you ever heard of anything like that?'

'No,' Sean admitted. 'No I haven't. So if he's not envious of their wealth, what is he envious of?'

'Like I said,' Anna reminded him, 'I don't believe envy is an element of his motivation.'

'Then here's something else for you to consider,' Sean moved on, although the question of envy still burned inside him. 'He's taking the victims at an increasingly high rate,

316

with less and less time between abductions, yet clearly he's carried out extensive research on each of them, all of which must have taken a significant amount of time.'

'So?' Anna asked.

'So logic suggests that pretty darn soon he's gonna run out of victims to take, or at least ones he's researched. Agree?'

'I suppose that's inevitable,' Anna conceded, 'and then he may very well start taking people he hasn't researched, which means he'll make more mistakes and therefore be easier to catch.'

'I don't think so,' Sean disagreed. 'I can't see that happening. Not this one. He's working to a finite list and when that list is complete, he'll stop.'

'You really believe that?'

'Yes,' he told her. 'Yes I do, but there's the problem. There's the problem with all of this, because if he's smart enough or cold enough to stop once his list of researched victims is complete, then it means he's highly disciplined and extremely organized. But if he's driven by revenge, driven into such a rage by the need for revenge that he's capable of murder and mutilation, then how could he still be in such control that he could simply stop?' He fell back into his chair and rubbed his temples hard with the tips of his fingers, as if the strain of trying to invade the mind of the man he hunted had pained and exhausted him.

'You all right?' Anna asked.

'I'm fine,' he lied.

Anna gave him a few seconds before continuing. 'Then if not revenge, what?'

Sean leaned forward again, his hands pressed together in front of his face as if he was praying, his eyes squinted. 'Maybe,' he began hesitantly, 'maybe it *is* about revenge, but if it is, then,' he paused, trying to let his tired mind catch up with his train of thought, the questions and answers a confused mass inside his head, 'then that must mean, if he's going to stop, that the victims are . . . that the victims are to him . . . to him they're . . . damn it. Jesus Christ, I don't know.' He fell back in his chair in frustration once more.

'Try and relax,' Anna encouraged him. 'Give it time. It'll come.'

He leaned forward again, gently tapping his forehead with the tips of his fingers, trying to tease the answers from the clouded recesses of his mind. 'Then the victims to him aren't . . . aren't random.'

'We already know they're not random,' Anna reminded him. 'They're clearly carefully chosen.'

'That's not what I mean,' he tried to explain. 'I mean they're not just not random, they're . . .' his eyes grew wide with anticipation, 'they're *personal* to him – not just objects that represent the thing he seeks revenge for, but they are *personally* the people he wants revenge against – the people who personally *damaged* him.'

'But none of the victims know each other,' Anna reminded him. 'They're strangers. Not friends. Not work colleagues – all from different banks. If this is more personal than we thought then there'd be a link – something to link the victims and hence something that links them all to the suspect.'

'Then we've missed it,' Sean snapped. 'Whatever links this whole thing together, we're missing it.'

'Do you really think so?' Anna asked. 'Do you really believe he has personal vendettas against each of the victims?'

Sean slumped back in his chair for the last time. 'I don't know,' he admitted with a sigh. 'Right now I'm not sure what I believe.' He looked hard into her dark brown eyes. A part of him was glad there were still other people in the main office – the two of them alone in a darkened office in the middle of the night would have been a difficult temptation to resist. He wondered if she felt the same way. 'It's late,' he finally told her. 'I'm tired. I'm going home. I suggest you do the same.'

318

'If that's what you want to do,' she answered, freezing him where he sat.

'It's not about what I want, Anna,' he explained. 'It's about what's the right thing to do. You were the one who told me that. Remember?'

'Maybe I was wrong?' she suggested, making his heart pound and his muscles tighten, the scent of her suddenly vivid and intoxicating.

'No,' he forced himself to say. 'You weren't wrong – you were right.' He hauled himself to his feet and pulled his coat over his jacket, loading the pockets with the usual items. He headed for the doorway, pausing when he reached Anna. He leaned over and gently kissed her on the cheek, his mind and body burning for more of her. 'Go home,' he told her, his hand brushing against the soft skin of her throat. 'Go home.'

13

Kate had been awake for what seemed like hours, although she'd hardly stirred at all as she lay in the marital bed listening to her husband sleeping fitfully next to her. She wasn't entirely sure what time he'd arrived home, just that it was some time early in the morning. As the first chink of light started to poke through the gap in the curtains she slipped silently from the bed and tiptoed from the room, gently closing the door behind her. She padded across the hallway to the children's room and peered inside at the sleeping mounds under colourful duvets. Such was her need to be alone in the quiet of the house, she was glad they were still in the land of childish dreams – for a while at least. Just a few minutes to herself to think.

She sneaked downstairs and checked there was still water in the kettle before she flipped it on, taking a cup from a nearby drawer and crossing the kitchen to the fridge for milk and then back across the room to the boiling kettle. She stared out of the window into their tiny garden and allowed her thoughts to wander to her own life – the life she shared with Sean.

He'd been even more distant than usual lately, as if he had more than just another difficult investigation on his mind – although the thought of Sean having an affair seemed somehow ridiculous, unless you counted his long-term love affair with the police. Damn his job, she thought. It was slowly but surely pulling him away from her and the children. If things didn't change it was only a matter of time before he was completely lost to them all. But how could she drag him away from the police or at least the Special Investigations Unit, without losing the Sean she loved? She didn't want his shell, but she didn't want the ghost of him either, which was all she felt she had right now. Getting him away from the police was like treating a cancer patient with chemotherapy: it could save them, but it could nearly destroy them in the process.

She poured hot water from the kettle into her coffee mug and was unloading the previous day's plates, cups and God knows what else from the dishwasher when Sean's voice behind her made her jump and almost drop one of the kids' bowls.

'Why didn't you wake me?' he accused her. 'It's almost six thirty.'

She looked him up and down with a hand still pressed to her chest. 'Jesus, Sean. You scared the hell out of me.'

'Sorry,' he apologized. 'I didn't want to wake the kids, but you shouldn't have let me sleep so late. I need to get to work.'

'Sean,' she snapped at him. 'You sound awful. You look awful. Work can wait. You need to rest.'

'No,' he argued. 'What I need is to get to work.'

'Sit down,' Kate ordered, 'and I'll make you some coffee. Then you're going to have a proper breakfast and then you're going to have a long hot shower and take your time to get dressed. You won't help anybody and you won't solve anything by self-destructing. Now sit.' Sean reluctantly pulled out a seat and slumped at the kitchen table, his eyes looking red and sunken, his skin grey and old. 'That's better,' Kate

321

told him as she headed for the fridge again to find something that would pass as a proper breakfast. 'Don't put yourself in an early grave,' she warned him. 'If you must do this job then treat it like a job and not an obsession.'

'Easier said than done,' he argued. 'You don't solve a case like this working nine to five.'

'How would you know?' she pointed out. 'You've never tried.'

'Let me get this case out of the way,' he assured her, 'and then I'll take some time off in lieu. At least it's the weekend,' he added.

'Weekend. Weekday. It hardly matters to you,' Kate answered as she took some eggs and butter from the under-stocked fridge, reminding her a trip to the supermarket was overdue.

'Because the Crown Courts aren't open at the weekend,' he explained.

'So?' she asked, puzzled.

'So at least I don't have to worry about Douglas Allen's trial at the Bailey.'

'Christ, Sean,' Kate told him, kicking the fridge door shut. 'You're running this new investigation and a murder trial at the same time? Are you completely mad?'

'I had no choice,' he argued. 'It's just the way the dice rolled.'

'You're going to kill yourself, Sean.'

'I can handle it.'

'From where I am,' she told him, 'it doesn't look like it.'

'I promise,' he assured her, 'I'll find this one and then I'll take some time off.'

'But when will that be?' she demanded. 'Days? Weeks? Months?'

'Days,' he answered without hesitation.

'How do you know?'

'Because I can feel it,' he tried to explain. 'It's like I don't know what I'm looking for yet, but I know what I'm not looking for.'

'Well, that makes a lot of sense,' Kate replied sarcastically.

'It's hard to explain,' Sean told her. 'It's like having the answer to a question on the tip of your tongue. So close, yet so far away, until suddenly one thing, one small thing, makes everything fall into place. Sometimes I dream about this giant machine with millions of cogs inside, but none of them are turning. I look down and in the palm of my hand I see I'm holding a tiny cog – the smallest of them all – and I know what I have to do: I have to work out where it goes in the machine to make it go. That's how I feel now: I have all the pieces I need . . . I just need something, one thing, to tell me where they fit.'

Kate listened with concern to her husband, the father of her two daughters. At times like this she realized how far away he was, not just from her and the girls, but from everybody: trapped in his own crippling world of death, pain and desperation, the responsibility of finding and stopping the bringers of suffering dragging him down into the dark depths of despair like an anchor of misery. How she'd like to cut the chains free and watch him swim back to the surface and breathe again.

'You need to get away from all this, Sean,' she told him, the sadness in her voice barely concealed.

'Like I said, I will,' he replied. 'As soon as I've found this one I'll take some time off. I'm owed plenty of leave.'

'That's not what I meant,' she answered. 'I meant *forever*. Before we lose you. Before you lose yourself.'

'Lose myself?' he questioned, his voice devoid of emotion. 'Have you ever thought that at last maybe I'm finally finding myself? Becoming whatever it is I'm *really* supposed to be.'

'And what the hell is that, Sean? What are you supposed to be?'

'I don't know,' he told her honestly, 'but am I really this?' He looked around the kitchen as if it was his world. 'Wife. Children. Terraced house in Dulwich – pretending to be *normal.*'

Kate sat next to him, pulling her chair close. 'So you can think *differently* from most people, but you still have the right to be happy. What your father did to you when you were a boy is in the past now. You don't have to carry it on your back for the rest of your life.'

'Don't I?' he snapped at her. 'How would you know? How would anyone know? The one good thing I can do is find the madmen and the evil men quicker than most, and the only reason I can do that is because of what my so-called father did to me.'

'You don't know that for sure,' Kate argued.

'Yes I do,' he insisted, 'and so do you. Whether I like it or not there's a part of him inside me. That's why I can think like *them*, or at least I used to be able to – right now I feel nothing.'

'Maybe that's a good thing,' Kate told him, 'a sign you're finally laying the ghosts of the past to rest.'

'You mean *changing*?' he asked.

'Like you said,' she explained. 'Perhaps you're finally finding that part of yourself as a man that your childhood took away.'

'But what if I don't want to change?' he argued. 'What if I . . . *liked* knowing there was something in me I couldn't control? Something no one can control. Maybe I don't want to become like everyone else. Maybe I *accept* what I am more than you think.'

Kate leaned away from him slightly and looked into his eyes. They were darker and more lifeless than she'd ever seen them before.

'Then I'd say you need help, Sean, before it overtakes you. Before you become something you *won't* like. Before you become like the people you've spent your whole career chasing. Before you end up having to hunt *yourself*.'

'You're being over-emotional,' he accused her. 'Hunt myself – I can't even hunt down this *clown*.'

'I'm not surprised,' Kate softened a little, despite her deepening concerns. 'You're exhausted. How can you think clearly enough to run your investigation properly? This bastard you're after can take all the time in the world, but you can't. He has the advantage, Sean.'

'It's not just that,' he explained, his eyes wide and fearful. 'It's not just all the day-to-day crap endlessly piling up on my desk or even Addis and his ridiculous demands that concern me. It's something else.'

'What?' Kate asked, though she was afraid of what the answer might be.

'Maybe I can't think like this one because we're nothing alike,' he told her. 'Because we're not the same.'

'Of course you're not the same,' Kate smiled with relief. 'He's a murderer and you're a cop.'

'That's not what I meant,' Sean told her. 'I'm not like this one, but I am like the others. That's what helps me catch them – the psychopaths. I am like them – a part of me is – a part of my mind at least. But not this one. That's why I can't think like him – because he's not *insane*, not even slightly.'

'And what?' she asked. 'You are – insane? You think you're insane?'

'No,' he answered quickly. 'At least not technically – not what most people would consider to be insanity. But if I can think like the madmen – exactly like them, as if I'm looking through their eyes sometimes – then there must be at least a part of me that's close to . . . *madness*.'

'And you don't believe this one is?' Kate questioned. 'Mad, I mean?'

'No,' he confirmed. 'He knows exactly what he's doing and why he's doing it. Cold logical efficiency. He's working rigidly,

325

unwaveringly to a plan – like a soldier following orders, bombing civilian cities even though he knows he'll kill innocent people because the final outcome demands it. A clarity of thought that people like me can never have. Our minds, our thought processes are . . . are a twisted vine of ever moving ideas and thoughts. We're never still, never at peace. We feel and think things that other people couldn't even hope to imagine. In a way I sometimes think we're more *alive* because we're so close to . . .'

'So close to what?' Kate managed to ask despite her trembling heart.

'I don't know,' he admitted, his bright blue eyes suddenly appearing quite black – like a shark's. 'To hell. To damnation. But I'm increasingly sure this one's more like *you* and everyone else than he is like me. He's not deranged. He has no voices screaming in his head telling him to do it. He doesn't spend hours talking to himself in the mirror of some filthy bathroom in some hovel and he doesn't self-harm out of self-loathing. He doesn't believe he's an agent of God or the devil. Instead he calculates and he plans and he doesn't make mistakes and he knows exactly what he wants.'

'And what's that?' Kate nervously asked.

'Revenge, emotionless revenge,' he told her. 'Like scratching an itch. I sense no rage or fury. Or even confusion or torment. Just a desire to . . . to even the score. I don't know.'

'How can you tell?' Kate couldn't help but ask. 'Behind that mask and sunglasses. You can't even hear his real voice. He just sounds like a machine. But his words seem angry enough.'

'Maybe,' Sean partially agreed, 'but even in his words there's something missing. Something just not quite right.'

'Like what?' she pressed.

'I don't know,' he answered, 'but he and I are nothing alike. I'll have to find another way of catching him.'

'I think you need to take a break,' Kate warned him. 'Get

away from all this before it drags you under. It wasn't so bad when you were at Peckham investigating – for want of a better word – *everyday* murders, but now, all you do is chase these *madmen*. It's all . . . too close to home for you, Sean. It's . . . it's unhinging you – resurrecting too many demons from your past. It has to stop, Sean. It has to stop.'

'I don't want it to stop,' he insisted. 'This is who I am and this is what I do. I don't want to take a break or walk away and I don't want to run off to New Zealand and live on a damn beach. I want to stay here and do what I do best. I like being out there hunting these so-called *madmen*. It's where I belong – where I need to be. It's where I feel alive. Without it I'd be nothing.'

'Well thanks,' Kate snapped at him. 'Thanks a bloody lot. So me, me and the kids are nothing to you? You'd rather be out there chasing bad people in the dark than be here with us? Jesus, Sean. What's the point?'

'That's not what I meant,' he tried to recover, spreading his arms. 'You, the children, home – you're my *sanctuary*. But I'm not defined by being a husband and a father. That's what I am, not what I need to do.'

'You just don't get it, do you?' Kate accused him.

'Get what?' he fought back. 'When people ask you what you do you don't say you're a mother and a wife. You tell them you're a doctor.'

'The difference is I could leave my job, Sean. If we could afford it I probably would. But you couldn't. It's not a job to you. It's an obsession.' He slumped at the table, unable to find an answer. 'Make your own damn breakfast,' Kate told him. 'I'm late for work.'

Donnelly arrived at work a little later than usual, but still early enough to be there before anyone else. He entered the main office and began to wander from desk to desk, checking on every detective under his charge, making sure each had enough work to be getting on with and that no one was either slacking or overstretching themselves. He couldn't afford anyone falling sick with stress and disappearing for God knows how long. He whistled the same tune he always whistled when he was engaged in clandestine activities and glanced around the office. It was the weekend, which meant no cleaners for a couple of days and the room was already showing the signs of strain: the bins full of takeaway food wrappers and polystyrene cups, the confidential waste sacks stuffed to bursting, although the team had still been using them as an old newspaper depository. It seemed every conceivable work surface was littered with yet more polystyrene cups and abandoned plates, some still with scraps of food on. The whole place would smell to high heaven by Sunday night unless he press-ganged a few unwilling volunteers into a clean-up crew before then.

'Jesus,' he complained. 'Look at the bloody state of this place.' But his moaning was interrupted by the sign of movement coming from Sean's office. Somehow he knew whoever it was it wasn't Sean.

He moved stealthily across the room, no longer whistling or stopping to flick through other detectives' diaries as he concentrated on the shadow of a figure sitting behind Sean's desk. Either the figure hadn't noticed him approaching or it didn't care as it showed no sign of trying to flee or hide. Donnelly walked the last few steps slowly to the doorway and peered inside. Anna looked up slowly, her own tiredness etched across her face.

'You're in early,' Donnelly greeted her, his eyes narrowing a little with suspicion. It wasn't often he was beaten into the office of a morning.

'Couldn't sleep,' Anna confided to him.

'Oh.' Donnelly shrugged and slumped in the chair opposite. 'Problems?'

'Just a lot going on in my head right now,' she told him, 'with the investigation and everything.'

'Yeah,' Donnelly smiled condescendingly. 'It's a lot easier studying these lunatics than it is catching them, eh?'

'I'm not sure I approve of the label "lunatic", but yes, this is a little more demanding.'

'You can bet your buns on that,' Donnelly quipped before looking more serious. 'To tell you the truth I was surprised you came back for another stint. I thought after the Thomas Keller investigation you would have had enough.'

'Really? Why's that?'

'The guv'nor didn't exactly welcome you with open arms, did he?'

'He was understandably suspicious at first,' Anna admitted, 'but we soon established a working relationship.'

'A *working* relationship?' Donnelly's smile returned.

'Yes.' Anna locked eyes with him. 'A *working* relationship.'

'Strange that,' Donnelly faked confusion, 'because usually the guv'nor won't have anything to do with your kind.'

'My kind?'

'Yeah – you know – *shrinks*. Psychiatrists, psychologists, criminologists. Anybody who thinks they can tell him his business. He really can't stand them.'

'Well then, I'm glad I've managed to change his opinion.'

'Change his opinion?' Donnelly shook his head. 'I'm not so sure about that. Perhaps if you'd been right about Thomas Keller. But as I remember it you weren't – Corrigan was.'

'We had some clinical disagreements, but our overall assessments converged.'

'All the same – I'm surprised he didn't kick up more of a fuss when you were attached to another of his investigations. I expected to see him put up a bit of a fight.'

'Perhaps he realized it would have been pointless, given that it was Assistant Commissioner Addis who asked me to help with the investigation.'

'Of course it was,' Donnelly smiled wryly, 'although that puzzles me a little too.'

'Oh.' Anna swallowed. 'In what way?'

'Addis may be a pain in the arse bastard, but he's still a cop – at least of sorts. He doesn't strike me as the type who'd want outsiders involved in a major investigation – not unless he felt he needed them for something – something specific he couldn't get from the guv'nor. As much as he and Corrigan can't stand the sight of each other at times, Addis trusts him to get the job done, despite all his shouting and threats. He knows the guv'nor's his best chance and he knows he doesn't need any shrink to tell him how to do it.'

'What's your point?'

'My point is, if Addis didn't put you on this investigation to help us find The Jackdaw, then why did he put you on it at all?'

'I doubt anything I can say would dispel your suspicions,' Anna explained, 'so I think it's best we just agree to disagree.'

'Very well,' Donnelly agreed with a smile that faded as fast as it arrived. 'So long as we all know where our loyalties stand. We detectives have a nasty habit of unearthing the truth.'

'I know where my loyalties lie.'

'Good.' Donnelly smiled again and stood to leave.

'And you might find DI Corrigan needs my help more than you think.' Anna stopped him. 'I sense his growing frustration at not being able to get into this one's mind.'

'So?'

'So I can help point him in the right direction. I don't know how or why but he has psychological similarities to some of the previous offenders he's investigated and it helped him find them. It helped him stop them.'

'Well, this is all news to me,' Donnelly lied.

'Cut the crap, Dave,' Anna warned him. 'You know what I'm talking about.'

'Go on,' he admitted without saying as much.

'Well, I don't think he shares any similarities with this one. In some ways you could say whoever The Jackdaw is, is more . . .'

'Sane?' Donnelly interrupted.

'I was going to say *balanced*,' Anna continued. 'At least, in some ways. Less emotional, more able to understand the fears and desires of the general public. He understands empathy enough to believe he can control it – how much sympathy the public will have for his victims.'

'And the guv'nor can't?' Donnelly asked.

'I think he struggles with empathy,' Anna explained. 'I don't think he has the same fears and desires as, say, you and I. Emotionally he's on a different scale to most of the rest of us – a scale that runs parallel to our own. When he comes across other people on the same emotional scale as he is he finds it relatively easy to empathize and understand them and therefore find them. But this one isn't like that which is why I believe I can help him with this investigation more than the others. I can *profile* The Jackdaw better than he can.'

'Let me get this straight.' Donnelly narrowed his eyes. 'You think the guv'nor can't profile this one because The Jackdaw is less *insane* than he is?'

'I don't believe either are insane,' she argued. 'Certainly not DI Corrigan. He's just *different*. He thinks differently. If I didn't know better I'd say he was still suffering from post-traumatic stress disorder.'

'If you didn't know better?'

'I checked into his past,' Anna explained. 'There was nothing that could have caused PTSD, except being shot by Thomas Keller, but that happened long after he was already displaying the symptoms.'

'I'm not sure about any of this psychological mumbo-jumbo,' Donnelly dismissed it. 'But what I do know is that

331

he's one of the best I've ever worked with – one of the best I've ever seen. If you're in any way trying to undermine him, or *betray* him, then things won't go well for you.'

Anna's mouth opened to speak, but no words came out as Donnelly spun on his heel and strode from the office, leaving his words spinning around inside her head, tightening her chest and making her feel sick in her stomach. She'd been around detectives enough to have learnt their greatest of all taboos – the thing they detested more than anything: the unforgivable act of betrayal.

Sean drove for miles across the light morning London traffic until he reached the derelict building outside Walton-on-Thames that Jackson had unwittingly led them to the previous night, only for them all to be snared in The Jackdaw's trap. He wasn't sure what had drawn him back to the scene – he was pretty certain neither he and Sally nor forensics had missed anything – but still he found himself taking the long drive back to the abandoned building, thoughts from the night before spinning in his mind, mixing with the words of the conversation he'd had with Kate only an hour or so before. All his adult life he'd thought he wanted to slay the demons of his past, but now he genuinely feared losing them – was afraid of what he might become without them. He'd rather be damaged goods than live in a picture-postcard world that he knew didn't really exist. He liked being able to walk down the street and pick out the muggers, burglars and paedophiles from the daydreamers with little more than a glance. He liked being able to predict trouble about to erupt inside a pub or restaurant before anyone else even suspected there was a problem. He liked being able to shake a man's hand and know whether he could trust him before they even spoke. For the first time he was beginning to see it as a gift, not a handicap.

He used the old service road to reach the building, avoiding the need to walk back through the woods of the previous night, and rolled to a halt outside the entrance to the deserted Forestry Commission facility, switching off the engine and stepping out into the crisp morning air. Free from the darkness of night the surrounding forest no longer felt dangerous and intimidating. It looked beautiful in the glow of the early sunshine, the mist and dew reflecting and refracting the rays into a hundred variant colours.

Did you stand here like I am now? Sean asked inside his mind. *Did you take time to look at what I'm looking at – when you were setting the trap I walked straight into? If you're the man you want everyone to believe you are then I think you did, but if you're something else you wouldn't have even noticed the beauty of the trees or the sound of their leaves in the breeze. None of those things would have meant anything to you. You're too consumed with revenge and envy.*

He walked to the front door and climbed the stairs to the room into which he had charged only hours before expecting to catch The Jackdaw in the process of torturing his latest victim. How quickly glorious victory had turned to humiliating defeat. The room was bathed in daylight now – the black bin liners used to cover the windows and the battery-operated lights used in the trap had been removed to the lab for close forensic examination along with everything else. Sean paced around the circumference of the room, looking towards its centre, imagining a victim sitting in the old wooden chair, The Jackdaw circling and threatening – preaching to his watching flock, waiting for the chosen moment when he would kill or maim his helpless victim.

'The Jackdaw,' he mocked the emptiness. 'More like The Vulture. Fucking Jackson.'

Finally he walked into the centre of the room and slowly spun around where he stood, looking and waiting for something – anything.

'There's nothing here,' he whispered. 'I'm wasting my time.

Nothing but an empty room in an abandoned . . .' His own words suddenly stopped him. 'You didn't have to search to find this building before setting your trap, did you? You already knew it was here. It has everything you needed – abandoned and forgotten – derelict and isolated with no fear of being discovered. So when Jackson became interested in you, you came up with the idea of using it for your trap. But the question is, why didn't you use it to commit your crimes in? What was wrong with it? Is it too far from your home? Would such a long absence be missed by your wife or your work colleagues, so you had to find somewhere closer?'

Again he waited for something startling to leap into the front of his mind, but nothing happened.

'Ah, Jesus Christ,' he muttered in frustration. 'Who cares why he didn't choose this building? It doesn't mean anything. All that matters is that he wasn't here.' He walked to the window and sat on the windowsill, not caring whether it was filthy or hid some shards of broken glass. Early morning and he was already exhausted – drained by the previous days of seemingly futile investigation. And now he was further dragged down by an avalanche of fruitless questions. He needed to sit, no matter what.

As he sat on the windowsill with his chin held in the palm of an upturned hand, his mind slowly rewinding the conversation with Kate, while at the same time remembering the image of Anna sitting in the semi-darkness of his office the night before, he found himself watching a fly struggling to escape from a spider's web it had become entangled in – its wings beating hundreds of times a second in a forlorn attempt to escape death. He watched as a black spider appeared from a gap in the window frame, its front legs dragging its body from its lair. It paused for a second, stretching out its foremost two legs, resting them on the silver strands that led to the web itself for a moment, before moving at a speed that almost made Sean recoil – defying gravity as it appeared to slide upwards and wrap the doomed fly in an inescapable grip. Sean's mind magnified the scene so he could see the spider's fangs puncture through the fly's thorax and pump its lethal flesh-dissolving toxin into its prey. The fly's wings beat only sporadically and then not at all. The spider began to spin the fly's dead body around and around, wrapping it in a silver coffin before sliding back down the strand that had led it to the scene of the crime and disappearing into the gap in the window frame, its back legs trailing behind the rest of its robot-like body, its insect meal seemingly left for another time.

Sean continued to look on, hypnotized by the macabre little scene, all thoughts of Kate, Anna and the investigation cleared from his mind as he considered the brutal simplicity of the spider's actions. He leaned closer to better see the fly's suspended cocoon as it ever so slightly swayed in the tiny breeze.

'Such clarity,' he whispered. 'You detect prey – you kill it. But did any type of thought go through your mind at all? You're not hungry, otherwise you would have already eaten it. Did you consider not killing it – letting it live – or is it simply in your nature to kill on sight?' For some reason the words of the young priest jumped into his mind – *envy and revenge*. 'Is that why you killed it?' he asked, 'because you envied its freedom – its freedom to go anywhere it likes while you're stuck in your little hole there – your entire life spent in a rotting window frame? Was it killed because of envy or was it just a means to an end – just another meal for some other time?'

He leaned away and shook his head in disbelief. 'Jesus Christ, I must be going mad. I'm talking to a bloody spider.' He stood, brushed the dust from his coat and took a step towards the door before his own words echoed inside his mind and froze him.

'A means to an end,' he repeated slowly. 'A means to an end. What? What? What does that mean? Why are those words in my mind? A means to an end. A means to an end. Is that what these victims are to you – merely a means to an end? No social revolution. No hero of the common man. Just a means to an end. But what is it you're trying to achieve? What is it you're trying to end? Have we all been looking in the wrong direction – the direction you deliberately turned our heads towards?' He rubbed his tired eyes in confusion and frustration. 'Do I even know what I'm doing any more?' he questioned himself. 'One thing's for sure – there are no answers here. Only more questions.'

Addis sat behind his desk in New Scotland Yard, it was impossible to tell that he hadn't been home the night before, dressed as he was in a crisp, fresh uniform, smelling like a man who'd just stepped out of the shower, looking alert and awake as he scanned the morning papers looking for good or bad news about the Metropolitan Police. Most still headlined with The Jackdaw, as they liked to call him, especially *The World,* which had added 'police incompetence' and 'lack of political will' to the various angles of the story. He ground his teeth slightly as he read about the trap Corrigan and the surveillance team had somehow managed to walk into. The phone ringing on his desk momentarily subdued his anger.

'Assistant Commissioner Addis speaking.'

'For Christ's sake, Robert,' the minister asked, 'have you read this morning's papers yet? Now we're getting the blame for police incompetence.'

'No doubt they're aware of cuts to the police budget,' Addis provoked him.

'I'd be careful if I were you, Robert,' the minister warned him. 'Plenty of other people are qualified to become the next Commissioner. Some are women and one's even *black* and the Home Secretary's oh so very keen on equal opportunities.

I'm sure I don't have to tell you what that could mean for you. Some people are already saying you could be considered to be a bit of a dinosaur and we all know what happened to them, don't we? You're on borrowed time, Robert. Get this case solved. How you do it – that's your business.'

Addis sensed the minister was about to hang up. 'I was just wondering,' he stopped him, 'if you've been to a certain address in Pimlico lately?'

'Pimlico?' the minister asked, sounding slightly confused.

'Yes. You see, after our little conversation last night I decided to check back through some old intelligence reports I keep here in my office. Quite a few contain rather good quality surveillance photographs.'

'And?'

'And I was wondering if the name Catrina Duvall meant anything to you?' Addis twisted the knife a little further. 'I'm sure the fact she has several convictions for prostitution isn't important.'

'I don't know what you're talking about,' the minister answered unconvincingly.

'Really?' Addis asked, dragging the word out slowly. 'Well, any time you'd like to pop into my office and take a look at the surveillance photographs, please let me know. Or would you rather I posted copies to your parliamentary office or perhaps your home, addressed to your wife?'

'Christ, Robert. Are you trying to blackmail me?'

'I'm terribly sorry,' Addis apologized. 'I seem to have given you the wrong impression. I'll pop the photographs in the post immediately.'

'No,' the minister answered quickly. 'No, no. That . . . that won't be necessary. Perhaps it's best if I don't contact you for a while – give you a little breathing space whilst you're in the middle of this high-profile investigation.'

'I think,' Addis agreed, sounding completely sincere, 'I think that would be an excellent idea. Oh and, Minister, you would do well to remember I've been playing this game for a very long time. A very long time indeed.'

Sean arrived back in his office by mid-morning, still unable to make sense of the three things he could neither organize in his mind nor get out of his head. Envy. The spider. A means to an end. But he knew himself well enough to know that if they wouldn't leave him, they must mean something. He was tempted to take his journal from the locked drawer and see if writing down all the thoughts in his head would somehow help him visualize and comprehend their importance, but he was too fearful someone would enter his office and see him. He was considered unconventional enough without having his anguish and confusion laid bare in the journal.

Sally stuck her head around his door, startling him slightly. 'You all right?' she asked.

'Yeah, fine,' he lied, but his face betrayed him.

'Just thought you should know the victims have been after updates,' she told him, 'wanting to know when we're going to catch The Jackdaw.' She pulled a face to mock the name the media had given the man they hunted. 'They're not exactly happy with our progress.'

'Nor am I,' he reminded her. 'Any particular victim?'

'From what I'm told,' she admitted, 'all of them.'

'Shit,' he swore. Now even the victims were turning on him. How long before Addis came storming through the office full of not-so-veiled threats? 'And what have we been telling them, exactly?'

'Standard updates,' Sally assured him, 'nothing critical. Just trying to keep them happy we're making progress without compromising the investigation. But they're pushy – more than one of them, or their representatives, have been after sensitive information.'

Sean shook his head in disbelief. 'What's the matter with

these people? Don't they understand we're trying to find the bastard who did this to them? Why can't they just leave me alone to get on with it?'

'I'm sure they're just concerned.' Sally tried to be the voice of reason. 'These are good people.'

'Try telling that to the thousands who voted for them to be tortured and maimed,' he countered.

'Maybe,' Sally shrugged, 'but the tide of opinion's turning. People don't want this any more.'

'Don't they?' Sean countered, rubbing the pain in the sides of his head with his knuckles. He needed to do something to take his mind off the human distractions that seemed to surround him and concentrate on the investigation. The Your View videos, he told himself. I need to see the videos. He pulled his laptop from its case and laid it on the desk in front of him. He flipped it open and within a few seconds was watching the footage of the first victim – Paul Elkins – The Jackdaw circling him, preaching to the viewers, reciting the alleged crimes he'd decided Elkins had committed against the people, while his victim writhed and struggled in the familiar wooden chair. Finally Elkins was hoisted into the air to die a grotesque death. Sean wanted to look away, but forced himself to observe and consider everything in the footage, trying to find anything he might have missed, but he saw nothing that leapt out at him.

Once the scene had played out he moved onto the next victim – Georgina Vaughan, young and attractive with long, wavy, dark brown hair that reminded him of Anna's. Again The Jackdaw circled her, preaching into the camera, broad-casting his special brand of hatred to the ever-increasing audience of eager participants – detailing her crimes as she protested her innocence.

'From a CEO to a project manager,' Sean spoke quietly out loud. 'Why her? Was she an easy target, or the *real* reason for your envy and revenge? Was she your lover, or did she turn you down? And why . . . why film it differently from the first victim?' He watched as The Jackdaw turned on her, using his knife to forever brand her on the chest with the sign of the dollar, ignoring her screams as he cut deep enough to hit bone. 'Bastard,' Sean muttered, but still he watched every second and listened to every word, until the screen went blank.

Without allowing himself any respite he loaded the next Your View video, showing Jeremy Goldsboro taped to the old wooden chair, hooded and gagged as the masked man lectured into the camera in his electronic voice, the usual accusations and promise of recriminations as the camera continued to film them – torturer and victim, side by side. Sean clicked the pause icon and stared at the screen, his eyes narrowing with concentration.

Why did you leave the hood over his head? Was it really so he couldn't see, or was it to stop us seeing? Are you trying to hide something from me?

He un-paused the footage and continued to watch as The Jackdaw took his victim's little finger between the blades of the pruners and slowly cut through flesh and bone, Goldsboro's cries of agony and terror making him shiver. Eventually the cries died down and the masked face of Goldsboro's torturer grew larger on the screen as he approached the camera, holding the severed finger up for the world to see, boasting that he had been merciful and forgiving, claims that made Sean feel a little nauseous. *There was nothing forgiving about The Jackdaw*. Again he forced himself to watch every second of the film, but this time he allowed himself some time before loading the footage of the last victim. *The final victim?*

He sank back in his chair and considered the video of Goldsboro's ordeal. It wasn't the first time he'd watched the footage since seeing it live, but it was the first time that the fact the victim had been left hooded and gagged bothered him. The first two videos were different from each other, but he'd allowed his victims to see and be seen. Sean reflected on The Jackdaw's words for a few seconds: *His greedy lips and deceitful eyes.* Now, seeing all the videos one after the other, it didn't feel right. The Jackdaw wanted to humiliate his victims – wanted their humiliation to continue even after their release. But no one had seen Goldsboro's suffering – his fall from grace – his fall from a rich and powerful man to a helpless victim. His destruction had been hidden under a cloth hood.

'Why?' Sean asked the room. 'Why didn't you want us to see the suffering on his face? Why didn't you want his face to be shown all over the Internet – all over the world, over and over until he would barely be able to leave his house without being recognized and ridiculed? That's what you want, isn't it? So why spare him from public humiliation?'

A sudden sense of urgency washed over him as he leaned forward and as quickly as he could loaded the fourth video, his heart beating a little faster now, his tiredness forgotten. It began as the others had, the victim sitting taped to the chair, the hood still pulled over his head, but as the video progressed the hood and gag were removed – his fear plain for everyone to see — and he was allowed to speak, to plead his case, to try to convince the watching 'jury' of his innocence. So why had Goldsboro not been allowed the same privilege?

As soon as the brutal replay of Barrowgate's suffering was over Sean reloaded and watched the video of Goldsboro again – his eyes moving from the hooded victim to the masked assailant and back – Goldsboro squirming in the chair, trying to free himself, his muffled appeals turned to distorted screams as once more The Jackdaw cut through flesh and bone to sever his finger from his hand.

'I don't believe what you say,' Sean whispered. 'If you believed his mouth was used for lies you would have cut out

341

his tongue and cut off his lips. If you believed his eyes were deceitful, you would have burnt them out, just like you did to David Barrowgate. So why leave the hood on – why really?'

He leaned back in his chair, plucked a pencil from his pen-pot and began to tap it on his desk – its rhythm unconsciously synching to the beat of his heart as he castigated himself for failing to consider the importance of the hood not being removed before – the pure volume of mundane inquiries and administrative work the investigation had created blocking his ability to think clearly and see what sometimes existed between the lines. His mind had been so cluttered that at times he couldn't even recognize the obvious things, let alone free his thinking enough to reach inside the mind of The Jackdaw and predict his next move or see the truth of why he did what he did. He needed to cut away the fat of the investigation and deal with the lean, crucial facts and leads. He'd seen too many detectives lose the very thing that had made them special once they became swamped under workloads and deadlines and now it had almost happened to him.

'Did you know Goldsboro?' he asked the screen. 'Is that it? You knew him and he knew you – from the past. Were you afraid that somehow he'd recognize you – even through your mask and distorted voice – that he knew you so well some small thing would make him recognize you. The way you moved perhaps? Or am I just clutching at straws?' Sean needed someone else to see what he was seeing, to tell him he wasn't imagining it, that it was indeed something important – or that it meant nothing.

He stood and walked the very short distance to Donnelly's office next door and leaned inside, making Donnelly break off from the conversation he was having with Zukov and look up.

'Can I borrow you a minute?' Sean asked.

'Problem?' Donnelly replied in his usual way.

'I just need you to take a look at something.'

'Sure,' Donnelly answered, heaving his thick body from the small chair.

'You found Jason Howard yet?' Sean quickly asked Zukov.

'He's on the PNC as wanted,' Zukov explained, 'and I've circulated his photograph to all Borough Intelligence Units in the Met, but still nothing. He's done a Lord Lucan on us.'

'Find him,' Sean demanded and headed back to his own office. Donnelly fired Zukov a quick look of irritation before following Sean next door and sitting on the opposite side of the desk.

'So, what is it you want me to look at?' he asked as he landed in his seat.

Sean spun his laptop through ninety degrees to an angle at which they could both see the screen.

'This,' he answered and pressed the play icon that started the Your View video of Jeremy Goldsboro once again.

'Goldsboro's video,' Donnelly said, sounding unimpressed. 'So what of it?'

'Just watch,' Sean told him, allowing the footage to play while they silently watched. After thirty seconds or so Donnelly cracked.

'What am I supposed to be looking for?' he asked.

'Keep watching,' Sean told him and let the video play for several more minutes before hitting the pause button. 'What's the most striking difference between this video and the others?'

'I haven't studied the others that closely,' Donnelly admitted. 'That's being done at the lab for me – breaking it down frame by frame.'

'You don't need to study them closely,' Sean argued. 'You just need to watch and to *see*.'

'OK,' Donnelly played along. 'It's . . . it's not as violent?'

'No,' Sean dismissed his observation. 'Something else.'

'Looks like the same place,' Donnelly tried. 'The same chair

343

and placement of the bags over the windows and the suspect's wearing the same clothing and . . .'

'And?' Sean pushed him.

'And the victim remains hooded and gagged throughout,' Donnelly finally gave him the answer he was waiting for. 'The other victims had their hoods removed and were allowed to talk – to plead their case, so to speak.'

'Do you think publicly humiliating them is important to him?'

'I . . . suppose so,' Donnelly agreed unconvincingly. 'I mean possibly – or perhaps it's just about making his point.'

'Which is?' Sean asked.

'Which is the bankers screwed up and yet it seems to be the likes of you and me that are paying for it.'

'And you still believe that?' Sean asked; he was using Donnelly as a sounding board for his own doubts and suspicions.

'Why not?' Donnelly answered with a question. 'There's a lot of anger out there towards the sort of people he's been taking. Why wouldn't someone who's a little unhinged decide to turn himself into a latter-day avenging angel? We'll find him soon enough and he'll be another two-time loser looking to make a name for himself. You'll see.'

'Maybe,' Sean answered, blinking rapidly as he tried to keep pace with his own thoughts, 'but this *different* treatment of Goldsboro . . . it just makes me feel . . .'

'Makes you feel what?' Donnelly asked.

'Makes me feel there's a link between him and Goldsboro – something personal between them.'

'Then what about the other victims?' Donnelly questioned his theory. 'Do they have a personal link to the suspect too?'

'Possibly,' Sean admitted.

'But if they are all linked to the suspect,' Donnelly explained, 'then the chances are they'd be linked to each other somehow, agreed?'

'Yes,' Sean played along. 'That's what I'd expect.'

'But there isn't a link,' Donnelly ambushed him. 'We've already checked and none of the victims know each other. They all work for different companies. Sorry. No links.'

'Work.' Sean seized on one of Donnelly's words. 'Maybe that's the link.'

'But like I just said,' Donnelly reminded him, 'they don't work together.'

'Not in the same company,' Sean argued, 'but maybe, some time in the past their paths crossed – too fleetingly for them to remember, but something that brought them into contact with either Goldsboro or the man who took them.'

'Like what?' Donnelly asked, his arms spread wide.

'I don't know,' Sean admitted before slumping back in his chair and then immediately sitting bolt upright. 'You said the victims don't work for the same company now, but what about in the past?'

'I couldn't tell you,' Donnelly told him. 'Sally's been looking after victim research.' Sean sprang to his feet and paced to his doorway from where he shouted across the office.

'Sally,' he called out and waited for her to look in his direction. 'My office please.' He moved back inside. 'Do we have Goldsboro's medical evidence yet?' he asked Donnelly while they waited for Sally's imminent arrival.

'You mean the statement from the A&E doctor who treated him?'

'Yeah,' Sean confirmed.

'No,' Donnelly admitted.

'Jesus Christ,' Sean complained. 'Why the hell not?'

'It's an A&E doctor,' Donnelly reminded him. 'Getting a statement out of them is like trying to get blood out of a stone. What's the urgency anyway? Goldsboro had his little finger clipped off. That's not going to change, no matter how quickly we get the statement. What's bothering you, guv'nor?

345

What's the sudden urgency for the medical evidence? It's not going to take us any further.'

Sally strolled into the office before Sean could answer. He quickly turned his attention to her. 'Dave says you've been looking into the victims' backgrounds – in particular their employment?'

'Well,' Sally answered guardedly, 'I've been overseeing it, if that's what you mean. I haven't exactly been doing it myself.'

'Whatever,' Sean told her, uninterested in the details of whose task it was. 'And what have we found?'

Sally looked at Donnelly for support before answering, confusion etched on her face. 'That they all work in the City,' she shrugged, 'for banks and financial institutions.'

'I know that,' he snapped a little. 'What I mean is, have any of them worked together in the same company? I'm looking for a connection between them.'

'They all worked for different companies,' Sally explained. 'There is no connection and Goldsboro hasn't worked for anyone for five or six years. There is no connection between the victims. What's this all about anyway?'

'He didn't take the hood or gag off Goldsboro,' Donnelly tried to explain.

'So?' Sally asked.

'So the guv'nor thinks that means he must somehow know him.'

'I don't get it,' Sally admitted.

'It's just an idea,' Sean answered, beginning to feel a little self-conscious.

'Well I hate to shoot it down,' Sally apologized, 'but we even asked the victims if they knew each other, and they didn't. Georgina Vaughan and David Barrowgate had apparently heard of Paul Elkins, he was a very senior and well-known figure in the City, but they don't know him.'

'And Goldsboro,' Sean asked, 'did any of them know Goldsboro or he them?'

'No,' Sally explained. 'He retired too long ago for them to probably even remember him.'

'Young blood, eh?' Donnelly offered. 'No time for the old guard.'

'But did he know Paul Elkins?' Sean persisted, refusing to let go of the feeling in his gut that at least some of the victims were connected to each other and The Jackdaw to them.

'We asked him,' Sally deflated him, 'but he doesn't know him.'

Sean slumped in his chair, drumming his fingers in thought and frustration on his desk. *What was he missing? What was he missing?* His eyes narrowed as he leaned forward. 'How far did you go back,' he asked Sally, 'how far did you go back into their employment history?'

'We didn't,' Sally admitted. 'There was no need. They've all been with their current companies for several years, except for Goldsboro who's retired. We just checked their current jobs.'

'No,' Sean almost shouted, getting to his feet. 'We need to go back further – back through their previous jobs and even further if we have to – at least back to when Goldsboro was still working.'

'Boss,' Sally warned him. 'That would take hundreds of man hours. We're trying to run a murder investigation while also handling a murder trial. We don't have the people to do that.'

'Then I'll do it myself,' Sean told them, the disappointment thick in his voice as he started pulling his coat on.

'Where do you think you're going, boss?' Sally asked him, her concern matching his anger.

'To speak to Jeremy Goldsboro,' he insisted. 'Maybe he can give me the answers I need, since it seems nobody here can.'

Donnelly sprang to his feet. 'Want some company?'

347

'No,' Sean answered too quickly.

'Why don't you just call him?' Sally tried to stop him.

'No,' Sean explained. 'I need to see him. I need to pump him for information. I can't do that down a phone.'

'You don't even know where he is,' Sally argued.

'I'll find him,' Sean snapped, fixing Sally with a look she couldn't remember him ever using on her before. The sound of the phone ringing broke the atmosphere. Sean hesitated, not sure if he would even answer it until curiosity got the better of him and he snatched it up. 'DI Corrigan.'

'Sean,' DS Aden O'Brien answered. 'How you been keeping? Haven't seen you since that little job we pulled in Liverpool.'

'Long time ago now, Aden.' Sean avoided reminiscing. 'You got something for me?'

'That shotgun DS Donnelly wanted me to take a look at,' O'Brien began. 'Very interesting.'

'I'm listening,' Sean assured him.

'Not your usual sawn-off,' O'Brien told him. 'Hope they haven't been robbing banks with it – gun's probably worth more than any haul would be.'

'What are you saying?' Sean asked.

'I'm telling you that shotgun's a rare and valuable item. More specifically, it's a David McKay Brown, over/under double-barrelled round-action shotgun with a twenty-nine-inch barrel and some very beautiful Celtic engravings. Any decent villain who got his hands on this would sell it, not saw the bloody barrels off it, so either whoever has it doesn't know what he has, or he doesn't care.'

'Or it's his own,' Sean said quietly.

'What's that?' O'Brien asked.

'Nothing ,' Sean lied. 'Thanks, Aden.'

'One more thing,' O'Brien said before Sean could hang up. 'I checked the register of stolen firearms. A gun like this should show up pretty quickly.'

'But?' Sean encouraged him.

'I got a big fat no trace.'

'Meaning no one's reported one as being stolen,' Sean surmised.

'Correct,' O'Brien confirmed. 'Listen. There's probably only a couple of hundred of these guns in the UK. Shouldn't take you too long to find out who's missing one.'

'Long enough,' Sean replied. 'Thanks, Aden.'

'No problem. Sorry I couldn't pin it down a bit more for you.'

'Trust me, Sean told him. 'You've given me plenty.' He hung up slowly as another brick in the wall The Jackdaw had built seemingly crumbled.

'Everything all right?' Donnelly asked.

'The shotgun our boy's been using,' Sean explained, 'it's valuable and reasonably rare, but not reported as stolen.'

'Then the owner doesn't know it's missing yet,' Donnelly offered the logical explanation.

'I don't see how,' Sean argued.

'Overseas maybe.'

'I don't think so,' Sean told him. 'I think it's not reported stolen because it's not stolen. I think it's *his* gun, whoever *he* is. He's not a criminal, or at least he wasn't, and neither does he associate with them, so he can't use his criminal contacts to get a gun and he can't just walk into his local boozer and quietly ask around. So he uses his own shotgun. But this isn't the sort of gun a farmer or gamekeeper would own, this is a rich man's plaything.'

'Maybe the rich man owner's dead,' Donnelly suggested. 'Our boy's first victim, hiding somewhere in a shallow grave. Can't report the shooter missing if you're dead and no one knows.'

'It's his gun,' Sean insisted. 'I'm telling you, it's his own gun, and he's no working-class hero. He's right under all our noses, only we can't see him.'

349

'But the Celtic markings on the gun,' Donnelly argued. 'Surely he'd know we'd identify it?'

'Then he has a plan for that too,' Sean insisted. 'He has a plan for everything, remember.'

'I'm not sure,' Donnelly shook his head. 'We should concentrate on looking for someone who's lost everything – someone with a vendetta against these City types.'

'No,' Sean told him. 'It's personal. It always was.' He quickly finished filling his coat pockets with everything he thought he might need and headed for the door.

'You sure you don't want me to come?' Donnelly asked.

'No,' Sean told him. 'I'll call you if I need you.' He swept past Donnelly into the main office and was gone, leaving Donnelly sitting open-mouthed in his office.

'Once in a while,' Donnelly complained to Sally, 'I wish he'd tell me what the fuck's going on in that mind of his.'

'Would you really want to know?' Sally asked.

'No,' Donnelly shook his head. 'D'you want me to go with him – even if he doesn't want me to?'

'No,' Sally replied. 'He's best left on his own – sometimes.'

'You sure?' Donnelly checked. 'This thing about Goldsboro and the hood – I wonder if this is one high-profile investigation too far.'

'If he thinks he's on to something we should trust him,' Sally rounded on him. 'Don't you?' Donnelly just shrugged. 'Let him work it through,' Sally ordered. 'Just give him time to work it through.'

As Sean reached the exit to the main office he almost bumped into Anna coming the other way. Instinctively he grabbed her by the shoulders and spun her around to avoid a painful collision – moving as if they were dancing.

'Sean,' she panted, flustered. 'I was hoping to see you.'

'Not now, Anna,' he apologized. 'I need to be somewhere else.'

'It's important. I've already waited too long to tell you.' Her eyes told him she was serious.

'OK,' he relented. 'What is it?'

'Not here,' she told him. 'We need to speak in private.'

'Walk me to my car,' he instructed her. 'We can speak on the way. If we're moving we won't be overheard.' She nodded her agreement and followed him out of the door and along the corridor heading to the lifts. 'So what's so important it can't wait?'

'Christ,' Anna tried to begin, drawing in a deep breath. 'This is not going to be easy for me to say.'

Sean smiled nervously as they strode along the thin corridor. 'This already doesn't sound good.'

'It's about Assistant Commissioner Addis,' she explained.

'Addis,' Sean said dismissively as he pushed open the doors that led to the small foyer and the lifts. 'What's Addis got to do with anything?'

Anna checked all around them to make sure they were alone as Sean impatiently stabbed at the lift button. Still he didn't sense her anxiety as his mind wandered ahead to Jeremy Goldsboro and what he was going to ask him. No doubt Goldsboro would think he was as mad as everyone else did once he started questioning him about why his captor hadn't removed the hood.

'It was Addis who made sure I was attached to the Thomas Keller investigation,' she reminded him.

'So?' Sean shrugged as the empty lift arrived, the doors parted and they stepped inside alone.

'And it was Addis again who arranged for me to be attached to this investigation,' Anna continued.

'I know,' Sean told her, sounding increasingly irritated. 'Listen, if you've got something to tell me then just say it.' The doors of the lift slid shut as they began their juddering descent.

'My job was and is to profile the offenders for you – to help you find them.'

'I know what you're here for,' Sean sighed.

'Only, that's not entirely true,' she explained. 'I'm not here to profile the offenders for you, Sean, I'm here to profile *you* for Addis.' Sean's eyes grew large and wild, before narrowing to thin slits – his pupils turning to little more than black pinpricks. Anna reached out to touch his arm, but he pulled it away. 'I'm so sorry. It was before I met you. Before I got to know you. If I'd known then what I know now I would never have agreed to it.'

'What was in it for you?' he managed to ask through thin white lips.

'It sounded an interesting case study,' she answered, knowing only honesty could save her now. 'A detective who could seemingly see things that others could not – see evidence that others had missed. One who could profile the people he hunted better than any psychiatrist or psychologist I've ever known.'

'Is that all?' he snarled as the lift bounced to a halt and the doors creaked open, revealing the underground car park sprawling out ahead of them. Sean stepped into the gloominess and walked fast, Anna trailing behind him.

'That and unparalleled access to investigations and any suspects arrested,' she said, trying to justify accepting Addis's offer. 'If you'd been in my position you'd have done the same. I didn't know things were going to become so . . . complicated.'

'You should have told me,' he said over his shoulder as she struggled to keep up. 'Once things got, as you say – *complicated* – you should have told me. Not carried on being Addis's *spy*.'

'Wait, Sean,' she pleaded. 'Just wait a minute.' She reached out and managed to get a hold of his jacket and pull him to a stop, although he still wouldn't look at her. 'I wanted to tell you—'

'Then why didn't you?' he interrupted her.

'Because I was afraid,' she admitted, finally getting him to look at her. 'I was afraid of what Addis would do. I was afraid of what he might do to you.'

'I can look after myself,' he assured her. 'I'm not afraid of Addis.'

'You should be,' she warned him. 'He's more dangerous than you think.'

'Maybe it's me who's more dangerous than people think,' he couldn't help himself from saying.

'No you're not,' she argued. 'You and I both know there's something in your past you're hiding – something . . . *dark*, but it doesn't mean you're a danger to anyone.'

'Doesn't it?'

'No,' she insisted, 'and now we won't be working with each other any more perhaps you can talk to me about it. Maybe I can help you.'

'What d'you mean, not working with each other any more?' he asked.

'Now I've told you, I can tell Addis I won't be staying,' she explained.

'No.' Sean stopped her. 'No. I have a better idea.'

'Such as?'

'You stay and you tell Addis nothing about this conversation.'

'I don't understand,' she admitted.

'You let him think you're still working for him,' he explained. 'Still watching me and reporting to him – but you tell him only what *we* want you to tell him. And anything he says about me, or anyone else on my team for that matter, you tell me.'

'You basically want me to be a double-agent?'

'If you like. You want to make things up to me then this is how you do it. Addis will never know and sooner or later he'll move on to bigger and better things and forget we ever existed. Believe me – I know his type.'

'I'm not sure I can do that,' Anna shook her head. 'I'm not sure I want to be used any more.'

'No one will be using you,' Sean tried to reassure her. 'You'll just be levelling the playing pitch – keeping Addis off my back. You owe me that much at least.'

'Wait a minute,' Anna suddenly accused him, taking a step backwards. 'You thought all this up pretty quickly. You already knew, didn't you? Someone told you? Was it Donnelly?'

'No one told me anything,' he answered, 'but yes – I suspected as much.'

'Jesus Christ,' Anna shook her head and closed her eyes. 'How long?'

'Since we first met,' he admitted.

'How?'

'You asked a few too many questions – that's all.'

'I can't remember asking any questions.'

'Must have been something else then. I can't remember now.'

'And everything else?' she pressed. 'Our *friendship*?'

'It was real,' he assured her. 'Is real. Sometimes too real.'

'Then why didn't you say something?'

'I could have been wrong,' he answered unconvincingly, 'and besides it was better to wait until you told me yourself.'

'And your little charade back there in the lift – your Mr Angry impersonation – all just for my benefit?'

'Sorry,' he confessed. 'I figured it would be best if you didn't know that I already knew.'

'So if I hadn't said anything you would never have told me?' Sean shrugged silently. 'Christ,' she continued. 'All this time I've been feeling like a betraying bitch and all the time *you* were using *me*.'

'I wasn't using you,' he argued. 'I never *fed* you anything that I wanted to get back to Addis. I just didn't tell you everything I was thinking.' Anna sighed, unable to think of anything else to say. 'Well?' Sean asked. 'Will you do it?'

'Cops,' she complained loudly. 'You're unbelievable. You're all as bad as each other.'

'I told you,' he reassured her, 'I'm not out to hurt Addis – I'm just looking for a little insurance. Plus you still get to help on the case and pick the suspect's mind when I catch him. Should be an interesting experience.'

'What choice do I have?' she asked.

'Every choice,' he insisted. 'You don't want to do it, don't do it. Walk away. I won't think any less of you. I won't blame you. At least think about it. Just think about it. I have to go now.' He rested his hand on her shoulder for a second before heading towards his car, leaving Anna standing alone feeling dazed and confused and wondering if she really knew anything about Sean at all.

Jackson entered the Three Greyhounds pub in Greek Street and searched the tables for the man he was looking for, finding him sitting towards the rear of the pub with his back to the wall facing the entrance reading a newspaper. Jackson noted it wasn't a copy of *The World*. He crossed the pub, slid into a chair opposite the man and patiently waited for him to lower his paper and acknowledge his presence. After a long thirty seconds he got his wish as the man, tall and slim and in his early fifties, neatly folded his paper and laid it on the table in front of him before looking up directly into Jackson's eyes.

'So what's this all about, Geoff?' DCI Ryan Ramsay asked him straight in his London accent. 'Why have you dragged me into the West End on a weekend?'

'Just thought we could have a quiet little chat,' Jackson told Ramsay.

'Oh yeah?' Ramsay replied suspiciously, running his hands through his short, thick salt-and-pepper hair before readjusting his wire-frame spectacles. 'What about – exactly?'

'No need to be defensive,' Jackson explained. 'We've

worked together before. You know me. You know you can trust me.'

'I was working on cases you were interested in,' Ramsay reminded him, 'and I needed the media exposure to help solve them. A mutually beneficial partnership, all sanctioned by the Press Bureau. But as far as I'm aware I'm not working on anything right now you'd be interested in. So why am I here, Geoff?'

Jackson took a deep breath. 'DI Sean Corrigan,' he simply stated. Apparently the name alone was enough to make Ramsay sink deep into his chair.

'You want to ask me about a fellow cop? A detective?'

'He interests me,' Jackson admitted. 'He's different.'

'I couldn't give a fat man's arse how different he is,' Ramsay told him. 'I don't talk about other cops.'

'Come on,' Jackson smiled as he encouraged him. 'Corrigan's a story. I know he is and you do too.'

'What makes you think I even know him?'

'I did my research,' Jackson explained. 'Back in 2006 – the Mao Ma case. You were on that together, right?'

'So?'

'So you must have *heard* things. *Seen* things.'

'Maybe,' Ramsay answered cagily, 'but like I said – I don't talk about other Old Bill.'

Jackson leaned back to consider his next move before leaning in towards Ramsay once more. 'How long you got left?' he asked. 'How long until you retire? Two, three years?' Ramsay just shrugged. 'Then what you gonna do – get a job as a security adviser to Tesco's or NCP, if you're lucky. If you're thinking of getting a job with some bank in the City investigating frauds and picking up a few big fat bonuses, you can forget it. Those jobs are strictly for the ex-Serious Fraud Squad boys. They're not interested in ex-Flying Squad or Murder Squad. They want the number crunchers.'

'What's your point?' Ramsay demanded.

'My point is,' Jackson explained, 'that you could come work with me at *The World* – straight in as the deputy crime editor. You'd still be doing proper police work – covering proper investigations – only you'd be getting paid about three times as much for doing it. I could even introduce you to my publisher – you could maybe write books about some of your old cases.'

'If,' Ramsay stopped him, 'if I talk about Corrigan?'

Jackson spread his arms apart. 'Come on. I'm not asking you to throw him under the bus, it's just the man's turning into the Grim Reaper: wherever he turns up, things get interesting. He's a walking front-page story.'

'I'll think about it,' Ramsay told him not too encouragingly.

'Come on, Ryan,' Jackson persisted. 'This could be as good for Corrigan as it would be for you. I'm going to make him a celebrity. A celebrity cop. The public will love him. It'll keep the brass off his arse.'

'You're out of touch,' Ramsay insisted. 'This isn't LA. The powers that be in the Met wouldn't stand for a celebrity cop, not unless they *are* the celebrity. As far as the brass is concerned, detectives these days have one purpose and one purpose only: to make them look good. They won't tolerate sharing the limelight with the likes of Corrigan.'

'We'll see,' Jackson answered with a grin.

'I'm telling you,' Ramsay reiterated, 'you're wasting your time.'

'Just promise me you'll think about my offer.'

'Fine,' Ramsay agreed, getting to his feet. 'I'll think about it. Don't call me. I'll call you.' He picked up his folded newspaper and walked towards the exit.

Jackson was left alone with his thoughts, but no sooner had Ramsay headed through the door and out into the street than his mobile began to ring.

'Shit,' he cursed. 'What now?' But when he pulled the phone from his pocket he realized it wasn't ringing. It was his *other* phone. 'Shit,' he cursed again as he scrambled to find it hiding somewhere in the many pockets of his coat, finally locating it and answering like a man slightly out of breath. 'Hello.' He waited for a reply. 'Hello,' he repeated impatiently.

'You still have the phone, I see,' the unearthly voice told him.

'Of course,' Jackson stammered.

'Then you must believe you deserve another chance.'

'No,' Jackson tried to sound contrite. 'I just hoped. You said you might contact me.'

'Don't grovel, Mr Jackson,' the voice told him. 'Your false platitudes aren't what I need now. I need your attention and your skills as a journalist.'

'For what?'

'For the finale,' the voice answered. 'All good things must come to an end, as must this.'

'What do you want me to do?' Jackson asked.

'Simply keep watching,' The Jackdaw told him. 'Just simply keep watching.'

14

The Jackdaw moved quickly and nimbly around the white room, ensuring everything was just how he wanted it – just how it needed to be for his penultimate broadcast. As he checked the computer equipment and the camera it was attached to, a mumbling, sobbing sound distracted him and made him look over his shoulder at the man who lay bound, gagged and hooded on the floor – his pleas nothing more than an unintelligible grumbling. His captor sighed through the electronic voice distorter hanging in front of his mouth, rendering the sound metallic and threatening. He moved away from the computer and walked slowly over to the forlorn figure on the floor, speaking as he approached.

'Your constant babbling is distracting me,' he accused his victim. 'I need to concentrate.' But the man's groans only grew louder and more desperate as he tried to appeal to the captor he couldn't see. 'Be quiet,' the hooded figure demanded, and he pulled back his leg and kicked the man in his stomach hard enough to make him curl into a ball. 'You're disturbing me,' he shouted, lifting his boot above the man's head and stamping down with a sickening thump as it hit the concrete floor, the man's body falling limp. Electronic laughter filled the room as the figure looked down on his doomed victim.

'The police won't notice a few bruises to your head,' he laughed. 'Not once I've blown it off.'

He walked back to the table and the equipment laid out on it, making several small adjustments before clearing his throat and turning everything on. Within a few seconds he was watching his own image on the Your View broadcast. He stood still staring into the camera for several minutes while the number of people logging in to the broadcast grew, until he was satisfied there were enough to spread the message. It mattered not to him if people watched it live or later – just so long as he was seen and heard, almost for the last time.

'Brothers and sisters,' he began. 'We have woken up the world. We have changed things forever. Never again will the rich, greedy and powerful take us for granted. Never again will they believe they can act without consequence. Never again will they live without fear. Together we have made all this possible. However, I am a hunted man, and they will find me. This much is inevitable. But I won't let them lock me in a cage for their own amusement – won't let them build a fabric of lies around my living body to denigrate all that we have achieved. Better to die a martyr than to live in captivity. From the very beginning I have known this must be so and have accepted it. This is what *they* could never understand: sacrifice. Sacrifice for the greater good. The needs of the many outweighing the needs of the few.

'But the war has begun. My goals have been achieved and I am not sad. I am joyful. Soon I will leave this world satisfied and happy, knowing the legacy I have left behind and that *you*, my brothers and my sisters, will carry on this righteous struggle for our justice and equality. For now there is still time. Time for me to strike one last blow into the heart of the devil before I show them our true strength of purpose and belief. If the authorities attempt to block or interfere with my broadcasts I will kill the next person I take. Keep watching

360

and wait for my signal. Soon it will be over.' He stepped forward and turned the connection off. As soon as the screen went blank he disconnected the voice distorter, removed his wraparound sunglasses and pulled the ski-mask from his head, the cool air invigorating against his skin. He closed his eyes to better enjoy and remember the moment, smiling to himself as he thought of the tens of thousands of people hanging on his every word – ready to march on the City of London if he just gave the command.

The sound of the stricken man's moaning spoilt his moment, the smile falling slowly from his face as he remembered where he was and what he must do. His eyes searched the table in front of him until he found what he was looking for – the small leather-clad cosh. He picked it up and ceremonially tapped it in the palm of his hand as he walked to the man who was beginning to struggle on the floor.

'Almost the end now for you, my friend,' he told the hooded figure before violently striking him over the back of his head with the cosh, the man's body falling instantly limp, the only sound the air rushing from his lungs. 'Or should I say . . . The Jackdaw?'

Sean enjoyed the silence and tranquillity of the car as he drove from the Yard to Holland Park thinking about Anna and her revelation, which although he'd long suspected, he'd hoped wasn't true. No matter. Now it was out in the open and there to be used to his advantage. He also used the time to question his own theory – to try to see it how everyone else probably saw it. But he simply couldn't reconcile The Jackdaw leaving the hood over Goldsboro's head with anything other than there being a connection between the two – a personal connection. The hood hid something, something he didn't want them to see. He reached Goldsboro's home street and parked in a residents-only bay and tossed the vehicle logbook on the dashboard in the hope of

361

dissuading any passing parking meter attendants from giving him a ticket.

He climbed quickly from the car and walked along the quiet, upmarket street until he found what he was looking for – the six-storey Georgian house towering above him. He looked up at the imposing building before climbing the short flight of steps to the shiny black door. Sean pressed the intercom and waited. A clear but electronic-sounding female voice answered cheerfully. 'Hello.'

'Hello,' Sean tried to sound relaxed. 'Sorry to disturb you. I'm Detective Inspector Corrigan, from the Special Investigations Unit.'

'Who?' the voice asked, not so cheerful now.

'Detective Inspector Corrigan,' Sean repeated, trying not to let his frustration tell in his voice, holding his warrant card towards the intercom, which he assumed would have a camera in it. 'I'm investigating what happened to Mr Goldsboro. From the police,' he added to be sure.

'Oh. Jeremy's not here at the moment,' she replied. 'Perhaps you could come back later.'

'This can't really wait,' Sean insisted. 'Maybe you could tell me where he is?' There was a long silence. 'It's very important.' There was another pause.

'He said he was going fishing,' she finally answered.

'Shit,' Sean cursed under his breath while he considered his next move. 'Perhaps you might be able to answer some of my questions,' he tried.

'Very well,' she eventually agreed. 'You'd better come in.' A second later he heard locks being turned and pushed aside before the door swung slowly open to reveal a tall, slim woman in her mid-forties, her short blonde hair framing her attractive face. 'Sorry about all the security,' she apologized. 'Since what happened to Jeremy, well, I've been a bit on edge.'

'No need to apologize,' Sean told her, faking a smile. 'It's totally understandable. Mrs Goldsboro, I assume.'

362

'Sorry,' she apologized again. 'Yes . . . I'm Mrs Goldsboro, but please, call me Sarah.'

'Sarah it is,' he replied. 'Perhaps it's best if I come inside?'

'Yes,' she answered without hesitation. 'Sorry. Please come in.' She opened the door fully and stepped aside, allowing him to enter. Sean quickly scanned his surroundings to get his bearings, paying little attention to the beautiful high ceilings and artwork that adorned them. He had too many questions dancing around inside his head to care about anything else but how he was going to ask them.

'You have a beautiful house here,' he managed to say, trying to sound like a normal person.

'Thank you,' Mrs Goldsboro answered. 'We've thought about moving to the country, since Jeremy retired,' she explained, 'but we'd miss London too much, I think. Please, this way,' she told him and headed towards the kitchen.

'I know what you mean,' he played along. 'I imagine Mr Goldsboro misses work. Sometimes. Must have been a buzz, working in the City.'

'He says not,' she told him, 'but I have my doubts. He locks himself away in his office for hours some days. Heaven knows what he does in there. Still playing with stocks and shares, I imagine.'

'Still keeping his hand in?' Sean asked as they entered the huge kitchen-cum-dining room.

'It's in his blood,' she answered, 'although lately he's been selling a lot of our portfolio and buying up precious metals and diamonds – gold, silver, even palladium, if you please. Turned into quite the magpie. Please, take a seat.'

Sean recalled Addis's attempt at a joke when he warned him that The Jackdaw's crimes were affecting share prices in The City: *If you have any shares, Inspector, now would be a good time to sell them and buy yourself some gold, or silver perhaps.*

'I hear a lot of people are getting out of stocks and shares in favour of something a little more solid,' he said.

'Yes,' she agreed. 'Gold's always been seen a safe haven in troubled times. This lunatic's not just hurting people physic-ally – he's hurting them financially too.'

'It's the physical hurt I'm interested in,' Sean told her. 'Like the physical harm he did to your husband.'

The reminder of what had happened to her husband seemed to freeze her for a second before she answered. 'Yes. Yes I suppose you are.'

'You all right?' Sean asked as he sensed her fear.

'I'll be fine,' she tried to assure him.

'You probably shouldn't be here on your own,' he advised. 'Not until we catch him or you feel less afraid.'

'I'm not alone,' she explained. 'My housekeeper's here – upstairs doing something or another.'

'And Mr Goldsboro's gone fishing?' he checked.

'His new hobby,' she complained. 'He's only been doing it a year or so, but he appears hooked – no pun intended. His . . . *ordeal* doesn't appear to have affected Jeremy too much, but that's typical of him. Can't let these things stop you, he always says, as if he had just been mugged or something.'

'Probably best he gets on with his life,' Sean told her. 'So long as he's not hiding any psychological effects his ordeal had on him.'

'Psychological effects?' she scoffed. 'Jeremy? If that was this lunatic's intention then he picked on the wrong man. You don't get to the top of a company like King and Melbourn by being some sort of wallflower. You have to be a fighter.'

'I'm sure you do,' Sean agreed, remembering what Anna had told him about CEOs – that a significant proportion of them had psychopathic personality traits. Could this be the first ever case where the victims were the psychopaths and the assailant was normal?

'So,' she finally worked round to asking, taking a breath and preparing herself for the business of this unannounced visit, 'what can I do for you?'

'Like I said,' Sean told her, 'I was really hoping to speak with Mr Goldsboro, but as he's not here I thought you might be able to help.'

'With what – exactly?' she asked.

Sean stalled, suddenly unsure of himself and everything he suspected about The Jackdaw. Was his theory about why he hadn't removed Goldsboro's hood really worth causing Mrs Goldsboro even more anguish and fear? Could his compassion overrule his need to know? He already knew the answer.

'It's just,' he began, 'I'm not so sure these attacks are random any more.'

'Jeremy's already told me that,' she told him, looking and sounding confused. 'He was picked because of what he used to do.'

'That's not what I mean,' Sean shook his head. 'I mean I think some, if not all, of the victims could be connected to each other somehow and that connection somehow links them to whoever abducted them. Something we've not found yet.'

'Like what?' she asked.

'I don't know,' he admitted. 'Not yet. That's why I'm asking questions. Perhaps he knew the other victims?'

'If he did, then he would have already told you,' she argued.

'Maybe he just knew them in passing,' Sean struggled, 'and didn't think it could be important.'

'I'm sure he would have mentioned it,' she insisted, 'even if he did only know them in passing.'

'Maybe in the past he's mentioned their names? Paul Elkins – did he ever mention that name?'

'No,' she answered flatly.

'Georgina Vaughan?' he pushed.

'No. Never.'

'David Barrowgate?'

'I've never heard those names before this awful business,'

she shook her head, 'and Jeremy retired almost six years ago. I probably wouldn't remember even if he had mentioned them, but since he retired he never talks about work – not his old colleagues, nothing. Typical Jeremy – says that's all in the past – better to concentrate on the future.'

'Then maybe at some point some of the victims worked for the same company?' Sean persisted, desperate to find something tangible. 'Paul Elkins worked for Fairfield's Bank. Maybe your husband used to work for them?'

'No, no,' she dismissed the possibility. 'Jeremy was with King and Melbourn for almost fifteen years. It was his life. He joined as a middle manager and worked his way up to the top.'

'But before that,' Sean kept at her, 'who did he work for?'

'Oh gosh,' she shook her head. 'This bank, that bank, I really can't remember. You'd need to ask Jeremy these questions. I'm sure he could help you more than I can.'

Sean ignored her. 'The other two victims – one worked at Glenhope Investments and the other at Chaucer and Vale Bank. Do those names mean anything to you?'

'No.' She raised her voice. 'I'm really sorry, Inspector. I'd like to help, but I can't. These names mean nothing to me. Nothing at all. I'm sorry. If you'd like to leave a note then I'd be happy to get Jeremy to look at them for you.'

Sean knew she was finished. She had nothing he could use – nothing to move his own theory forward. Maybe the route to the connection lay elsewhere? Perhaps the other victims had worked for King and Melbourn some time in the past? Or maybe he was wrong – driven to believe in something that didn't really exist in a vain effort to make an unsolvable case solvable by looking for a connection that wasn't there. But the hood bothered him – bothered him too much to ignore.

'Inspector.' Mrs Goldsboro's voice brought him back. 'Are you finished?'

'Yes,' he weakly answered. 'I'm finished. Sorry to have bothered you.'

She seemed almost to take pity on him. 'What will you do now?' she asked, although he knew she just wanted him to leave.

'Only thing I can do,' he told her. 'Go to King and Melbourn.'

'Why?'

'To ask them the same questions I've just asked you,' he admitted, 'and pray they can give me the answers I need to find the man who took your husband before he acts out his final scene. I need to go,' he told her. 'Thanks for your time.'

He pulled the cut-down branches away from the white van, freeing it from its pace of hiding. He'd been sure to cover the roof especially thoroughly to conceal it from the police helicopters that circled above from time to time. He carefully scattered the branches randomly around the van's hiding place so they wouldn't draw any attention. Not that there were many passers-by in this part of the forest, except the occasional illicit couple. The police had come that one time, but their visit was now to be seen as a blessing — he was sure they'd reported the deserted building as having been searched with a negative result. Eventually he knew they'd realize their mistake and re-search the building, which was exactly what he needed them to do. After The Jackdaw had killed himself live on Your View the laptop he used would of course be left on – eventually leading the police straight to the white room.

Carefully he picked any loose leaves from the white van and brushed the dust away before opening the side door and retrieving a cardboard box containing a front and rear number plate he'd made himself, copied from another white Renault Trafic van he'd spotted driving through west London one day which, according to the sign on the side, belonged to an electrician. He used an electric screwdriver to attach them. Next he took another cardboard box containing stick-on letters and numbers he'd bought years before from a giant DIY store. He'd paid cash – The Jackdaw was nothing if not careful. He used the letters to spell the name of the electrician he'd seen plastered to the side of the van and even added the correct telephone number for complete authenticity. He took a few seconds to stand back and admire his work before climbing into the van's cab and opening the glovebox from which he took an oversized pair of wraparound mirrored sunglasses and a plain, black baseball cap. He pulled the collar of his black boiler suit up over his chin and checked himself in the driver's mirror. He doubted even his own wife would be able to recognize him. It would do fine until he had his next – his *last* – victim in sight. Then he would switch to the full face mask and voice-altering equipment that sat on the seat next to him covered with a copy of *The World* newspaper, bearing a headline that was all of his own making.

He reached for the ignition key, but suddenly paused, as if the significance of the moment had almost overwhelmed him. For years he'd waited for this – waited until the time was absolutely right – the time when he couldn't be connected to the two men who'd stripped him of everything he loved most – everything he'd worked for. First Paul Elkins, and now the one he'd yearned for more than any of the others – the kingpin in his downfall. Georgina Vaughan and David Barrowgate had meant nothing to him in particular, although he knew who they were and where they worked and what they wanted out of life. But they made perfect victims for The Jackdaw, as did Jeremy Goldsboro – another wealthy banker, albeit retired, who *deserved* his punishment. He smiled at the simple cleverness of his deception.

Years he'd spent in the wilderness – years being the forgotten man. But he'd never forgotten his humiliation and pain and now the time had finally come for his revenge. His long-time tormentor would become the tormented before he was put to death in front of the watching thousands, or perhaps millions. One thing he already knew, one thing he'd long, long ago decided, nothing could save his final victim now – not the vote of the people's jury and not DI Corrigan. Within the next few hours the game would be over and he would have won.

Sean stood outside the tower block in Bath Street, in the heart of the City of London, all thirty floors of which belonged to King and Melbourn Capital Associates, one of the City's largest trading firms. He looked up from the entrance to the very top of the gleaming building that reflected all the other buildings around it as well as Sean's own tiny image standing, shimmering, at the foot of this testament to power and wealth. It would take more than a banking crisis to topple these financial monoliths. They'd been built to survive the ages.

He walked to the giant building's entrance and into the ground-floor atrium. A long, thin, brown wooden desk with enough seats for ten receptionists stretched across the middle of the expanse, but today was Saturday and only two of the seats were occupied. He walked to the youngest and friendliest-looking of the two and flashed his warrant card.

'DI Sean Corrigan,' he introduced himself. 'Special Investigations Unit. I'm here to see Amanda Coppolaro.'

'Is she expecting you?' the receptionist asked.

'I phoned ahead,' Sean explained. 'She said she'd see me.'

'OK,' the young receptionist replied, sounding a little unsure. 'I'll call her office and let her know you're here.'

'Fine,' Sean agreed. 'I'll wait.'

'You can take a seat,' she told him looking up at the empty foyer. 'Anywhere you like.'

'Thanks,' Sean told her without smiling and wandered off to pace the atrium and think about what he was going to ask Coppolaro, but his mobile ringing destroyed his preparations. It was Sally.

'Christ, Sean.' She used his Christian name, which told him she was probably alone, their relationship having grown more personal since both had nearly died at the hands of two different killers. 'Where the hell have you been? Our man's been up to his old tricks on Your View again. I take it you saw it?'

'No,' Sean admitted, his mouth suddenly so dry he could hardly speak as his stomach tightened with anxiety and frustration. 'And the victim?' he managed to ask.

'No victim,' Sally told him, making his body suddenly relax again as he looked to the heavens in thanks. 'Just a lot of preaching and telling everyone to get ready for the finale. Sounds like he's beginning to lose it too – shouting about justice and equality, like some civil rights leader from the sixties. I'm beginning to think he actually believes in what he's saying.' Sean's eyes darted from side to side as he tried to process this new information. *What was going on?* He felt so close to the truth, so close to finding the thing – the one thing that connected the victims and therefore The Jackdaw to them. He just needed to keep asking questions, keep digging, even if he was digging blind, until that one small, precious thing opened the shutters and allowed the light to come flooding in and reveal everything.

'There's something else, too,' Sally continued. 'He's said he's going to kill himself, as soon as he's finished with one last victim. He sounded like he meant it.'

'One last victim and then martyr himself,' Sean spoke his thoughts out loud. 'Why would he do that?'

'Says he knows that eventually he'll be caught and doesn't want to vilified by the rich and powerful making up lies about him,' Sally explained. 'Says he'd rather die and prove his commitment to the cause.'

'His own cause,' he replied, his mind already wandering

from their conversation, trying to make sense of what he was being told. 'OK, Sally. Thanks for letting me know.' Why hadn't he seen The Jackdaw's self-destructive potential earlier? Now that he'd said he was going to take his own life it seemed so obvious that was what he always intended. Sean should have seen it coming and somehow used it against the man he was beginning to feel closer and closer to.

'What do you want me to do?' Sally asked.

'Just wait for my call.'

'Wait a minute,' she stopped him. 'Where are you? Everything's going mad back here. Addis has been charging around trying to find you.'

'What did you tell him?'

'I didn't,' Sally explained. 'I saw or should I say heard him coming and ducked out the office.'

'Good,' Sean told her. 'Best keep a low profile for now.'

'Fine,' she replied, 'but where are you?'

'King and Melbourn, in the City,' he admitted.

'What are you doing there?' Sally argued. 'There's nothing there for us.'

'We didn't go back far enough,' Sean insisted. 'We need to check back to when Jeremy Goldsboro worked here.'

'Yes,' Sally sighed. 'So you said – because he didn't remove his hood?'

'He was hiding something,' Sean again tried to convince her. 'His connection to Goldsboro is the key.'

'OK,' she played along, sounding concerned. 'Just don't. Just don't . . .' She couldn't finish what she'd started to say.

'Don't what?'

'Promise me if you find something you won't go charging in on your own. You'll wait until you have back-up.'

'I won't,' he told her, trying to sound genuine. 'I promise I won't.'

'Good,' she replied, sounding relieved. 'Call me when you decide what you're going to do or if you find something.' He heard the line go dead, slowly lowering the phone and slipping it back into his pocket, the questions racing in his head making him all but oblivious to his surroundings.

'Inspector Corrigan.' He thought he heard a distant voice. 'Inspector Corrigan,' the voice repeated until he realized it was the young receptionist calling his name. He half turned towards her, still in a semi-daydream.

'Yes,' he answered.

'Mrs Coppolaro will see you now,' she told him. 'Take lift number five to the twenty-fifth. Mrs Coppolaro will meet you there.' He followed her eyes to the lifts lined up next to each other like silver boxes.

'Thank you,' he replied. As soon as he pressed the call button, the doors to lift number five slid open with an electronic *whoosh* and invited him to step into the emptiness. He paused – the quietness of the huge building feeling somehow wrong and unnerving. He could sense the receptionists looking at him and glanced back from the corner of his eye before stepping inside the lift and pressing the button for the twenty-fifth floor. The doors closed with the same sound while the arrow on the display panel told him he was ascending, although the lift moved so smoothly he had no sensation of climbing at all. After only few seconds the arrow stopped flashing and the doors once more slid open. For a second he thought he'd been tricked and was about to step back out into the atrium, to the amusement of the waiting receptionist. He thought of the lifts back at the Yard, jolting and juddering at every stop – when and if they worked at all. But when he stepped out he was indeed on a new level of the building, facing another reception, only this one was unmanned and the office beyond apparently empty. He looked around for signs of life, but could find none in the dark corridors that seemed to run in every direction.

He circled the reception self-consciously, beginning to seriously wonder whether he'd got off on the wrong level, before

372

a distant light flickered on along one of the corridors, illuminating the figure of a slim woman. More and more lights blinked on as she walked towards him, activated by her mere presence. She walked into the reception area as if on rails, stopping directly in front of him, a smile appearing on her face as if she'd had to download it from her memory banks.

'Inspector Corrigan, I presume.' She held her slender arm out like an android.

Sean accepted her hand and tried to read her blue eyes. They sparkled with intelligence, the magnification of her glasses making them look childlike in her stern, but attractive face. He guessed she was in her forties, though she could have been older, preserved by all the advantages that money could buy.

'And you must be Amanda Coppolaro.' Sean tried to appear as friendly as he knew how. 'Thanks for seeing me at such short notice.'

'It's a pleasure,' she told him without a hint of irony, before clearing her throat. 'If I could just see your identification,' she asked a little awkwardly.

'Of course,' Sean answered and fumbled for his warrant card, eventually retrieving it and holding it out in front of him.

She bent forward a little, squinting her eyes to better see before straightening, her business-like smile returning. 'Thank you,' she told him. 'Can't be too careful. We hold a lot of valuable, not to mention sensitive, material in this building, hence the reason I wasn't prepared to discuss the matter over the telephone.'

'I understand,' Sean assured her, hiding his frustration at being forced to drive to the City, although he'd been glad of the time to think in solitude.

'If you'd like to follow me,' she said and spun on her heels, heading back along the corridor she'd come from with Sean in close pursuit. 'I took the liberty of pulling the file

373

for the person you mentioned from our human resources department.'

'Jeremy Goldsboro?' Sean checked. 'And?'

'Well, he hasn't worked here for quite some time,' she informed him. 'I don't know him myself, as I've only worked here for the last two years, although I was aware of his existence. He was, after all, a very senior figure.'

'What was his position?' Sean checked.

'He was a vice president here,' she answered over her shoulder as they kept walking.

'I remember him telling me now,' Sean lied. 'Sounds like a very prestigious position to hold – why give it up so young?'

'Who knows,' Coppolaro answered. 'Maybe he'd just had enough. He certainly would have been comfortable enough, financially anyway.'

'He is,' Sean confirmed.

'Anything else I can help you with?' she asked as they entered a large office surrounded by windows that gave an incredible view of the City below.

'Yeah,' Sean continued. 'Did a man called Paul Elkins ever work here – round about the same time as Jeremy Goldsboro?'

Coppolaro suddenly looked at the floor. 'Poor Paul,' she told him, shaking her head. 'What that awful man on Your View did to him is quite beyond belief.'

'Then you knew him?' Sean jumped in as his heart missed a skip. He was getting closer, he could feel it – feel him – *The Jackdaw.*

'Only a little,' she admitted. 'He was here when I first arrived, before he moved on.'

'But he was here at the same time as Jeremy Goldsboro?' Sean pushed, desperate to try to bring order to the jumble of puzzle pieces swimming around inside his mind.

'No,' she explained, the tone of her voice telling Sean she was about to reveal something she almost assumed he already

374

knew. 'Paul was Goldsboro's replacement. When Goldsboro left, Paul was brought in from outside as the new vice president. They did the same job, just at different times.'

Sean actually felt lightheaded and a little dizzy at what he was being told. He waited for his head to clear before speaking again. 'It's this company,' he spoke out loud. 'This man's fight is with your company. Whatever happened to him, happened because of something this company did.'

'Are you sure?' Coppolaro asked, unconvinced.

'Didn't you think that was a coincidence – two men who did the same job at this company both become victims of the same man?'

'But neither have worked here for years, Inspector,' she explained. 'Jeremy Goldsboro not for almost six, and they weren't here at the same time. Clearly if the other victims had worked here also then I and others would have become suspicious of a link between this madman and the company.'

'And did they?' Sean asked urgently. 'Did the others work here?'

'No,' she dismissed the suggestion. 'I'd know if they did.'

'Not now,' Sean explained. 'In the past.'

Coppolaro sighed before answering. 'I'd have to check.'

'If you could,' Sean encouraged her.

'Very well,' she agreed and strode to the huge glass table that dominated the room – a neat, silver, slim laptop one of the very few things on its surface. 'What are their names?' she asked.

'Georgina Vaughan and David Barrowgate,' Sean told her.

She leaned over the computer and typed rapid-fire instructions before straightening and resting her chin between her index finger and thumb as she waited for a response. 'No,' she eventually told him. 'They were never employed here.'

Sean felt the excitement leave his body. For a moment he'd allowed himself to believe they might have missed something as obvious as all the victims having at some point in time worked for the same firm, but his hopes had been quickly dashed. *Think*, he demanded of himself. *Think*.

'Both Elkins and Goldsboro had been threatened by the same man,' he began. 'Someone who blamed King and Melbourn for losing his business, home, family.'

'Because of the banking crisis,' Coppolaro pre-empted him. 'There was a lot of that at the time – people blaming us for their own failings.'

'City of London Police told us they were threatened by a man called Jason Howard,' Sean explained, 'but what we didn't check was whether he too worked here.'

'As a banker,' Coppolaro sounded incredulous. 'I really don't think so.'

'Not as a banker,' Sean told her, 'but maybe as a cleaner, security, something else.'

Coppolaro sighed again before turning back to the laptop. 'What did you say his name was?'

'Jason Howard,' he repeated and watched her type in the name as the uncomfortable excitement returned to his stomach.

'Sorry, no,' she quickly told him, shaking her head. 'No one by that name on record.'

'Damn it,' Sean said quietly as another door appeared to slam shut. 'Then it must be something else. Something I'm just not seeing.' Coppolaro didn't answer as Sean walked away and leaned against the window looking out over the City of London. 'You're missing something,' he whispered to himself. 'Something right here.' He was silent for a few seconds before he spoke his thoughts again. 'Two men have the same job in the same firm, only at different times. One ends up dead, the other disfigured, but the other two victims have no apparent connection to them. The men from here were both vice presidents – the other two were relatively junior, so . . . so why were they taken? What's their connection to these other men?'

'Whatever the connection is, it's not King and Melbourn,' Coppolaro insisted.

'Then maybe it's nothing.' Sean spoke out loud rather than to her. 'Whatever his motivation is, it's something to do with this company, but he doesn't want us to know that, because there's also something that connects him to King and Melbourn.'

'Such as?' Coppolaro asked.

'I don't know,' Sean admitted, shaking his head, 'but he needed to keep me off his scent. He took Vaughan and Barrowgate precisely because they're not connected to King and Melbourn, to try and make me believe this is all random, but it's not, it's personal – personal against the top people in this firm.' Sean reflected on his own words for a moment. *The top people. The top people.* 'You said that both Goldsboro and Elkins were vice presidents here?'

'Correct,' Coppolaro agreed.

'Then who was the top-dog, when Goldsboro was still here – just before he left?'

'That would have been Francis Waldegrave,' she told him, 'but he left a couple of years ago to join Dean, Pembridge and Villiers.'

Sean paced around the room trying to align his thoughts, trying to imagine The Jackdaw sitting alone in the white room formulating his plans – considering his next move.

'Why take out the two people who were second in command and leave the top man untouched? If the others needed to be punished for something they did to you, then doesn't he?' One last trial, The Jackdaw had warned them. There would be one last trial before he took his own life. 'Waldegrave,' Sean whispered to himself, the revelation so obvious now he had the answer. Who cared if finally the connection was there to be seen? The men he was burning to have his revenge on would have been punished and The Jackdaw would be dead. 'I need Francis Waldegrave's home address.' he snapped at Coppolaro.

377

'Is he in danger?' she asked.

'Maybe,' Sean told her. 'I don't have time to explain, but I do need his address.'

She raised her eyebrows and sighed. 'Very well,' she agreed and once again danced her fingers over the laptop's keyboard. 'Here it is – 127 Cadogan Square, Brompton. But I can't guarantee it's current.'

'And his telephone numbers,' Sean pushed. 'Home and mobile.'

'Here,' she told him and pointed at the screen, 'although again, I can't be sure they're still current.'

Sean moved close enough to see the numbers and as quickly as he could dialled the mobile number on his own phone and waited for an answer, not quite sure what he'd say when it came, but after a few rings he heard it go to voicemail.

'Shit,' he cursed, hanging up.

'No good?' Coppolaro asked.

'Voicemail,' Sean replied. 'But at least we know we've got the right number.'

'You didn't leave a message?' Coppolaro questioned him.

'And say what?' Sean queried as he tried Waldegrave's home number, the endless ringing tone stretching his patience to breaking point, until a foreign-sounding female voice answered tentatively.

'Hello.'

'I need to speak with Francis Waldegrave,' Sean demanded.

'He's not in right now,' the voice told him. 'Can I take a message?'

'I really need to speak to him,' Sean insisted.

'Have you tried his mobile?'

'Yes,' Sean told them, 'but he's not answering. Is there anyone there who can get a message to him?'

'Only on his mobile,' said the voice, 'or you could try his golf club.'

'His golf club?' Sean seized on it.

'Yes, sir,' the woman confirmed. 'He said he was going to play golf today, just before he left.'

'When did he leave?' Sean asked, speaking as fast as he could without becoming incoherent.

'Just a few minutes ago,' the voice answered.

'Damn it,' Sean cursed into the phone.

'Sir?'

'Where's his golf club?' he asked. 'Where does he play?'

'Hampstead,' she told him. 'He always plays at Hampstead Golf Club.'

Sean thought for a few seconds, but could think of nothing else the woman could help him with. 'Thank you,' he told her. 'If he gets in touch I need you to get him to call me on this number. Tell him I'm Detective Inspector Corrigan and I urgently need to speak to him. Do you have a pen ready?'

'One second,' the woman told him. 'OK. I'm ready for the number now.' Sean gave her his mobile number and hung up.

'No luck?' Coppolaro asked.

'Gone to play golf,' Sean explained, the picture of a golf course flashing in his mind – trees and open land – just how The Jackdaw liked it. He tried to slow his racing mind and organize his thoughts. He turned to Coppolaro. 'Is there anything you can remember that all three men – Waldegrave, Goldsboro and Elkins – could have been involved with that might have particularly upset someone inside the company or connected to it? Something they maybe tried to keep quiet? Something they tried to keep between themselves?'

'Elkins and Goldsboro weren't here at the same time,' she reminded him.

'Sure, but there could have been a crossover period when they were. They were troubled times.'

'Well, if there was it all happened long before I was there,' she pointed out. 'You'd be better off speaking to someone who would have been here then.'

'Such as?' Sean hurried her.

'Perhaps my predecessor,' she suggested. 'The previous HR director.'

'OK,' Sean relented and pulled out his warrant card from which he took one of his business cards and handed it to her. 'Get hold of her and get her to call me on this mobile number.'

'Me?' Coppolaro complained.

'Yes, you,' Sean insisted. 'I can't wait around here any longer. I need to get to Hampstead and find Waldegrave. Get him somewhere safe. If you can't find her you can't find her,' he told her, already heading back towards the corridor and the lifts. 'But I need you to try. I'll see myself out.' He left Coppolaro in the bright office and headed back into the dimness of the hallway, the overhead lights coming on one by one as he walked. He slid his phone from his coat pocket and called Donnelly's number. It was answered after only one ring.

'Guv'nor. Where are you? Addis has been stalking around looking for you.'

'Forget Addis,' Sean told him. 'I need you to do something for me.'

'Fine,' Donnelly agreed, sounding a little flustered, 'but where are you?'

'Just leaving King and Melbourn Capital Associates – in the City.'

'Jeremy Goldsboro's old company?' Donnelly asked.

'And Paul Elkins's,' Sean broke the news. 'When Goldsboro left he was replaced by Elkins, but a few years later he also left and we didn't go back far enough so we missed it. We missed the connection. Goldsboro and Elkins were both vice presidents, but the top man was Francis Waldegrave. What better way for our man to sign off than taking out the top-dog?'

'You think this Waldegrave is going to be his last victim?'

'I'm sure of it,' Sean told him as he pressed to call the lift.

'Is it Jason Howard?' Donnelly asked. 'He threatened both Elkins and Goldsboro. He may have threatened Waldegrave too.'

'He probably did,' Sean agreed, 'but Howard threatened a lot of people from a lot of different City firms. This feels more personal – more organized.'

'But it could be him?' Donnelly pushed.

'It could be,' Sean had to concede.

'And the other victims?' Donnelly questioned. 'Are they connected to King and Melbourn too?'

'No,' Sean tried to explain. 'They were just decoys to keep us off balance. They meant nothing to him.'

'I don't understand,' Donnelly admitted.

'I'll explain later,' Sean told him, 'but right now I need you to book out a firearm.'

'What?' Donnelly almost shouted.

'Your certification hasn't lapsed, has it?' Sean asked.

'No,' Donnelly assured him. 'It's still valid, but why the hell am I booking out a forearm?'

'Don't worry.' Sean tried to calm his fears. 'It's just for back-up. If it comes to doing a hard stop we'll get an ARV to do it. Yours will be just in case.'

'Just in case what?'

'I'll explain everything later,' Sean insisted. 'Just get the firearm then get over to Hampstead Golf Course. Apparently Waldegrave's heading there. Don't approach anyone until I'm with you. Park up out the way somewhere and wait for me to meet you.'

'I don't like how this is going,' Donnelly admitted. 'You're not thinking of doing anything rash, are you?'

'Me?' Sean managed to joke. 'I'll call you when I'm there.' He pressed call end just as the lifts arrived. The doors quietly slid open with little more than the sound of a breeze and allowed him to step inside – the doors closing as he was carried back towards the streets where he felt so much more at home. His finger hovered over Sally's number on his phone, the lack of reception frustrating him until finally the doors opened and released him into the atrium. As soon as he stepped out he pressed call and kept walking, heading through the huge glass doors just as Sally answered.

'Shit, Sean. What's going on?'

'You with anyone?'

'Yeah,' she said without enthusiasm. 'I got DC Bishop with me.'

'Good,' Sean replied. 'Has he got any closer to pinpointing the broadcast location?'

'That's something else we need to talk about,' Sally told him.

'Meaning?' Sean asked.

'Meaning after his earlier broadcast today we got the location down to just a couple of square miles in Surrey,' she explained. 'Only trouble is that area's already been searched. The local police found three derelict buildings and searched them all with no sign of our man.'

Sean thought quietly for a few seconds. 'How sure is Bishop that he got it right?'

'Says he's completely sure,' she told him. 'He can't understand what went wrong.'

Again Sean thought silently for a few seconds. 'Then he's not,' he said. 'Whoever searched the buildings missed something.'

'I don't know,' Sally disagreed. 'I checked the reports myself. All are recorded as being fully searched.'

'Mistakes happen,' he reminded her. 'This is what I need you to do. Get hold of at least two ARVs. Take one with you to Surrey and search those buildings again. Get the other one over to the golf course in Hampstead ASAP and tell them find and secure a guy called Francis Waldegrave as a matter of urgency. I'll meet them there as soon as I can.'

'Francis Waldegrave?' Sally asked. 'Who the hell is Francis Waldegrave?'

'The Jackdaw's next victim,' he told her.

'What?' She tried to understand. 'How could you possibly know who his next victim is going to be?'

'I found something,' he assured her, 'but I don't have time to explain right now. You're just going to have to trust me, Sally.'

A few seconds passed before Sally answered. 'They won't like it,' she warned him. 'You know what ARV crews are like: they're going to want a bit more information than we're giving them.'

'I can't help that. Just get them to meet me there and make sure they know to keep Waldegrave out of the way.'

'OK,' she hesitantly agreed, 'but wouldn't you rather check out the buildings in Surrey and leave the golf course to us? You could be in Surrey quicker than us from where you are.'

'No,' he insisted. 'Leave the golf course to me.'

'Why are you so keen to get to the golf course?' Sally asked.

'I need to speak to Waldegrave,' Sean half lied.

'Bollocks,' Sally accused him. 'You think The Jackdaw's going to be there, don't you? Somehow you know – you know he's going to try and abduct Waldegrave from the golf course.'

'I don't know anything,' Sean tried to convince her. 'Not for sure.'

'You want to confront him, don't you?'

'No,' he answered, not even sure within himself if he was telling the truth or not. 'I just need to check something out.'

'Then let me get local uniform units to swamp the area and scare him off,' Sally suggested.

'No,' Sean answered too quickly. 'This could be our best chance to catch him. He's made a trap for himself. Let's let him walk into it.'

'I don't know, Sean,' she appealed to him. 'Don't stick your neck out again. Your children, Sean. They're so young.'

He sighed into his phone. He knew she was right, but he also knew he wouldn't be able to stop himself. He never could. 'I have no intention of confronting him,' he told her what he knew she wanted to hear, 'but if we end up crossing paths, Dave will be with me and he'll be armed.'

'Dave's armed?' she asked disbelievingly.

'As a precaution,' he tried to calm her. 'If we're the ones who have to arrest him then it'll be Dave making the approach, not me.'

'No it won't,' she told him. 'Just be careful. I'll call you once we've checked out the buildings in Surrey.'

Sean listened to the phone go dead.

15

Mark Hudson sat in his squalid bedroom staring at the blank square on his computer screen, waiting for The Jackdaw to return. He felt like he'd been watching the screen for days, but he didn't dare take a break and run the risk of missing his idol – not even to use the toilet or to eat or drink. Nothing could pull him away from the old computer he'd stolen during a burglary a few months before. The thrill of being an intruder in somebody else's home had been one of the greatest feelings he'd had in his short life, but it would have been oh so much more *satisfying* if the occupants had been in while he rifled through the house. Next time he'd make sure they were. He'd do it at night. Wait outside hidden in trees as he watched them go to bed one by one, the house turning to darkness, and then he'd slip from the trees and find a way in. Before he left with his stolen haul he'd be sure to defecate somewhere prominent inside the house – a final act of defiling the house and family who lived inside. He had no way of knowing that such acts would soon fail to satisfy his needs. Soon he would need more.

'What the fuck's going on?' he shouted at the blank screen. 'What are you waiting for?' He flopped backwards on his bed, but kept his eyes on the screen. He needed this. He lived for this. The Jackdaw had shown him the way forward. Shown him what he could achieve with his life. And now he was going to slay another rich pig live on the Internet – for his *entertainment*. And after that, he'd as good as promised to end his own life.

Hudson leaned forward, suddenly interested in his own thoughts. How did The Jackdaw plan to kill his next and seemingly final victim? Would he hang him like he did his first, or would he use the shotgun? He hoped it would be the shotgun. He'd already seen people hanged – hundreds of them on the Internet – victims of the Holocaust, victims of other conflicts, but prisoners too and even Saddam Hussein's execution by hanging had made it onto the Net. He'd even seen his fair share of decapitations – nearly all the victims of jihadists and terrorists — but he'd never seen anyone shot, not live and close up with a shotgun. He hoped he shot him in the chest or better still the abdomen, so the victim could be seen to be suffering. Somehow that would make it all the more *real*.

And how would The Jackdaw end his own life? With courage and strength? No fear. He'd show the world how strong he was. The Jackdaw was just like him – he lived his life hard and fast and wouldn't let anyone fuck with him. If they did he made them pay, just as Hudson did. They were kindred spirits. The Jackdaw had shown him the true way forward. From now on he'd never look back. He knew what he had to do with his life.

But right now he just wanted the small black square with the words 'Your View' in its centre to blink into life and for The Jackdaw to once again take centre stage.

Over a hundred miles away from Hudson's squalid bedroom, Gabriel Westbrook sat at the breakfast bar in the kitchen of his house in Hoxton. Once a tough and depressed area of the East End of London housing dockers and their families, famous for lunatic asylums and workhouses, in the 1980s it had been taken over by young artists and then inevitably the rich had moved in, taking advantage of its proximity to the City to make it their own.

He looked up from his laptop's screen for a few seconds to see his beautiful young wife playing with his beautiful children in their modest-sized garden. She waved through the glass kitchen extension and encouraged the children to do the same. He faked an eager smile and waved back, pointing at his screen to let her know he still had work to do. Only it wasn't work on his computer – it was the same black Your View picture that, unbeknown to him, a young psychopath in Birmingham was waiting to come alive.

Westbrook had planned on meeting some work colleagues for a game of golf, but had decided against it when he saw The Jackdaw's earlier broadcast. He'd bent a few rules and regulations back in the bad old days, when the banking crisis was the only thing in the news, and in his heart he'd always known that his actions had probably made somebody, some- where, suffer because of his own greed and impatience to climb the corporate and financial ladder. He always managed to console himself with the thought that if he hadn't, then someone else would have, and since then he'd been as white as white. However, the thought of The Jackdaw still roaming the streets a free man was enough to put him off leaving the house. How could he know? How could he be sure he hadn't already been selected to be his next victim? But The Jackdaw had all but promised to take his own life once he'd taken his final victim. All Westbrook had to do was see out these last few hours and he'd be in the clear. No more looking over his shoulder whenever he was out and about. No more feeling paranoid on the Underground – every stranger's glance making him on edge. No more nightmares about being taped to that old wooden chair as the monster burnt out his eyes and hacked off his fingers before hoisting him in the air to hang to death. He just had to get through the next few hours.

With The Jackdaw out of the way everything could get back to normal. The City could relax and breathe again – stocks and shares would quickly recover and the money and bonuses could once again begin to roll in. He, like his colleagues, knew the get rich quick and stay rich formula. It was simple enough: get your bonus, take the cash out of the increasingly regulated banking sector and use it to buy property across London. Who cared if the middle and working classes got pushed out of London altogether? There was fast money to be made. At least, that was what he used to think. The Jackdaw was nothing other than a vengeful lunatic, as far as he was concerned, but the amount of people watching and voting had deeply troubled him, especially the amount who had voted the defendants guilty and thus encouraged The Jackdaw to maim and kill. Locked in his bubble of work and wealth, he'd had no idea how much the majority of people hated his kind. But it was those who voted not guilty who had affected him most – tens of thousands of ordinary people, no doubt many who had suffered as a result of the banking crisis, but who showed mercy and compassion – they were the ones who had truly changed him. He didn't want to spend the rest of his life making money for people who already had money. He wanted to do more with his life now, something that mattered. Something that made a difference – if he could just see out this day. Come Monday he would hand in his resignation then take some time out to think about what he really wanted from life. A slight smile spread across his lips at the irony. The Jackdaw represented nothing but hate and revenge – a man who wanted to turn the country on itself. But somehow he couldn't help but believe that The Jackdaw, in trying to destroy him, had saved him.

Phil Taylor sat in his small, cluttered office in his small terraced house in Hull, his chin propped in the palm of one hand while the other circled the arrow icon round and round on his computer screen as he waited for what was promised to be the final broadcast ever from the man the media had been calling The Jackdaw. He wasn't even sure why he was watching any more – any sympathy or admiration he'd ever had for the self-proclaimed messiah had long since faded.

At first he'd hung on The Jackdaw's every word, agreeing with everything he had to say and the need to say it in the first place – even to the point where he felt no sympathy for the man he'd murdered. But since the torture of the young woman and the blinding of the young man, he'd seen The Jackdaw in a new light and now his latest ranting, preaching diatribe had confirmed in his mind that he was nothing more than a madman – just another murdering psychopath looking to become infamous.

The Jackdaw blamed others for his plight, just like he himself had been doing since his small business went under. But Taylor didn't want to be like The Jackdaw – didn't want anything in common with him. The time for bitter recrimin-ations and self-pity was over. It was time to build again.

'I don't need this any more,' he told the room. He moved the cursor over the quit icon and clicked. The Jackdaw was gone forever. He clicked the cursor on the Internet search space and typed 'Loans for small businesses' into the box and pressed search just as his wife came into the room.

'You all right, love?' she asked.

'Sure,' he told her. 'I've wasted enough life. It's time to start over.'

Father Jones sipped his tea and tried to concentrate on preparing his sermon for the following morning, but the black computer screen with the words 'Your View' embla-zoned across it continued to distract him. He felt he had no choice but to watch what he expected to be the last of the troubled soul's broadcasts, no matter how abhorrent they were to him. Rarely had he felt so close to such evil as he did when he watched and listened to the man who hid behind a bird's name, but he had to be there in spirit and mind when the dreadful broadcast began – to pray for both victim and persecutor.

He looked down at the blank pages of the book he recorded all his sermons in – giving them marks out of ten according to how well his listeners had responded to them, most of the marks being five or less.

'Tut, tut,' he reprimanded himself. 'Not many ten out of tens in here. Perhaps I'm in the wrong job?' His thoughts turned to the policeman, the detective who came to see him very irregularly and always at times when it was all but certain no one else would be about. He wondered what he would be doing right now. Not sitting down trying to write some half-baked sermon, that was for sure. How would he be feeling knowing the 'troubled soul' was planning on taking another victim and then, if he was to be believed, his own life? How desperate and sick the detective must be feeling right now – the life of another human being in his hands. The weight of his responsibility must be crushing. No wonder he felt the occasional need to unburden his soul – even if it was just to an under-qualified priest hidden away in the depths of southeast London. But Father Jones sensed a strength in the man he'd rarely detected, and a darkness too that ran like a vein of evil through his core – an evil he somehow managed to control – unlike the 'troubled soul' who'd thrown his lot in with the devil the moment he'd taken a life. The policeman had secrets – troubling secrets he needed to unburden himself of before they consumed him and dragged him to a place where not even God could help him.

He looked at the blank screen and then the blank page in his book. 'Jesus,' he blasphemed, 'what am I supposed to say? I've got young kids stabbing each other because they walked down the wrong street. I've got young mothers using their family allowance to buy crack instead of baby food and a man who can draw an audience of hundreds of thousands because he tortures and kills people, while I'll be lucky if forty people turn up to listen to me on a Sunday morning. Dear Lord, give me strength. Give me a sign of why I should carry on.'

He breathed in deeply through his nose and began to write his sermon. *The other day,* he began. *A man came to see me in the middle of the night – long after everyone else had left. A policeman. A policeman who carried a terrible burden.*

'Do you really have to play golf today?' Jennifer Waldegrave asked her husband as they inched along in the heavy traffic along Hampstead High Street.

'I'm afraid so,' Francis Waldegrave answered. 'It's all for a good cause.'

'But I was really looking forward to doing something together,' she complained. 'You work so hard I hardly ever get to see you. You're either at work or going to some charity do or another. You practically missed seeing Evie grow up and now she's away at university and it'll only be another couple of years before Harry's off too. You've sacrificed so much.'

He ran a thin hand through his neat, greying black hair and checked his reflection in the rearview mirror. Although at a glance he appeared handsome and tanned, he also looked tired. Not the sort of tired you can look after a late night, but a deep-set tiredness born of years of relentless hard work and dedication to his profession. What little spare time he had he split between his family and the charity work he'd come to take increasingly seriously. But it was all beginning to take its toll.

'It won't be for much longer,' he assured her in a kindly tone. 'I'm fifty-six now. In another couple of years I'll be able to retire and spend more time with you and the kids.'

'But the children won't be children any more,' she warned him. 'In so many ways they're already young adults.'

'And fine young adults they are too,' he told her with a smile. 'Thanks to you.'

'And the best education money can buy,' she reminded him.

'It all helps,' he agreed, 'but at least they're not arse-holes. They understand they're privileged. They know how lucky they've been. They don't look down their noses at anyone. They don't think they're special just because their parents can afford things most people can't.'

'You certainly made sure of that,' she said approvingly.

'It's important,' he insisted, stealing a look at his still beautiful wife as he eased the Jaguar through the traffic. 'They need to know the value of money. I'll give them the best start I can then it's down to them: they have to make it themselves. Nobody helped me when I first started. I paid my own way through university before getting a job in the City. I started at the bottom and worked my way to the top. It wasn't easy. I didn't have an old school tie to wave around.'

'I know,' she assured him, 'and that's what sets you aside – that's what makes you better than the others.'

'There's more like me than you think,' he tried to convince her.

'Really?' she argued. 'I bet there's not many giving up their day off to run a charity golf day. You know you hate golf.'

'I may hate golf,' he agreed, 'but it can sometimes be a better place to do business than the boardroom. At least I get some fresh air and exercise.'

'But on your day off,' his wife complained. 'Can't you skip it – just this once – and take your poor neglected wife out for a long, lazy lunch?'

'I can't,' he sighed. 'Most of the people are only coming because I persuaded them to. We need their money. Twenty-first-century London and people are still living on the streets. Hard to believe.'

'And a lot of people blaming you and your kind for it,' she reminded him.

'There were plenty of homeless people before the banking crisis,' he explained. 'Although I won't deny it didn't help. Some of us got greedy, became lost in the search for easy, fast wealth. Once I knew who they were I got rid of them quickly enough. I didn't try to protect them – no matter how much people wanted me to. We all have to take responsibility for our actions.'

'I remember your *actions* cost us quite a few friendships,' she recalled. 'No one could ever accuse you of trying to win a popularity contest.'

'Integrity is not negotiable,' he explained. 'They had to go.' For a second his mind wandered back through the years to the time when he was the CEO of King and Melbourn Capital Associates, the mismanagement of funds he'd helped uncover and the subsequent letting-go of a number of its employees – some senior officials amongst them. Those who had done wrong must pay for their mistakes and greed – in part at least. 'If I had to do the same tomorrow I would,' he eventually continued. 'I wouldn't hesitate for a second.'

'Sometimes I think you're an out-and-out socialist,' she accused him.

'Maybe I am,' he admitted, 'or maybe I just believe in capitalism with a conscience.'

'Whatever you are,' she told him, 'you should be safe from that lunatic the media are calling The Jackdaw. You're hardly his . . . *type.*'

'Was Paul Elkins his type?' he questioned.

'More than you.'

'I hired Paul to come and work at King and Melbourn when I was there because he was a good man as well as a good banker,' Francis Waldegrave explained. 'Most of the things the so-called Jackdaw said about him were lies.'

'I know,' she agreed, 'but maybe he'd changed in the years

393

since you worked with him. Certainly some of the things the newspapers said about him would suggest so.'

'You shouldn't read the papers,' he warned her. 'Especially the tabloid rags. They like the idea of this lunatic being something more – a man of the people standing up against their greedy oppressors. It's more interesting than just another killer with mental health problems. It's a story they can spin out for months or at least as long as it takes to catch him.'

They were both silent for a few seconds until Jennifer Waldegrave spoke again. 'Have you spoken to Jeremy Goldsboro again?'

'No,' he answered. 'He wasn't too happy when I contacted him the first time. I thought it best not to call him again.'

'Well, you did fire him and end his career,' she unnecessarily reminded him.

'No,' he corrected her, 'I let him go with a golden handshake he didn't deserve. We never liked each other, but when I saw he'd been one of The Jackdaw's victims it seemed the least I could do. Once he got over the shock of me calling him he was polite enough – I suppose – although his tone made it clear he didn't want to hear from me again.'

'You can't blame him,' she smiled. 'You were never going to be on his Christmas card list.'

'No,' he agreed. 'I don't suppose I was and nor did I want to be.'

'Quite,' she replied, a shadow casting across her face. 'But when you spoke to him, did he mention it seemed a bit of a coincidence that both he and Paul had been victims, given they had both worked at King and Melbourn – even if it was years ago?'

'No,' he told her, 'but I did.'

'And?'

'We agreed it was probably just bad luck, given neither of them have worked there for years, but Jeremy said he'd mentioned it to the police anyway – just in case.'

'Then it must have come to nothing,' she decided, 'otherwise I'm sure the police would have come to see you by now.'

'Exactly,' he assured her, 'and there are the other victims too. None of them have a connection to me or King and Melbourn. It all appears quite random. You're better off jumping out here and walking the rest of the way,' he told her. 'The traffic's not going to get any better.'

'Good idea,' she agreed, undoing her seat belt and reaching for the handle before pausing. 'Just be careful,' she warned him. 'There's still a madman running around out there.'

'Remember what Franklin D Roosevelt said,' he smiled. 'We have nothing to fear except fear itself.'

Sally allowed the unmarked car to roll to a silent stop on the dirt road in the Surrey countryside, out of sight of the derelict building. The fully marked Armed Response Vehicle rolled up behind them. She felt as if butterflies were fluttering uncontrollably in her stomach. She had good reason to be afraid of the men who stalked the woods with shotguns, but it was her dread of not being able to control her anxiety that scared her most.

'We have nothing to fear, but fear itself,' she whispered a little too loud as she unconsciously rubbed the scars on her chest that hid under her clothes.

'Excuse me?' Bishop asked.

'What?' Sally asked, surprised to remember she was not alone. 'Oh. Nothing. Just something somebody said once.'

'Franklin D Roosevelt,' Bishop told her. 'During the Great Depression. He said it.'

'Whatever,' Sally replied. She climbed quickly out of the car and indicated with a wave for the uniformed armed officers in the other vehicle to join them. Bishop climbed out the other side and spoke over the roof.

'Wonder what they used this old place for?' Bishop asked.

'The information report said it used to be some kind of electricity sub-station or something.'

'And it's already been searched?'

'Apparently,' Sally told him. 'As have all the other possible buildings in this area.'

'Then why are we here?' Bishop questioned her. 'He must have been broadcasting from somewhere in this area we haven't found yet.'

'Sean said to double check, so that's what we're doing,' she snapped at him a little. By now the uniformed officers from the Armed Response Team had joined them.

'Fair enough,' Bishop gave in. 'You sure you want to start with this one and not one of the other buildings?'

'Yes,' Sally answered. 'From the reports this looks the most likely – so we start here. And we'd better both hope I'm right, because any second now Sean and Dave will be arriving at the golf course in Hampstead. If we can find something here to end this bloody thing then there's less chance of Sean doing something . . . Well, let's just say it would be better for everyone.'

'I don't follow,' Bishop admitted.

'You don't have to,' Sally dismissed him and turned to the three armed officers – two fit-looking middle-aged men and a young woman who Sally reckoned couldn't be more than thirty, but she looked strong and confident, her Heckler & Koch nine-millimetre sub-machine gun cradled in the crook of her arm. One of the men carried the same weapon, whereas the driver was armed only with a semi-automatic pistol still holstered on his right thigh.

'This is about as bad a scenario as I can imagine,' the driver, apparently the leader, told her, keeping his voice to little more than a whisper. 'One dirt road in – trees on either side and a large derelict building you want us to search at the end of it. You couldn't have picked a worse spot. Take an army to search this area safely. This is ambush paradise.'

'No one's asking you to go in alone,' she told him, her patience already wearing thin as her desperation to find The Jackdaw before Sean made her irritable.

'If this is an armed operation then we go in first,' the driver explained. 'We wouldn't want to shoot you by mistake.'

'We'll hang back,' Sally assured him.

'Or we could wait until we have more armed units,' the driver argued. 'I could probably get them here in ten minutes.'

'No,' Sally insisted. 'We can't wait.'

'Mind telling me why?' the driver asked.

'Because he may have already abducted a member of the public he intends to kill,' she half lied, keeping her fears for Sean to herself. 'We can't let that happen.' The driver just shrugged. 'So, how d'you want this to go down?'

The driver theatrically drew his pistol from its nylon holster and slid the top half of the gun back before releasing it forward to load a round into the chamber and clicking the safety on. Next he unclipped his iPhone, called up Google Maps and expanded the area around the derelict building as much as he could.

'We use the woods for cover as we approach,' he explained. 'Stay close to the road, but in the trees. According to the map there's a degree of clearing all around the building, although it could be more overgrown than it's showing. If not we're going to have to cover the ground between the treeline and the front of the building quickly and quietly.' He turned to his two colleagues. 'Jonnie, you go left. Head for a ground-floor window that's got no glass in it and cover the inside. Jenny, you go right and do the same.' They both nodded that they understood. 'I'll go straight for the front door, but no shouting and screaming. Let's try and rely on stealth to get this done. There's not enough of us to cover the sides and back at the same time. Once we're in there we'll need eyes in the backs of our heads, so that means sticking together.' His colleagues nodded their agreement with

397

his assessment. He turned back to Sally. 'You wait in the treeline until I call you forward. Understand?' She didn't argue. The driver looked her up and down one more time. 'You sure you don't want to wait for back-up? If this man's the person you say he is then I could have half the Met here in less than twenty minutes.'

'No.' Sally stood by her decision. 'We go now. No waiting.'

'It's your call,' he told her before summoning the others forward with a nod of his head. Sally watched them all but disappear into the trees at the side of the road before turning to Bishop.

'Come on, Bob,' she encouraged him, 'and try not to get shot.' Bishop turned a pale shade of grey as Sally followed the armed officers into the trees and headed towards the derelict building, pushing branches out of the way as she walked, careful not to let them spring back and hit Bishop in the face, watching where she placed her feet as her eyes darted around the forest looking for any sign of movement.

Jesus Christ, she thought. *He could be hiding anywhere in this mess. He could be five feet in front of me, pointing his shotgun straight at my head and I wouldn't be able to do anything about it.* She hoped the armed cops ahead of her had better instincts for an ambush than she did.

As they headed further through the trees she couldn't help but be reminded of the Thomas Keller case – she and Sean walking through what seemed like endless forest as they searched for the bodies of his victims and then finally as they searched for Keller himself.

'Forests,' she whispered. 'Why does it always have to be forests?'

'What?' Bishop asked as loudly as he dared.

'Nothing,' she told him. 'Just keep up.'

She picked her way through the trees and undergrowth for what seemed an age, always trying to keep the armed officers within sight, a sense of panic making her heart rate jump every time she momentarily lost sight of them. Eventually they stopped, the leader holding up his hand behind him and signalling for them all to get down before he turned and summoned Sally forward. She took a deep breath and headed towards him, crouching next to him. His eyes were firmly fixed on the building that lay just beyond the last line of trees.

'There's no more cover between here and the building,' he whispered. 'That's thirty feet of open ground. More than enough distance for him to get off both shots from a shotgun. You both wearing your body armour?'

'Yes,' she truthfully assured him.

'Close up it probably won't save you,' he told her seriously, 'but at this range it should do the job – unless he goes for a head shot, or he's using illegal single or five shot, in which case . . .' Sally tried not to think about the damage a lead ball over half an inch thick travelling at more than a thousand feet per second could do to a human body.

'Thanks,' she said with a sarcastic smile. 'That's very reassuring.'

'Just remember to wait for my signal,' the leader reminded her. He turned his back on her and tapped his colleagues one after the other on the shoulder, causing them to rise simultaneously and break from the treeline, crouched down and moving fast across the open ground, the sub-machine guns wedged in their shoulders sweeping back and forth across the front of the building, the leader with his pistol held out in front of him in a two-handed grip, elbows slightly bent. Within a few seconds they were at the front of the building, bodies pressed against the wall, weapons pointing to the ground. The leader held out three fingers and started to count them down. Once all digits were folded into a fist the three of them stepped slightly back from the building – the two with the Heckler & Kochs pointing their weapons through open windows, the light from the Maglite torches attached to the guns sweeping the darkness inside, while the leader pushed open the front door and dropped back into a crouched position as he flicked on the small torch hung underneath his pistol – the three beams of light occasionally crossing as they searched the ground floor for signs of life.

Sally watched from the sanctuary of the trees, almost wincing with tension as she waited for the outbreak of gunfire she felt would surely come, but no deafening sounds interfered with the gentle rustling of the leaves above. She watched as the leader looked from colleague to colleague and, with a sideways nod of his head, moved forward into the darkness, the others moving quickly from the windows to the door and also disappearing inside. For what seemed an eternity Sally saw and heard nothing other than the occasional flash of torchlight until without warning the leader emerged from the front door and walked backwards about six feet from the building, his pistol trained on it the whole time. He quickly looked over his shoulder at Sally's position and summoned her forward.

'Shit,' she muttered and grabbed Bishop by the arm. 'Our turn.' She broke from the treeline dragging Bishop along with her and all but sprinted in a squat across the ground, past the leader and into the building. Once inside she leant against the wall and took a few deep breaths to steady herself. She noticed Bishop was doing the same, only he seemed to be taking a lot longer to compose himself. 'You all right?' Sally whispered.

Bishop gulped air before answering. 'Yeah,' he managed to answer. 'Just . . . I haven't been out of the office for quite a while.'

'I understand,' Sally told him sympathetically. 'Just stay behind the people with guns and do what I tell you to.' He nodded a nervous agreement.

The leader re-entered the building and stood next to Sally looking relaxed, but with his pistol still at the ready, the light from his torch forming a circle on the ceiling as they all watched the beams of light from the other armed units still moving about, mainly pointing at the ground.

'Ground floor's clear,' he told Sally in a matter-of-fact tone.

'Then what are they still looking for?' Bishop asked, looking increasingly concerned.

'Signs of recent life,' the leader whispered. 'Evidence someone one could have been using the building.'

'Let's just get on with it,' Sally insisted. 'If he's here then by now the chances are he knows we're here. Let's just find him and get this over with.' Creeping around in the dark and damp brought back too many vivid memories for Sally, memories she'd rather forget. She wanted this over – no matter what the outcome.

'If that's the way you want to play it,' the leader told her before whispering into his radio's mouthpiece. 'All right, guys. Let's check out the first floor.'

Sally watched as the beams of light once more came together and formed up, making their way to the foot of the open-plan staircase that doglegged its way up to the first floor. The leader took a long hard look before putting a foot on the first step as he began his ascent – the rest of his small team following one at a time, five steps apart, all still with their weapons raised, the light from their torches showing the way ahead. Once the leader had reached the first floor Sally tugged on Bishop's sleeve.

'Come on,' she told him.

'Aren't we supposed to wait for a signal?' Bishop asked, the fear etched on his face in the dimness.

'If we stay here, we won't be able to see the signal, will we?' she explained and headed off towards the stairs, looking over her shoulder to see Bishop still rooted to the spot. 'Come on,' she whispered as loudly as she could, watching him until he finally moved away from the wall that had become his sanctuary. Sally shook her head a little and almost tiptoed the rest of the way to the foot of the stairs just in time to see the light beams fade as they moved inside the first room off the corridor. She took a deep breath and headed up the stairs, making herself look as conspicuous as possible so as not to spook the gun carriers.

When she reached the top step she froze, arms raised to shoulder height and slightly spread as the light beams came back through the doorway. She neither moved nor spoke until she was sure they'd registered her presence in the semi-darkness, their lights appearing to scan her body like alien invaders trying to decide what she was.

'Anything?' she asked, the shakiness in her voice catching her by surprise.

'You're supposed to wait until I signal for you,' the leader chastised her. 'I don't want to have to explain a dead detective to my boss.'

'Sorry,' she apologized without meaning it, 'but, anything?'

'No,' he whispered, never looking at her, constantly sweeping the corridor ahead. 'It's clear. Stay behind us.' He gave his colleagues one nod and they set off further along the corridor, like something out of a video game. Sally's heart was beating so loudly she felt sure it must be audible to everyone in the dark, damp building – felt sure it would betray their presence if by some miracle *he* didn't already know they were there – waiting to strike like a hidden snake.

Again she watched as the lights swept into the next room, a quiet voice behind her making her visibly jump.

'They found anything yet?' Bishop practically whispered in her ear.

'Jesus Christ,' she quietly snapped at him. 'D'you mind not doing that? And no – they haven't found anything.'

After only a few seconds the lights found their way back out into the corridor – searching the walls, floor and ceiling in circular patterns, heading towards the next door.

'We should have waited outside,' Bishop complained.

'And not know what the hell was going on?' Sally whispered back. 'I don't think so. Just say close enough not to get shot by one of our own and far enough away not to get shot by whoever might be hiding in here.' Bishop's mouth opened as if he was about ask how, but Sally had already moved away, following the lights until they stopped outside the next door. She sensed their hesitation before entering, as if something was different about this one. She moved a few steps closer to the leader. 'What is it?'

'Closed door,' he hissed back. 'The others were open.' His words alone made Sally take several steps backwards as the leader crouched by the wall next to the door, his female colleague standing tall, but her back also pressed against the wall, while the other armed officer stood on the opposite side of the frame. They all pointed their weapons towards the ceiling, standing as still as statues, as if someone had pressed pause on the video game, but Sally could sense their heightened state of anxiety and excitement as the leader raised a gloved hand and held out three fingers, beginning the now familiar countdown. Once the last finger was folded back into the palm of his hand his female colleague stepped around him and gave the door a firm kick before swinging back against the wall as the crouching leader poked his gun and head just around the corner and the other male cop did the same.

Sally held her breath and waited for the sound of gunfire, but none came. After a few seconds the female cop stepped past the men and walked slowly into the room, her colleagues waiting a few seconds before following her in, one after the other a few seconds apart. Sally assumed the distancing was to ensure that anyone lying in wait wouldn't be able to hit them all with one burst. Suddenly she heard the words she'd been praying to hear – the words that meant Sean wouldn't be able to rush head-on into danger, even if he'd wanted to. It was the female officer's voice she heard.

'Freeze,' she yelled, her voice incredibly loud and shocking after minutes of nothing more than whispered silence. 'Armed police. Don't you fucking move. Put your hands where I can see them.' Sally listened to no more than two seconds of silence. 'I said, put your hands where I can see them or I'll open fire.'

'Hold it a second,' the leader's voice cut in. 'For Christ's sake, hold your fire.' For some reason his words made Sally's heart sink and her stomach churn. 'Check it out, Jonnie,' she heard him tell the other male officer. 'Leave me a line of fire.' She started creeping along the corridor to the room, praying they had The Jackdaw, dead or alive, she didn't care any more. But some detective instinct burnt inside her telling her something was wrong.

'He's not armed,' she heard Jonnie tell the leader.

'Signs of life?' the leader asked.

'He's alive,' Jonnie replied just as Sally entered the room, the light spill from their torches enough for her to just make out the black bin liners over the windows, the old wooden chair at its centre and what looked like a table against the wall behind the door. All three torches were pointing towards a hooded figure lying bound at the ankles on the floor, his hands tied behind his back.

'Jesus Christ,' Sally exclaimed. She stepped quickly to the prostrate figure and pulled the hood from his head – terrified, wild eyes staring at her as the man tried to scramble away.

'Police,' she told him. 'I'm a police officer – take it easy. You're safe now.' The man's crazed eyes darted around the room, blinking against the light of their torches as he tried to see his liberators. 'Get the light off him,' Sally demanded, holding up her hand to shield him. Once they were illuminated only by the ambient light Sally reached out towards the tape over the man's mouth, making him recoil slightly, his chest still rising and falling rapidly.

'It's OK,' Sally tried to reassure him, reaching out again,

noting the multiple cuts and bruises on his face – some old and almost healed, although not cleaned, while others appeared new. 'I just need to take the tape off your mouth so you can speak to me.'

She pinched the edge of the tape and began to peel it from his face as he closed his eyes against the pain. As gently as she could she managed to pull the tape back, his unkempt facial hair making the task more difficult. Once off she had the presence of mind to drop the tape into a small plastic evidence bag before doing anything else, giving the injured man a few seconds to calm down and take in what was happening.

Sally helped him into a sitting position and looked at the knotted nylon rope used to bind his hands. It would need to be cut off to preserve the evidence of the knot-tying. And there was something else – a blood-soaked strip of material tied around the man's hand, covering the place where his little finger used to be.

'Bloody hell,' she cursed as she tried to comprehend what it could mean. She rested her hands on the man's shoulders and looked deeply into his terrified eyes. 'Who are you?' she asked. 'I need to know your name.'

Sean drove fast along Winnington Road approaching Hampstead Golf Course, the blue light attached to his roof spinning and flashing as the siren wailed. Dozens of different thoughts and possibilities were swirling inside his head – Elkins, Goldsboro, Waldegrave. Were they really all connected, or was he making things up in his own mind in the desperate and forlorn hope of finally catching The Jackdaw? Was he so desperate to remain in charge of the Special Investigations Unit and avoid a return to mundane investigations that he was speeding to an answer that didn't really exist and therefore the destruction of his own credibility? What had these men done to The Jackdaw to turn him into a torturer and murderer? And why had he kept Goldsboro hooded and allowed him to live? Had they been friends? Were they maybe even family? So that, when it came down to it, The Jackdaw simply couldn't bring himself to kill him?

He could just make out the phone ringing on the hands-free system and quickly killed the siren, reduced his speed and pressed answer. 'Yes.'

'Detective Inspector Corrigan?' the distinctive, mature female voice asked.

He knew he didn't have time to be too guarded, even though he had no idea who was calling him. 'It is,' he admitted.

'My name is Felicity George.' It still meant nothing to him. 'Amanda Coppolaro over at King and Melbourn asked me to give you a call. She said it was rather urgent.' Still Sean didn't understand. 'Amanda was my replacement when I retired from being the HR director there.' Finally Sean realized who she was.

'Of course. I'm sorry,' he apologized. 'Thanks for calling.'

'If I can help catch the man who did those terrible things to Jeremy and of course poor Paul, then I'm only too happy to help.'

'Then you know what this is about?' Sean asked.

'Amanda informed me,' she told him. 'But I was already fully aware of what's been happening. And now I believe you suspect Mr Waldegrave could also be in danger?'

'Yes I do,' he admitted. 'Which means none of this is random. It has to have something to do with these three men. Something they did when they were at King and Melbourn. Something that made someone very angry. Something they never forgot about, even all these years later.'

'I don't see how,' she replied. 'They were never there all together, you see. Mr Elkins was Jeremy's replacement.'

'Was there something maybe they did?' Sean kept probing. 'Something they did then tried to keep quiet or cover up?'

'Not possible,' she dismissed it. 'Jeremy had already gone before Mr Elkins arrived.' She gave a long sigh before continuing. 'It's all so ironic really.'

'What is?' Sean asked, confused.

'That this monster should choose Jeremy as one of his victims, when the very thing this madman seems to hate was also the thing that turned its back on Jeremy.'

'What d'you mean, turned its back on him?'

'I mean when Jeremy was let go by the company,' she explained. 'I know things were very difficult for him for a while.'

'*Let go*?' Sean questioned her. 'I thought he retired.'

'Not exactly,' she told him. 'I'm afraid things all got a little confusing and unpleasant. I felt so sorry for Jeremy.'

'What happened?' Sean demanded, his body stiff with tension as he sensed a whole new avenue of the investigation was about to open up. Something none of them had considered before. 'Tell me exactly what happened.'

'Goodness,' she stalled. 'This is difficult. Jeremy had worked for King and Melbourn for almost fifteen years, working his way up from middle management all the way to vice president. He was so sure he was set for the top job, but then the shareholders gave it to Francis Waldegrave, an outsider.'

'The shareholders?' Sean asked.

'King and Melbourn only has major shareholders,' she explained. 'A small collection of wealthy people from around the world, who believed Waldegrave would best serve their interests. Jeremy was so cross. I think that's when things started to go wrong. He was so determined to prove he was the man to take King and Melbourn forward that he started to take increased risks – investing large amounts in high-risk overseas markets, encouraging his subordinates to do the same and to lend money to individuals who probably could never afford to repay it. Then the banking crisis hit the entire sector and people started looking closely at Jeremy's actions. It was just the excuse Mr Waldegrave was looking for. That sort of thing was bad for business, once people knew about it.'

'So they paid him off?' Sean told her more than asked.

'He was allowed to keep his pension and his bonus,' she continued, 'just so long as he didn't make a fuss, but it hurt him very badly. He and Mr Waldegrave could barely stand the sight of each other. As far as Jeremy was concerned Francis had taken what was rightfully his, so when he was also the one to tell him his time at King and Melbourn was over . . . well, it was almost too much for him to bear.'

'But he did,' Sean reminded her. 'He did bear it. He never tried to make trouble for anyone. He kept quiet.'

'What choice did he have? What choice did anyone have? I know he tried to find another job in the financial sector, but Francis quietly made sure no one would touch him. Jeremy was a tiger, Inspector. He lived for his work – his position and status. The thought of retirement must have almost killed him.'

'And he blamed Waldegrave,' Sean spoke his thoughts out loud, the hairs all over his body standing on end and bristling as the solution to the puzzle finally began slot into place. 'He blamed Waldegrave for taking it all away.'

'Inspector,' she told him. 'I truly believe he hated him.'

'Jesus Christ.' Sean tried to comprehend the enormity of what he was hearing, Jeremy Goldsboro's face fixed in the front of his mind – the years of planning and waiting for his revenge finally making Sean realize what sort of animal he'd been looking for all along: a vengeful, envious, bitter man, yes – but no man of the people striking at the rich and powerful. Instead, a man who was institutionally part of the very thing The Jackdaw claimed to hate. *So that's why you left Goldsboro hooded. You were hiding something from me – that you, The Jackdaw, are Jeremy Goldsboro. So who the hell was the hooded man in the chair?*

408

'Jesus Christ,' he blasphemed again.

'Are you all right?' she asked him.

'Yeah,' he lied before another question jumped into his mind. 'Why didn't you call us?' he asked. 'When you realized both Paul Elkins and Jeremy Goldsboro had been taken by the same man. It must have struck you as a coincidence?'

'Of course it did,' she admitted. 'I spoke to Jeremy, after I found out what happened to him, and I mentioned to him that it seemed strange. He told me he'd already told the police all about it.'

Sean physically shrunk as he realized how much Goldsboro had been playing him. How else had he fooled them? How many more times had he led them by the nose? He remembered the constant phone calls from all the victims, their families and friends demanding information on the progress of the investigation. *Damn you. That's why you made yourself a victim, isn't it? So you could become part of the investigation – find out if we were getting closer to you. You couldn't bear not knowing, could you?*

'You clever bastard,' he accidentally said out loud.

'Excuse me?' George reminded him she existed.

'Who else knows about this?' he demanded.

'Very few,' she confessed. 'It was all kept very, very quiet.'

'I have to go,' he told her. 'I'll be in touch.' He hung up just as the entrance to Hampstead Golf Course came into view. 'I know who you are, my friend. I know who you are.' His phone ringing momentarily distracted him. It was Sally. 'D'you find it?' Sean asked as soon as he answered.

'Yeah,' Sally told him, 'and that's not all.'

'Go on,' he encouraged her, sensing the concern in her voice.

'We found someone,' she explained. 'It's Jason Howard, Sean. We found Jason Howard and amongst other injuries he's missing his left little finger. What the hell's going on, Sean?'

Sean felt instantaneously lightheaded and confused. Only

seconds before he'd discounted Howard from all his thoughts, but now he was back and he was real.

'My God.' Howard's role in the unfolding events clicked into place in Sean's mind. 'Howard was the man in the hood,' he told Sally. 'The man we thought was Goldsboro was Howard. He was faking his own torture – that's why he couldn't take the hood off.'

'Then where the hell was Goldsboro?' Sally questioned, the confusion thick in her voice.

'Don't you understand yet?' he unfairly asked. 'Jeremy Goldsboro is The Jackdaw, Sally. He cut Howard's finger off then he did it to himself. Fuck,' he cursed. 'He must have been planning this since the day they made him walk away from everything he really loved – his job, the prestige it brought him.'

'But why keep Howard alive? Why keep him here?'

'To take the fall,' Sean explained, shaking his head at Goldsboro's cunning. 'Howard made the perfect suspect – the perfect Jackdaw. He was on police records as threatening Goldsboro and Elkins and God knows how many others in the City. He blamed everything he'd lost on the banking sector. He was perfect. Bloody hell, Goldsboro must have been watching him for years, tracking him – waiting for the time when he needed him, then he took him – took him and kept him until it was time to fake the video of his own torture.'

'Why keep him after that?' Sally asked. 'Tied up in this place?'

'Because The Jackdaw has told the world he's going to kill himself live on Your View – for everybody to witness. Only the real Jackdaw was never going to commit suicide. Goldsboro was going to fake it, then blow Howard's brains out and leave him for us to find. Case closed and Goldsboro walks away. He has his revenge on the people he believes stabbed him in the back.'

'How d'you know all this?' Sally asked. 'How can you be sure it's Goldsboro?'

'It's him,' he insisted as he pulled into the long drive that led to the golf course car park. 'Everything I've found and everything you've just told me proves it has to be him.'

'I don't know, Sean,' Sally poured doubt on his belief. 'Goldsboro is still a very wealthy man. Why risk it all to take revenge for something that happened years ago?'

'Because he's not like you,' Sean told her, his voice slightly raised. 'Not like other people. Money means nothing to him without power and respect. Without fear. People feared him when he was a vice president. They took all that away from him and he couldn't bear it. He's a lion, not a lamb.'

'So I can't understand him?' Sally asked accusingly. 'But you can?' Sean didn't answer, but kept driving, the car park next to the clubhouse drawing ever nearer until he was close enough to see the scene unfolding in the near distance. 'Is that what you mean?'

'Shit,' Sean said as his eyes focused on what he didn't want to believe he was seeing – the man in a ski-mask, dressed all in black, walking backwards slowly towards the white Renault Trafic van on the edge of the car park, a white man in his fifties held in front of him, – one of the masked man's arms locked around his neck, while the other held the sawn-off shotgun under his chin as three armed uniformed officers edged towards him.

'I have to go,' he told Sally and cut her off before she could reply. He snatched the light from the roof and allowed the car to roll to a quiet halt behind a small copse of trees. He should have listened to Sally, he told himself. Had the area swamped with local uniformed units to scare Goldsboro away. Now he'd gambled with Waldegrave's life. If matters got even worse, if Waldegrave was killed, he'd be hung out to dry. But Sean knew he needed it to happen this way. He

411

needed to confront Goldsboro – needed to finally stand in front of The Jackdaw.

He flipped the glovebox open, revealing the main set radio concealed in most unmarked police cars. He snatched up the mouthpiece and spoke across the already busy radio traffic. 'MP. MP, this is an urgent active message from DI Corrigan, SIU.'

There was a second's silence before a calm, clear female voice came out of the radio. 'DI Corrigan, go ahead with your message over. All over units stand by unless urgent.'

'I've just arrived on scene at Hampstead Golf Course to liaise with an ARV unit – do you have that ARV unit assigned, MP?'

'Be aware, SIU,' the voice came back, 'the ARV crew are now on scene and dealing with an armed incident at that location. You are advised to keep clear, SIU – over.'

'The suspect has a hostage,' Sean pleaded.

'SIU, be advised – we are aware of the situation – over.'

'No,' Sean argued. 'The suspect has the upper hand. The suspect has the upper hand. He's going to drive away with the victim and there's nothing they can do to stop him. They can't take a shot while he has the victim.'

'SIU, be advised, you are being ordered to leave this to the armed units.'

'Listen to me.' Sean wouldn't give up. 'I need you to speak to the ARV crew on their headsets. Tell them to back away – all the way back to the clubhouse and make sure the suspect sees them do it.'

'SIU, the on duty commander is ordering you to leave the incident to the armed units.'

'Speak to Assistant Commissioner Addis if you have to,' Sean demanded, 'but get the armed units to back away. This suspect will open fire if he feels he has to.' He desperately tried to think of something to convince the people he knew would be sitting in the control room cursing his meddling.

412

'It's The Jackdaw,' he found himself saying into the mouth-piece. 'The suspect is The Jackdaw.'

There was a moment's silence before the voice answered. 'Stand by, SIU.' He waited for what seemed an age, watching from his concealed position as first the armed units held their ground and then slowly started to walk backwards away from the masked man and his hostage, their sub-machine guns still pointing at him until they were about twenty metres from the target, where they crouched and held.

Sean spoke urgently into the radio. 'No,' he barked. 'I need them all the way back. I need the suspect to see them go.'

'Stand by,' the voice told him. A few seconds later the armed units stood again and kept moving backwards as both he and The Jackdaw looked on until they were eventually all but out of sight – the man Sean knew he had to face down quickly dragging his hostage to the waiting van, the shotgun still pressed under his chin. As he slid the side panel door open Sean spoke into the radio.

'Keep all other units away from the scene until I say other-wise,' he insisted.

'All received, SIU,' the woman's voice replied. 'All units stay away from the scene and await details of a RVP – MP over.'

He slipped silently from the car, leaving the door swinging open as he quickly and quietly weaved between the parked cars until there were no more left to provide him with cover. He felt no fear of physical pain or even death. In that moment he was glad he was alone, spared the need to consider how other people, other cops, might feel in the same situation. It was beyond him to understand why other cops wouldn't be prepared to risk everything for a chance to confront the man they'd been hunting for days – thinking about all day and dreaming about each night. His only fear at that precise moment was seeing The Jackdaw escape.

He peeked around the back of the last car just in time to see the dark figure slide a hood on the now bound and gagged man he assumed was Waldegrave and slide the door shut. He knew this would be his only chance. He was close enough to reach the masked man before he could unbind his hostage and again use him as a human shield, but if he rushed him The Jackdaw would have only two choices – kill him or surrender.

'Shit,' he whispered to himself as the masked man headed for the driver's door, but looked back towards where the armed units had headed – his shotgun raised in the same direction. 'Shit,' Sean cursed again. But he already knew what he was going to do – already knew he wouldn't be able to stop himself. Slowly he stood up behind the car and walked into the clear where he could be seen, his hands held out to his side. The dark figure spun towards him and raised the shotgun, pointing it directly at Sean's head, but he kept walking slowly forward.

'You should have changed locations,' Sean explained. 'It was only a matter of time before we found where you were broadcasting from.' He kept edging forward.

'That's close enough,' the man told him in the now familiar mechanical voice. Sean could feel his quarry looking him carefully over from behind the sunglasses – searching for any signs of a weapon or weakness.

'You thought you were safe, didn't you, Jeremy? You see I was thinking about it and then I realized we must have made a mistake – must have missed something when we were searching possible buildings in the area you were broadcasting from. Then the answer seemed so clear to me: we *did* search the building you were using, but somehow didn't realize it. And you must have been there at the time. That's why you felt safe to keep using it, because you never thought we'd search it again. But we have, Jeremy, and we've found him. We've found Jason Howard.'

'You know nothing,' the unearthly voice insisted and moved towards the driver's door.

'We know everything,' Sean tried to convince him. 'That you were sacked from King and Melbourn by a man you already hated and that he replaced you with Paul Elkins. That you sold nearly all your shares and invested the money in precious metals. And that McKay Brown shotgun you're holding now – it's yours, isn't it? I know everything because I did the one thing you never thought I'd do: I went back years to when you were still at King and Melbourn. I found the people who were there when you were there. I even spoke to Felicity George – just a few minutes ago. She told me everything, Jeremy – about you and Francis Waldegrave. That must have really burnt you up inside, being passed over for the top job and then being sacked by the same man – your nemesis. Did you lie awake thinking about him? Did you fantasise about killing him? All those nights alone in your office planning his death – did it give you relief from the burning hate you felt inside, or did it just make you feel worse?' He took a couple of steps forward.

'Careful,' the man stopped him. 'I don't want to kill you, but I will if I have to.'

'It's over, Jeremy. I worked you out.'

'I don't think so,' he doubted Sean. 'Perhaps you're not as clever as you think you are. Francis Waldegrave must be judged by the people.'

'Stop,' Sean interrupted him. 'Can't you see it's over?'

'It's over when the people and I say it's over.'

Sean ignored him. 'I even know why you killed the others. They were just decoys. Apart from Elkins they meant nothing to you. Kidnapped and tortured to strengthen the illusion of The Jackdaw – nothing else. All so you could have your petty, meaningless revenge and get away with murder.' Sean knew that behind the mirrored glasses the other man's eyes were burning with rage.

'You think what I've done is *petty*?' the awful voice asked. '*Meaningless*? Then you understand nothing. I am The Jackdaw.'

Sean tried to detect any doubt or weakness in the disguised voice, but he couldn't. He knew The Jackdaw would shoot him if he had to and not feel a thing – especially if he was the man he thought he was.

'Where you gonna go?' he asked. 'It's over. You can't run. Not forever. Your escape plan's gone. We have Jason Howard. You've made too many mistakes, Jeremy. You should have sought your revenge in the boardroom – where you belong. You don't know this world. This is my world. I belong here, not you. Once you stepped into my world you'd already lost.' Sean stole two steps forward. 'You can't beat me, Jeremy.'

'One more step and I'll kill you where you stand,' the alien voice warned him, 'and what would your pretty young wife and your beautiful two girls think of that? Their husband and father dying a fool's death. Dying for a stranger, instead of living for them.'

The mention of his family rocked him for a second. The Jackdaw had researched him. What else did he know? Had Jackson told him something – found out something – something from his past? He recovered himself quickly. 'I can't let you take him.'

'I know you can't,' the dark figure answered, slightly lowering his aim. 'Which is why you have to die.'

Sean's heart seemed to stop and time stood virtually still as he watched the gun again being raised, buried deep in gunman's shoulder as he rested his cheek against the wooden stock and lined up the barrels for the head shot. But Sean felt no fear. He felt nothing other than an inner peace and acceptance – a feeling that this had always been inevitable. The destiny of the damned. His destiny.

He heard the deafening *crack* of a gunshot – like a lightning strike in the dead of night — but he saw no slow-motion explosion of fire from the end of the shotgun, no flames coiling towards him, and he felt no pain. There was just the dark figure staggering backwards, colliding into the side of his white van, momentarily looking down in disbelief at his own chest, foaming pink blood spluttering from his mouth as he tried to breathe out, the shotgun still in his hand, but fallen by his side.

He looked straight at Sean and began to level the gun in his direction, but instantaneously two more lightning strikes cracked in the air, each making Sean flinch and hammering The Jackdaw back against the van. His dark glasses flew from his face, his legs seeming to fold neatly underneath him, and he slid down the side of the van like a collapsing tower block until he was sitting on the floor. He seemed to take two more bloody breaths, his grey eyes peering through the holes in the mask staring straight at Sean, before his head fell forward and the shotgun dropped from his clawed fingers.

Sean was unable to move or speak, or even take a breath, his eyes fixed on the body lying lifeless against the van, the sound of the gunfire still rumbling across the golf course. Eventually he managed to turn to where the shots had come from. Slowly Donnelly appeared from behind a parked car only a few feet away, his pistol held out in front of him and pointing at the stricken man, his eyes wide and wild, never leaving his downed target.

'You all right?' Sean asked, his voice quieter than he'd expected, his mouth dry and his throat constricted, but Donnelly neither answered nor looked at him. 'Dave,' Sean called to him. 'Dave.'

Donnelly blinked repeatedly before turning towards him, although his eyes still never left his victim. 'Are you all right?' Sean asked, his voice stronger now, his mind already coldly processing what he'd seen – working out what had happened and evidencing every aspect of the violent death of another human being.

Still unable to speak, Donnelly answered with a slow, juddering nod of his head. Sean nodded back as both men stood in the now eerie silence of the car park, both dealing with the immediate aftermath of what they'd just witnessed – what they'd been a part of, in their own very individual ways.

'Who is he?' Donnelly finally asked. 'I heard you call him Jeremy.'

'I'm not sure,' Sean explained. 'I thought I was, but now . . . everything feels too surreal to be sure of anything any more. Seeing a man die in front of you can rock the deepest of beliefs.'

'Only one way to find out,' Donnelly told him.

Sean nodded he understood and walked towards the body, growing more excited with each step he took – the fact that a man was dead becoming secondary to his burning need to know who was hiding underneath the bloodied balaclava. When he reached the fallen man he pulled a pair of latex gloves from his coat pocket and crouched next to him. He watched the man's chest closely for a few seconds, watching for the telltale signs of life, but his body was still. He held the man's head upright and rolled up the ski-mask, exposing the man's throat, pushing his index and middle finger hard into the area next to his trachea as he searched for a pulse; but he felt nothing.

'Is he dead?' he heard Donnelly call from behind. He looked back over his shoulder.

'Yeah,' he confirmed. 'He's dead.' Donnelly finally lowered his pistol and seemed to shrink smaller than Sean could ever remember seeing him. For a second he wished he'd been the one to have fired the fatal shots – wished he'd been the one who'd have to carry the burden of taking a life for the rest of his. A burden he knew he'd be able to bear better than almost anyone. *The darkness isn't my weakness. It's my strength.* His fingers coiled under the bottom of the mask as he began to roll it back from the man's face, slowly revealing more and more of his bloodied features until he could see it in its entirety – the dead eyes of Jeremy Goldsboro staring back at him – the features he had in life already beginning to desert him in death. Sean felt a calmness washing over him as he realized it was over and that he'd been right.

'Well?' Donnelly's voice broke into his world. 'Who is it?'

Sean answered without looking away from Goldsboro's dead eyes. 'It's him. It's Jeremy Goldsboro.'

'You knew it was going to be him, didn't you?' Donnelly asked.

'Only at the very end,' Sean admitted. 'Only at the very end.'

'How did you know?'

'Like I told you,' Sean reminded him. 'I found things out – at King and Melbourn.

'Not that,' Donnelly pushed. 'I mean, what sent you there in the first place?'

'The video,' Sean explained, still looking at Goldsboro, as if he was speaking to the body. 'It was the video of his own supposed torture. Leaving the hood on just didn't feel right.'

'That's all?' Donnelly questioned. 'That's all you had to put you onto Goldsboro?'

'It didn't put me onto Goldsboro,' Sean shook his head. 'It just told me there was a connection, between Goldsboro and The Jackdaw. But honestly, I never saw this – not until I spoke to Felicity George less than twenty minutes ago.'

'Who?' Donnelly asked.

'It doesn't matter,' Sean told him. 'Not right now. The man's dead. That's all that matters.'

Donnelly sat on the bonnet of his unmarked car smoking another cigarette and looking down the slight incline of the car park to where Sean stood next to the body of Jeremy Goldsboro talking to the uniformed units from the Armed

Response Team. He couldn't hear what they were saying, but he watched as every now and then Sean would point in one direction or another while they nodded their understanding. They'd already surrounded the entire car park with blue and white police tape. It flapped in the breeze and made a strange whistling sound that almost drowned out the noise of approaching sirens – more police units, an ambulance and God knows what else. He watched Sean make a final gesture to the ARV crew and start to walk across the car park towards him. Without knowing why, Donnelly opened his coat and jacket to look at the pistol he'd killed Goldsboro with tucked into its holster. The heavy nausea he'd felt since pulling the trigger began to swell again. He covered the weapon and concentrated on the approaching Sean who looked grey and exhausted, but with a detectable spring in his step.

'You all right?' Sean asked when he reached him.

'Not really,' Donnelly answered.

Sean looked him in the eyes. 'I'm sorry,' he told him. 'I didn't know it would go down like this.'

'Really?' Donnelly asked. 'Then why did you make me bring the gun – if you didn't know it would come to this?'

'Just in case,' Sean tried to reassure him.

'You never thought it was Howard, did you?'

'He was a good suspect,' Sean explained, 'but he lacked envy.'

'I don't understand,' Donnelly admitted. 'What's envy got to do with it?'

'It doesn't matter now,' Sean told him. 'It was Goldsboro and now he's dead. It's over.'

'I know,' Donnelly reminded him with barely concealed bitterness.

'There'll be an investigation,' Sean warned him.

'Aye,' Donnelly agreed, 'that's what worries me. Ethics and Standards, IPCC, the media – they're all going to murder me when they find out I didn't shout a warning before firing.'

'You didn't have time,' Sean argued. 'By the time you shouted a warning he would have killed me.'

'They won't care about that,' Donnelly explained. 'All they'll care about is procedure. I didn't warn him – so that's me fucked.'

'But you did shout a warning,' Sean told him, 'just before he started to raise the shotgun at me and just after he'd said he would kill me. You remember now, don't you?'

Donnelly nodded he understood before looking towards the ARV crew. 'And them? What about what they heard?'

'They were too far away to hear anything other than the shots,' Sean assured him. 'They couldn't have heard you warning him to drop the gun – not from that distance.'

'No,' Donnelly agreed. 'I suppose not.'

'And . . . thanks,' Sean added. 'He was going to do it. He was going to shoot me. You saved my arse.'

'Aye,' Donnelly replied, 'but to be honest, I'm not really sure how I feel about that right now. I had to kill a man because of you.'

Before Sean could answer, his phone rang. It was Sally.

'Sean,' she began. 'What the hell's going on? The ARV crew are telling me there's been shots fired at the Hampstead Golf Course – that someone's been killed?'

'It's all right,' he reassured her. 'We're fine.'

'Goldsboro?' she asked.

'Yeah,' Sean confirmed. 'Killed. We had no choice.'

'*We* had no choice?'

Sean took a few steps away from Donnelly, as if it would prevent him from hearing. 'Dave was the shooter. He had to. Goldsboro was about to fire on me.'

'Jesus Christ,' Sally reprimanded him. 'You were supposed to let the ARV crew make the arrest. You promised.'

'I couldn't,' he tried to explain. 'He had a hostage. He was going to get away. I had no choice.' There was a long silence.

'OK,' Sally eventually softened and took a breath before

continuing. 'I can't believe he thought he'd get away with it. Arrogant bastard. We'd have found out eventually,' she reasoned. 'Something would have given him away – forensics, a witness. Something.'

'But you're forgetting one thing,' Sean told her. 'We wouldn't have been looking any more. Nobody would be.'

'You would be,' she accused him, 'because you knew, didn't you?'

'No,' Sean answered solemnly. 'Not a hundred per cent. Not until I lifted the mask.'

'Don't play games with us any more, Sean,' Sally whispered down the phone. 'You went to that golf course alone because you wanted to face him, even if it meant getting yourself killed.'

'That's not true,' Sean tried to convince her. 'I was just trying to stop him from taking Waldegrave. I had no choice.'

'No,' Sally argued. 'You had a choice. You just made the wrong one. Question is, Sean, why?'

He sighed before giving up. 'I'll see you later. I'll explain more then.' He pressed the end call icon and walked the few steps back to a morose-looking Donnelly.

'Problem?' he asked.

'Sally,' Sean explained. 'She's pissed off with me.'

'*She's* pissed off with you!' Donnelly shrugged his shoulders, already starting to rebuild his detective's façade. 'Ah well. She'll get over it. She always does.'

'Maybe,' Sean replied, expressionless.

'One thing does bother me though,' Donnelly changed the subject, 'what you said to Sally – about how we could never have proved it was Goldsboro. There's one thing both you and she seem to have forgotten.'

'What's that?'

'The shotgun,' Donnelly answered. 'If he killed Howard in the white room then he'd have to have left the shotgun at the scene otherwise we would have known someone else must have been involved. And if he had to leave it we would have easily traced it back to Goldsboro. He would have had a hell of a job explaining how his shotgun ended up there.'

'He'd have thought of it,' Sean told him. 'Would have had it covered. I doubt he kept his guns in his London place – with his sort of money he's probably got a place in the country. Somewhere a burglary could easily be staged – and guess what was stolen?'

'A McKay Brown shotgun,' Donnelly answered.

'I'd bet my pension on it.'

'But why would Howard take a gun belonging to one of the people he also abducted and tortured?'

'Why not?' Sean explained. 'Even when we still thought this was all about someone taking revenge on the bankers we didn't have him down as a criminal who had the connections to get his hands on a gun. So why not take one from one of the people we thought he'd been following – learning everything about – including the fact they had shotguns and where they kept them?'

'Jesus,' Donnelly sighed. 'You got this whole thing worked out, don't you?'

'Now I do,' Sean answered. 'Easy to see the picture once the puzzle's been solved. Not so easy until then.'

'And now you've stood in front of him,' Donnelly asked, 'd'you think he always had the potential to be a killer?'

'I suppose.' Sean considered it. 'Deep down inside. But I don't believe he was a psychopath. If anything he was something more – something even colder.'

'A sociopath then?' Donnelly almost whispered.

'Maybe,' Sean partially agreed – understanding more and more how Goldsboro had managed to lock him out of his mind. 'If such a person really exists. His job kept it all at bay, satisfied his needs for dominance and power, but once that was taken away he changed – stepped into our world.'

'A killer in the boardroom, eh?' Donnelly half joked.

'You could say that,' Sean agreed.

Donnelly looked down at the body of Jeremy Goldsboro as the uniformed officers covered him with a large, blue plastic sheet. 'At least there won't be any trial this time, except maybe mine.'

'You'll be fine,' Sean assured him, even managing to rest a hand in his shoulder. 'It might just take a little time. It always just takes a little time.'

'Well, there'll be a lot of disappointed people out there,' Donnelly told him. 'A lot of people actually believed in The Jackdaw – felt empowered by him. Finally someone was standing up for them. But in the end it was nothing more than a rich man's revenge. The Jackdaw stood for something, meant something – but this means nothing.'

'It's better this way,' Sean explained. 'It's better it meant nothing. Better for everyone.'

Geoff Jackson sat at his desk in the open-plan office of *The World* thinking about how best to maximize the coverage of The Jackdaw's final victim, not to mention his own suicide, when something coming from the large TV screen adorning the room made him look up from his computer screen. Sky News was showing a smartly dressed woman in her thirties, who looked more like a model than a reporter, standing on the edge of some car park or another. The caption in the bottom left-hand corner of the screen read, 'Shooting at Hampstead Golf Course', while the rolling news bar on the bottom of the screen said, 'Police shooting in Hampstead, north London. Unconfirmed reports say man shot is The Jackdaw'.

'Shit,' Jackson cursed loudly as he saw the story of the year coming to an untimely conclusion.

'Bad luck,' one of his colleagues told him with a grin. 'Bloody Sky. Already all over it. I guess there'll be no more interviews with The Jackdaw then.'

'Bollocks,' Jackson told no one in particular.

'Better luck next time, eh,' the colleague told him and walked off as Jackson continued to watch the coverage – the footage cutting away from the reporter to a slightly older shot taken through a long-range lens, making the pictures from deep inside the car park appear a little grainy and ever so slightly out of focus, but good enough for him to be able to make out the dark-haired man as he walked to the white van where a blue sheet of plastic covered something on the ground. His experience told him it was a body – the body of The Jackdaw.

'Corrigan,' Jackson hissed through gritted teeth before leaning back in his chair with his hands behind his head, the thought of the money he'd earn from the book rights already softening the blow of losing the main character in the best story he'd had for years. 'Corrigan,' he repeated as he stared at the images on the TV, a slight grin spreading across his pale lips. 'Rest assured I'll be keeping a close eye on you, Detective Inspector Corrigan. A very close eye indeed.'

Acknowledgements

A quick thank you to all the team at Harper Collins – particularly Kate Elton – the Publisher, the entire sales team and also the marketing team, especially Hannah Gamon for all her hard and inventive work. A special note to my editor – Sarah Hodgson – who having been set a demanding task with *The Jackdaw*, did a fantastic job.

A big thank you to the Harper Collins team over in America, lead by Trish Daly, for all the hard work they put in on the last three books that were published over there. Much appreciated.

Here's to the future.

LD

STIRLING COUNCIL LIBRARIES

3804802 111373 8